NAMELESS

EILEEN ENWRIGHT HODGETTS

ISBN: 978-0-9982154-9-5

CHAPTER ONE

August 1952
Tooting, London, England
Buddy, the Boy from Canada

Buddy stood in the neat front garden and stared up at the house. He saw the twitch of a curtain. Someone was watching. Was that someone his mother? Ma and Pa Stewart stood on the front doorstep, and Ma was telling Pa to knock again. Buddy took a step back and studied the house and the street, searching for something to jog his memory. Had he really lived here, on this depressing London street, when he was a child? He sniffed the air heavy with exhaust fumes from cars and buses rumbling by. He sniffed again, recognizing the hint of ozone that lay beneath the stink of the great city.

Ma turned to look at him, her face hopeful. He shook his head. No, nothing here was familiar. Pa knocked on the door again, and the curtain fell back into place. Perhaps she was going to open the door, and perhaps he would recognize her, but he doubted it. If this was the place where he had lived for the first eight years of his life, surely being here should stir something in his memory. The only thing that stirred was a strong desire to return to Canada and get on with his life. He looked at Ma, small and plump, with her graying hair held back in an untidy bun. She shouldn't be here; she should be tending to her garden at home. As for Pa, his hand raised to knock again, he was too big for this cramped little house and cramped little country. With his broad shoulders and weather-beaten complexion, he belonged to the lakeshore and the pine forest. They didn't need to do this for him. He didn't need to meet his mother or find out why she had not written to him in the last twelve years.

The front door opened. Buddy's stomach lurched. He didn't want to look. He didn't want to see the mother who had abandoned him. He was almost an adult, and he was doing just fine without her.

The dark-haired woman who stood on the doorstep was as plump as Ma but not as pretty. Her dark hair was trapped under a hairnet. She wore a flowered apron, as though she had been disturbed in the midst of some domestic task, and her face was set in an unwelcoming scowl.

"Go away."

Ma and Pa both took a step backward.

"Go on, get out of here. I'm a good Christian woman, and I don't need a Jehovah's Witness to tell me how to get to heaven."

Her voice was sharp and nasal, and suffered in contrast to Ma's gentle Canadian tones.

"Are you Mrs. Powley?" Ma asked.

Buddy studied the scowling woman. If she was his mother, surely he should remember something.

The image formed in his mind. A headscarf knotted under a woman's chin, eyes red with crying. Steam or smoke, thick and sulfurous.

Pa reestablished himself on the doorstep. "Are you Mrs. Elizabeth Powley?" he asked.

The woman's expression turned from a scowl to a suspicious frown.

"I am."

Pa gestured toward Buddy. "We've come about your son."

Buddy saw that Mrs. Powley ... his mother was looking at him with worried interest.

"Are you a friend of Eddie's?" she asked. "Has something happened to him?"

Buddy felt a surge of relief. She didn't know him. He didn't know her and she didn't know him, so surely she was not his mother, and that meant that this noisy, dirty, ruined city was not his home.

"Has something happened to my son?" Mrs. Powley demanded.

"No," Pa said, "nothing's happened to him. We've taken good care of him."

"What do you mean?"

"This is your son. We've brought him back from Canada."

Mrs. Powley's eyes widened as she searched Buddy's face with an expression that could have been recognition. His heart sank. Was this scowling woman really his mother? Her face was not the face in his memory.

The woman on the doorstep shook her head with angry vigor. "That's not my son."

6

Ma set her shoulders indignantly, and her voice acquired a sharp edge. "I know you haven't answered a single one of his letters, and perhaps you'd like to forget he exists, but this is your son. This is the boy you sent to Canada when he was eight years old. We've raised him to be a man."

Buddy saw a look of panic flick across Mrs. Powley's face and heard her sharp intake of breath. When she spoke, her voice shook slightly. "You're all mad," she hissed. "Go away before I call the police. I didn't send my son to Canada; he's here in London, attending university. I don't know who that young man is, but he's nothing to do with me."

Mrs. Powley's panic turned to angry action as she turned away and slammed the door. In the silence that followed, Buddy heard the rattle of a chain sliding into place. Mrs. Powley did not intend to be disturbed again.

Pa rested a hand on Buddy's shoulder. "Come on, son. There's nothing we can do here."

"Be glad that woman isn't your mother," Ma said. She looked at Pa. "We should go back to Canada now. We did our best."

Pa tightened his grip on Buddy's shoulder. "If you don't remember her ..."

"I don't."

"Do you remember anything else?"

Buddy pressed against a barrier in his mind. He had always known that the barrier existed and whatever was behind it was forbidden, but now a piece of information floated free of its restrictions. Was this forbidden? No, he thought not. Now that he did not have to believe his name was Edward Powley, he was free to remember the address.

He was very little, and his cheek smarted from a stinging blow. The man towered above him, glaring and impatient. "You're old enough to know your own address. I don't have time to run all over Brighton looking for you, and I don't want your mother calling the police again to help her useless brat. One thirty-four St. Godric Street, Brighton, Sussex. Don't forget it."

"I know where I used to live," Buddy said. "Do you think we should go there? It's a place called Brighton."

Ma's voice was firm. "No, we shouldn't. We should go home. No good will come of this."

"We've come all this way," Pa said. "We have to do what we can. It might help Buddy to remember his name. Obviously, he's not Edward Powley."

Another memory surfaced.

A candle flickered, and a woman knelt beside him. Her hands gripped his shoulders so tightly that he could not move. She held him with her gaze.

"Your name is Edward Powley."

7

"No, it's not."

She moved her hand to his forehead, stroking and smoothing. "Your new name is Edward Powley. Forget your old name."

Ma clutched at his arm. For a moment, he tried to resist. He grasped at another onrushing memory of steam swirling and writhing through a vast, echoing space, of children shouting, and a hectoring voice from a loudspeaker, announcing the imminent departure of the train to Liverpool. Ma's touch dragged him back to reality, and the fact that he was standing outside a door that had been closed and bolted against him.

"We could just go home," Ma said, and Buddy found himself in complete agreement with her. He wanted to go home, and this was not home. Home was a place where he was made welcome. Home was Canada, and when he reached Canada, he would force himself to forget Mrs. Powley and her fleeting glance of recognition.

"We'll ask our solicitor," Pa said.

"Ask him what?" Ma snapped. "If that woman says that Buddy is not her son, there's nothing else to ask. We've done our best, and now we should go home." She took a deep breath and stood back, looking from Pa to Buddy and then at the shuttered house of Mrs. Elizabeth Powley. "There's something going on here," she said. "Someone had a good reason for putting Buddy on that ship and sending him away, and if it was a good reason then, it's a good reason now. We need to leave."

Pa's face took on a stubborn set that Buddy recognized only too well. It was the same expression that crossed Pa's face when storms and blizzards brought down telegraph wires across the Bruce Peninsula, and Pa went out in the night to climb poles and untangle live wires. This was Pa's expression of courage, the face he wore when he had to do something he was afraid to do. It was an expression that meant Pa was not ready to give up.

"We'll ask our solicitor to find us a lawyer in Brighton, and we'll go to the address that Buddy remembers," Pa declared.

"We don't even know where Brighton is," Ma wailed.

Pa clasped Ma's hand firmly. "We'll find out where it is," he said, "and we'll find another solicitor there, and we'll start all over again. We are not going home until Buddy is legally our son. That's what we came to do, and that's what we're going to do."

August 1952
Brighton, Sussex, England
Toby Whitby

Anthea Clark entered Toby's office. Her gray hair was held in place by its usual quota of hairpins, and her posture was rigidly upright, but Toby thought that a hint of excitement lurked at the corner of her thin lips. She set a folded paper on his desk.

"Your new clients are here. They brought a letter of introduction."

"Which new clients would that be?" Toby asked. He could not resist teasing her and seeing her look of irritation.

"How many new clients do you think we have?" she hissed. "It's Mr. and Mrs. Stewart and their foster son. Such an interesting case."

Toby picked up the letter with studied nonchalance.

"Mr. and Mrs. Stewart?" he repeated.

Anthea folded her arms in exasperation. "The clients referred by your former employers Mr. Squires and Mr. Parson; the boy from Canada who cannot find his mother."

Toby nodded and studied the letter. "Apparently, the woman they thought was his mother disclaims all knowledge of him," he said.

"Disgraceful," Anthea snapped. "I don't know what the world's coming to."

"Neither do I," Toby agreed.

He set the letter back on the desk. "Parson gave me a quick rundown on the phone," he said. "I have an address and I've made arrangements. Unfortunately, the house the boy remembers is scheduled for demolition, so we have no time to waste."

Anthea's disapproving sigh suggested that she was not the one wasting time.

"I think," Toby said, "that you should offer Mr. and Mrs. Stewart a cup of tea and—"

"I have already done so."

"—and then find a taxi to take them to their hotel," Toby continued. "Slater and I will take the boy with us."

Anthea raised her eyebrows. "Why have you involved Inspector Slater? There's no suggestion of a crime, is there?"

"Not yet," Toby replied, "but I need Slater's influence to get onto the site. They're about to begin demolition, and the houses are not safe. They haven't been lived in or even looked at in the past twelve years."

Anthea looked at him dubiously. "What do you expect the boy to do when he sees them?"

Toby shrugged. "I don't know, but nothing else has jogged his memory, so we have to give it a try. Even though they're practically falling down, he may still recognize something. I don't know what else I can do."

Toby took his suit coat from the back of his chair, ran a hand through his unruly hair, and removed his glasses to polish them with his handkerchief.

As he took a step toward the door, Anthea stopped him and made an effort to straighten his tie.

"Have to make a good impression," she whispered. "We need the business."

"And the boy needs to find his mother," Toby said.

Anthea nodded. "Of course."

Toby paused. "I wonder what this is really about."

Anthea looked at him quizzically.

"Mothers don't just disappear," Toby said, "not even in wartime."

CHAPTER TWO

Toby stood beside Detective Inspector Percy Slater and studied the address that Buddy had given to him.

"These houses took a direct hit July 1940," Slater said, waving his left arm to indicate the row of tumbled houses.

Toby turned to the young man at his side. "Well, Buddy, does anything look familiar?"

Buddy stared fixedly at the ruined buildings, squinting against the morning sun and saying nothing. Toby studied his new client's face, worried brown eyes, straight dark hair, and the shadow of a youthful beard.

"Well?" Toby asked again.

Buddy shook his head. "I don't recognize the houses." He gave Toby a despondent glance. "But that doesn't mean anything. I mean, there's not much left, is there? I don't understand why they're still here. Why wait so long to pull them down?"

"Town planning," Toby said. "Our elected government is still trying to decide where we all should live, what to do with the empty spaces left by bombed houses, how to find the owners when so many people are dead, or whether we should all just live like communists, with the state owning everything."

He saw Buddy's shocked expression and smiled. "I'm not serious. It's a matter of priorities, and these houses had no priority while there were hotels down on the seafront that needed to be repaired, and a beach that still needs to be cleared. This site has only just made its way to the top of the list for demolition. We're lucky that we found out in time to make them stop work. You can thank Inspector Slater for calling a halt. This isn't part of his job, but he's a friend, and lawyers and policemen are very rarely friends."

He smiled to himself. He had never expected to call Percy Slater a friend, but it was a relief to find that his relationship with Slater had now turned from a prickly rivalry to a comfortable friendship.

He turned back to look at his client. "You must have been very shocked when Mrs. Powley said that you were not her son."

Buddy hesitated for a moment before shaking his head. "No, I wasn't surprised. When I saw the house she lived in, I knew I had never been there before. She says she's not my mother, and I believe her. I always knew that my name wasn't Edward, but no one would believe me until now. I had a label, you see, on a string around my neck, and the label said I was Edward Powley. None of this makes sense. Why did someone give me her son's name, and why can't I remember my own name?"

He lifted a hand to shade his eyes. "That view looks familiar. I think I've been here before."

Toby turned to follow Buddy's uncertain gaze. They stood at the top of a road that meandered up from the backstreets of Brighton. Behind them the cramped houses gave way to the green slopes of the South Downs, and below them the English Channel stretched to the horizon. On the seafront, the white walls and minarets of the Royal Pavilion sparkled in the summer sunshine.

Buddy pointed. "That," he said. "I remember that building, I think."

Toby shrugged. "Everyone who has ever been to Brighton remembers the Royal Pavilion. It's quite possible that your parents, whoever they are, brought you here for a visit when you were a little kid, and that's why you remember."

He waved a hand to indicate the demolition machinery idling in front of the destroyed houses. "This is the address you gave me, one thirty-four St. Godric Street. It has to mean something. Take a good long look at the house, Buddy. Tell me you recognize something."

Buddy's mouth trembled, and an expression of such anguish crossed his young face that Toby regretted his impatience, but he couldn't back down. Unless something of significance was found here, the houses on St. Godric Street would be gone by evening; nothing but a pile of rubble.

"Well?"

"I wasn't a baby when I left," Buddy said. "I was eight. I should be able to remember."

Toby thought of himself as an eight-year-old in the happy days between the wars. When he was eight years old, the world had been reveling in the joy that came from the end of the Great War. He could remember everything with clarity: the aunt who bobbed her hair and shortened her skirts, the drudgery of school, and the joy of holidays. When he was eight, life had been simple, but it was not the same for Buddy. When Buddy was eight, he had somehow or other changed his name, boarded a boat to Canada, and spent the next twelve years forgetting where he came from.

"You remembered this address," Toby prompted.

Some of the anguish fell from Buddy's expression. "Yes. I am absolutely sure about that; it was something I was not supposed to forget, but I have a feeling that I wasn't supposed to tell anyone. Perhaps I shouldn't have told you."

"No point in keeping it a secret now," Toby said. "The war's over. This is St. Godric Street, and there doesn't seem to be any reason to keep it secret. It's just a row of ruined houses."

"Hey, Whitby, over here."

Toby turned to see Slater, a tin hat jammed on his head, calling to him from the splintered framework that marked the place where a front door had once stood. He looked at Buddy. "Are you ready to go inside?"

A look of panic crossed Buddy's face. "I have a bad feeling about this. What if I remember something I'm not supposed to remember?"

Toby sighed. "Your foster parents retained me to find out who you are," he said, "so let's get on with it."

He strained for patience. Buddy's fear seemed so much at odds with everything Toby thought he knew about Canadians. Of course, his learning had come from tales of adventure he had read as a child, but he was disappointed that Buddy did not fit the same mold. Canadians were people who lived in log cabins they had built with their own hands; they paddled across the wilds in canoes; they wrestled with bears and survived winters in the Arctic. They did not tremble in fear at the thought of going into a bombed house in suburban Brighton.

"I can't go," Buddy protested. "You go."

"I'm not the one who needs to remember," Toby snapped.

Slater gestured impatiently and stepped through the gaping entrance to the house. Toby grasped Buddy's arm and urged him forward. Buddy picked his way reluctantly through the rubble of the front yard, where the ruined front door lay in the weeds. A flush of emotion suffused his face.

"Do you remember?" Toby asked.

Buddy stopped abruptly.

"Well?" Toby asked.

Buddy shook his head. "I can't go in there. Please, don't make me."

Slater reemerged from the doorway and looked at Toby impatiently. "Is he coming?"

Toby shook his head. "Not yet."

13

Slater scowled at Buddy. "We don't have all day. The demolition crew needs to get on with their work."

Buddy hung his head and remained mulishly silent.

Toby felt a wave of sympathy and a conviction that something very bad had happened to Buddy; something he could not yet bear to remember. He released Buddy's arm. "Maybe you need more time. Stay out here for a minute, and try to pull yourself together. I'll go in."

He took the tin hat that Slater held out for him and followed Slater through the weeds to the front door.

"What's the matter with him?" Slater asked.

"I don't know. Some kind of shock or trauma from the evacuation, I think. He doesn't seem to be ready to face it yet."

"Nonsense," Slater declared. "Thousands of kiddies were evacuated, and they seem to be fine now. Best thing he can do is face it like a man, and none of this mumbo jumbo about not remembering. He remembers; he just doesn't want to say what he remembers."

Toby settled the tin hat on his head. "Let's take a look for ourselves. We can leave him out there for the moment."

Slater stepped into the shattered shell of the house. "Step carefully," he warned. "It's all a bit precarious."

Morning light slanted through the remnants of the roof, revealing the outlines of a kitchen. Toby could see a black stove partially buried in the rubble, and the remnants of a sink clinging to one wall. A shattered staircase led to a now nonexistent second story. The splintered remains of a Welsh dresser lay facedown beneath the weight of a blackened roof beam that had crashed down into the room, shattering furniture and crockery.

Slater kicked gingerly at a chair leg. "You got me out here," he said, "so tell me what we're looking for."

"Something to jog my client's memory."

Slater cocked his head to one side and looked at Toby. "How are we supposed to do that when your client refuses to come in here?"

"I don't know. Look around and see if you can see anything personal. He was just a kid, so maybe a teacup or a photo or something."

"A teacup," Slater scoffed. "You think a teacup could survive this?"

Toby pointed at the dresser pinned beneath the beam. "That's probably where they kept their china."

Slater shook his head. "I don't suppose there's anything left now." He stirred the debris with his foot, exposing a small section of linoleum. Toby heard him give a slight grunt of surprise, and he suddenly dropped to one knee and began to brush aside the accumulated dirt of twelve winters.

"What is it?" Toby asked. "Did you find something?"

"Not anything I expected to find," Slater said quietly, "but there's something here, and I don't like the look of it."

He pushed himself back to his feet and pointed down to the floor. "See that?"

Toby bent to look. "I don't see anything."

"Well, I do," Slater said emphatically. "I see a bone. Just a small one."

"What kind of bone?"

Slater reached into his pocket and produced a flashlight. The light beam picked up a small white object. Toby bent lower. He saw that the object was really just a splinter of bone, disturbingly ornamented with tooth marks.

"Rat?" Toby asked.

"A rat's done the chewing," Slater said, "but he hasn't been chewing another rat. This is from something much bigger. Possibly human."

Toby took a step back. "These houses were cleared out years ago. No one was reported missing."

Slater surveyed the scene. "We'll have to get that beam lifted. My guess is that the rest of the bones are under the dresser."

"Family dog?" Toby asked hopefully.

"Did your client mention a dog?"

"No."

"Better go ask him," Slater said, "and I'll go and talk to the work crew to see if we can get them to lift the beam."

Toby found Buddy standing in a trancelike state, staring up at the green hills of the South Downs rising behind the houses.

"We've found something," Toby said.

Buddy kept his eyes on the hills.

"Did you have a dog, Buddy?"

"No, I don't think so. Why?"

"Just wondering," Toby said. "Wait here, Buddy. Don't go inside."

Buddy shook his head. "I won't."

The workers had been celebrating their unexpected break time by brewing tea on a Primus stove. The whistling kettle drowned out Slater's voice as he spoke with them. Toby couldn't hear Slater's instructions, but he could see that his friend was making a forceful argument for abandoning the tea break and starting up the crane.

One of the workers took the kettle off the stove, and another climbed into the cab of the crane. The ground trembled as the crane rumbled forward. A broad-shouldered worker with a sailor's tattoo on his muscular arms came to stand by Toby.

"We should get danger money for this," he grumbled.

"Why? This is your job, isn't it?"

"We're here to knock the house down," the worker agreed, "but we're not here to pick stuff out of the rubble like we're playing hot potato. I'd stay out of the way if I were you. The whole house could come down when he lifts that beam. This had better be important."

"I promise you it is," Toby said.

"Everyone makes promises," the workman muttered. "No one keeps them. You want to hook up the crane, or shall I do it?"

"Me?" Toby stammered. "Me? I don't know how to ..."

"No, of course you don't." The workman spat on the ground. "Suits," he said. "Just like officers. No bloody use."

He walked away from Toby and into the ruined house, reemerging almost immediately. A few minutes later, Toby saw the massive roof beam being lifted up through a hole in the roof. The crane operator left it dangling and climbed out of his cab. He walked over to Slater. "All right, mate. I've done what you want."

"I need you to go inside," Slater said, "and help me lift a—"

"No. No way. You go and do whatever it is you're going to do, and when you're finished, we'll get on with knocking the house down, but we ain't going inside."

Toby looked at the beam dangling from its hook, and the workmen shuffling back to their tea kettle. Slater stood in the rubble of the front garden and gave Toby an inquiring glance. Toby groaned. He knew what his friend wanted, and he knew he couldn't refuse, not just because Slater asked, but because the workman had spat on the ground, called him a "suit," and bracketed him in with every officer who had ever given a foolish order.

"Buddy," Toby called.

The boy turned to look at him.

"Stand clear of the house, Buddy."

Buddy nodded.

Toby settled the tin hat firmly on his head and followed Slater back into the house, where the dangling beam cast a long shadow across the floor. They stood together for a moment, looking down at the remnants of the dresser.

"You'll have to lift that for me," Slater said.

Toby nodded. It was not necessary to mention the reason why Toby would have to do the lifting. They rarely spoke of the fact that Slater had lost his right arm in Normandy, and Slater rarely offered the lack of an arm as an excuse.

Toby looked up at the beam. "We'd better be quick about this. Don't forget you have a family who are going to be very sorry if a house collapses on your head."

Slater grinned, his whole face brightening and years of worry dropping from his expression. "So do you."

Toby gave a momentary thought to his wife and stepdaughter before he squatted down and searched for a fingerhold on the edge of the dresser. He wondered if Carol and Anita would understand why he was taking this risk; why he could not help taking risks. He could hardly understand it himself, so why would he expect Carol to understand?

His fingers curled into a space beneath the dresser, and he lifted. Slater dropped to his knees and shone his flashlight into the space beneath. He grunted and spoke in a strained voice. "Lift it higher."

Toby strained against the weight of the dresser as Slater shone his light into the void.

"Hurry it up," Toby gasped. "I'm going to drop it."

Slater slid backward and away from the possibility of Toby dropping the dresser on his head.

"All right. Put it down. I've seen what I want to see."

"Well?"

"We need help. Get everyone you can. We have to lift the dresser aside."

"Are they …?"

"I think so. I think they're human bones."

Toby went to the door and called to the idling workers, who had the kettle steaming again. "In here. Inspector Slater needs your help."

They came slowly, reluctant to leave their teapot again, and clustered sullenly at the entrance to the house.

Slater glared at them. "Get in here."

The foreman, his hair coated in brick dust, looked up at the swinging beam. "It ain't stable. We need danger money to go in there."

Toby saw that Slater was winding up to giving an angry command. He caught Slater's eye and pointed to himself. *Let me talk to them.* He took the foreman aside. "Look. I know you don't want to go in there, but the fact is we've found some bones, and they could be human."

The foreman shook his head. "I don't see how they can be. The wardens would have cleared the place out right after it happened. They'd know if someone was in there."

"Not necessarily," Toby said. "It looks like he or she, or it, was in the kitchen when the bomb dropped. The blast knocked the dresser over, and then the roof beam came down. No one would have known there was a body there."

The foreman creased his brow. "But if someone was in there, they'd be reported as missing. They're probably dog bones. Do you want me to risk my life for a few dog bones?"

Toby looked him in the eye. "I just did."

The foreman looked up at the beam swinging lazily on the crane hook. "Yes, you did. Perhaps you ain't so bad after all." He raised his voice and gestured to the workmen. "All right, lads, let's give the police a hand here, but make it quick."

The men shuffled toward the hole where the door should have been. Toby glanced around, looking for Buddy. He was nowhere in sight, and Toby did not have time to look for him.

The men were standing in a silent, nervous knot in the center of the destroyed kitchen.

"All right," Toby said with a confidence he did not feel. He pointed to the fallen dresser. "We need to lift that."

The workers made light work of lifting the dresser, and they stayed in place, holding it upright while Slater played the beam of his flashlight across smashed crockery and splintered wood.

"There," said Slater, steadying the beam and allowing the light to give its own answer. The bones peeked out from rotting clothing, and a hand stretched as though reaching for help. The ribs, smashed flat, had retained their original pattern. Slater stirred the debris with his feet and uncovered a skull with remnants of hair and flesh still clinging to it. He turned the skull with a dusty shoe to reveal empty eye sockets, a scattering of teeth, and a small round hole. Toby did not need to hear Slater's verdict; he knew what he had seen.

"Bullet hole," Slater said. He looked at the foreman. "Set that dresser down over there, and get out of here while you can. And don't talk about what you've seen."

Slater waited until the workmen had shuffled back outside. "Why couldn't it be a dog?" he grunted. "We're short-staffed, and this is a mountain of paperwork. You'd better go get your client and see if he knows more than he's telling us."

Toby stepped outside into the bright August sunshine, relieved to be away from the bones and the reminder of the price so many had paid when their houses had crashed down around their heads. Of course, this person, man or woman, had paid a different price; a bullet to the head. Why? Was this death the nightmare that had haunted his young client and stoppered his memory?

Buddy was still nowhere in sight, and the workmen were gathered in a whispering knot. *No chance they'll stay silent*, Toby thought. *This will be all over Brighton by this evening.*

He sheltered his eyes from the glare of the sun and looked up and down the street. He had a new prescription in his glasses, and he should have been able to spot Buddy even at a distance. No one was moving. He looked up toward the green of the South Downs and back down the hill to the seafront. No sign of his client.

He returned reluctantly to the ruined house. Slater was still inside, still studying the bones in the beam of his flashlight.

Slater looked up at him. "Where's your client?"

"I don't know."

It was a testament to Slater's new domestic arrangements, and the unexpected happiness of having a wife and child, that the detective remained calm. He merely raised his eyebrows and shook his head before turning his attention to the bones.

"You can't keep this a secret," Toby warned. "Those men will talk."

Slater nodded. "Yes, I know. I'd better call this in before the story reaches every pub in Sussex, and you had better find your client. He must be around here somewhere."

"Perhaps he overheard us, or overheard the workmen," Toby said. "He'll know we've found a body. He may have run."

"Why would he run?" Slater asked.

Toby looked down at the bones. "Suppose he remembered something. Maybe hearing there was a body in here made him panic."

"I don't like it," Slater said, tapping his nose thoughtfully. "Call it copper's instinct. When you've been on this job long enough, you just know when something isn't right, and your client running off is not right. I think he knows something about this."

"How could he?" Toby argued. "He was in Canada."

Slater shook his head. "Maybe this happened before he went to Canada."

Toby shrugged. "What does it matter? Even if he was here, he was just a kid."

"How old is he now?" Slater asked.

"Twenty."

"So he was eight years old when this house was bombed."

"I suppose so."

"But he can't remember anything about his life here."

"Right."

Slater looked down at the bones and back at Toby. "I can't keep this to myself. I have to report it, and after that the case will be out of my hands. I'm on special duty, and I can't follow up on local cases. You need to find your client before the police find him."

"Why?"

"Because when they find him, they're going to arrest him."

"He was a kid."

"He was eight. You know what the law says about eight-year-olds."

Toby closed his eyes, remembering his hours spent under the tutelage of first Cedric Squires and then Edwin Champion, studying dusty, irrelevant law books citing laws that were rarely enforced but had never been repealed. The law said that a child of eight could understand right and wrong. A child of eight was old enough to be held responsible for their actions. A child of eight was old enough to be charged with murder.

Buddy

Memories flooded his mind. He tried to catch them, but they were slippery. The view had brought one of his memories to the surface. He recognized the ornate pier jutting out into the sea, and the fanciful palace with its white walls and minarets. That memory seemed to be willing to stay around and let him inspect it, but the memory of the house at 134 St. Godric Street would not stay to be examined. It slipped away from him, replaced by images of his childhood and his new life with new parents.

August 1940
Tobermory, Ontario, Canada

The boy had a bedroom of his own in a snug little house, with a window that gave him a view of the lake and the pine forest, but the walls were thin, and he could hear even whispered words.

"Poor little mite. We don't even know if his house is still standing or if his parents are ..."

Pa hushed her. "Don't talk about it, Evvie. No point in worrying him. He seems to be settling in."

"But it's strange, isn't it," Ma whispered, "the way he says that his name isn't Edward?"

"Shock," Pa said. "Wouldn't you be shocked if you were sent off all alone to Canada with nothing but a suitcase and a promise that someone would meet you, and no one comes to meet you, and so you sit all alone and wait for some stranger to pick you and take you to God knows where?"

"He seems to be happy to call us Ma and Pa," Ma said, "but what shall we do about his name? He says he's not Edward, but he won't give us another name to call him. Do you think someone made a mistake on his paperwork?"

"No," Pa said decisively. "He's Edward Powley. Some of his paperwork is missing, but his name and his number are on that little plastic disk they all wear."

"It looks like a disk you'd put on cattle," Ma sniffed. "They sent us children like sending cattle to market."

"Just trying to keep them safe from the Germans," Pa said.

Ma returned to her previous complaint. "Why won't he let us call him Edward, or maybe even Eddie?"

"He's trying to disassociate himself from past trauma," Pa declared.

"Those are some big words you're using," Ma complained.

"I talked to the child welfare officer," Pa said. "She says a lot of the children are having trouble assimilating. She said we shouldn't argue. She has the paperwork to say who he is, but if he wants to use another name, we should go along with it."

"Buddy," Ma said.

"That's a dog's name."

"No, it isn't. We don't have a dog called Buddy. We've never had a dog called Buddy. Ask him if wants to be called Buddy."

Buddy! It was as good a name as any, and far better than Edward.

August 1952
Brighton, Sussex

Buddy liked Toby Whitby, the lawyer that Ma and Pa had hired for him. He was young and energetic, and seemed full of confidence. Buddy felt bad about hiding from him. He wished he could tell Mr. Whitby why he was so reluctant to go inside the house; why he associated that dark interior room with pain and loss. His memories flashed and sparked like a faltering neon sign, but they would not stay to be examined. He remembered a dresser and white teacups, a woman in an apron. He tried to see her face, but she would not stay with him, not even in memory.

The workmen filed out of the house. They whispered anxiously among themselves and didn't notice him as he emerged from his hiding place and crossed the rubble-strewn yard.

Pull yourself together. Yes, he owed it to Ma and Pa to face whatever memory lay hidden in that house. They had come all the way from Canada to help him find his family and get permission to legally adopt him. He was not a blood relative; he was just a boy who had turned up in Canada like an unwanted, unordered package.

He approached the gaping hole that had once contained the front door. He forced himself to look in at the shattered room and gasped at the shock of memory. The dresser that had housed the white plates leaned against a wall. The white plates were nothing but shards on the floor. The stairs that had once led to his bedroom clung to a section of wall, but there could be no bedroom. The second story was gone completely. The shreds of linoleum that lay scattered on the floor still showed their blue-and-white pattern. This was the kitchen. This was where he had eaten breakfast, because his mother had insisted that a good breakfast would lead to a good day. He stepped back. If he could grasp that memory, perhaps he could grasp another. What was the name of the schoolboy who had eaten breakfast with his mother?

Someone was holding his hand and dragging him through a crowd of people in a train station. Steam swirled around them as the engine panted impatiently. Somewhere a guard was blowing shrill blasts on a whistle.

The woman paused for a moment, with her face just inches from his own. "Tell me your name."

"My name is…" He felt a rush of rebellion. He knew what he was supposed to say, but he couldn't say it. '

He watched tears forming in the woman's eyes. She gave him a gentle shake. "What is your name?"

A power beyond his understanding forced himself to say the words. "Edward Powley."

"Good boy. Now tell me where you come from."

He thought the deceitful words would choke him as they spilled from his mouth. "I'm Edward Powley from London."

"That's right, love, you're Edward Powley from London and don't ever say anything different. No one must know who you are. We have to hurry, the train will be leaving."

"Where am I going?"

A tear trickled down the woman's pale tired face. "Far away, dear. You're going far, far away."

"Why do I have to go? Have I been naughty? Is that why you're sending me away?"

The solitary tear was joined by another and then another and when she spoke she choked back a sob. "No you haven't been naughty. You're a good boy. When the war is over …" The tears flowed very freely now. "When the war is over and you come back to England—"

"Back from where?"

"Never you mind where. You're going somewhere safe; that's all you need to know. Your name is Edward Powley. Say it for me, love. Repeat it."

He resisted stubbornly.. "I don't like that name."

"Do you think you have another name?"

He searched his mind. "I don't know. I just don't like being Edward."

Her grip tightened on his shoulders and she hissed at him impatiently. "We don't have time for this. If you don't want to be Edward, pick another name, any name, when you arrive."

He startled as the locomotive issued another shrill blast of steam. The woman leaned down and kissed his cheek. "It will all be over by the time you come home and then you'll remember."

Mr. Whitby's voice interrupted Buddy's train of thought. The lawyer and the detective were still inside the house.

"We haven't had a case like that in the last fifty years," the lawyer said. "We don't try children for murder, not these days."

"Maybe not," the detective said. His London voice contrasted with the lawyer's refined tones, sounding hard and uncompromising. "The fact is we have a body with a bullet wound to the skull, obviously a murder—"

"Could be a suicide."

"Not at that angle. No, it's a murder, and all we have to go on is your client, eight years old at the time, and suffering from a convenient memory loss. We can't ignore it, Whitby. We have to ask him some hard questions, and whether you like it or not, eight is the age of responsibility under English law."

The conversation echoed in Buddy's head. They had found someone inside; someone with a bullet wound to the skull. The detective hadn't said a bullet wound to the head, he had said a bullet wound to the skull, and that implied a skeleton rather than a body. They had found a skeleton inside that had been there ever since the house had been bombed, ever since Buddy had gone to Canada, and the detective wanted to blame Buddy's eight-year-old self for the murder.

Buddy stepped away from the door. He couldn't let this happen. He couldn't let his absence of memory lead to a murder charge. He had to remember. He had to tease every last strand of information from his reluctant brain. He would begin here. This was where he ate breakfast before school. School! Yes, he knew how to get to school.

He walked away from the ruined house, following a map that unrolled behind his eyes. Turn left from St. Godric Street; be careful of the buses as you cross St. Swithin Avenue; don't dawdle outside the newsagent; you can read the comics when you get home. Go straight into school, and don't waste time talking.

His feet traced a path through the ruins. So this was what the Germans had done. Ma had told him that he would be shocked. No bombs had landed on his quiet Canadian town, so far from the war, so far from anywhere, but he knew, because he'd read it in the newspapers, that some English cities had been bombed into rubble.

He followed the ruined street, turning right, turning left, and feeling no surprise as he came to a wider boulevard. A memory flickered to life. This was St. Swithin Avenue, where he had to watch out for buses, but no buses could run here now among the potholes and rubble. Nonetheless, his mind insisted on showing him this same street crowded with schoolchildren, walking in twos and threes, and he was among them but walking alone. Why alone?

The street was deserted now, apart from an old man with a white beard who sat on the remnants of a garden wall, with a pipe in one hand and a box of matches in the other. He looked up and nodded as Buddy passed him, and then returned to lighting his pipe.

Buddy nodded in return, wondering if the man was even real or if he was part of the kaleidoscope of people tumbling and twisting in his head.

He left the man behind and walked a few more paces before turning to face the sea and a view that was surely familiar. From here he could see down to the seafront and the sparkling minarets of the Royal Pavilion. He was a small boy again, forbidden to go down into the town, with its crowded streets and people who would ... What? What would people do?

He wasn't a child now, and he was not afraid of the town streets, but he knew his answer was not down there among the stores and hotels. He turned his back on the sea and looked up to the wide expanse of the South Downs, where a grove of trees stood atop a hill. This was the way he should go.

CHAPTER THREE

Toby Whitby

Toby could see pain and panic written on Evvie Stewart's face as she sat in the bleak interview room at Brighton Police Station, twisting her hands in her lap.

"Why aren't you looking for him?" she asked. "He's all on his own here. He doesn't know anyone. What will he do?"

Roy caught hold of his wife's hand, and Toby looked at the way Evvie's plump fingers returned Roy's grip. He saw the dusting of gray hairs on the back of Roy's calloused hand, and the way that Evvie's wedding ring had embedded itself into the flesh of her finger. He thought of his own wife, with her brand-new wedding ring, and his own hands, where the only calluses were the result of holding a pen. He imagined how he would feel if his stepdaughter ran away.

Buddy had not even entered the house and seen the skeletal remains trapped beneath the dresser, so why had he run? Where had he gone?

Percy Slater sat back in his chair on the opposite side of the table. Toby realized with sudden disappointment that the table between them marked Slater as an adversary. In fact, simply by requesting that Buddy's parents meet him at the station and not at Toby's office, Slater had already gained the upper hand.

"Well?" Evvie asked. "Are you going to look for him?"

Slater nodded. "Of course, but we're short-staffed, Mrs. Stewart, and we have …" He fell silent for a moment. "We have an important event this week, and that has most of the manpower tied up." He looked at Toby and then back at Evvie. "I'm not sure who is going to be put in charge of this case. I'm only here as a favor to Mr. Whitby. This isn't my normal beat."

He leaned forward and spoke in a low voice. "There's only one reason why we would mount a full-scale search for your son, and you're not going to like it."

His eyes flicked from the Stewarts to Toby and seemed to ask a question. *Should I tell them?*

Toby nodded. *Might as well. It will come out sooner or later.*

Slater turned his attention back to the Stewarts. "English law deems that an eight-year-old child is capable of knowing right from wrong and is therefore capable of knowingly committing a crime. Buddy led you to a house where he lived when he was eight, and we found the remains of a murder victim."

Roy was suddenly on his feet. "Now wait a minute."

"I am waiting," Slater said, "and I am hoping that your son will make his way back to you and will have a reasonable explanation for his actions. If we launch a search for him, I don't know what might happen. I'm asking you to be patient and let me work this out behind the scenes the best way I can."

Toby flashed his friend a grateful smile. "He's trying to help you."

Roy shook his head. "This makes no sense. He was just a little kid when he left here. He didn't kill anyone."

"Probably not," Slater agreed. "But I can't do anything to help until he shows up and explains himself. As I told you, we have an important event this week, and we're short-staffed. It will be better if he comes in by himself."

Evvie buried her face in her hands, and Roy sat down again to put his arm around her.

While Toby groped for words, the door was abruptly flung open, and a short, balding man in a tan raincoat bounced eagerly into the room.

"I was just passing by, you know, been to see your chief constable, and I heard you had an interesting case in here, so I thought I'd come and help you, you being shorthanded."

The man's accent was pure Yorkshire, and his red face spoke of a life spent outdoors. Toby's eyes were drawn to the newcomer's eyebrows, thick and yellow, as if to make up for the lack of hair on his head.

Slater was on his feet. "What the—?"

"Cameron," said the newcomer, extending a hand to Slater. "Detective Inspector Robert Cameron, on secondment from the North Riding of Yorkshire Constabulary for the … you know … for the event."

"I didn't know anything about—" Slater stuttered.

"Of course not," Cameron agreed. "It was all worked out by the bigwigs upstairs. There's a contingent of us coming down to help you all out with security. I came by to introduce myself to your chief, and I heard you had this interesting case." He looked at Roy and Evvie, and grinned. "Are these the parents?"

For a moment, Slater seemed lost for words, and in that moment of hesitation, Cameron hooked a chair with his foot and dragged it over to place it beside Slater.

Slater remained standing. Cameron patted Slater's chair. "Sit down, sit down. We're all friends here. I had it from your chief himself, that I should give you a hand. Oops!" His hand flew up to cover his mouth. "Sorry about that. Tactless, I know. Didn't mean to refer to your … well, you know, your missing—"

Slater cut him off abruptly. "I don't need your help."

"Ah, well," Cameron said thoughtfully, "I think you do. I see you have the parents of the young murderer here."

"He's not a murderer," Evvie hissed.

"Maybe not," Cameron allowed, "but from what I hear, he's not who he says he is. His name is not Edward Powley."

"He doesn't know his real name," Evvie explained. "He has some kind of amnesia."

"Amnesia," Cameron repeated. "Very handy."

Roy was on his feet again. "Now you hold on a minute."

Cameron sat back in his chair and turned to Slater. "I'm just trying to help out," he declared.

Slater's voice was an angry hiss. "We don't need help."

"Well, you should take that up with your chief constable. I told him I had a couple of days before I was needed at the … you know, the big event, and he told me I should pitch in and help you. I expect you want to detain the parents. We can hold them for bringing him into the country on a false passport."

Toby surged to his feet and spread his hands on the table so that he was eye to eye with the newcomer.

"The Stewarts are my clients. They obtained his passport with the same paperwork that accompanied the boy to Canada as a child. They had no way of knowing that he wasn't Edward Powley."

"Really?" Cameron sniffed. "He's lived with them for twelve years, and he only answers to a nickname. He won't let them call him Edward …" His gaze flicked from Toby to Evvie. "Well, Mrs. Stewart, didn't you find that suspicious?"

"He was just a poor, frightened little mite," Evvie said. "We didn't want to upset him any more than he was already upset."

"What do you think upset him?" Cameron asked.

"Being dragged away from his home and put on a ship," Evvie said forcefully. "It's enough to upset anyone."

"Maybe," Cameron said, "but most children managed to remember their own names. Maybe it wasn't the voyage that upset him. Maybe it was what happened before he left. Maybe—"

Cameron stopped speaking as Slater's hand descended, and Toby saw Slater's knuckles turn white as he squeezed Cameron's shoulder. Slater had built up considerable strength in his five remaining fingers, and the squeeze was enough to silence the other man, if only for a moment.

"Let's not get ahead of ourselves," Slater said.

Cameron spread his hands. "Sorry about that. You know how it is with us Yorkshire folk. We like to speak our minds. I'm only trying to help."

Slater returned to his seat. "Maybe you should stop talking and start listening."

Toby stared at Slater in astonishment. "Are you going to let him do this?"

Cameron gave Toby a smile that was all teeth but very little warmth. "The chief constable thought I could help. We all like to do what the chief constable wants."

"But—" Toby bit off his next words. He knew that Slater was on an undercover special assignment and no longer answered to Reginald Peacock, the chief constable, but he suspected that Slater's new assignment was not generally known. For the moment at least, he would have to pretend he was still answerable to the chief constable, and that meant he would have to allow Cameron to share in the inquiry.

Slater released Cameron's shoulder. "I think you should listen to what Mr. and Mrs. Stewart have to say before you start talking about arresting them."

"They brought the children up from Quebec to Toronto," Roy said. "We read about it in the paper. Most of them had a place to go, but not all of them. Some arrangements fell through, and homes had to be found. We didn't have any children, and Evvie said we should take one. I wasn't so sure. I told her she could get her heart broken by loving a child who had to be returned at the end of the war."

Evvie smiled, ignoring Cameron's beetling brows. "We decided we'd go and look. It's a long ride from Tobermory to Toronto, and all the way there, I kept thinking about how we would get a little girl and I could teach her to sew, and cook and ..." She shook her head. "You have to understand, Inspector Cameron, that every little girl in Canada has read *Anne of Green Gables*, and—"

"Evvie," Roy said, "I don't think these officers wants to know about *Anne of Green Gables*."

"No, of course not. I'm sorry. Well, anyway, when we got to the office of the Children's Overseas Reception Board, the girls had all been taken away, and just a few boys were left. They were wearing school uniforms, blazers, caps, short pants, all except one. He didn't look like the others."

Cameron looked at her quizzically.

"I knew he was the one," Evvie said.

August 1940
Toronto, Canada
Evvie Stewart

Five boys aged from six to twelve sat disconsolately in the echoing dining hall of the hostel. They had thin, pinched faces, as though they were in need of a good meal and clean country air. Evvie and Roy joined the small group of men and women who stood uncomfortably in the doorway, eyeing the children.

"Well?" Roy asked. "Do you want one?"

Evvie's heart sank. Roy spoke as though choosing a child was like choosing a puppy, or even a new hat. She knew that she was only borrowing someone else's child for the duration of the war, and that could be a matter of months or a matter of years. She had lost hope of ever having a child of her own, but she knew she could love someone else's child. She had love to give, but looking at the hostile faces of the English boys, she couldn't imagine that any of them would be willing to receive her love.

A woman, tall, dark haired, with the confident stride of a farm woman, stepped forward abruptly and positioned herself in front of the largest of the boys.

"This one," she said. "We will take this one. He looks strong. Where's his paperwork?"

Mrs. McKinder, the welfare officer, handed her a sheaf of papers.

The farm woman shuffled the paperwork and looked appraisingly at the boy. "Michael Johnson, aged twelve. Yes, we will take Michael."

Michael grinned triumphantly and looked back at the other children. Evvie could read his expression. His future was decided; he had been chosen.

She wondered what would happen to the boys who were not chosen. They were all here because the authorities had failed to find the host families who were supposed to meet them. Well, surely they couldn't be sent back across the treacherous Atlantic to England, so where would they go? Would they be forced upon families who didn't want them? If Roy would let her, she would take them all. They were nothing but poor little scruffians fleeing the coming destruction.

She turned to whisper to Roy. "That woman is only looking for a farm laborer. That shouldn't be allowed. Can't we—?"

"No," Roy hissed. "We can't take them all. Choose one."

One boy sat apart from the others, separated not just by distance but by the defensive set of his shoulders. He was afraid of the other boys. Why? She examined his face. His eyes were brown and shadowed with fear. The other boys had pale skin and cheeks reddened by exposure to the sun on the voyage over, but this boy's skin was darker,

29

almost olive, and marked with the bruised remnants of a black eye. The other boys had neatly cropped hair, but this boy's hair fell in lank dark curls almost to his collar. When he looked at Evvie from under sweeping dark lashes, her heart melted.

"That one," she said to Roy. "He's not like the others."

She knew that Roy couldn't see what she saw. He saw a boy like all the other boys in a gray school blazer, but she saw that the blazer was too big for him, that he wore stained khaki shorts instead of gray flannel school uniform shorts, and instead of school shoes, he wore sandals. This boy did not belong.

"That one," she said again.

She approached tentatively and lifted the plastic disk tied on a cord around his neck. That, she vowed, would be the first thing to go.

"Hello, Edward," she said.

"I'm not Edward," he replied.

"Who are you?"

"Don't know."

Evvie looked back at Mrs. McKinder, the welfare officer, who stood in the doorway, watching the dispersal of her charges.

"He says he's not Edward."

Mrs. McKinder shrugged. She seemed tired and impatient. Perhaps she'd had her fill of small, unhappy boys. "Some of them are very confused. His paperwork is missing, and we know very little about him. We don't know who is supposed to meet him. All I know from his registration number is that he is Edward Powley, Franciscan Primary School, Tooting Broadway, SW16. Aged eight. We have an address for his mother. He must have passed his medical before he left England, or he wouldn't be here. That's as much as I can tell you. Do you want him or not?"

Evvie longed to reach out and hug the small boy, to hold him until the fear receded from his eyes. "Yes," she said. "We want him."

August 1952
Brighton, Sussex
Toby Whitby

Toby laid a comforting hand on Evvie Stewart's arm as she stumbled into unhappy silence. "No one is blaming you, Mrs. Stewart. You could not have known."

He turned to look at Slater and Cameron. He could not see how they could resist Evvie's pained honesty, and yet doubt was written on both their faces. He had a sinking feeling that Slater was no longer operating as his friend and had formed a partnership with Cameron. Now Slater was just another police officer, filled with suspicion and ready to believe the worst.

"My clients were told that the boy's name was Edward Powley and he came from London," Toby said firmly. "He was evacuated along with a group of approved evacuees. No one had any reason to believe that he was not who he claimed to be."

Evvie corrected him quietly. "He didn't claim to be anyone. He only said that he didn't want to be called Edward or Eddie, and he didn't want to talk about his life in London. He was obviously very disturbed."

"Murder will do that to a kid," Cameron said.

Roy leaned forward, but it was Evvie who spoke. "You will not speak that way about my son."

"He's not your son," Cameron replied.

Evvie's tone was fierce. "I'm the only mother he has, and Roy's the only father. We never heard another word from England. I made him write letters to his mother. I mailed them myself. When we didn't get any replies, I thought it was because of the war, but then after the war, we still heard nothing. She didn't want him back, or at least that's what I thought. Of course, now I know the truth."

"And what is that?" Cameron asked.

"We came here together," Roy said, "me and Evvie and Buddy, to find Buddy's mother so we could adopt him properly. He's almost twenty-one, almost an adult, so we want to make it legal before he comes of age. Our solicitor in Canada wrote letters to the address in London, but we got no replies, so we came here. We figured that his mother or father, if he has one, couldn't object, as they'd shown no interest in him. We thought it would be easy."

"We went to the house," Evvie said. "We went to the address where I had been writing letters to. It was still standing. It hadn't been bombed." She paused and seemed to be searching for words. "London," she said eventually. "The greatest city in the world ... ruined ... It's hard to believe."

"It's better than it was," Cameron said coldly, making a hand gesture that indicated Evvie should get on with her story and stop bewailing the fate of London.

Toby looked at Slater, and Slater shook his head. He was not going to interfere. Toby was on his own.

"My clients went to the address they had been given," Toby said, "and they found Mrs. Elizabeth Powley. She's a widow. Her husband died in the war. She has a son. He is twenty years old and his name is Edward. He was a student at Franciscan Primary, but he was not evacuated to Canada. He is studying in London. She knows nothing about the boy who arrived in Canada wearing Edward's label."

"Of course not," Cameron sniffed.

"There's no 'of course' about it," Toby snapped, "and I would appreciate you changing your tone. My clients have done nothing. They took in a boy. His paperwork was in order. They have come here with the very best of intentions to legalize their son's adoption."

Cameron gave Toby a small, knowing smile. "So if the boy came from London and wore a blazer from a London school, what are they doing in Brighton?"

Evvie tried to answer, but Toby silenced her. He had no intention of giving Cameron any additional ammunition. "I can see no grounds for charging my clients with a crime. I assume we are free to leave."

Slater's hand descended on Cameron's shoulder again. He nodded to Roy and Evvie. "You're free to leave."

Toby helped Evvie to her feet.

"What do we do now?" she asked.

"We find your son," Toby said.

Buddy

Buddy reached the place where ruined pavement gave way to tall weeds and the remnants of a footpath. He pushed through a patch of goldenrod and found his way barred by a tangle of blackberry bushes heavily burdened with fruit and determined to entrap him.

Not this time, he thought. *I'm taller now.* The memory arose from the depths of his mind.

The goldenrod was as tall as he was, but the path was well-worn, and he could walk without brushing against the bright blooms and coating himself in pollen. He should stay clear of the blackberry bushes, because their thorns could snag his sweater, the one that had been knitted by ...

He struggled to complete the thought. Who? Who had knitted him a sweater? Not his mother, someone else; someone who had loved him enough to give him a blue woolen sweater knitted in a complicated pattern and far too warm to wear on such a hot summer day.

As Buddy pushed through the grasping blackberry bushes, he reached out and plucked a handful of berries. Their taste was sweet and familiar, but that familiarity meant nothing. Blackberries grew in Tobermory and all around on the Bruce Peninsula, and so did goldenrod. He was not sure he was even accessing a memory of his life before he reinvented himself in Canada. Pollen, blackberries, a hand-knitted sweater. Ma had knitted him sweaters. Had one of them been blue?

The weeds and blackberries gave way to chalky soil and patchy grass and a barbed wire fence. Beyond the fence, he could see the open space of the Downs and hear the familiar bleating of sheep. All right, that was definitely a memory from his time before Canada. The pinewoods around Tobermory were home to deer, moose, and elk but not sheep, and yet he seemed to know about sheep. He knew that if the goldenrod was blooming, the lambs would be almost fully grown. He knew that the purple daisies dotting the hillside were Michaelmas daisies; he knew that the sheep would not be interested in him; he knew that he would have to climb a stile ... and there was the stile, just as he remembered. His way was barred by a barbed wire fence, but he stepped up on the stile and crossed the fence without difficulty.

The path was clear now, chalk white where the grass had been worn away by a thousand years of peasants and pilgrims traveling from the coast to the cities. He followed his shadow as it stretched out before him, growing longer and longer as the sun began to set.

"Make sure you're home before dark, and don't let your father know where you've been."

Toby Whitby

Toby would be late for dinner. He was unaccustomed to having a wife to cook for him and wait impatiently for his return, and his old habits resurfaced easily. He needed to get to the bottom of this case, and he would do whatever it took to find out Buddy's true identity. Evvie Stewart was reluctant to let him leave the hotel where she and Roy were staying. While he saw a restrained anger in Roy Stewart's face, he saw only panic in Evvie's.

"I know he's not our own flesh and blood," Evvie said in her soft Canadian voice, "but we've raised him like a son. I can't bear the thought of him alone in the town. He's not used to towns. He's never even been to Toronto on his own."

"He's a big lad," Roy said, "and he's got a smart head on his shoulders. He'll survive a night on his own. It's summer and it's warm. It's not as bad as a night in the woods in the dead of winter, and he's survived that many a time with the Boy Scouts."

"A night in the town is not the same as a night in the woods," Evvie snapped. "Why did he run away?"

"I'm not sure that he ran," Toby said mildly. "He may just have wandered, you know, following a memory. I'm sure he'll be found."

"And then he'll be treated like a criminal," Evvie wailed. "Those policemen accused him of murder. He was just a little boy when he left. How can he be a murderer? Anyone could have done it. Why are they picking on our boy?"

Toby bought himself time by taking off his glasses and wiping at a smudge. He smiled, not a happy smile but a smile intended to convey the fact that the accusations against Buddy were nonsense.

"I don't know of any case in the last fifty years when that statute has been applied—"

Roy Stewart cut him off, his tone sharp and angry. "Give it to us straight, Mr. Whitby. Can our boy be charged with murder?"

Toby nodded reluctantly. "It's possible but highly unlikely. They have no evidence, and they haven't even begun an investigation."

"But does the law really say that a little kid can be charged?"

Toby sighed. "Yes, it does. Eight is the age of criminal responsibility under British law. At the age of eight, a child is said to know the difference between right and wrong, so in theory, they can knowingly commit a crime."

"Buddy is not a murderer," Roy declared, "not now and not when he was a little kid. When he came to us, he was just a frightened little boy, not a murderer running away from a crime."

Toby could not resist asking the obvious question. "Why do you think he wouldn't tell you his real name?"

"I don't know," Roy snapped, "but it wasn't because he'd just shot someone. He didn't know one end of a gun from the other. I'm the one who had to teach him. If you're going to talk like that, I don't want you as our lawyer."

Evvie laid a hand on her husband's arm. "It's all right, Roy. Mr. Whitby is on our side."

"That remains to be seen," Roy said suspiciously, "but we'll let it go for the moment. You go on home, Mr. Whitby. You've frightened my wife enough for one night. We'll start again in the morning, but we won't be talking to your friend Slater again, and you can tell him that if he asks."

Toby was still concentrating on the case as he drove home. Winning Slater's trust, and finally his friendship, had been no easy task for Toby. He thought they now understood each other, and yet Slater had done nothing to protect the Stewarts from Cameron's accusations. In fact, Slater had been the first person to voice his suspicions. Faced with a twelve-year-old murder, Slater had been ready to accuse the first person who came to mind, a boy who could not remember his own name, and he had even remained silent when Cameron had leveled his absurd charge that the Stewarts had falsified Buddy's passport. Surely he could understand that the Stewarts had simply obtained a passport in the name that had been given to their foster child by the authorities. There was no crime involved, but Slater had done nothing to protect them.

Toby tried to turn the case on its head and look at it from Slater's point of view. Why had the boy refused to give his real name? At eight years old, he had been old enough to know his name, even to write his name, so why had he refused? What secret had sent Buddy to Canada under a false name and with instructions not to speak of his past? As Roy and Evvie Stewart's lawyer, Toby wanted to protect their interests, but he was also an officer of the court. If a crime had been committed, he had a duty to report it, but an eight-year-old boy? No, something was not right, and tomorrow …

Toby shook his head and refused to think of tomorrow. Tonight was happiness enough. He put his questions aside and entered his new home.

Carol was in the kitchen, fussing over something on the stove, and Anita was at the kitchen table, reading a book. Toby's troubles melted away at the sight. This was all so new and yet so perfect. He had met Carol Elliot in February and married her at the end of July. In February he had been an unhappy bachelor, and now he was stepfather to a seven-year-old daughter. He slipped his arms around Carol's waist and nuzzled her neck.

"Sorry I'm late."

She reached up and patted his cheek. "I expect I'll have to get used to it."

"Is my dinner ruined?"

"I'm trying to cook you something else, but you can't eat yet."

"Why not?"

"You have a visitor."

Toby's heart sank. All he wanted was to be alone with Carol. Anita would be going to bed in just a few minutes, and …

"It's Percy Slater. He's waiting for you in the living room."

"Slater?"

"Yes."

"Why?"

"I don't know, but he seems quite agitated. Go in and talk to him, Toby."

He spun her around and kissed her on the mouth. "I'll be back."

She grinned. "I know you will."

Percy Slater rose and set his teacup down on a side table as Toby entered the small sitting room. He had shed his suit coat and tie, and wore an open-neck, long-sleeved shirt, with the empty sleeve held out of the way by a safety pin. Toby wondered idly whether Slater was ready to consider a prosthetic arm, or whether he thought about prosthesis the way that Toby thought about contact lenses; an unnecessary vanity when he could manage quite well without.

"Sorry to disturb you at home," Slater said, "but I felt bad about the way we had left things."

Toby nodded. "So did I. Why did you let Cameron do that? You have no idea how upset Mrs. Stewart is."

"I'm sure she is," Slater agreed. "He was pretty brutal."

"And you let him just take over."

"He had instructions from the chief constable."

"But it was your case."

Slater shook his head. "No, it's not my case. I'm on secondment to the Met. I'm not supposed to take cases in Brighton. I went to the house with you as a favor, that's all."

"So is it Cameron's case now?" Toby asked with a sinking heart.

"No, it's not. Cameron's just down here for special duties."

"What does that mean?"

"It means that if you leave it alone for a few days, Cameron will be gone back to Yorkshire, and Peacock will find someone else to put on the case. Right now we have no one, so don't expect a big manhunt. It's an old case, and it'll keep a few days longer. Meantime, Cameron's just poking around to pass the time. He won't find anything."

"Are you sure?"

"Well," Slater said, "he won't know about this." He held out a slip of paper.

"What is it?"

"It's the address of Randall Powley, Elizabeth Powley's estranged husband."

"She said he was dead."

"Well, he's not. He has a small place in Surrey, and he's growing watercress."

Toby paused. "Growing watercress?" he queried.

"Someone has to."

"I've never thought about it," Toby admitted. "Watercress is just something that people put in sandwiches."

Slater nodded his head to indicate the scrap of paper. "Do you want this address or not?"

"Yes, of course. I'm pretty much convinced that Buddy isn't Powley's son, but maybe he'll say more than his wife is saying. Apart from anything else, I have to wonder why she told the Stewarts that her husband is dead. Something is most definitely wrong here. I'll go and see Randall Powley and see what he has to say for himself." He took the paper and studied the address. "You're sure Cameron doesn't know about this?"

"I haven't told him. He'll forget about Buddy as soon as we open our operation in Arundel. That's what's taking all of our best lads."

"What's going on at Arundel?" Toby asked, thinking of the sleepy little river town just a few miles inland.

"It's the seat of the Duke of Norfolk," Slater explained. His grin faded. "He's not just duke of Norfolk, he's also earl of Arundel, and that makes him the Earl Marshal of England, traditionally responsible for planning state events. He arranged the coronation of George the Sixth, and he's arranging the coronation of young Queen Elizabeth."

"Why does that require a police presence in Arundel now?" Toby asked.

"The coronation is not universally popular," Slater said. "There are people who think Elizabeth's too young. The fact that she's married to a Greek prince with Nazi-sympathizer sisters is not going down well. No one wants Philip as the power behind the throne, the uncrowned king of England."

"Really? Is that what people are saying?" Toby asked. "People I talk to are excited about the coronation."

Slater shook his head. "You're talking to the wrong people. The people I talk to are very worried, and they're the ones with their ears to the ground."

Toby looked at his friend's face, now set in an unhappy frown. "So this is your new job?" he asked. "Is this why you say you've been seconded to the Met at Scotland Yard?"

Slater raised an eyebrow. "Yes, that's what I say."

"But it's not really the Met?"

"No comment."

"Why?"

Slater shook his head. "The mood of the country is turning ugly, and you can expect to see riots. Hitler's been defeated, but the war isn't over, and the Soviets are waiting in the wings. Hitler brought us all together, but he's gone now, and we're left to pick up the pieces. Seems we're not picking them up fast enough for some people, and they're ready to turn on their own government. So if they're looking for someone to blame, they might as well blame the new queen and her foreign husband."

"And because of that, you personally have to guard the Duke of Norfolk?" Toby asked.

Slater's frown remained in place. "No, not me personally, and it's not a matter of guarding. There's a meeting of the Coronation Commission planned for Arundel Castle. The Duke will be there, of course, because it's where he lives, and Philip will be there because he won't keep his nose out of the whole business, and that's why we're taking extra precautions. We're putting in a strong police presence, and that includes bringing in reinforcements from all over the country. Cameron's come with a squad from Northallerton."

"What are you expecting?" Toby asked. "Bombs? Riots?"

Slater waved a dismissive hand. "We're expecting trouble; just leave it at that. I only told you about it because you wanted to know why no one can work your case at the moment. It's a twelve-year-old murder; it can wait a few days, but Arundel can't."

"What about the body?" Toby asked. "What's happened to the body? You can't leave that lying around."

"No, of course not. It's been sent over to Colin Patel at the mortuary," Slater said grudgingly. "He'll take a look and let us know what he finds out. At this point, we don't even know if it's male or female, and I didn't get a good look at the clothing."

"But you're sure it's murder, not suicide?" Toby asked.

Slater shook his head. "I'm not willing to give an opinion. It's not my case."

Toby studied the paper again. He had already made up his mind. "I'm going to see Randall Powley tomorrow morning. Are you sure you don't want to come with me? Unofficially? Just to keep me company in case I lose my way?"

Slater scowled. "Haven't you heard a word I told you?"

"Aren't you even curious?" Toby asked.

"Of course I'm bloody curious," Slater snapped, "but ..."

"It won't take long." Toby tried to hide the note of desperation behind his words. He needed the authority that Slater would bring to the interview. He wondered if the secretive government agency employing Slater had allowed him to keep his warrant card.

"I've always wondered where watercress comes from," Slater muttered.

Toby grinned. "Haven't we all?"

Slater rolled his eyes and looked thoughtfully at the ceiling. "Well," he said slowly, "I might be able to kill two birds with one stone. I'm off to London on the early train, but I'm due in Arundel later in the afternoon to talk about arrangements, so you can drive me there. I'll meet you at Hackbridge station late morning. Let's say eleven. We'll have a word with this watercress grower, and then you can take me to Arundel." He held up a warning hand. "Not a word to anyone, not even your clients."

Toby accompanied Slater down the stairs and unlocked the front door. He opened the door and stepped out into the night air. Buddy was out there somewhere, alone, and no one was even looking for him. The moon was bright in a cloudless sky, and Toby briefly considered going back to St. Godric Street and starting his own search.

Carol called to him from the top of the stairs. "Your dinner's ready and Anita's gone to bed."

CHAPTER FOUR

Evvie Stewart

Roy was asleep. Evvie envied his ability to put his worries aside and fall into the oblivion of slumber. He had always been that way, even in the hardest times. In the anxious months after the war began, when Canadian troops were already being shipped across the Atlantic, Roy had been able to sleep, while Evvie sat up all night worrying. Roy had been confident that his work on the telegraph would be considered a reserved occupation, and even if he wanted to volunteer to fight, he would not be allowed. Telegraph wires had to be kept humming. Canada could not help in the war, or send food or shelter refugees, without a communication network.

Of course, he wasn't a young man anymore, and she was not a young woman. Neither one of them would see fifty-five again. Maybe she should have learned by now that worrying accomplished nothing, and yet here she was, still dressed, staring down at her sleeping husband and knowing that she could not close her eyes for even five minutes.

She looked out of the window. The moon was high in a cloudless sky, illuminating the waves that broke on the shingle beach. The rhythm of grinding pebbles carried in and out on each wave was alien to her and nothing like the rhythm of waves on Lake Huron. She could find no comfort in the view or the sounds, or the unfamiliar tang of salt air.

Was this really Buddy's hometown? His memory of an address on St. Godric Street, Brighton, had brought them here; just one clear memory emerging from the fog that obscured his early childhood. She wondered if he had remembered something else. Was that why he had run away and left them to answer questions that had no answers? He wasn't a shy boy; in fact, he was a very confident young man. He had a drawer full of Boy Scout badges to prove his capabilities, and dozens of friends as evidence that he was happy in Tobermory. Why had he run? What was his secret?

She picked up her cardigan and slipped quietly out of the room. Roy would not stir; he would not notice her absence until morning, and perhaps she would be back by then.

Earlier in the evening, she had asked at the front desk for a map.

"Just the local streets," she had said. "In case I want to go shopping."

The young woman at reception had pushed a printed map across the counter, her painted nails showing up red against the white paper. "It's prewar," she said, "but most of the buildings are still in the same place, if they haven't been pulled down." She made marks with a pencil. "Royal Pavilion, some people call it the Regent's Palace. This is the Palace Pier, and this is the East Pier. If you want shopping, this is Woolworths, and there are shops all along here, but you'll need a ration book for some things. Do you have one?"

"No," Evvie said. "We don't need them in Canada."

"Lucky you," the girl said. "Well, you could still go sightseeing, I suppose."

"Can you show me St. Godric Street?"

"St. Godric?" The receptionist chewed on the end of her pencil. "Saint …" she muttered. "There are some streets up behind the Royal Pavilion that all have saints' names. St. Swithin, St. Andrew, there's probably a St. Godric." She removed the pencil from her mouth, the top stained with lipstick, and made a mark on the map. "In here somewhere. It's not far. You could walk."

Evvie walked, and as she walked, she thought. She had known from the first day that something was very wrong, but she had dismissed her doubts. She wanted this boy to be her son, and she would not worry that he couldn't or wouldn't tell her his name.

She had kept her other doubts to herself, but they were still bright in her memory.

August 1940
Toronto, Canada

His school blazer was too big, but not in the way of a boy who was expected to grow into his clothes in just a few months. This blazer was made for a boy with a bigger build, a boy far sturdier than this boy would ever be. Beneath the blazer, he wore a voluminous white shirt with the cuffs rolled up and the collar loose around his neck. His khaki shorts were a good fit, but surely they were not part of a school uniform. The other boys who waited at the hostel wore short pants of gray flannel to match their school blazers.

Mrs. McKinder handed her a box of the boy's possessions.

"He brought this with him, and he has a gas mask."

"Why does he need a gas mask?" Evvie asked.

A sadness crossed the welfare officer's face. "No one knows if the Germans will use gas like they did in the last war. The children in London have to carry their gas mask everywhere they go."

"But not here," Evvie protested. "He won't need it here."

"It's what they've been taught," Mrs. McKinder said. "It will be up to you to unteach him. They are all very frightened, even the ones who look tough and confident. Underneath it all, they're just little kiddies who've been living in fear of being bombed and gassed. It has an effect, even on the strong ones."

The boy was silent on the long ride from Toronto to Tobermory, staring out of the truck window as suburbs gave way to farmland and eventually to the pine forests of the Bruce Peninsula. She saw his eyes widen as he caught glimpses of the blue waters of Lake Huron.

She had made several attempts to talk to him as they jostled elbows in the cab of the pickup, but his answers, when he answered at all, were monosyllabic.

She tried again. "Nearly there. That's Lake Huron, one of the Great Lakes. I expect you learned about them in school."

"It doesn't smell right," the boy said.

"What do you mean?"

"I know what he means," Roy said, breaking a silence that had lasted for hours. While Evvie had chattered at the child, Roy had kept his eyes fixed on the road ahead, but now he chose to speak.

"He means it doesn't smell like the sea," Roy said.

"Oh." Evvie had nothing else to add to the conversation. She had never seen the sea, only the endless waters of Lake Huron and Lake Ontario.

They drove on in silence until the road led them from the shelter of the pine forest to the stone harbor at Tobermory, where the fishing fleet lay at anchor and blue water stretched to the horizon. The boy jumped down from the cab and ran eagerly to the harbor arm, where he stood staring at the vast expanse of water that blended into the horizon.

"That boy's used to water," Roy said.

"His papers say that he comes from London," Evvie replied. "That's not on the coast, is it? Perhaps he's thinking about the Thames."

"No," Roy insisted. "He's thinking about the sea. He's wondering how to get home."

Evvie's heart was filled with sadness for the little boy in oversize clothes, looking longingly across the water to the horizon. Perhaps he was imagining that these waters that lapped against the harbor wall in Tobermory were the same waters that also lapped against the white cliffs of England. If that gave him comfort, it was only a false comfort. The waters of Lake Huron would not carry him home; they would only carry him deeper into the unknown.

That evening, while Roy brought out an atlas and showed him the Canadian provinces and told him of the rivers and forests and all the things they could do together, Evvie unpacked the boy's box. These, she thought, *are not his clothes. Every item bore a label or a laundry mark to indicate that they belonged to Edward Powley. They were, no doubt, what the parents had been told to pack: an overcoat, a pullover, underpants, undershirts, socks, gym shoes, boots, and pajamas. They were all clean and neatly folded, but they were so large as to be ludicrous. She was certain that they had not been purchased for the skinny boy who stood before her in tattered khaki shorts; the boy who would not allow them to call him Edward.*

August 1952
Brighton, Sussex

Evvie walked the length of the promenade before she turned her back on the ocean. She knew now what Buddy had meant when he'd said that the lake did not smell right. In those far-off days, she had never been to the ocean and didn't know the tang of ozone and the smell of seaweed. Now, of course, she had crossed the Atlantic on a liner, and she knew perfectly well the difference between lake air and sea air. On the whole, she preferred lake air. She wished she had never come to this ancient, broken country, the motherland of the Dominion. They should just have stayed home and made no attempt to formally adopt Buddy as their son. Instead of giving him security, they had destroyed the solid Canadian ground under his feet and brought him to a place where memory had sent him fleeing from them.

She stood beneath a streetlamp and studied her map before setting out along a wide boulevard where a number of houses showed signs of occupation. Lights shone from windows, and the sidewalk looked new and smooth. She saw a bus stop and a sign attached to a wall. St. Swithin Avenue. She was getting close.

After a short while, the new sidewalk petered out, and she was back in the ruins, with only the moonlight to show her the way. She had not seen the house for herself; Buddy had gone without her and with only the one-armed policeman and the lawyer. She should have been with him. Perhaps if she had been there, he would not have run away. The moonlight showed her construction equipment, a crane, and a bulldozer. She was close.

She saw the remains of abandoned houses on either side of a narrow street. A group of houses in the center of a terrace lacked a roof and a second story. Moonlight shone on a rubble-strewn front yard, and a row of sawhorses sat across the road. Were they intended as a barrier to prevent entry? Evvie ignored them. She had to know if Buddy was inside. If one of these houses had been his home, perhaps he had returned here. She pictured him sitting in a once familiar room, remembering his childhood in the misty years when he had been another woman's son. Who was she? Who was the mother who had sent him to Canada under a false name?

Mr. Whitby had said that human remains had been found in the ruins, and the odious Detective Inspector Cameron had even suggested that Buddy was the person who had put a bullet hole in its skull and the remains were all that was left of Buddy's mother. Now that she had a moment here in the nighttime quiet to think about it, Evvie knew that the suggestion was impossible. It wasn't just that Buddy had been only eight years old when he left England; it wasn't that he didn't know how to fire a gun, or that he was one of the kindest, most generous young men in Tobermory, and the last person anyone would ever suspect of a murder. Even if all those facts were ignored, Evvie knew that this was not Buddy's crime. Only a mother could have persuaded Buddy to join the line of children boarding the train that would take them to the docks and onto a hulking ocean liner. He would have run from anyone else, but he trusted the person who took him and told him to take a false name. Obviously, his mother could not have taken him to the train if she had also been lying dead in the ruins of her home. If this was his mother, she had been killed later, after Buddy was on board the boat to Canada. It was nonsense to think that anything else could possibly be the case.

She hesitated, struck by an unwelcome thought. The police inspector had said that they had found human remains; he had not said whether the remains were male or female; she had only assumed that the remains were female. What if a man had been killed and left to rot beneath the ruined house? A woman, presumably his mother, had taken Buddy to the train. The remains they had found could have belonged to Buddy's father. If that was the case, Buddy was not in the clear.

She made her way carefully past the sawhorses and set a tentative foot in the rubble-strewn front yard.

"Buddy, are you in here?"

A hand descended onto her shoulder. She spun around and found herself facing Detective Inspector Cameron.

"So," he said, "it appears you know more than you are telling me."

Buddy

For a brief, blessed moment, he thought he was back on the Bruce Peninsula, sleeping rough among the pine trees. If he opened his eyes, he would see Pa pulling the canoe ashore and coming into camp with a stringer of fish.

He tried to hold on to that thought as he blinked away the remnants of sleep, but he knew it was nothing but an illusion. Everything was wrong, from the coarse grass beneath him to the distant bleating of sheep, and the air that smelled of ozone and seaweed.

He staggered to his feet, stretching and yawning and very, very hungry. He looked around. The chalk path he had walked the night before had brought him to the crest of the Downs and the shelter of a grove of ancient oaks. He had followed the path until the moon had set and he'd found himself tripping over stones and snagging on blackberry bushes. He had finally been halted by an encounter with a surprised sheep, who had headbutted him before staggering off into darkness. He remembered thinking that it would be a good idea to stop walking and sit down in the midst of an outcrop of rocks, where he would be sheltered from woolly-coated attackers.

The sun blazed down from high in the sky. How long had he slept? He studied his surroundings. Something stirred in the back of his mind. He knew this place. He knew the shape of the trees and the rocks that created a circle within the grove. He had been here before.

He was wearing summer sandals, and little pieces of stony chalk crept through the holes and wriggled their way under his toes. He sat on a sun-warmed rock and unbuckled his shoes. He shook the stones out and wiped the soles of his feet with his hands. His mother had told him to wear socks, but he had said he was too hot. If he was so hot, why was he wearing the thick blue sweater?

Buddy was wide awake now and knew that this was where he had come, so long ago, in his sandals and his blue sweater. Why? He studied the rocks. The circle was not a natural phenomenon. The stones had been placed in position, but they showed no signs of having been cut or shaped; they were not the remnants of a building.

He paced around the circle, looking for a clue as to who had placed the stones. In one area, the rocks were smoke blackened, and he saw the remains of a campfire. He stirred the long-dead ashes with his foot, revealing the singed remains of a matchbox, but nothing else remained of whoever had made the stone circle. The absence filled him with an unexpected, unexplainable sadness. He felt as though he had forgotten something. No, not something, someone! This place, the stone circle, this grove of trees, was where he had once come to find someone who loved him.

His heart skipped a beat, and he remembered stern words of warning. He was not to mention the people who lived here. He was to forget that he had ever known them. Why? Why had he been told to forget about someone who loved him?

He stared in frustration at the trees and the rocks and the shadows on the ground, but nothing more would come to mind. From his viewpoint on the crest of a chalk hill, he could no longer see the town of Brighton, and the sea was a distant blue smudge beneath a cloudless sky. The path must have taken him eastward, away from the town. He knew he should go back and tell Ma and Pa that he was safe, but if he went back, the one-armed police inspector would find him and charge him with murder.

Perhaps he should wait until night and make his way into town under cover of darkness. If he could talk to Pa and tell him what had happened, he was sure that Pa would know what to do. Pa would find a way to put him on the next ship back to Canada without anyone knowing. He could return to the lake and forests of the Bruce Peninsula, and never leave again. He didn't need to know who he was; he had never needed to know. He should have put up more of an argument when Ma had suggested bringing him to England. What did it matter where he came from?

He studied his surroundings, looking for the path he'd followed the night before. He saw it as a white chalk trail across the hillside. It would be easy to follow this path even at night. Of course, he would need to avoid the destroyed houses where the police were probably still waiting. He would find another way through the side streets.

St. Hilda Avenue would take him to St. Swithin and past the school without passing St. Godric.

If he knew the names of the streets, why didn't he know who had lived on the hilltop?

A piercing whistle shattered the morning silence. Buddy took a step backward as a half dozen sheep, bleating and complaining, crossed his path at a run. A black-and-white dog harried them from behind, alternately running and crouching.

The shepherd came into view and stopped suddenly as he saw Buddy.

He wore no hat, and the rising sun illuminated the horror of his ruined face. Buddy took a deep breath and fought to prevent his shock from showing. He knew that such men existed, and he knew why. He also knew that horror had no place here, and neither did pity. The very least he could do was greet this man, smile, move on, and pretend that nothing was wrong.

The man fumbled at the scarf looped around his neck, pulling it up to hide his scars. When he spoke, his voice was muffled. "They're not here," he said. "They're long gone."

CHAPTER FIVE

Hackbridge, Surrey, England
Detective Inspector Percy Slater
With a hiss of steam and a squeal of brakes, the train from Victoria announced its arrival at Hackbridge station. Percy Slater stepped down onto the platform and flashed his police pass at the ticket collector, receiving a desultory salute in return. He located Toby Whitby's Morris Oxford, parked in the station forecourt, and Toby himself involved in an argument with a uniformed police constable.

Slater palmed his warrant card and approached the constable. "Is there a problem?"

"Illegal parking, and who are you?"

Slater looked at the young police officer's pugnacious face, his sharply pressed uniform, and the lack of chevrons on his sleeve. This constable was spoiling for trouble. Another few minutes, and Toby's car would have been impounded, or Toby himself would have been issued a summons.

Slater opened his palm to reveal his warrant card. The constable, PC 37, according to his badge, gave it a dubious glance, and Slater felt a familiar annoyance. So he thinks a one-armed man with graying hair and an undeniable paunch can't be in possession of this very special warrant card giving free access to all branches of all constabularies. Well, think again, sonny.

"Take a good look," Slater commanded.

PC 37 studied the card and then snapped to attention. "Sorry, sir. I didn't know he was waiting for you."

"I told him," Toby said.

Slater raised his eyebrows. "Is that the truth, Constable? Did my associate tell you that he was waiting for me?"

"People will say almost anything to avoid paying to park their car," said PC 37.

"And sometimes they'll tell the truth," Slater said. "You have a lot to learn, sunshine."

Toby opened the passenger door with a flourish.

"Here you are, sir. Sorry for the delay."

Slater leaned forward and removed a brown paper bag from the front seat. "What's this?"

"Lunch," Toby replied. "Carol never lets me leave home without a sandwich."

Slater tossed the package into the back of the car and settled into the passenger seat.

"Quite comfortable, sir?" Toby asked with exaggerated courtesy.

"Quite comfortable," Slater assured him, "now that I'm not sitting on your lunch."

Toby slammed the door and returned to the driver's seat. "Carol thinks I'm too thin. She's forever trying to feed me."

His expression conveyed impatience with his new wife, but Slater heard pride behind the words. Toby had a woman who loved him; life was good.

"I enjoyed watching you throwing your weight around," Toby said as he started the engine. "It's a long way from being almost demoted to being a member of an elite Scotland Yard squad."

Slater grinned. "Yes, it is, so let's try to keep out of trouble from now on. I'll do this one thing for you, but after that you have to deal with Cameron or someone like him."

Toby gave Slater a sideways glance. "You're curious. Come on, admit it."

"All right, I admit it. Let's go and see the watercress farmer and see what we can find out."

Randall Powley, the not-deceased husband of Elizabeth Powley, was hard to find. Slater had the address, but once they left the main road, they were soon immersed in a maze of leafy lanes and hedges.

Slater was a Londoner who had slowly accustomed himself to the wide-open spaces of the Sussex Downs, where trees were few and far between and the sparse grass was cropped short by sheep. Now he was in Surrey, in a countryside dominated by ancient trees and tall undergrowth.

He grunted impatiently as Toby drove at a snail's pace, searching among the overgrown hedges for a sight of Randall Powley's watercress farm.

They passed a gap in the endless procession of hedges, and Slater caught a glimpse of water. He tapped Toby's arm. "There. That's the river."

Toby backed up and looked through the gap. He took off his glasses and wiped them on his handkerchief and looked again. "I wouldn't call that a river."

Slater punched Toby's arm. "Not every river has to be deep enough for you to try to drown yourself in. That's the River Wandle, not much of a thing but very clean and fast flowing, perfect for watercress. Pull in here."

"It's not a road," Toby argued.

"It doesn't have to be. His address is Wandle Lane. Well, that's the Wandle, and that's a lane if ever I saw one."

Toby turned the car in through the gap in hedge, and a small cottage came into view. It squatted beside the stream with its feet almost in the water and its rear wall hidden under a cloak of ivy, turning red in the late-August sunshine.

They bounced across a barely discernable track and pulled up next to the cottage. Slater climbed out and stood for a moment, enjoying the warmth of the sun and the babble of the river as he watched a man walking toward them along the edge of the stream. He was short and broad shouldered, wearing a straw hat, a blue shirt, and baggy pants tucked into wellington boots. He carried a sickle in one hand and a basket overflowing with greenery in the other hand. As he approached them, he removed his hat and wiped his bald head with his shirt sleeve.

"Have you come from The Dorchester Hotel?" he asked.

"The Dorchester?" Toby muttered. "Do we look like the kind of people that go to The Dorchester?"

"Suit and tie," Slater said softly. "Don't suppose he sees that much around here. I'm assuming he sells his watercress to hotels and restaurants, and you can't get much fancier than The Dorchester. Let me deal with this."

Toby nodded. "You're the one with the warrant card."

"Yes, I am."

Slater raised his voice. "Randall Powley?"

The man in the wellington boots came closer. His face and forearms had been burned brown by the unusually warm summer, and his eyes were light gray and curious. He bore no physical resemblance to the skinny, dark-eyed boy from Canada, and Slater could not hold out any hope that Randall Powley was Buddy's father.

In his extensive experience of questioning suspects, Slater had found the element of surprise to be very useful. He didn't have a lot of time for beating around the bush; he was due at Arundel Castle. He came straight to the point.

"Your wife says that you are dead."

Powley came closer, his face twisted into an expression of wry amusement. "She wishes."

It was not the response Slater had expected. He found himself wanting to like this man.

"What about your son?"

Powley's mouth dropped open and he stared. "My son? Has something happened to Eddie?"

"You tell me," Slater said.

Toby elbowed Slater aside. "Wait a minute; just wait a minute. You're frightening the man. Nothing has happened to his son."

"We don't know that," Slater said, confident that Randall Powley was now off-balance and unlikely to lie. "Mr. Powley, let's start again." He flashed his warrant card. "Slater, Metropolitan Police. Can you confirm that you have a son named Edward?"

"Yes, I can. What's happened?"

Slater kept the other man off-balance by asking another question. "Was your son evacuated to Canada in 1940?"

Powley set down his basket of watercress and his sickle, and sighed. "I see. I thought this might happen one day. I told her she couldn't get away with it. You'd better come inside."

They followed Powley into the cool, dark interior of the cottage. They stopped in the kitchen, where Powley set his basket of watercress in the deep stone sink and turned on the tap.

"Have to rinse it off before the buyers get here," he said. "Slugs. They're a sign of a good, healthy environment, but buyers don't like to see them."

"Have you always grown cress?" Toby asked. "Did you do this before the war?"

Slater could see that the questing curiosity in the young lawyer's face would have to be satisfied before they could get down to the real purpose of their visit.

"I've been here for a while," Powley said. "This place had been in my family, but it was derelict. After the war, I needed someplace quiet and a way to make a living. I'd had enough of being ordered about, so I decided I could make a go of this. I do all right, and it's a peaceful place, just me and the river and the cress."

He shifted his gaze to Slater's empty sleeve. "You know how it was. Where did you get yours?"

"We're not here to talk about me," Slater said, sensing that Powley was trying to put off the moment when he had to talk about his son.

"Let's get down to business," Toby said.

Toby's abruptness came as no surprise to Slater. He knew that Toby was discomfited by conversations that involved comparing war experiences. Toby's poor eyesight had kept him out of uniform, and he avoided any discussion that would force him to admit that he had spent the war years in an office in London.

"Let me tell you about my client," Toby said. "His passport says that he is Edward Powley and he traveled to Canada in 1940 as a child evacuee, using your son's identity papers. However, your wife says that your son never went to Canada. She says that he is in London."

"She's a lying ..." Powley fell silent, apparently unable to find a word to describe his wife.

"Are you saying that your son isn't in London?" Slater asked.

Powley shook his head. "No, I'm not saying that. He's in London. He's studying at the London School of Economics. I see him sometimes, although my wife doesn't know it."

"You said that she lied," Slater prompted.

"She's not lying about Eddie being in London, but she lied about Canada. Eddie never went to Canada. She kept him in London. She swore to me that she'd send him to safety, but she lied."

Powley's face twisted with remembered anger. "All she thought about was herself. She didn't think about what might happen to Eddie. He could have been safe in Canada, but she kept him in London all the way through the Blitz."

He walked over to the sink and began to pick his way through the watercress leaves, pausing occasionally to pinch a slug and drop it into a bucket.

"I think she expected me to die," he said. "She thought I wouldn't come back, and so I would never find out. She was almost right. After Dunkirk things looked hopeless."

Slater thought back to the early years of the war, to the time when the people of Britain were beginning to realize that this new war might finally be the one that they would lose.

"Were you at Dunkirk?" Slater asked.

Powley nodded without looking up. "Went over to France in 1939 with the Middlesex Regiment. By the new year, we could see the writing on the wall. Things looked really bad. It didn't matter what the generals were telling us, we could see for ourselves that we were losing ground, and we had to retreat back to Blighty or surrender where we stood."

Powley's hand trembled slightly as he brought out a ball of string and began to bundle the watercress. Toby was about to speak, but Slater silenced him with a gesture. Powley needed to talk.

May 1940
Dunkirk, France
Randall Powley

He was too exhausted to protest, not that protesting would have done any good. He was a corporal, and no one listened to a corporal, not even the sergeant.

"Keep your opinions to yourself, Powley."

"We should never have been in Belgium," Powley complained. "Anyone with an ounce of sense could see that Hitler was going to take it, and now we're on the run."

"We're not running," his sergeant declared. "We are making a strategic retreat."

Powley settled for a snort of derision in place of any additional argument. The sergeant was as exhausted as everyone else. Even their young lieutenant was exhausted. The Luftwaffe had attacked relentlessly as they straggled through the flooded Belgian dikes on the long road back to France, carrying only their rifles and small packs. He felt an overwhelming sense of guilt as the column of retreating troops pushed refugees from the road. He knew a boat would be waiting for him at Dunkirk to take him out of this hellhole, but where would the refugees go? Who would send a boat to carry them away from the advancing German army?

His thoughts turned inevitably to his own family and neighbors. With the way the war was going, would they soon be refugees, dragging their few possessions and fleeing in panic from the German invaders?

The lieutenant, as bedraggled and exhausted as the troops under his command, pointed to a column of smoke on the horizon. "Dunkirk," he said. "We're almost home."

When they came in sight of docks, Powley could see a huge boat waiting in the harbor; waiting to give them a ride across the narrow English Channel. He joined a column of troops shuffling forward and waiting to board. This was not so bad. They had retreated ignominiously from Belgium, and the Germans had harried them all the way across France, but they would live to fight another day.

He heard the siren whine of the Junkers before he saw them. For a moment, he stood still in paralyzed disbelief. He was so close to boarding; so close to finding a way home. He dropped to the ground as the first explosions shook the docks and sent up spouts of water. The ship that was to carry him home lurched over onto its side. The Junkers came again, strafing the decks and the men in the water. The ship's engines exploded and sent up a column of oily black smoke.

Powley's unit ran for shelter in the stone buildings that lined the seafront, and there they remained, day after day, watching helplessly as the Luftwaffe rained destruction on the harbor and the docks. The ships that would take them across the Channel to

England could no longer approach. He caught glimpses of them well beyond reach, waiting helplessly on the horizon while the Luftwaffe flew raid after raid across the countryside to mow down the remnants of the British and French armies straggling back from the front lines. The long retreat across Belgium and France had brought the army to a place of no return. With their backs to the sea, their supplies low, and the harbor destroyed, it was only a matter of time before Hitler launched a full attack, and surrender seemed the only option.

On the eighth day, the lieutenant, hollow eyed but rigid with determination, gave the order to abandon their shelter and take to the beach. A desperate plan had been hatched by Churchill, and hope was reborn.

The lieutenant took the sergeant aside and spoke softly. Powley strained to hear.

"Can't abandon discipline."

"No, sir."

"But in the end, it'll be every man for himself. A fleet of private small craft is on its way. They'll come in as close as they can and pick up whoever they can. We have a designated place to enter the water, and we're assigned to a minesweeper, if it can get close enough and if it can stay afloat. Get your men into the water. It's low tide now, so they'll have to wade out as far as they can. If we lose the minesweeper, tell them to get on board anything that floats. We have to get this army back to England."

Powley crossed the seawall and got his first full view of the thousands of troops already swarming across the sand, as thick and disciplined as ants swarming out of a nest. He saw a scattering of large vessels out beyond the surf line and watched hundreds of small boats shuttling back and forth to carry anyone who could wade through surf. A flight of German planes screamed low across the beach, strafing the columns of men. Powley fell to the ground. When he rose again, he saw nothing but bodies between him and the surf.

The lieutenant was beside him. "Keep going, men. Can't do anything for these chaps. Grab that rowboat and row for your lives. Get on board anything that will take you. Go."

Powley waded into the surf. The salt water stung the blisters and scrapes he had acquired on the long march from Belgium. He dropped his rifle. What did it matter? Who could he shoot? He reached out for the abandoned rowboat. It was riddled with bullet holes and low in the water, but he managed to heave himself on board and fumble for the oars while the boat threatened to sink under the weight of the men clinging to the gunwales; men who saw the boat as their last faint hope.

Powley pulled on the oars. A vision of home swam into his mind as he drew closer to the waiting minesweeper. With each stroke of the oars, he told himself that he was not going to die on this beach, and he was not going to starve in a German POW camp. He was going home.

He looked back at the chaos he was leaving behind and was struck by a despairing thought. The next time he stood on a beach, would it be a British beach? Would he be there to stand against a German invasion?

As he rowed out toward the minesweeper, he set his mind on one goal. He would find a way to get his son out of England before the Germans crossed the Channel. Whatever happened, Eddie would survive.

August 1952
Hackbridge, Surrey
Detective Inspector Percy Slater
Slater laid a hand on Powley's shoulder. "You don't need to tell us the rest."

"Yes, I do," Powley said grimly. His fingers worked automatically, tying the watercress into neat bundles. "You have to know what it felt like."

"I was in Normandy," Slater said.

"Normandy," Powley said without raising his head. "You were winners, heroes, soldiers in the army that won the war. At Dunkirk we were losers. We let ourselves be pushed out of Europe. We ran back to England with our tails between our legs."

"No one thought of it that way," Toby said.

Powley tied a knot with savage intensity. "I did."

He lifted another bundle of watercress.

"They gave us home leave, enough time for a bath and a quick cup of tea while the generals decided what to do next. So I went home to my wife and told her what I wanted. We knew children were being sent to Canada. I knew some people, distant relatives, and I had some money set aside. I told her to do whatever it would take to get him passage on a ship, and she said she would."

Powley gathered another handful of watercress and tied another knot before he spoke again.

"Two days, that was all we had. Two days, and my unit was on its way up to East Anglia to protect the airfields. I saw it for myself then, wave after wave of bombers heading for London, but I knew Eddie was okay because he was being evacuated. I wrote home, and Elizabeth told me she'd taken care of it and Eddie was going to Vancouver."

Powley picked a slug from the watercress and squeezed it between his fingers. His voice was tight as he spoke. "It was six months before I got another weekend pass and I went down to London. Coming into London on the train, I could see the damage, and all I could think was how good it was that Edward was safely on the other side of the Atlantic. Imagine my surprise when Elizabeth greeted me at the door, all smiles and happiness, and Eddie in the kitchen, doing his homework."

Powley turned away from the sink and dried his hands on a towel. "She sold his papers."

Slater heard Toby's surprised grunt.

"Sold?" Toby asked.

"That's what I'd call it," Powley said truculently. "She had Eddie ready to leave, or so she says. She even took him to the station, and then a woman came up to her and begged her to let the children change places."

Slater met Toby's satisfied gaze. A piece of the puzzle had taken shape. No doubt there were many other pieces of the puzzle to be found, but this was a beginning.

"Do you know who the woman was?" Toby asked.

"No idea," Powley said.

"I happen to know that he was a boy from Brighton. Could he have been a relative of your wife, or someone she owed a favor?"

"She says the woman was a total stranger."

"How about you, Mr. Powley? Do you have any connections in Brighton?"

Powley shook his head. "I wasn't even there. It's nothing to do with me. It was a total stranger, and my wife didn't even ask her any questions. She couldn't wait to sell Eddie's chance of safety to the highest bidder."

"I wonder how this other woman knew what day and what time the train was leaving," Slater mused.

Powley shrugged. "No idea."

"Well," Toby said in a placating tone, "it seems that everything worked out for the best. Your son is safe, and—"

"No thanks to her," Powley snapped. "She gave it all up for the sake of a few trinkets."

Slater met Toby's eyes again.

"Trinkets?" Toby asked.

"Apparently, the other mother was desperate," Powley said, "although I don't know why she couldn't just put her son on the list like everyone else. According to Elizabeth, she was willing to pay ..." He trembled with remembered anger. "She was willing to pay for our son to stay and face the Blitz so that her son would not have to."

"You said she paid with trinkets," Slater said. "What kind of trinkets? Are you able to describe them?"

"I can do better than describe them," Powley said. "I can show them to you. Elizabeth still had them when I came home for good. She said she had been keeping them for after the war in case I didn't come back. She'd been quite ready for me to die. I think she'd been looking forward to it. I took them and put them in a safe place."

"Where are they now?" Toby asked.

"Here, in this cottage. I'll fetch them."

Powley set down the towel he had been using and walked away. A moment later the floor creaked above Slater's head.

Toby lifted his eyes up toward the ceiling and spoke softly. "Do you think he'll part with them?"

Slater fingered his warrant card. "He won't have any choice. They're evidence."

Toby grinned. "Of course."

Powley returned to the kitchen and tipped the contents of a small cloth bag onto the table. The meager light from the kitchen window glinted on gemstones and drew Slater forward. These were not trinkets. He saw the green glint of an emerald ring, white fire from diamonds set in a pin, and the warm gold of a man's signet ring. He gathered up the treasure and moved to the window, where he could take a closer look.

He felt Toby beside him, looking over his shoulder.

"These are worth a lot of money," Toby said softly.

"A small fortune," Slater agreed. "I'm surprised his wife parted with them." He thought of Powley's smoldering anger. "He was very angry. Might have been some domestic violence involved. War will do that to a man." He fingered the emerald ring. "European cut. No hallmarks. These aren't British; they come from somewhere on the Continent. France, Germany, I'm not sure."

"Spoils of war?" Toby asked. "Something brought back from World War One?"

Slater sighed. "It's a sad day, isn't it, when we have to number our world wars."

"It's over now," Toby said.

Slater thought of the stream of top-secret information that passed across his desk on a daily basis. He didn't share Toby's confidence that the war was over.

"What about the signet ring?" Toby asked, taking the ring and bringing it close to his face, where he could examine it through his spectacles. "It seems unusually thick. I think it has a ..." He investigated with his fingers, and the bezel sprang open, revealing a hidden interior.

Slater dropped the ring and the pin he was holding and grasped Toby's wrist. "Don't move."

"What?" Toby asked, and then, "Damn, is that what I think it is?" Slater looked at the tiny white pill nestled in the hidden compartment. "Cyanide," he said.

CHAPTER SIX

Brighton, Sussex
Buddy

The shepherd's eyes were bright blue and seemingly undamaged. His nose and the lower half of his face was now hidden behind the scarf, but the left side of his forehead was decorated with a web of scars, and the hair on that side of his head was patchy. He held his shepherd's crook in a scarred left hand as he adjusted the scarf with his right hand. He kept his eyes focused on Buddy.

He's expecting me to run away, Buddy thought. He was certain that small children would run from this man, maybe even unthinking adults, but Ma had taught him better than that. This man had paid a high enough price; he shouldn't have to keep paying.

Ma spoke softly in his head. *Most likely he was a pilot or a gunner, a brave man shot down in flames by the Luftwaffe, and now he has to live without a face, or only half a face. Some would say it would have been better to die a hero instead of living like that. Show him respect, Buddy. Don't turn away; look him in the eye.*

Buddy kept his voice steady. "Why do you say they've gone away? Do you know who lived here?"

"They didn't exactly live here," the shepherd said. "They don't really live anywhere. They keep on the move."

The shepherd's scarf slipped as he spoke, revealing a web of scars on his left cheek and a glimpse of a bright pink nose. Buddy was determined not to look away. He would carry on a conversation with this man just as he would carry on a conversation with any man.

"Who are they?"

"Gypsies."

Gypsies! Buddy rummaged among this scant trove of memories. Gypsies? Why would he remember Gypsies? He pushed against the barrier in his mind, and the memory surfaced.

"Gypsies. You took my son to see those filthy animals."

His father's voice carried up the stairs and through the closed bedroom door. He pulled the pillow over his head to muffle his father's curses and his mother's screams. He knew better than to go down the stairs to confront his father.

At long last the screaming came to an end, and he heard the slam of the front door and the sound of his father's heavy footsteps on the graveled path. His mother came into the room, nursing a bruised wrist. He sat up in bed.

"Mum?"

"I'm all right, Henry. Don't worry about me."

"When I'm a man, I'm going to kill him. I'll shoot him."

"No, you won't."

"Why not? I'll be a soldier, and I'll have a gun, and I'll just walk in the front door and kill him where he stands. That way, he won't hurt you ever again."

Buddy buried his head in his hands as the forbidden name came to the surface. "Henry," he muttered. "My name is Henry."

"Pleased to meet you, Henry. I'm Leo."

Buddy looked up. Had he spoken aloud?

"No, I'm not Henry."

"You just said—"

"That's not my name. I'm Buddy."

That was better. He couldn't be Henry. He didn't know how to be Henry, but he knew how to be Buddy from Canada.

The shepherd extended his undamaged right hand. Well," he said, "you may have changed your name, but I haven't changed mine. I'm still Leo."

Buddy gathered his scattered thoughts and took the shepherd's hand. "Pleased to meet you, Leo."

Leo's scarf was in place again, and Buddy could see little of his face except the pain in his blue eyes. "Most people are not pleased to meet me," Leo said.

Buddy shook his head. "I mean it. I am pleased to see you. I was on my own up here all night, and I—"

"Why?"

"What?"

"Why are you up here on your own? You're not from here, are you? Are you American?"

"Canadian, well not really, but almost."

"Not really but almost," Leo repeated. "Sounds like you have a story to tell."

"No, I can't. I can't tell anyone."

Leo turned away to whistle a command to his sheepdog, who was holding the little flock of sheep in abeyance. At Leo's command, the dog leaped to her feet and stood expectantly.

"Would you care to join me for lunch?" Leo asked.

Buddy wanted to refuse the offer. What he should do was stay hidden until nightfall and then make his way back into town. Leo's eyes were expectant.

He's expecting me to refuse, Buddy thought. *He's waiting to be rejected.*

"Lunch?" Buddy said. "Sure, lunch sounds good."

Toby Whitby

Toby parked the Morris behind the Armstrong limousine that stood at the curb outside the offices of Champion and Company. He reached into the back seat and retrieved his sandwich lunch, hoping he would have time to eat before another emergency crossed his desk.

As he walked past the Armstrong, he stopped and leaned in the open window to greet Mr. Champion's chauffeur, who was sitting in the back seat, reading a newspaper. "Afternoon."

Morton looked up and pushed his reading glasses to the end of his nose. "Afternoon, Mr. Whitby."

"How's the boss today?"

Morton's eyes were noncommittal as he looked at Toby over the top of his spectacles. "Same as usual."

Toby nodded. Same as usual. That meant that his employer would be wearing his old-fashioned lawyer clothes, complete with striped cravat; that he would be teetering on the edge of an attack of bronchitis; that he would be impatient with what he called "the state of the country"; and last but not least, he would have a great many questions about their new Canadian clients.

The fact that Mr. Champion was in residence in his office meant that Miss Anthea Clark would be at her desk, outside Mr. Champion's office. Toby grinned as he looked forward to the opportunity of teasing Mr. Champion's faithful secretary.

He climbed the steps and opened the heavy front door. Miss Clark looked up from her typewriter and gave him a welcoming grin. Just a few months ago, she had been a woman devoid of warmth or joy, but events had changed that. More specifically, a geriatric romance with an elderly

Cornishman had brought a blush to her cheeks, a loosening of her iron-gray hair. She had even shown a grudging willingness to indulge Toby in his habit of unpunctuality, and to forgive his insufficient disciplining of his unruly hair.

Toby noticed that Mr. Champion's dark raincoat and homburg hat were adorning the coat stand. Despite the fact that they were enjoying the hottest, driest August since before the war, Mr. Champion was always prepared for inclement weather. Toby had long since abandoned the wearing of a hat or the carrying of an umbrella. He admired his employer's skills and long years of legal knowledge, but he had no wish to emulate him.

"Afternoon, Miss Clark."

"Good afternoon, Mr. Whitby. Mr. Champion would like to know where you have been."

"I have been about our clients' business," Toby replied. "Why is Mr. Champion here? I thought he was still recovering from bronchitis."

Anthea Clark sniffed. "No one knew where you were. Your wife … I hope she's quite well …"

"Yes, thank you. She's very well. What about my wife?"

"Your wife could only tell us that you had taken your car to London."

"Not all the way to London," Toby said cheerfully. "Just as far as Hackbridge station. I went to visit a watercress farmer."

If he had hoped to provoke a puzzled reaction from Miss Clark, he was doomed to disappointment. He had not known how watercress was grown, but Miss Clark was apparently well aware of watercress culture.

"Oh yes, the watercress beds on the Wandle," she said. "But …"

"Yes."

"But," she continued, her pale eyes determined, "I don't imagine Mr. Champion will find watercress growing to be a valid excuse for tardiness, not when he has one of your clients in his office and ready to raise the roof."

Toby felt a flood of relief. So Buddy had been found.

"Where did they find him?"

"Find who?" Anthea said, and then corrected herself. "Find whom?"

"The boy, Buddy."

"I'm afraid he has not been found. His foster father is talking to Mr. Champion now."

Toby's heart sank. He had hoped that Buddy would choose to return from wandering the Downs in search of his memories. The night had been warm and dry, and he would come to no harm from sleeping in the open, but where was he now? What was he looking for, and where had his memory led him?

"Mrs. Stewart must be beside herself," Toby said. "She seems very fond of the boy."

"Mrs. Stewart is in custody, brought in by an Inspector Cameron."

Toby's anger flared. "Cameron!"

"Yes, that is his name."

"He's an ass."

"He certainly appears to be," Anthea said. "If only we had Inspector Slater on the case."

Toby perched himself on the edge of Anthea's desk and began to unwrap his sandwich. "We do."

"Really?"

"Yes. Something happened while we were at the watercress farm."

Anthea gave him a quizzical and somewhat skeptical glance. "At the watercress farm?"

Toby spoke with his mouth full. "At the farm that belongs to Edward Powley's father; the father who is supposed to be dead. He's not dead. He's growing watercress in deepest Surrey, and—"

Anthea interrupted him as she brushed breadcrumbs from her desk. "I'd love to hear about this," she said, "but you'd better go in and talk to the boss. He has hearing like a bat's. He knows you're out here."

Toby stood up, rewrapped the remains of his sandwich, and set it on the corner of Anthea's desk. As he turned away, she called out softly. "Toby, come back. You have crumbs on your tie."

He flicked away the offending crumbs and straightened his shoulders. "Once more unto the breach," he said cheerfully. "I'll go and tell our employer all about our new Canadian clients."

He was ready with a justification for taking on clients who were not landed gentry. Many of the old, aristocratic clients who had kept Champion and Company in business had perished or lost their fortunes in the last two wars. The survival of Champion and Company demanded that they should broaden their reach and move beyond tradition. The new era under the new queen required new thinking.

Thinking of the new queen turned Toby's thoughts toward Slater and his canceled visit to Arundel Castle.

"Someone else can go and talk to the Duke," Slater had said as Toby took the road to Brighton. "The cyanide capsule changes everything."

Toby had felt a twinge of disappointment. He had only ever seen Arundel Castle from a distance, and a small part of him wanted to take a look inside its gothic fortifications and to meet the Duke of Norfolk, the Earl Marshal of England. That would really be something to tell Carol. Instead, Slater had insisted on being taken directly to Brighton Police Station, where he would take control of the investigation into the Powley affair and move it up the ladder of priorities.

Toby knocked on Mr. Champion's door, waited for a bark of admission, and turned the handle.

Roy Stewart sat with his broad shoulders slumped and his calloused hands twisting in a restless knot in his lap. He looked up hopefully as Toby entered. "Did you find him?"

"Not yet," Toby replied.

"Well, you'd better find him before that ass ..." Roy looked at Mr. Champion, sitting impassively behind his heavy oak desk. "Sorry, sir. Pardon my language. We tend to be plain spoken where I come from."

Edwin Champion arranged his lips into a thin but not unkind smile. "I expect that you have made a correct assessment of Inspector Cameron," he said. "Now that Mr. Whitby has finally arrived, I am sure we can manage to have your wife released. I can't imagine he has any grounds for keeping her."

"I went to the police station myself," Roy said. "He wouldn't tell me anything, and I wasn't allowed to speak to her. I don't even know how Cameron got his hands on her. She was gone when I woke up this morning. The receptionist at the hotel said she'd asked for a map earlier in the evening. Then she came down last night and went out." He shook his head. "I know she's upset about not being able to find Buddy's mother, but I don't know what set her off wandering in the middle of the night."

Mr. Champion looked up at Toby. "What do you think, Whitby? Can you get Mr. Stewart's wife released?"

Toby looked at his employer with a tinge of impatience. Edwin Champion was on good terms with the chief constable; surely he could have gone over Cameron's head to Reginald Peacock himself. Cameron wasn't even a member of Peacock's staff. What gave him the authority to start arresting people?

Mr. Champion returned Toby's glance and understood that he was being challenged. Yes, Mr. Champion could pull strings, but why should he? The problem of Evvie Stewart's arrest was something he expected Toby to solve.

"He can't hold her without charging her," Toby said. "I'll go and see what I can do."

Roy rose, straightening his long legs and unlocking his fingers. "I'll come with you."

Toby shot a glance at Mr. Champion, hoping that the old man would read something into that one meaningful glance. *Tell him to go to his hotel and wait. Don't let him come with me. There's more going on here than meets the eye.*

"Yes, of course," Mr. Champion replied. "Mr. Whitby will drive you in his Morris."

Toby sighed. It had been too much to expect. Obviously, Mr. Champion was not a mind reader.

Roy folded his long legs into the passenger seat of the Morris and stared impatiently ahead as Toby started the car.

"Evvie's right; we should have left as soon as that Powley woman said that Buddy isn't her son. I was just being stubborn. What does it matter if Buddy isn't really Edward Powley? We have a passport that says he is, and we have a return ticket to Canada. Evvie wanted us to adopt him legally so that there could be no doubt that he's our son, but that doesn't matter now. We just need to get home and get on with our lives."

"Has Buddy ever said anything," Toby asked, "that would give you a clue as to who he is?"

"We weren't looking for clues," Roy grunted. "We thought it a bit strange that he wouldn't let us call him Eddie, but we assumed he was just shocked and upset at being dragged away from home with no warning. He was in a bad state when we picked him up in Toronto."

"Bad state?"

"I think he'd had a hard voyage. He seemed to be in a state of shock."

"That makes sense," Toby said. "The other children on the boat had all been told what was going to happen. Their parents had made all the arrangements and made sure that the children were fully prepared, but Buddy knew nothing. One minute he's with his mother, and the next he's being crammed into some other boy's clothes and pushed on board a train. I don't suppose he even knew where he was going."

He must have been terrified, Toby thought. Why hadn't he said something to one of the chaperones on the ship? What had his mother said to keep him quiet, to keep him from saying that he should not even be on the ship?

"Are you sure he didn't say anything to you?" Toby asked again. "You must have known something was wrong."

"No," Roy snapped. "He said nothing. Of course, we knew something was wrong, but we thought it was just because of the journey and because there had been no one to claim him when he arrived. When we picked him up, there were only a few boys left, and they all looked a bit sorry for themselves." He swiveled in his seat. "If we could find one of those children that went over on the boat with Buddy, do you think they'd talk to us? Maybe he said something to one of them."

"You're right," Toby said. "That's a good idea. I'll get Miss Clark onto it. She's very good at that kind of thing."

"Really? I thought she was just a secretary."

Toby grinned. "Don't tell her that. She loves a challenge. Wait here a moment, and I'll go back inside and tell her what we want. She can be working on it while we drive down to the police station and get your wife released."

Buddy

Buddy walked for several minutes, following the little flock of sheep and admiring the stop-and-go tactics of Leo's sheepdog. They crested a small rise, and Buddy caught a brief glimpse of the white chalk footpath, where a lone hiker plodded toward some unknown and distant destination.

Leo caught his arm and turned him around. "This is my place."

Buddy saw a cottage nestled into a fold in the hills, where it was protected from the weather and hidden from the view of passersby. The dog harried the sheep into a pen, and Leo closed the gate.

"I'm late with the shearing," he said. "I should have taken care of that a couple of months ago. Now they'll be a real bugger to handle." He looked at Buddy. "Don't suppose you'd like to ..."

Buddy studied the sheep, seeing the sprigs of tangled gorse and bracken matted into their lumpy gray wool. They were sheep, the gentle, helpless creatures of his Sunday school classes; how hard could it be to hold them still and give them a haircut? More to the point, who would think to look for him here? The burned man had found himself a perfect hiding place in a cottage so old that it seemed to have sunk into the ground, its thatched roof at one with the surrounding vegetation.

Buddy made up his mind. "I'll help you."

"Great," Leo said. "Thanks, old chap."

Old chap! Leo's speech dripped with education. Buddy had never met an aristocrat, but he'd seen movies. Leo's voice was the voice of a duke or an earl, or a commanding officer. Perhaps Leo had once been in command. Maybe he'd grown up with privilege, expecting a bright future, even a seat in the House of Lords. It was all gone now. Now he was a shepherd, and not a very good one if the state of his flock was anything to go by.

"Come on inside," Leo said. "Lunch will be on the table."

"How?"

"Oh, I have a woman who helps. Mrs. Widdicome, Winnie, she gets my shopping in and makes my meals. Saves me going out, you know, in public. Most people don't ..." Leo's voice faded into uncertain silence.

Buddy nodded. "I understand."

Leo ducked his head and entered through the low door of the cottage. Buddy was about to follow him when he heard a woman's voice speaking from inside.

"Lunch is ready, Your Lordship."

Your Lordship. Buddy gave himself full marks for detecting Leo's origins. Leo should be in a manor house somewhere, with a titled wife, and sons who would be sent to Eton.

"I've brought a guest," Leo said. "Any chance we can stretch the supplies to feed another mouth?"

"A guest?"

"Yes, a young Canadian chappy. Hungry as a horse, I don't doubt. What can we do for him, Winnie?"

"There's a meat pie in the larder, brought it over for your supper, and there's bread, and I put in a new jar of pickled onions, and some cheese from the estate."

Buddy's stomach growled in anticipation as the woman continued her recitation of the foods available. Her voice crackled slightly, the voice of an old woman, and her country accent stood in contrast to Leo's enthusiastic drawl.

"I've brought you over some butter and the blackberry preserves from last year."

"Splendid, Winnie. Well done."

"And there's a Victoria sponge cake for your tea."

"Wonderful."

Leo's head appeared in the doorway. "Come on in, Buddy. No need to stand out there when there's food on the table."

Buddy ducked through the front door and found himself in a dim, low-ceilinged room dominated by a table set with blue-and-white-striped china. The white linen cloth caught the light from a small lattice window and drew Buddy forward in anticipation of putting an end to his two-day fast.

Winnie Widdicome was a small, birdlike woman. Her sharp face was crowned with a halo of white, wispy curls, and her eyes alighted on Buddy with interest.

"Did you say he's Canadian?" she queried.

"Yes," said Leo cheerfully, turning away and opening a cupboard. "I found him up on the Downs. He's going to help me with the shearing."

"You'll need all the help you can get," Winnie warned. "They've been let go too long."

"I am well aware of that," Leo said with a hint of irritation. He snapped his fingers, suddenly the aristocrat who would not be lectured by a housekeeper. "Where the devil is the chutney? Why can't I ever find anything in this cupboard?"

"Maybe you've eaten it all," Winnie said. "Shall I bring you some tomorrow from the big house?"

Leo continued to rummage impatiently through the cupboard, and Winnie turned her attention to Buddy. As the light caught her face, Buddy thought that he saw something hopeful in the way she looked at him.

"So, was you born in Canada?" she asked.

He hesitated, wondering if he should tell her the truth, that he had once lived just a few miles away and that his life had somehow been connected with someone who lived up here on the Downs. He studied her hands, strong, thin fingers and a slim gold wedding band. Did he know her? Were these the hands that had knitted a blue sweater?

He looked up at her face and struggled to find a memory. Her hair was white now, but what color had it been twelve years ago? He should tell her. He should just say it. *No, I wasn't born in Canada. I was born here, and my name is Henry.*

Leo turned from the cupboard with a glass jar in his hand. "Found it," he said triumphantly. "I knew there was some left."

Although he stood in a patch of shadow, his scars shone white and his light eyes glinted. He looked at Buddy and moved his head, a barely perceptible shaking, a warning perhaps.

Buddy smiled at the housekeeper. "Born and bred in Tobermory."

He saw the hope fade from her face, replaced with puzzled suspicion. "Tobermory's in Scotland, on the Isle of Mull."

"But also in Canada," Leo said. "Ontario, I believe."

Buddy nodded.

Leo's voice was cheerful but dismissive. "So there you are, Winnie. This is Buddy from Canada. We'll take it from here. No need for you to wait around. We'll eat a hearty luncheon, and then we'll take care of shearing the sheep."

Winnie took off her apron and hung it on a hook beside the door. "I'll be back with your supper."

"No need," Leo said. "You've brought plenty of food. We'll fend for ourselves."

Winnie's voice was still hopeful. "It's no trouble. I don't mind coming back."

Leo ushered her toward the door, but she hesitated and looked up at Buddy. "Did you ever meet any of the children who were evacuated? I knew someone who went."

Leo put a hand on Winnie's shoulder and propelled her forward. "Canada's a very big country, Winnie."

Winnie nodded. "I know that, Your Lordship, but I was just wondering."

"Of course you were," Leo said. "It's not every day you meet a boy from Canada. Off you go, Winnie. We'll take care of ourselves."

He stood in the doorway and watched until Winnie disappeared from sight beyond the rise of the hill. He turned back to Buddy. "Any reason she would recognize you?"

"No."

"Or you would recognize her?"

"No."

"And yet you did."

"No, I didn't."

Leo turned to the dresser and took down a striped plate. Buddy followed his every movement, fighting his unwelcome memory of a dresser with white plates and a man shouting.

Leo set the plate on the table. "I know you want to run, but don't do it, old chap. First rule of boarding school: never run away on an empty stomach. Sit down and eat."

Buddy watched as Leo cut into a meat pie. His stomach growled, and anticipatory saliva flooded his mouth. Leo set the slice of pie in front of him.

"Dig in. I'll talk; you eat."

Buddy crammed the pie into his mouth. He didn't think he'd ever been so hungry.

Leo cut himself a small slice of pie and added a pickled onion and a spoonful of chutney. He rested an elbow on the table and looked at Buddy. "I assume that your name is not Buddy and you were not born in Tobermory."

Buddy stuffed another forkful of pie into his mouth. After a moment, he nodded his head.

"And I assume," Leo continued, "that you recognized Winnie."

Buddy spoke with his mouth full. Ma would be so ashamed of him. "I don't know," he spluttered. "I don't know anything." He swallowed and spoke clearly. "I'm not sure I want to know."

Leo took a small mouthful of food. Buddy watched for a moment until he realized that Leo was struggling to chew. He looked away, embarrassed by Leo's difficulties, wishing that he had not stared. Ma had warned him. *They're heroes, Buddy. Don't stare; just smile. Treat them as you would treat anyone else.*

Leo set down his knife and fork, apparently losing interest in the food, or unwilling to eat while Buddy stared at him.

"I can't fault you for running away," Leo said. "I'm doing the same thing myself."

"But you live here," Buddy protested. "You're not running."

"I live here because I'm running," Leo said. "I should be living in the manor house. I should have claimed my seat in the House of Lords." His ruined face twisted in a wry expression. "Yes, I'm a lord. Or I was a lord. Lord Leonard Montard, Viscount Pulborough, hereditary heir to the Pulborough peerage." He shrugged his shoulders. "I had to give it up, of course. Can't take this face into polite company."

Buddy opened his mouth to protest, but Leo silenced him. "You're doing a good job of not being appalled by this mess of a face, and I thank you for that, but not everyone has your self-control. I am quite capable of frightening small children and causing people to cross the street to avoid me. I know that I'm a monster, and so I gave my inheritance to my brother. We're twins, but I beat him into the world by four minutes. That's all that stood between him and the title: four minutes. Well, it's his now. He'll represent the family in Westminster, and he and his wife will sit in the abbey for the coronation. He has children who will inherit, and I will never have children."

Before he could control himself, Buddy's eyes slid downward toward Leo's lap. Leo gave a barking laugh. "No, no, it's all in working condition down there, but I doubt I'll have the chance to use it. What woman would want me?"

"I don't—"

"You don't have to answer me," Leo said, "unless you know someone who would want to live with me in a shepherd's hut and abandon all contact with the outside world." He sighed. "That's what I mean by *running away*. I stay here, and Winnie brings me my food. Every now and then, I travel to the hospital in East Grinstead, where the surgeons make additional attempts to fix my face, but it's a bit of a lost cause. It's better than it was, but it will never be pretty."

Buddy wondered if he should ask what had happened. Would Leo want to talk about it, or would the memory be too painful?

Leo leaned back in his chair, and his eyes appeared to lose their focus. He looked up at the ceiling, but it seemed that his gaze went beyond the dusty old beams and out into the high blue heavens.

"It's very quiet, you know, once the parachute pops. Everything slows down. I could see my kite, a Lysander; I expect you've seen pictures. She was a ball of fire. Funny thing, I didn't feel the heat. Didn't feel anything much, just floating."

He lifted a scarred hand and touched his face. "If I'd known about this, I would have punched the release, sent the parachute on its way, and it would have been just me, the earth below, and God in his heaven, waiting for me." He shook his head, all semblance of a smile erased. "Instead, it was hospital and all the torments of hell."

"I don't understand," Buddy said. "Were you captured? Was it a prison camp?"

Leo shook his head. "No, nothing like that. I made it down safely. They tell me I was fortunate that I dropped into the Channel. Apparently, salt water is good for burns. I swam around for a while, and then I was picked up. I'm one of the lucky ones."

"So you weren't captured?"

Leo shook his head. "God bless the Royal Navy. They scooped me up, and off I went to Queen Victoria Hospital. They have a special ward for men like me, men without faces. It's not so bad when we're together and there's a surgeon there who tries."

He lifted a finger and tapped the end of his nose. "What do you think?"

"About ...?"

"About my nose. It's an Archibald McIndoe special. The bone was once part of my hip, and the skin was on my arm." He sighed. "Believe it or not, it's an improvement on what Jerry left me with."

Buddy glanced quickly at the smooth pink skin of Leo's nose, a contrast to the scarring of his left cheek. "It looks okay."

"Okay?" Leo said. "Okay? It's a bloody work of art, or so they tell me."

September 1944
Queen Victoria Hospital, East Grinstead, England
Lord Leonard Montard

Leo awoke with a start. For one short, blessed moment, his dream stayed with him. From his seat on the terrace at Montard Hall, he could see Daisy and Daphne playing tennis, long, suntanned legs in white shorts. He heard the thwack of the ball and Daphne's cry of triumph as the ball hit the white line, sending up a cloud of dried paint and skidding beyond Daisy's reach. He tried to hang on to the moment, the distant calling of seagulls, and the heat of the sun on his face.

The wisps of dream curled away. The heat of the sun was pain, not as bad as before, just a pulling and stretching and a steady throb.

"He's coming round. Keep his hands still. Don't let him touch."

Leo was awake now, still keeping his eyes closed, still wishing to be anywhere but here. He didn't want to see, just to feel, but hands clamped his wrists to restrain him before he could reach out and touch the abomination that the surgeon had attached to his face. The burns, the scars, surely they were enough; surely he didn't need ... this.

He opened his eyes and looked into the face of the surgeon who had committed this final indignity. He told himself that he had been passive too long. He had suffered silently through the saline baths and the wrapping and unwrapping of bandages. He had given in to the insistence that he get out of bed and socialize, join in the bonhomie with mutilated hands on the piano keys, exchange banter with the nurses. He had forced his numb, burned lips to join with his fellow faceless sufferers in singing bawdy soldier songs and fierce patriotic hymns.

He had done all these things while he waited for the surgeon to bring forth his pièce de résistance.

Sir Archibald McIndoe, the man behind the knife, smiled, and an expression of pride illuminated his unscarred, unmutilated face as he looked from Leo to the white-coated doctors and students who surrounded the bed.

"We call it a walking-stalk skin graft," he said. "It's a long process, but I'm confident of success. We began by raising a flap of skin on this young chappy's arm, forming it into a tube and attaching the loose end to his shoulder."

He poked at a patch of pink skin on Leo's upper arm. "This is where we started. Over time we've walked the tube up his arm, along his shoulder, and up toward his face, all the time keeping the blood supply intact. Now, we've attached one end to the place where we can build him a new nose. We'll take a bone graft from his hip to make the structure."

He touched Leo's shoulder and looked into his eyes. Leo tried to read the expression on the faces that surrounded him. Fascination and awe at the surgeon's achievement, but underneath it all, horror and sympathy.

"I want to see."

The surgeon nodded. "Of course you do. Bring the lieutenant a mirror." His hand remained on Leo's shoulder. "It's just temporary, Lieutenant. Try to keep that in mind."

A nurse approached. Her white apron rustled as she moved. She held out a mirror. Leo forced himself to look and not to flinch, not to shy away.

In the reflection, he saw what was left of his face. His eyes had been protected by his goggles. They gazed back at him, blue as ever, but bright with unshed tears as he looked at what had been done to his face. In place of his nose, burned beyond repair, the surgeon had sewn a tube of pink flesh as ugly and out of place as an elephant's trunk. The other end of the tube looped down to Leo's shoulder, giving him just enough slack to move his head a few inches in either direction.

He handed the mirror back to the nurse. For his whole life, he had shared a face with his twin: same eyes, same nose, same golden hair. Well, Victor was on his own now, the sole owner of the famous Montard good looks. Leo's mind was made up. He could never be Viscount Pulborough. He could never show this face to the world. Victor had the face, and now he could have the title.

August 1952
Brighton, Sussex

Leo's eyes came back into focus, and he looked down at the food on Buddy's plate. "Hope I haven't put you off your grub," he said. "It was kind of you to listen, but that's enough of my self-pity. Eat up. We have work to do. Have you ever shorn a sheep?"

Buddy shook his head. "No. We don't have sheep in Tobermory."

"And before you went there?"

"I can't remember."

"Can't, or won't?"

"I don't know. I think someone told me to forget."

Leo leaned across the table and looked into Buddy's face. "What about Winnie Widdicome? Were you told to forget her?"

Buddy felt a surge of anger. How many times did he have to say this? He had already told Ma and Pa; he'd told the policeman; he'd told the lawyer; and now he had to tell the shepherd. Why would no one believe him? Why did they insist on dragging his memories out into the daylight? What if he remembered a gun? What if he remembered shooting his mother?

Leo gave him a twisted smile. The right side of his mouth lifted and dragged the burned left side along. "It's all right. You'll remember when you're ready."

Buddy resented the reassurance. "I don't want to remember."

Leo shrugged. "I understand."

"How could you possibly …?"

Leo sprang to his feet. "Do you think you're the only one with bad memories?"

"I'm sorry. Of course, the crash—"

"Bugger the crash," Leo snapped. "I was on a night flight to France to pick up an agent. I didn't get there. I didn't pick her up. That's what I don't want to remember. What are you trying to forget?"

The words were out of Buddy's mouth before he could stop them. "I think I murdered my mother."

CHAPTER SEVEN

Toby Whitby

Toby pulled into the forecourt of Brighton Police Station and squeezed the Morris into a parking place between two hulking Wolseley police cars. He ushered Roy Stewart in through the front door and was pleased to find Slater waiting for him.

Roy released some of his pent-up frustration as he pulled himself to his full height and glared at Slater. "Where's my wife? Is this what you call justice? We don't do things this way in Canada."

Slater held up his hand to silence the big man. "All in good time, Mr. Stewart. I'm doing what I can, but this may turn out to be a very complicated case."

Slater met Toby's frown with an expression that said, *Trust me. I'm doing my best.*

"I want to see her," Roy declared.

"I'll have her brought up," Slater said.

Toby's frown deepened. "She's in the cells?"

"I'm afraid so. Our friend Cameron wants her up in front of the bench tomorrow morning, and he plans to keep her here overnight."

"What's the charge?"

"Buddy's false passport."

"That's nonsense."

Slater sighed a short, impatient sigh. "Of course it is, but I'm not ready to show my hand, not yet. I haven't told anyone here about what we found at Randall Powley's house, so Cameron is still meddling."

Toby looked at Slater in amazement. "But Cameron's a nobody. He's not even part of the Brighton Police."

Slater nodded. "I know. He's come down from Yorkshire to make up the numbers for the Arundel deployment. Unfortunately, he's made himself useful enough that the chief has welcomed him with open arms. I promise you that I'll get it all sorted out eventually, but right now I don't want to rock the boat."

Toby shook his head. "I'm sorry, but my duty is to my client, and I can't allow her to be detained. There's absolutely no reason. If you won't say anything, then I will."

Slater's voice was firm. "No, you won't. Your client is perfectly safe where she is. She's under the charge of our new woman police constable, WPC Connie Reynolds. Go over to the desk, and put in a request for Mr. Stewart to see his wife, and Connie will bring her upstairs. She might even make them both a cup of tea. Shouldn't be any trouble. Wait for me in the interview room."

Toby filed his request, left Roy Stewart under the care of the desk sergeant, and went into the interview room to wait for Slater. The room was stuffy with the windows firmly closed and barred. Toby stretched his long legs and made an attempt at patience.

The minutes ticked by. Toby took off his jacket and loosened his tie. If he wasn't going to see his client, he had no need to look like a lawyer; better to be comfortable.

At long last Slater appeared and closed the door firmly behind him. Toby sprang to his feet. "What's going on?"

Slater sat down behind the desk and indicated that Toby should return to his seat. "I've been busy in the records office, trying to find out who was living in the house on St. Godric Street. I thought it would be helpful if we had a name."

"Any luck?"

"No, none. The whole row of houses was owned by the Church Commissioners, and their records went up in smoke in the Blitz. After the bombing, the tenants scattered, and we have no idea where they went, so that's a dead end."

Toby thought of Evvie Stewart, who was facing the possibility of another night in the cells. He rose angrily to his feet. "So, if you don't know anything, why am I hanging around here waiting for you? I need to take care of my client."

"Your client is fine."

"No, she's not. I'm going to get her out. I can argue that Cameron has no authority here."

Slater nodded. "You can spend time doing that if you want to, or you can sit down again while I tell you what I do know."

Toby sat. "What?"

"I've had someone take a look at the jewelry Randall Powley gave us. Apparently, the style and cut are Central European, and I already noted that there's no hallmark, so they were not made in Britain. The initials on the signet ring are almost worn away, and the jeweler I spoke to was not even certain that they were initials. He thought that it could be a symbol."

Toby made an attempt to curb his impatience. "So what does that mean? How does that help my client?"

"It means that whoever brought young Buddy to the station paid his way onto the boat with jewelry from Central Europe, and that, combined with the presence of the cyanide pill, will give me a good reason to remove this entire investigation out of the hands of the Brighton Police."

Toby felt a lifting of his spirits. Cameron was an unwelcome unknown, but Slater was a friend. He could work with Slater. He reached for his jacket. "Let's get on with it."

Slater shook his head. "There's more."

"Yes?"

"The body in the house was female."

Female? Toby considered the implications before speaking. "Female," he repeated. "Well, if a woman was dead inside the house, it wasn't his mother. Obviously, his mother took him to the station and traded the jewelry for a place on a ship, and she couldn't do that with a bullet in her head. That lets Buddy off the hook, doesn't it? He didn't murder his mother."

Slater shook his head. "Suppose it wasn't his mother who took him to the train," he said. "It could have been his grandmother, or alternatively, suppose the dead woman isn't his mother or his grandmother; perhaps it's some other woman."

"You're not helping," Toby snapped.

Slater raised his eyebrows. "I'm helping," he said. "I'm asking the questions and drawing the conclusions that a prosecutor is going to draw. Buddy isn't in the clear yet. We need to go and see Patel at the mortuary ourselves. It's amazing what that man can tell you just by looking at bones."

"We need to find Buddy," Toby insisted.

"No," said Slater. "We need information. First let's find out what we're dealing with. Buddy will show up sooner or later. He has nowhere else to go."

Toby shook his head. "I can't just leave Mrs. Stewart here."

"Why not?" Slater asked. "I'll have a word with the desk sergeant and see that she's not taken back to a cell before you can get someone here to get her released or bailed if necessary."

"I need to do that myself," Toby insisted.

"No, you need to come with me. Call your office. Get your boss down here."

"No, I—"

Slater slapped him on the back. "Don't you know yet that you're the brains of the outfit? Champion's nothing without you. Let him do some work for a change."

Anthea Clark

People will think we're an old married couple, Anthea thought as she sat across the table from Colonel Hugh Trewin in the Bluebird Tea Room. The thought brought a blush to her cheeks. Really, she should not be blushing like this. She would never see sixty again, and neither would he. She was too old for blushing. Hugh was a charming man, but he had never done or said anything that could be considered inappropriate. He had asked to call her by her first name, but that was de rigueur in these casual postwar times, and once he had kissed her on the cheek.

Nothing else had happened; not so far. Nonetheless, here she was in the middle of the afternoon, when she should be at her desk, sitting in a cozy tearoom in the unchaperoned company of an unmarried man. Unchaperoned? Ridiculous. No one worried about chaperones these days. Her mother's face swam into view. *You are too rigid, Anthea.*

"So, the lad doesn't know who he is?" Hugh asked, and even those few words betrayed his Cornish origins.

"No idea at all," Anthea replied. "I'm sure it's very upsetting for him, but maybe not knowing his mother's identity is better than thinking that his mother is a woman who has been ignoring him for the past twelve years."

Hugh smoothed his neat gray military mustache. "It's still a bit of a rum go, isn't it? All these years, that poor boy has been writing from Canada to the woman he thinks is his mother, and she does nothing. It must have hurt his feelings."

"I don't think boys are as emotional as girls," Anthea said.

Hugh nodded. "That's true, Anthea, but boys do have emotions." He looked down at the crumbs of his tea cake resting on a Blue Willow pattern plate. "Even men have emotions."

She blushed again. Really, this blushing was becoming ridiculous. She would have to concentrate on the matter in hand. Toby Whitby had given her a task to accomplish. She was to find the names of other children who had accompanied their client across the Atlantic to Canada. Well, she had done that, and she had found an address and a phone number for a girl who had been on the ship and who was living in London.

Now she wanted to do more than find information in a phone book. She wanted to be useful, really useful. She didn't want to be a woman who sat behind a typewriter, transcribing other people's words, she wanted to be a partner, or if not a partner, at least an assistant. Yes, an assistant investigator. She should have a business card. No, she was getting ahead of herself. First she would have to prove that she could investigate. She had already phoned the girl and arranged to meet her.

So, she asked herself, why have you invited Hugh to join you? If you want to do this on your own, why are you including him? What has this to do with him? She found herself unwilling to answer her own question.

"I thought we could take the four thirty train to London Bridge," she said, "and then perhaps the bus to Catford."

Hugh shook his head. "I'll have a word with Champion, see if we can take his motor; no point in traveling in a sweltering train when we have an alternative. Who are we going to see?"

"A girl who went over with Edward Powley, or I should say, she went over with the boy that the authorities thought was Edward Powley. She probably owes her life to the fact that she was evacuated. Her house didn't survive the Blitz. Her name is Elspeth, and I'm afraid she lost her mother and father, but an aunt took over responsibility for her and brought her back from Canada. She's living on the Excalibur prefab estate in Catford and training to be a nurse. I've already spoken to her on the telephone, and she agreed to meet me this evening. I told her the truth, that the boy she knew as Edward Powley was really someone else, and I asked her if she could throw any light on that question. She said she'd think about it and see what she could remember."

"Well, then," said Hugh, rising abruptly from the table, "let's not waste any more time getting to the bottom of this. We'll get that Morton fellow to drive us, and we'll be in London by six o'clock."

Hugh offered her his arm as they left the tearoom, but she pretended not to notice, determined to keep the relationship on a professional basis. She knew she should be doing this alone, but it was very useful to have Hugh available to request the use of the motorcar and to direct Morton as they set out from Brighton.

At the end of the war, Anthea had gladly turned her back on London and retreated to her house on the south coast and her comfortable employment at Champion and Company. Now, as they drew close to the city, she was shocked to see how little of the bomb damage had been repaired.

Hugh, seated beside her in the back seat, fell silent as they passed from the leafy Surrey suburbs into the crowded streets of south London, where rows of houses remained boarded up and derelict.

"I haven't been up here since before the war," Hugh said. "We didn't see anything like this down in Cornwall. I wonder how they're going to get this all fixed up before the coronation."

"If there is a coronation," Anthea said.

Hugh frowned. "I know about the rumors," he said, "and the people who think Elizabeth is too young, and perhaps the Duke of Windsor should come back, but I don't put any store in such rumors. We have to be positive, Anthea. We have to welcome a new Elizabethan age; a fresh start."

"I certainly hope so," Anthea agreed.

She leaned forward to speak to Morton. "Do you still have the address? Do you know where we're going?"

Morton nodded. He had taken off his chauffeur's cap, and the oppressive heat had slicked his thinning gray hair down onto his scalp. They had driven up from Brighton with the car windows open, but now the windows were closed against the noise and exhaust fumes of the city traffic.

Morton turned from the main road and passed through an area of tall brick houses and sad, drought-stricken trees that crowded out the view of the sky. Eventually, they left the tall houses behind them and emerged onto an expanse of flat, treeless land crisscrossed with row after row of identical single-story houses.

Hugh wound down the window and looked out. "What is this? What happened here? Where did all these huts come from?"

Anthea stared out, momentarily disoriented. "Elspeth said she lived on the Excalibur Estate," she said. "I suppose this is it."

Hugh continued to stare. "I don't understand. Were they all built at once? Why are there so many?"

Oh dear, Anthea thought, *he really has been too long in the depths of Cornwall. It seems he doesn't even read the newspapers or listen to the radio. I will have to put a stop to that when ...* When what? Why would she need to change Hugh Trewin's behavior? What on earth was she thinking? *Pull yourself together, Anthea.*

"These are prefabs," Anthea said. "Prefabricated houses constructed in a factory and delivered in just a few pieces. I'm told they're really quite nice inside; two bedrooms, and an indoor bathroom, even a refrigerator and a stove. They're for people whose houses have been bombed. Temporary, of course."

"They don't look very temporary," Hugh remarked as they drew closer. "It looks as though people are settling in for the long haul, planting trees and rosebushes, and making themselves at home."

Morton turned his head. "It's better than the places they used to call home," he said. "When Hitler wiped out the docks in the East End, he wiped out houses that were little more than slums. For most of these people, this is the first time they've had indoor plumbing, or a nice piece of garden. You can't really blame them for settling in and hoping they can stay."

Anthea sat back in surprise. She had never given any thought to Morton as anything other than an extension of the big limousine he drove for Mr. Champion. She had never exchanged more than a few words with him, never thought of where he came from, never wondered where he went at night. Listening to him now, she recognized the London accent emerging as he spoke. So that was why he had navigated his way here to Catford without the benefit of a map, or stopping to ask for directions.

"Do you know people here, Morton?"

"A few."

"Relatives?"

"No, not relatives."

He reached into his pocket and produced a handkerchief to wipe his forehead. Anthea took this as a signal that he had told her as much as he intended to tell her, and that she should not ask any additional questions.

Morton drove on, guiding the car through a maze of streets bordered on all sides by little white bungalows. Although the houses were identical in size and construction, the occupants had expressed their individuality in a host of different ways, from colored front doors to painted nameplates, and extravagant flower gardens now drooping in the heat.

Morton brought the car to a halt. "Thirty-four Pelinor Road," he declared. "Will you be long, Colonel Trewin?"

Hugh shook his head. "I don't know."

Morton has someone he would like to visit, Anthea thought. *He may not have relatives here, but he has friends.*

"Come back in an hour," she said.

Morton climbed out to open the passenger door. "Thank you, Miss Clark."

Hugh, standing at the curb, gave Anthea a puzzled glance. "Why did you do that?"

"I'll explain later," Anthea replied. "Let's go and see Miss Elspeth Aleshire."

The front door was ornamented with an elaborate lion's-head knocker that had been intended for a much grander house. *Spoils of war,* Anthea thought as Hugh rapped firmly on the door.

Elspeth Aleshire was a petite, dark-haired young woman dressed in a striped shirt and white shorts. Her arms and legs were deeply tanned, and her feet were bare. *Perhaps she forgot we were coming,* Anthea thought, *and that's why she is not appropriately dressed.*

Elspeth greeted her enthusiastically. "Miss Clark, I'm so glad to see you. I've been waiting."

Apparently, she had not forgotten; apparently, she thought her clothing was totally appropriate. Anthea reminded herself that it was not her place to judge Elspeth's choice of clothing. She was not the girl's mother; in fact, the girl had no mother, only an aunt.

Anthea introduced Hugh, who bowed courteously and averted his eyes from Elspeth's legs.

"Do you mind if we sit in the back garden?" Elspeth asked. "It's really hot indoors."

Anthea nodded. She would have liked to see the inside of the prefab, with its miraculous indoor plumbing and refrigerator. Of course, Anthea had indoor plumbing at her house, but she had never thought to purchase a refrigerator, and yet here, where people had come from the worst of the slums, the government had felt it necessary to provide refrigerators.

Elspeth led them around the side of the house, where a mismatched group of kitchen chairs sat on the sun-browned lawn. Anthea looked beyond the low fence that surrounded the lawn, and saw row after row of identical houses, each with its patch of lawn, each with a low fence.

"Nice, isn't it?" Elspeth said. "Not as nice as Canada, but better than where we were before."

"I'm sorry about your parents," Anthea said.

Elspeth sighed. "It didn't seem real. I was so far away when it happened. My aunt wrote to tell me. She thought I'd want to stay in Canada, but I didn't. I was billeted with these two old people, brother and sister, distant relatives of my father. They were all right, but I didn't feel welcome. I came back as soon as I could."

Hugh waited for Elspeth and Anthea to be seated before he spoke. "Can you tell us anything about Edward Powley?"

"Miss Clark says that he stayed in Canada," Elspeth said. "I'm glad he was happy there. He had a really hard time on the crossing. I think that even the chaperones knew there was something wrong about him, but I don't think that anyone thought he was telling the truth, and he really wasn't Edward Powley, because no one could imagine how that could happen. You wouldn't believe the rigmarole we had to go through before we were approved for Canada: medical exams, references, school reports, our parents even had to pay money for our keep. We all knew where we were going and why; all except Eddie. He just seemed, you know, stunned."

She paused for a moment and looked into the distance as though remembering that long journey across the Atlantic. "I should have guessed from the way his clothes didn't fit. I thought maybe his parents had been too poor to buy him new clothes for the journey and they were hand-me-downs from a bigger boy, an older brother or something. It never occurred to me that they weren't his clothes at all."

"When did you first see him?" Anthea asked.

"At the station. We had to take the train to Liverpool, so we had to say goodbye to our parents at Euston station. It was pretty horrible. Some of the children were crying, girls mostly. The boys were trying to look like none of it mattered, and they were saying things like they were only going to Canada until they were old enough to come back and join the army. That was the first time I noticed Eddie. We were getting into our train carriages, and all the mothers were waving and trying to look brave, and we were waving back and trying to look equally brave, and then I heard this kid asking if we were really going to Canada. I thought he must be a bit stupid. We all knew where we were going, so it didn't make any sense for him to say that. That's the first time I really noticed him."

"And you thought he didn't fit in?" Hugh prompted.

"I thought it was strange," Elspeth agreed, "but I didn't see him again until we were halfway to Canada." She sighed. "I feel bad about that. If I'd known what was going on, maybe I could have done something to stop it. I was fifteen, older than some of the others, and I could have talked to one of the chaperones, but I didn't know."

August 1940
Mid-Atlantic, Five Days out from Liverpool
Elspeth Aleshire

Elspeth climbed the stairs from the girl's dormitory far below decks and stepped out into fresh air and sunshine. Their ship was steaming at full speed, creating a wind that ruffled her hair, but the ocean around her was calm and deep green in the hazy sunshine. The ship's speed, and the clouds of steam emitted from the engines driving at full thrust, spoke of the need to reach the safety of Canada as soon as possible. The seas might look calm, but who could say whether a German U-boat lurked beneath the surface, or whether a German destroyer might come steaming over the horizon? She clutched the life jacket that she was required to carry at all times, and decided to stop worrying and to enjoy the moment.

She breathed deeply, glad to be free of the stench of vomit that hung like a veil over the bunks in her dormitory. And, she admitted, she was glad to see that the boys were also on deck. Five days of being sequestered with nothing but girls had been quite long enough. The younger girls might not mind, but Elspeth was fifteen, and boys were important; not that she could form any long-lasting relationship with a boy on board the Duchess of Richmond. *She knew they would all go their separate ways when they reached Quebec.*

She stared out at the vista of endless ocean, broken only by the distant silhouettes of their escort vessels. She wondered what Canadian boys would be like. Her parents told her that she was going to Toronto, and although the city was not as large as

London, she would go to a good school, and she would have plenty of opportunities for entertainment. She was already mentally preparing her first letter home, which she would mail as soon as they reached land.

Dear Mum and Dad, having a wonderful time. We have so much food at every meal. No one seems to care about rationing. The other girls are nice …

She tore her thoughts away from her letter writing as she heard the sound of someone crying. She wasn't sure why she always felt the need to comfort anyone in distress. Her mother said that it meant she would be a nurse one day; her father said it was because she was a busybody and she just wanted to know what was going on. Well, whatever the reason, she felt compelled to investigate.

She found the boy concealed in a dark corner where a lifeboat protected him from view. She knelt and peered into the shadows, seeing untidy black curls and a frightened, tear-stained face. She recognized him as the boy she had seen on the train, the boy who had not known he was going to Canada.

"What's the matter?"

He stared at her silently. His eyes were red with weeping, and a purple bruise extended from his left eyebrow down to the corner of his mouth.

"Are you homesick?" she asked.

"We really are going to Canada, aren't we?" he said.

"Of course we are; in fact, we're almost there."

It was a lie; they were only halfway across the Atlantic, but she thought the lie would make him feel better. Obviously, someone had been beating him, but what could she do about that?

"What will happen when we arrive?"

"Your parents will have arranged somewhere for you to stay."

He shook his head. "Not my parents."

Elspeth showed him the cord around her neck and the little plastic disk with her name and number. "See this," she said. "This tells who you are and where you're going. You have one too."

"It's not mine."

"Of course it is."

"I'm not Edward Powley."

"Then who are you?"

"I'm not allowed to say. I'm not supposed to be here."

Elspeth heard a boy's voice behind her. "Why are you talking to him?"

She looked up into the admiring hazel eyes of a boy her own age.

"Why are you talking to him?" the newcomer asked again.

Elspeth scrambled to her feet and smoothed down her dress. "He says he's not supposed to be here."

The boy ... he was very handsome ... nodded. "I know. He's told that story to our chaperone as well. He's a bit squiffy, if you ask me."

To Elspeth's disappointment, another boy pushed himself forward and into the conversation. This one was not so handsome, with close-set eyes and a pock-marked face. "I'll tell you something else ..."

"What?"

"He's not English."

"He sounds English."

"He talks in his sleep. We think he talks in German. We think he's a spy."

August 1952
Brighton, Sussex
Anthea Clark

"A spy!" Hugh's voice was the bluster of an old soldier presented with an absurd piece of information. "He was an eight-year-old child on his way to Canada. What was he going to spy on in Canada? Did any of these boys even speak German? How would they even know?"

Anthea laid a hand on Hugh's arm as his face reddened with outrage. "She's only telling you what they said. I'm sure she didn't believe them. Boys can be very nasty little creatures."

Hugh would not be mollified. "Well," he demanded to Elspeth, "did you believe them?"

Elspeth sighed. "I'm afraid I didn't think much about it. The weather closed in again, and we were all kept below decks until we reached Quebec. I never saw any of the boys again beyond a glimpse at the train station; we were all going in separate directions."

"So that's all you can tell us?" Hugh asked.

"I think she's told us a good deal," Anthea insisted. "He spoke a foreign language in his sleep. Perhaps it wasn't German, but it was something that was not English. That's a piece of information we didn't have before."

"I might be able to talk to one of the boys," Elspeth interrupted abruptly. "I have a phone number for one of them. If he can tell me anything, I'll call you right away."

Hugh summoned a smile and, unfortunately, another glance at Elspeth's legs. "Thank you, my dear."

Anthea looked at her watch. Their visit to Elspeth had not taken as long as she had expected, and Morton would not yet have returned in the

Armstrong. She felt an inappropriate stab of jealousy as Hugh continued to smile at Elspeth. Surely it was just a grandfatherly smile. She wished Elspeth had worn a dress or something more appropriate.

Hugh turned his smile on Anthea. "I see that our driver is not yet here. Perhaps we should take a walk. It is a beautiful afternoon."

Anthea turned to Elspeth. "Is there a park or anything similar?"

Elspeth shook her head. "No, just rows and rows of prefabs, but it's interesting to see what people have done to make them their own."

"An Englishman's home is his castle," Hugh declared. He extended his arm for Anthea. "Come along, my dear, let's go and look at these castles of the future."

Having decided that she was now no longer in Catford in a professional capacity, Anthea took Hugh's arm and walked with him in the late evening sunlight.

CHAPTER EIGHT

Brighton Mortuary
Toby Whitby

Colin Patel had laid the bones out on a green sheet spread across the metal table where he carried out his forensic examinations. Toby was relieved to see that they had been cleaned of dirt and dust and any remaining remnants of flesh. He was also pleased to note that Patel had no other "clients" in his keeping and the air was only lightly perfumed with the odor of Dettol and formaldehyde.

"You say it's a woman?" Slater asked, looking down at the bones arranged as closely as possible to the way they would be arranged in life.

"A small woman, slightly built," Patel said, indicating the length of the legs and the fragility of the bones.

"How can you tell?" Toby asked.

"How can I tell it's a woman?" Patel queried. "Well ..."

He lifted a pointer from the tray of instruments beside the table and allowed a smile to linger on his sharp brown features. "I thought you were a married man now," he said. "In fact, I distinctly remember attending your wedding. Are you telling me you can't tell the difference between a man and a woman?"

Toby scowled at him without real menace. "I'm accustomed to women with flesh on their bones," he said. "Even the dead ones you've seen fit to show me before have not been actual skeletons."

Patel looked at Slater. "What do you think, Inspector? Can you tell the difference?"

"She had some bits and pieces of women's clothing," Slater replied. "I don't need anything else to know that she's a woman."

"Spoken like a policeman," Patel said.

"Spoken like a man who wants to get on with the job in hand," Slater grunted. "The victim is a woman. What else can you tell me?"

Patel gave him a sly grin. "I didn't need the clothing to know that the victim was a woman. I have … other ways."

Slater raised his eyebrows. "You're going to tell me whether I need to know or not, aren't you?"

"It's information you may find useful on another occasion where there are no remnants of clothing."

Slater heaved a sigh. "Go ahead. Dazzle me with your knowledge. Everyone says you're a genius. Everywhere I go, I hear about how Colin Patel, formerly of the First Punjab Regiment, is now the person to go to with forensic questions. I'm surprised you're still in Brighton. I would have expected you to be in London by now."

"I'm thinking of taking an advanced degree in anthropology," Patel said, "but until I make up my mind, you can have the benefit of my expertise."

He extended the pointer. "The pelvis is the first clue. The female pelvis is adapted for gestation." He looked at Toby. "That means pregnancy."

"I know that," Toby replied.

"Just get on with it," Slater snapped.

Patel's pointer tapped the fragile white pelvis. "I'm afraid this pelvis has been broken in several places, but the injuries are postmortem. I can't say the same for some of the other injuries. You will note that this entrance in the pelvis is wide and circular; this is to facilitate the passage of the newborn. If I only had this pelvis and none of the other bones, I would still be able to tell you that its owner was a woman."

He set the pointer back on the tray. "There you have the answer to how I know that our victim is a woman. I can tell you that she was either a very clumsy woman or a woman who had been subject to considerable abuse, as we can see from the partially healed bone fractures, especially in her wrists. I would say that someone was in the habit of grabbing her arms and twisting them."

Toby looked at the white bones so neatly arrayed. Was this Buddy's mother? Had Buddy seen what had happened to her? Had he known the person inflicting the damage?

"And the hole in the skull?" Slater asked. "I assume it's a bullet hole."

"Made by a Luger—"

"How could you possibly know that?" Slater asked.

Patel turned aside, picked up a set of forceps, and carefully removed a small object from the tray. "This is the slug that did the damage.

It was still in the skull. I can tell you from my own experience that it was fired from a German Luger."

"Can you prove that?" Slater asked.

Patel dropped the slug into the palm of Slater's outstretched hand. "To the untrained eye, this is just a hunk of metal, but to me, it is something I have seen many times before, something I have extracted from wounds inflicted on our troops by German weapons."

Slater studied the slug for a moment and then held it out to Toby. "Do you want to see?"

Toby shook his head. "I wouldn't know what to look for. I'll have to take Patel's word for it and assume that the victim was killed by a German."

"No," Patel replied. "That would be a false assumption. I am saying that she was killed by a German bullet; I cannot say that it was fired by an actual German, only that it is my professional opinion that it was fired from a German Luger, and even that I cannot prove without access to the shell casing."

"Nonetheless," Toby said, "this surely clears young Buddy. He was just a little kid; where would he get hold of a Luger?"

Slater shook his head. "Same place as anyone else: someone brought it home as a souvenir."

"Maybe they did," Toby argued, "but that would be after the war, and by then Buddy was in Canada."

"Not necessarily," Patel interrupted. "The Germans have been making Luger pistols since the beginning of the century. This slug could have come from a prewar Luger. It could have been fired from a pistol that was brought home from the First World War. In order to be sure, I would have to see the shell casing. Do you have such a thing?"

Toby thought of the fallen ceiling and teetering walls of the house on St. Godric Street. Was the shell casing buried somewhere under the rubble? He looked at Slater. "Do you think that Cameron would—?"

Slater shook his head. "He has no reason to go inside."

"But we do," Toby said.

Slater's voice was stiff with determination. "We do not. I'm committed to this case, Toby, but not so committed that I would risk my life. I have a wife now, and I'm not joining in any more of your harebrained schemes."

Toby, thinking back on the last time that he and Slater had risked their lives, felt genuine indignation. "That dip in the Channel was your idea, not mine. I was trying to help you."

"Well, don't try again," Slater grunted. "We are not going back into that house. It's probably already reduced to rubble."

Toby pushed the idea of investigating the ruins to the back of, but not entirely out of, his mind. He turned away from Slater, hoping that the detective would not see the speculative expression on his face. He looked down at the bones laid out on the green cloth, and then up at Patel. "Can you tell me anything else? Age, perhaps? Maybe this isn't even Buddy's mother."

He heard Slater draw in a sharp breath. Obviously, that thought had not occurred to him. Toby grinned. It felt good to be one step ahead of the professional.

"No sign of arthritis," Patel said, "and a full set of teeth. I would guess that she was young."

"Can you do better than guess?" Toby asked. "What about that thing you told me last time I was here, when you said that you could tell the age of someone by their skull?"

"It's an ongoing study, and some of it is still being disputed," Patel said with a note of warning in his voice. "However, I can tell you what I think." He picked up the pointer again. "As you know, when babies are born, their skulls are unfused. Fusion takes place in stages, and over time. We refer to the joining of each skull plate as a suture. Your victim still has two unfused sutures. This one, the sagittal, would normally close somewhere around thirty to forty years of age, and this other one, the lambdoid, at roughly the same time, and you will see that the fusion is not complete. Therefore, I would say that she was under forty, maybe even under thirty. It's not an exact science, but coupled with the lack of arthritis, the healthy teeth, and the strands of black hair that I found still clinging to her skull, I would say that this was a young woman."

"It has to be Buddy's mother," Toby said, "and that's why she hasn't tried to find him. She's been dead all this time." He took a deep breath. "Surely this clears him of any involvement. She could not have taken him to the station and bought him passage on a boat while she had a bullet in her head. He didn't kill her."

"What if the woman isn't his mother? What if he killed someone else?" Slater said.

"He was a little kid," Toby protested. "My stepdaughter is eight years old, and I can't imagine her having the strength to aim and fire a Luger."

"It's not an open-and-shut case," Slater argued.

Patel inclined his head in apology. "I'm sorry. I wish I could be more definite, but I've told you what I know."

Slater extended his left hand to Patel, who shook it without making an issue of the awkwardness of the gesture. "Thanks for the information."

"Glad to be of assistance. Let me know if you find the shell casing."

"That's not going to happen," Slater said firmly.

Toby felt an urge to cross his fingers behind his back. *Who says it's not going to happen?*

Toby stepped outside and found that the heat had drained from the day. The shadows had already lengthened, and the attendant on the promenade was collapsing and stacking the striped deckchairs.

Toby thought about Buddy. Where was he? Would he have to spend another night in the open, or would he find his way back to the hotel? He glanced at his watch. Carol would be getting ready to put dinner on the table. He couldn't be late again. He looked back at the discreetly inconspicuous door of the mortuary. Slater had not followed him out. What was he doing in there? Slater had a wife now to make him dinner. Why wasn't he in a hurry to get home?

He saw the lights blink on along the promenade and out along the length of the Palace Pier. He had a good mind to leave Slater behind. He had already pulled the car keys from his pocket when Slater finally put in an appearance.

"Another missed dinner," Slater said cheerily.

"No, I'm not missing dinner. What are you talking about?"

"I'm talking about your employer, Edwin Champion."

Toby's heart skipped a beat. Had something happened to the old man? He was always so frail, and he should not have asked him to go and speak for Mrs. Stewart.

Slater patted him on the back. "Don't worry. It's all good news. I stayed back to answer a phone call that had come through for me. It seems that Mr. Champion is even now in the office of the chief constable, arranging for Mrs. Stewart to be released immediately. According to the desk sergeant, who was kind enough to call me and tell me, Cameron is not happy." Slater grinned. "Not that anyone cares. I think they've all had enough of him and his helpfulness."

Toby raised his eyes heavenward in gratitude. "Good news all round," he said. "Can your desk sergeant arrange for a taxi to take the Stewarts to their hotel? I imagine that Mrs. Stewart is in need of a bath and Mr. Stewart is in need of a stiff drink."

Toby saw Slater glancing at his watch. "In a hurry to get home?" he asked.

"I'm taking Dorothy and Eric out for a treat," Slater said. "The beach has finally been declared safe, and we're going to the café that just reopened. I'll let you know if it's any good."

Toby shook his head. "I couldn't take Anita there. She's terrified of seagulls."

Slater frowned. "Why?"

"I took them on a picnic to Beachy Head, and she was mobbed by seagulls as soon as she unwrapped her sandwich. She was running around in a blind panic, and Carol thought she would go over the edge. I had a hard time of it, fighting of the bird and stopping her from running off the cliff. Those birds are vicious."

"Flying rats," Slater said.

"One of them landed on her head," Toby said, "and got itself tangled in her hair. Poor Anita was terrified, and I had a heck of a time untangling it, what with the flapping wings, its nasty, sharp beak, and Anita screaming. We ended up going home with Carol and Anita both in tears and me bleeding. Now Anita won't go anywhere near the beach or anyplace where seagulls will follow her, and I don't blame her."

"Well," Slater said, "I don't see how she's going to avoid seagulls if you stay here."

If we stay here. If I don't take the job in Africa. Are there seagulls in Rhodesia?

Toby consulted his own watch and thought of Carol and the baby she wanted him to make. Tonight would be a good night for that. "Do you want me to drop you off at your house on the way home?" he asked.

Slater shook his head. "Unfortunately, that won't work. Mr. Champion would like you to drive him to his house."

"In my Morris?" Toby asked, thinking of the sorry state of his car and the distance he would have to drive to return Mr. Champion to his home in Worthing. "Why isn't Morton driving him?"

Slater raised one eyebrow and grinned. "Morton has taken Miss Clark and Colonel Trewin up to London."

"What? Why?"

"To interview a witness."

"You're joking."

Slater shook his head. "No joke. Our friend Anthea is up in London, taking a shufti at a young lady who crossed over to Canada with Buddy, and for some reason, she's taken the colonel with her, so you're going to be late for dinner and whatever else you had planned, and I'm not."

CHAPTER NINE

"Well, young Whitby, what have you decided to do about that offer of employment in Rhodesia?"

Toby tightened his grip on the steering wheel. They had not yet left Brighton, and Mr. Champion had already inquired whether Toby had enough fuel to drive to Worthing, and whether the headlights on the Morris were working correctly, as it would soon be dark. Now he had arrived at the important question. Was Toby going to take the government position he'd been offered in Africa?

Mr. Champion emitted a dry chuckle when he saw the shock on Toby's face. "You thought I didn't know about the offer?" he said. "I wrote a reference for you, dear boy. I told them that you would make an excellent Crown prosecutor, and I thought you would fit in very well with the general way of life. They would certainly supply you with a better quality of motor vehicle."

Toby gritted his teeth. He had been proud of his ability to purchase the Morris Oxford, and he thought that having the car had helped him to court and to win his wife. It wasn't an Armstrong Siddeley limousine, but it was a perfectly good car, with room for two people in the front and as many as three children in the back.

Three children? Well, at least two.

"I haven't decided anything," Toby admitted.

Mr. Champion stared at the road ahead. "Well, you had better make up your mind soon, because I can't wait much longer to retire."

Toby turned his head, and Mr. Champion waved an impatient hand. "Keep your eyes on the road, young man. As I was saying, I will have to retire soon, and I need to know whether or not I can leave the firm in your hands."

"My hands?"

"Keep your eyes on the road."

"Yes, sir, but—"

"Do you speak German?"

Toby wondered if the events of the day had been too much for Mr. Champion. He rarely put in a full day at the office, and he always had the assistance of Miss Clark. Perhaps today had been too tiring, with Anthea taking off for London, and Mr. Champion having to make a personal visit to the chief constable. That, coupled with his anxiety about the roadworthiness of the Morris, may well have been too much. Perhaps the old man was simply babbling.

"Well, do you?"

"Do I speak German?"

"Yes."

"No, Mr. Champion, I do not. I have Latin and French but no German."

"Do you think that a boy attending school during the war years would have been taught German?"

"I would doubt it, sir. With Hitler storming across Europe, I think most schools would have discouraged all things German, unless they were training undercover agents."

"And an eight-year-old boy would hardly be an undercover agent, would he?"

"I don't understand exactly what—"

"I have received a telephone call from Miss Clark, who wished to bring me up to date on her investigations. She interviewed a young woman who traveled across to Canada with your client Buddy, and this young woman said that Buddy was given to speaking German in his sleep."

"Really?"

"That is what she said, although it was secondhand information given to her by another boy on board the ship. Perhaps he was not speaking German in his sleep; perhaps it was some other language."

"Perhaps it was just rubbish," Toby snapped. He had not meant to sound quite so short, but he was still dealing with the suggestion offered, and then apparently withdrawn, that Mr. Champion would leave the law firm in his hands.

Mr. Champion did not react to Toby's impatient tone and continued to ruminate on the possibility that Buddy had simply been babbling in his sleep. "Broken speech, fragments of words, anything is possible. However, according to Miss Clark's informant, the young man's nighttime loquacity earned him a black eye and made him an object of suspicion. If one couples that with the fact that the boy could not, or would not, remember his own name, it is certainly worth thinking about."

"Yes, sir."

"Do you have any idea where the boy might be?"

"No, sir, I don't, but I do know a little more about what happened to his mother."

"Oh, yes?"

"Mr. Patel at the mortuary believes that she was killed with a German weapon, possibly a Luger."

"A Luger, you say? Very efficient weapon. I remember ..." Mr. Champion's voice faded away, and he was briefly silent. Toby wondered what the old man was remembering. Had his mind taken him back to the Somme, back to the mud and the trenches and the hopelessness of the war of his youth, the war to end all wars?

Mr. Champion snapped back into the present. "Does Patel know this for certain?"

"No, not for certain. He has the slug but not the shell casing. Presumably, that is still somewhere in the ruins of the house."

"Unless the killer picked it up."

"Yes, unless the killer picked it up," Toby agreed.

Mr. Champion leaned back wearily. "I'm afraid your young client is not yet in the clear. I have managed to put an end to this nonsense about his foster parents falsifying his passport, but I can't change the law when it comes to the age of responsibility. It is still possible for that poor young fellow to be charged with murder."

"But he couldn't have—"

"Of course not, but you yourself discussed the possibility, didn't you?"

"Well, yes, but—"

"The whole thing has gone too far now," Mr. Champion warned. "That Cameron fellow has taken hold of the idea, and it can't just be swept under the rug."

"The sooner Cameron goes back to Yorkshire, the better for all of us," Toby said.

"Returning Cameron to Yorkshire will not change the facts."

Toby nodded. "I know. Of course, this would all be much easier if Buddy hadn't run away. It makes him look guilty. I can't help wondering if he overhead my conversation about children being charged with murder. I wish I'd never said it."

"No point in wishing," Mr. Champion said acerbically. "If wishes were horses, beggars would ride. Stop wishing, Whitby, and do something about it."

"What do you suggest?"

"Go back to the last place you saw him."

"Cameron has already done that."

"Cameron is not you, and he doesn't have half of your intelligence. Go back there first thing in the morning, before anyone else is around, and take a look. Put yourself in the boy's shoes, and see what direction you would have chosen if you had wanted to hide, and while you're there, see if you can find that shell casing."

Buddy

Buddy leaned back against the wall of Leo's cottage, where the old stones still retained the heat of the day. Leo slumped down beside him and looked at the pile of dirty gray fleece they had managed to harvest. He heaved an exhausted sigh.

"Sorry about that, old chap," Leo said. "I thought it would be easy. Who knew sheep could be so bloody-minded? I couldn't have done it without you."

Buddy grinned. For the past few hours, he had forgotten everything except the need to catch and hold the struggling sheep. Their symphony of complaining bleats had drowned the voices in his head, and his efforts to avoid their thrashing hooves had kept his mind occupied.

He wiped his hands on his pants, light-brown cavalry twill purchased in the general store in Tobermory. Ma said they were a good investment. Cavalry twill was good for every occasion. Now the pants were ruined. *Sorry, Ma.* The fleece had oozed lanolin, coating his clothes and hands, and making it doubly difficult to hang on to the recalcitrant sheep and keep them in a position where Leo could snip inexpertly with his antique shears.

He watched Nan, the sheepdog, rounding up the denuded sheep and herding them back toward the open grassland. Before long the sound of complaining sheep grew distant and faded into a silence broken only by the occasional screech of seagulls coming in from the sea.

"They're moving inland," Leo said, looking up at the birds passing overhead. "Storm coming. We'll need to find you somewhere to sleep."

"Oh, no, that's all right. I'm sure I ..." Buddy tried not to let his disappointment show. He had hoped that Leo would offer to take him in. In fact, he had built a whole scenario where he spent the rest of his life living in Leo's concealed cottage, tending the flock and being fed by Winnie Widdicome. Ridiculous, of course; the imaginings of a child.

Leo shook his head. "Don't worry. I'll find you a nice dry place, but I don't think you should stay in my cottage, just in case Winnie has mentioned seeing you. We have some rabble-rousers in the village who would love to make life unpleasant for us. Aristocrats are not so popular these days. The old order changeth, yielding place to new."

Buddy racked his brains. He should know that quote. "Is that from the Bible?"

"Tennyson," Leo said. "*Morte d'Arthur,* the death of the king and the birth of a new era. That's where we are now, old chap. The old king is dead, and the new queen is painfully young and not at all ready for the task ahead. There are those who think she should be told to wait, or maybe even told to bugger off and let the grown-ups take care of things."

"Is that what you think?"

"Me?" Leo's thin lips arranged themselves into a smile. "I'm not part of the discussion anymore. It's all up to my brother now." He cocked his head to one side and examined Buddy with wide, interested eyes. "I'm more interested in you. I could swear that Winnie recognized you."

Buddy hung his head. "Maybe she did. Maybe she knows who I am. Maybe she knows I'm a murderer."

Leo raised his eyebrows. "So you're going to stand by that story, are you? I thought I'd give you some time to think it over before I brought the subject up, but you seem to want to talk about it. So let's talk about it. Do you really want to tell me that you murdered your mother? Think carefully, Buddy. Is that what you really did?"

"Yes ... no ... I'm not sure. I don't remember."

"I see."

Leo shifted his position, making himself comfortable before he spoke again. "All right, Buddy, let's start from the beginning. How long ago did this supposed murder take place?"

"Before I left for Canada."

"So you were not born there; you were evacuated?"

"Yes."

"How old were you?"

"I was eight, and the police say that eight is old enough to be held responsible for—"

"Yes, yes, I know the law," Leo interrupted. "It's rubbish, old chap. What you need now is a good lawyer."

"I have a lawyer."

"Is he any good?"

"I don't know. I heard him talking to the police, and I ran. I just ran away. What does that make me? Does it make me a coward?"

"No. Sometimes all you can do is run and give yourself time to think."

"Is that what you're doing?" Buddy asked. "Are you giving yourself time to think, and then you'll go back into the world?"

Leo's voice crackled with annoyance. "I told you, I'm not going back. Look at me, Buddy." He ran his lanolin-soaked hands across his face.

The white scars and the impossibly smooth pink nose gleamed in the golden evening light. "This is not going to get any better."

"But people will get used to you," Buddy argued. "Ma always says that beauty is only skin-deep."

"Ma doesn't have a face like this," Leo snapped.

"But—"

Leo shook his head. "If I'd stayed on the ground and fought with the Royal Sussex, I'd be viscount now, with a wife and a clutch of children, but I had to get up in the air." He sighed. "I flew Spitfires in the Battle of Britain, and I was damned good."

"I'm sure you were."

Leo held up a hand to silence him. "Empty boasting; take no notice of me. I have nothing to boast about. To be honest, Buddy, any fool can fly a Spitfire. All it takes is training and not giving a damn about your own safety." He gestured to his face. "I didn't get this in a Spitfire."

September 1943
RAF Tempsford, England
Lord Leonard Montard

Leonard's pass gave him a priority place on the crowded and convoluted train journey from Duxford to Newmarket. His transfer papers felt heavy in his breast pocket, and he spent the train ride pondering the reason for his transfer. He'd been flying for No. 19 Squadron since 1940, and the fact that he was still alive was its own validation. Life expectancy among the newer pilots had dropped to just four weeks, but he was still here, still taking his Spitfire up into the wild blue to seek out enemy planes. Now he'd been pulled away and sent to join No. 138 Squadron. Why?

He asked the question again when he stood in front of the desk of his new commanding officer.

"Why me, sir?"

Group Captain Howard Crabtree's handlebar mustache bristled with indignation. "Why not you? Ours is not to reason why; ours is but to do or die."

Leo glowered, not at all mollified by Crabtree's quote from the ill-fated Charge of the Light Brigade. He was willing to die. He looked death in the face every time he took his Spitfire on patrol, but he could see no reason for being pulled away to fly for No. 138 Squadron, known only for its cloak of secrecy.

"You speak French like a native, don't you?" Crabtree asked.

"My mother was French."

"And you spent some years in Paris before the war?"

"Yes."

"Sir."

"Yes, sir."

Leo realized unhappily that his connections in Whitehall, even his distant relationship to Clementine Churchill, would not get him what he wanted. Group Captain Crabtree would not be swayed by Leo's family ties.

"England needs every man to do his duty," Crabtree said. He seemed to have a quote for every occasion.

Leo continued to protest. *"With all due respect, sir, I think I'm doing my duty."*

"We need you as more than a pilot. I know you can fly, but I think, given your history, that you could survive and pass for a Frenchman if you're forced down."

Leo straightened his shoulders, feeling his curiosity coming to life and overriding his resentment. *"Pilots are considered prisoners of war,"* he said. *"Why would I need to pass as a Frenchman?"*

"Because if and when you are shot down in occupied France, you will be in possession of vital secrets," Crabtree replied, *"and you will be expected to safeguard those secrets. People break under torture; it can't be helped. So we look for pilots who won't get caught, pilots who can mix in with the general population while they make their way back to Britain."*

Crabtree studied Leo's transfer papers. *"Everything here is in order. I didn't request your transfer. The request came from the top. It would seem that you have connections who are impressed with your abilities. It's not easy to find pilots for One Three Eight Squadron."*

Leo felt a puff of pride as he began to change his opinion of his new posting.

"You'll be flying a Lysander," Crabtree said. *"I know you Spitfire boys look down your noses at the Lysander, but she's a good craft for the work you'll be doing."*

"And what is that work, sir?"

Crabtree regarded him with grave blue eyes and an expression that belied the absurdity of his massive mustache. *"It's work that will change the course of the war. We no longer have a foothold in Europe, and unless and until the Americans join in, we're on our own. We need to know what's happening over there under German occupation."*

"Spying?" Leo asked.

"That's one word for it," Crabtree agreed. *"I'm not asking you to be a spy, of course. We have our agents already trained. You will be responsible for landing them in occupied France."*

Leo felt a shiver of fear. The war he had waged for the past three years was a wide-open combat, with no secrecy and no subterfuge. This was different. This war would be fought in secret by men and women whose names would not be known and whose *passings would not be mentioned. He would have the easiest part; no more than a bus driver taking them to their dangerous destinations.*

Crabtree was still talking. "Landing strips are short; that's why we give you the Lysander, and of course, the locations are secret. All you will see are a few flares at the very last minute. You land; you drop your agent; you pick up whoever is waiting for you; and you return. You say nothing to anyone. You do not tell your pals in the Spitfire squadrons, or your friends from Oxford, or your aristocratic relatives. Do you understand me?"

"Yes, sir."

"Dismissed."

"Yes, sir."

August 1952
Brighton, Sussex
Buddy

Leo fell silent, wrapped in memory, and Buddy could not find anything to say. In light of Leo's terrible injuries, Buddy's problems seemed minor. He didn't know who he was or why he had been sent to Canada, but his life up until now had been easy. He hadn't endured a fall from a burning plane. He hadn't lost his face or had someone attach a nose that looked like an elephant's trunk and call it an improvement.

Leo rose to his feet, groaning and stretching his back. "Never knew shepherds worked so bloody hard," he said. "Come on, old chap, I'll show you a good place to sleep. You can tell me the whole story while we walk, and tomorrow we'll see what we can do about it."

He pursed his lips and emitted a piercing whistle. "We'd better call Nan to heel before she drives the sheep all the way to Brighton."

CHAPTER TEN

Buddy and Leo emerged from a small stand of trees, and Buddy caught a glimpse of the great house dominating the surrounding parkland, with its redbrick chimneys glowing in the last rays of sunlight.

He set down the canvas bag containing his evening meal and turned to Leo. "Is this your house?"

The scars on Leo's face made his expression unreadable, but his voice was firm, his tone neutral. "Not anymore. My brother has it now."

"How could you—?"

"One has to do one's duty," Leo said. He waved a hand to indicate the sweep of lawn falling away to a large ornamental lake, the tall trees that lined the driveway, and the sprawl of outbuildings. "This place has been in my family ever since Henry the Eighth stole it from the church. Generations of Montards have ridden out from here to take their place on the world stage: generals, admirals, courtiers. We all know what's expected of us. Oldest son inherits; the next goes into the army; the third son goes into the church; and any remaining sons can either waste their lives on drinking and gambling, or throw themselves into adventuring: polar exploration, that kind of thing."

"What about girls?" Buddy asked.

"Oh, daughters are easy. Marry money and produce sons." Leo gave a dry chuckle. "I think it's the girls who'll bring the old order crashing down around us. My sisters went into war work: one of them flew all over the country, delivering planes, and the other one did some kind of hush-hush work at a place called Bletchley. Both of them refuse to marry, so the future is in my brother Victor's hands. He's off to a good start: two little boys and another baby on the way."

Leo turned away from the view of his ancestral home, squared his shoulders, and whistled Nan to heel. "I've done the right thing by the Montard legacy. Now let's see what we can do for you." He pointed to the lake. "I'll take you to the boathouse. No one ever goes there."

Buddy struggled to keep up with him as Leo strode away in the direction of a shabby wooden building set at the water's edge, where it sheltered a ramshackle dock that reached out into the dark water of the lake. Buddy paused for breath, but the dog, unable to resist her herding instincts, turned back to nip at his heels and keep him moving. It would have been funny if he had not been so tired. He thought of his Sunday school classes again; Jesus looking for the one lost sheep. Jesus had good intentions, no doubt about that, but Jesus was not the one looking for Buddy, and Inspector Cameron was not the Good Shepherd.

Leo put his shoulder to the door of the boathouse and forced it open. It gave way with a protest of rusty hinges, and Buddy followed him inside, breathing in the dust that hovered in the stale, musty air. Leo nodded his approval. "You'll be all right here; looks like no one's been in here since before the war. I don't know what's happened to the boats; I expect they were taken for the war effort."

He surveyed a pile of ropes and canvas stacked in a corner of the shed. "I think you'll find some seat cushions in there somewhere, so you can make a bed for yourself, better than sleeping on the ground. I'll leave you a torch, but don't use it unless you really have to. Don't want to draw attention to yourself."

Buddy shivered. He told himself he was not afraid; he was just tired. If he ate the supper that Leo had brought for him and made a bed with the cushions, he would surely feel better in the morning. And in the morning …

He felt a prickle of tears forming at the corners of his eyes and turned away so that Leo could not see his face. He would not feel sorry for himself.

Leo's hand descended onto his shoulder. Buddy stared down at the ground, refusing to acknowledge the rebellious teardrop working its way down his cheek.

Leo's hand tightened its grasp. "You'll be safe in here, old man. No one comes here. Don't worry if you hear noises in the night. We're plagued by poachers. Can't blame them really, with meat in short supply and the whole estate crawling with rabbits. You may hear a rifle shot or two, but don't go and investigate. Just leave it alone."

He patted Buddy's shoulder. "Tell me the name of your solicitor, and I'll give him a ring in the morning. You can't keep running like this, and you can't stay in my old boathouse forever, so let me talk to your solicitor and see what we can work out. I may not be lord of the manor any longer, but the Montard name still means something around these parts."

Buddy sniffed and wiped away the tear. "Toby Whitby, Champion and Company. I don't remember the address, but it was in Brighton, right on the seafront. You could see the sea from his office window."

Leo spun Buddy around so they were face-to-face, and Buddy tried not to flinch as he saw that Leo's smooth, pink, unnatural nose had no nostrils. Leo's mouth dragged itself into a smile. "You're going to be all right. This is all nonsense, and I'm sure your solicitor has it under control already."

"What about your housekeeper?" Buddy asked. "She saw me."

"Yes, she did," Leo agreed, "and she seemed very interested in you. I think it was good that you didn't tell her anything."

"I saw you shaking your head," Buddy said. "Why did you do that?"

"Just a feeling," Leo replied. "Best to be careful. Winnie doesn't need to know you're still here. She'll assume you've gone back to Brighton. Her cottage is just down the road, but she won't even be showing a light now. She goes to bed early so she can get up at the crack of dawn to light the Aga and make bread."

Buddy's mind gave him a sudden memory of a striped tea towel covering a basket of warm bread. *"For your mam."*

Leo patted his shoulder. "Try not to worry. Get a good night's sleep, and in the morning, we'll sort it all out."

Leo let his gaze wander around the dim space until it came to rest on an old canoe gathering dust in a corner. He grinned. "That's my old canoe. We had some fun with that in the good old days, before everything went pear-shaped."

He stooped suddenly and pulled at a scrap of red fabric caught between the canoe and the wall, gripping it with his damaged hand.

"What is it?" Buddy asked.

Leo answered in a whisper. "An old bathing suit."

"Yours?"

Leo shook his head. "No, Buddy. This belonged to a girl."

The silence grew long and uncomfortable. Leo's pain seemed to have a life of its own and crackled around him like a shield. Buddy groped for words and found none. Leo dropped to his knees.

"I let her down," he said softly. "I wasn't there."

September 1943,
RAF Tempsford, England
Lord Leonard Montard

Leo leaned against the bar in the makeshift officers' mess and lit a cigarette offered to him by Squadron Leader Dougal McDermott. In the three weeks since Leo had been seconded to No. 138 Squadron, all he had done was practice short-field takeoffs and landings under McDermott's direction. He was bored and more than ready for action.

He looked at his watch. The sun had already set, and the airfield was bathed in the light of a three-quarter moon. Two Lysanders, painted matte black, waited beside the runway.

McDermott leaned forward, propping his elbows on the bar but not looking directly at Leo. "Full moon coming up," he said.

"I know."

"You're ready."

Leo drew a deep breath. "Do you know where or when?"

"Provence," McDermott replied.

Leo saw the map in his head and imagined the long flight across the Massif Central and deep into occupied France. "When?"

"Can't say, old chap, not for sure. Depends on the weather and local conditions. We won't know until the local Resistance says they can get out onto the landing strip with their flares. It's a lavender field. At least you'll smell good."

"Who am I taking?"

"It's a woman this time. She's finished her training in Beaulieu, and she's ready, as much as anyone can be ready." McDermott sighed. "These women are really something. Every minute in France could be their last minute, and they have no protection. We drop them in, fly away, and nine times out of ten, that's the last any of us will see of them."

"Will I meet her before we take off? Can we talk?"

McDermott lifted his head as the door opened with a complaining squeak. "She's here now."

Leo looked at the woman who stood in the doorway, dressed in a blue woolen coat, her long dark hair held back by a patterned scarf. He saw that she had lost weight, perhaps to make her indistinguishable from the half-starved population of France. Her eyes, huge in her gaunt face, opened wide in surprise at the sight of him.

"Leo."

"Daphne, I didn't know you ..."

She put a finger to her lips. "It's a secret."

August 1952
Brighton, Sussex
Leo stumbled to his feet and stuffed the scrap of fabric into his pocket. "Best not talk about her," he said, his voice bright with forced cheerfulness. "Official Secrets Act and all that stuff. Loose lips sink ships, and so on and so on."

"But the war's over," Buddy protested.

"Wars are never really over," Leo said. He patted his pant leg, and Nan came to stand beside him. He looked around the boathouse and whispered a snatch of song. "'Twas in the day of careless youth, when life was fair and bright, and ne'er a tear and scarce a fear o'ercast my day and night."

He turned abruptly on his heel and headed for the door. "Good night, Buddy. I'll see you in the morning."

Anthea Clark
Anthea could not imagine what had possessed her to do such a thing, but she had done it, and now she would have to deal with the situation. Hugh Trewin had accepted her sudden invitation to come in for a cup of tea, and now he stood in front of the empty fireplace in her living room with his hands clasped behind his back while Anthea peeked at him from the kitchen. She believed that his stance was what the army called "at ease," a position from which he would be able to spring into action, but what kind of action?

The tea kettle emitted a shriek of alarm as the water came to a boil. She turned away from the door and busied herself with the tea leaves and the teapot. She searched her cupboard for another teacup. How long had it been since she had shared tea with anyone in this house? The last time had been before the war, on the occasion of her mother's funeral.

She set the two teacups on the tray. Before the war ... So long since she'd had company. Mother and Father had entertained, of course, and for a very brief period before his death on the Somme, she'd received formal visits from her fiancé, but that was so very long ago, almost forty years. Forty years had passed since anyone had looked at her the way Hugh looked at her, with a kind of questioning hunger.

She was alarmed to find that an unwelcome warmth was not only spreading across her cheeks but also creeping downward below her high-collared blouse, down toward her navel. *Oh my goodness! Really, Anthea, take hold of yourself. This will never do.*

She heard Hugh's footsteps approaching from the hall. Her hand trembled as she poured milk into the little silver jug.

"Is everything all right, Anthea?"

She could not prevent the tremor in her voice. "Yes, of course. I'm just coming."

He was in the doorway now. Tall, broad shouldered, handsome, very spry for his age. *But what about me? No one would ever call me spry.* She couldn't look at him. If she did this ... thing ... she had never done before, she would be a changed woman. She thought of the romance stories in the magazines she kept in the nightstand beside her bed. The lovers were always young and beautiful, not old and dried up and worn out by two world wars. Lovers! How could she even think of the word? A cup of tea, that's all it was. They would have a nice cup of tea, and then he would leave. Where would he go? Morton had taken the car and gone home. The buses had stopped running an hour ago, and where would he find a taxi?

"Anthea."

He was behind her now, taking the milk bottle from her unresisting hand.

"Anthea."

She set down the little milk jug. So it was now or never. Her body was uncomfortably warm. She needed to do something about that. She needed to ... She knew what she needed to do. She knew herself to be an old, dried-up stick of a woman, with her knitted cardigans and her hairpins and her flannel nighties. *Nighties? Oh my goodness, do I have a clean nightie?*

She turned into Hugh's embrace with only a fleeting thought left to think. *I won't need a nightie.*

Buddy

Buddy startled awake with the sound of a rifle shot still ringing in his ears. His heart pounded, and he grasped at the blanket tangled around his shoulders. Memory shot through his fingers as he recognized the texture of the knitted squares.

Someone had made a blanket for him from scraps of yarn. In the daylight, it was a riot of colors, but the daylight was long gone, and now he was just a child in a dark room. He could feel the softness of the pillow beneath his cheek, and the damp patch where he had cried himself to sleep, muffling his sobs so that his father would not hear him.

His mother had screamed, but he knew he could not go to her. One day ... one day ...

"Get up, Henry. We're leaving."

The voice did not belong to his mother, but it was a voice he recognized; someone he could trust. He stretched out his arm to turn on the light beside his bed, but a hand, thin and strong, with a clawlike grip, clutched his wrist.

"No light. You can dress in the dark."

He heard his own voice, young, weak, terrified. "He'll hear me."

"He's gone, but he'll be back. Hurry up."

The woman with the strong fingers helped him out of his pajamas and into the school clothes he had discarded the night before. "Hurry," she said, "before he comes back."

The rifle cracked again, and the memory slid away as Buddy took a firm hold on reality. He was in the boathouse. He had made a bed of the boat cushions, wrapped himself in an old blanket, and fallen asleep almost immediately. He blinked and rubbed sleep sand from his eyes.

Why was he awake? Had the gunshots been real, or were they part of a dream? Poachers! Leo had said something about poachers coming after rabbits. He sat up and took stock of his surroundings. A pale predawn light crept through the gaps in the weather-beaten walls, illuminating the debris of Leo's aristocratic youth. Buddy imagined Leo as he had once been, golden haired and handsome, with his heart fixed on a girl in a red bathing suit. Seeing the boathouse like this, the old canoe, the coiled ropes, an abandoned picnic basket, he realized how much Leo had lost. The war that had sent Buddy into exile in Canada and stolen his memories had stolen even more from Leo: his heritage, his title, and even his face.

Buddy crawled from beneath the musty blanket and wondered what he should do now. He peered through a gap in the wall. The sun had not yet risen, but the birds were beginning to stir and make tentative cheeps and whistles as they prepared for their dawn chorus. The waters of the lake were dark and still. No lights shone in the windows of the great house, but to the west, where the sky was still deeply dark, he could see the flickering orange glow of an oil lamp. Winnie Widdicome was up and about, probably baking bread. His stomach growled at the thought of warm bread.

A wicker basket and a striped tea towel to cover the bread. *"For your mam."*

He was suddenly impatient with himself. He shouldn't be here, hiding and wondering where his next meal would come from. He should not have run from the house on St. Godric Street. He should have stayed and declared his innocence. He had not killed his mother. The idea was absurd. So what if he couldn't remember what had actually happened in that unhappy little house? Not remembering didn't make him guilty.

He stared out at the beckoning light of Winnie's cottage. He was not a child; he was a man, and he would get to the bottom of this himself. He didn't need Mr. Whitby or the one-armed policeman to tell him what to do. He would take his fate into his own hands.

He would begin with Winnie, and if she couldn't or wouldn't help him, he would go to London and face the mother of Edward Powley. He remembered Mrs. Powley's expression and the quick flash of fear on her face when she saw him. She most certainly was not his mother, but she knew something.

His mind was made up. He would not surrender. London was a long way. He would need to take a train, and he would need money for a ticket. Perhaps Winnie would give him the money. It would be a loan, of course. Pa would pay her back once this was all over and Buddy had proved his innocence.

What if he couldn't prove his innocence? What if Mrs. Powley refused to talk?

Ma's voice spoke a gentle warning. *No need to meet trouble halfway; cross that bridge when you come to it.* She was right, of course. He couldn't give up before he'd even started. He'd made a plan, and he would stick to it. London! He would go to London.

He stepped out of the boathouse and into the breezy morning air. The sun, still below the horizon, was already sending a glow into the sky and turning the scudding clouds a bright and ominous red. Leo had said the seagulls were heading inland and a storm was coming.

Dawn was breaking on Bruce Peninsula. Pa pulled the boys out of their tents to hammer in the tent pegs and tighten the guy ropes. He pointed at the sunlight on the clouds. Red sky in the morning, sailors take warning.

A well-worn path along the lakeshore led Buddy toward the light from Winnie's cottage. Thunder rumbled in the distance but no rain. Not yet. He wondered if Winnie had a raincoat he could borrow if he had to go to London. Perhaps it would not come to that. Perhaps Winnie would tell him everything he needed to know. There had been nothing threatening in the way Winnie had looked at him, only sadness. He would begin by telling her the truth. *No, I was not born in Tobermory; I was born here. You know who I am. You brought me bread. Help me, please.*

Winnie's cottage was whitewashed and half-timbered and surrounded by a garden of flowers. The roof was red tile. Smoke rose from the chimney and was whipped away in the rising wind. He pushed the wicket gate, but it would not open all the way. He pushed harder and slipped impatiently through the gap. He stumbled over the obstruction and grasped at the trellis of roses to keep from falling. Thorns stabbed at his hands, and the roses shed their petals in protest; or perhaps in mourning.

Winnie Widdicome lay on the garden path. Bright summer blossoms crowded around her, and her eyes were wide and empty, oblivious of the falling rose petals and the blood that pooled beneath her and oozed between the mossy paving stones.

CHAPTER ELEVEN

Toby Whitby

Toby eased his way out of from beneath the covers. Carol had fallen asleep with her head on his shoulder and her arm flung across his chest. He wanted to stay and make love to her again. She wanted another child, and she had his full cooperation. Anita was eight already and old enough to ask for a baby sister. She was even willing to accept that the new arrival could be a baby brother, although she insisted that, in the case of a baby brother, the error should be remedied as soon as possible with another baby, this time a sister.

Toby was quite certain that Anita did not believe babies were delivered by the stork, but he didn't think she knew the whole story. He would leave those questions to Carol to answer in the fullness of time.

As he tiptoed from the bedroom into the bathroom, with his clothes under his arm, he thought of his conversation with Mr. Champion. Emigrating to Rhodesia, once his only aim in life, was losing its allure, and another baby would surely make it impossible. What of Mr. Champion's wish to retire and leave the firm in Toby's hands? Could that really happen?

Although he had walked on tiptoe and dressed as quietly as possible, he emerged from the bathroom to discover that the kitchen light was on and Carol was toasting bread.

"What are you doing?" he asked.

A grin lit her freckled face. "You thought you could sneak past me," she whispered. "You're not leaving without something to eat."

Toby shook his head. "You don't need to do this."

"Yes, I do," Carol argued. "I like looking after you."

"I don't have time."

Carol produced a sheet of greaseproof paper and hurriedly wrapped two slices of toast. "It's not much, but it will keep the wolf at bay," she said. "Now take it and go, and please be careful."

He let himself out of the front door and looked up at the sky. A warm wind was blowing in from the south, with the red-tinged light of dawn reflecting on a bank of clouds that hovered over the town. He had a feeling that the spell of dry weather was about to come to an abrupt close.

He drove through deserted streets and succeeded in arriving at the St. Godric Street house long before the demolition crew were due to put in an appearance. Buddy's house was still standing but only just. It looked as though a strong gust of wind or even a mild rainstorm would bring it down around an intruder's ears, and the ever-increasing cloud cover seemed to promise that either one of those things would be happening before the morning was over. As if to remind him of the danger, a gust of wind tugged at the blackened beam that still swung from the crane arm. Surely someone should have taken care of that. Were the workers on strike?

Toby spared a thought for Carol. If something happened to him, she would not be happy, and if that something was anything less than death, she would let him know how unhappy she was. She had married him despite his tendency to take risks, but she had been clear that she expected him to look after himself in future and not risk his life for the sake of his clients. Well, at least this time, he hadn't involved Percy Slater. He would not have to face the ire of Slater's wife, Dorothy. He was taking this risk on his own.

He picked his way through the rubble in the front garden and stepped gingerly through the gaping hole that had once contained a front door. The Welsh dresser was still propped against the crumbling outer wall, and a roughly swept area of floor showed him where the skeletal remains had lain for so many years. He still didn't have a name for the abused woman who had died here, shot in the head by a bullet from a Luger, and that would be his defense if Carol were to find out about his exploits. He would say that he didn't want the woman's tombstone to bear the sad inscription that had been engraved on so many markers since the war: "Known unto God."

He kept clear of the area that had already been swept. If the casing had been there, it would not be there now. He looked at the dresser and hoped he would not have to move it.

"Was the body moved after she fell? That's the question, isn't it?"

Toby spun around and saw Slater standing in the doorway in his rumpled raincoat. The detective laughed. "I knew you'd be here."

"And I knew you'd come," Toby said.

Slater shook his head. "No, you didn't, because if you knew I was coming, you would have offered me a lift in your car instead of making me drive that abomination."

Toby peered past Slater and saw a black Wolseley police car standing at the curb. "Still not used to it?" he asked.

"It's a bugger," Slater said. "Handicap adapted, my foot. It might be all right for a one-armed monkey, but I can't get the hang of the thing. Anyway, I'm here now, so what have you found?"

"Nothing yet. I'm not even sure what I'm looking for."

Slater stepped in and surveyed the room. "Better make this quick. There's a storm coming."

"I'm not sure what the casing would look like," Toby admitted.

"You'll know it when you see it," Slater said. "Round brass thing, flat on the bottom." He held up the finger and thumb of his left hand. "About yay long. If you find anything like that, you've struck gold. Be good if it has a serial number on it."

"How about a 'made in Deutschland' mark?"

"Just a letter D will do."

Toby circled the room, aimlessly scuffing at the debris on the floor.

"It's easy to see you're not a copper," Slater said. "Did you bring a light?"

"No."

"Well, I did. Let's hope the casing is still shiny."

"Let hope it's not under the dresser."

Slater nodded abstractedly and occupied himself in sweeping the beam of light across the floor in a disciplined grid pattern. A gust of wind shook dust from ruined rafters, and Toby was forced to wipe his spectacles before he could refocus his attention on the light and the search for a glint of metal.

A shadow on the floor caught his eye and deflected him from his purpose. He wiped his glasses again. The shadow was still there.

"Shine your light over here."

"Did you see something?"

"It's not the casing, but it's something."

Slater focused the beam. "I don't see anything."

"It's not a shell casing. It's something else."

Toby was not sure about what had caught his eye, but he went down on one knee and examined the floorboards.

"What are you doing?" Slater demanded. "That's where the body was. There's nothing there."

"There's a gap in the floorboards."

"Not surprising, seeing that the house is falling down."

Toby looked up. "Do you have a screwdriver?"

"Why would I have a screwdriver?"

"A pocketknife? Do you have a pocketknife?"

Slater handed Toby the torch and fumbled in his pocket. Once again Toby was reminded of the difficulty of Slater's life with only one arm. Slater dropped the knife into Toby's hand, and Toby eased out the blade while Slater retrieved the light.

"What are you thinking?" Slater asked.

"I'm thinking that there's an opening under the floorboards and it's been hidden by the dresser all these years."

Toby brushed away the recent accumulation of dust and revealed the place where the boards showed a separation.

Slater was already on one knee beside him. "Careful."

"You think I should preserve fingerprints?"

"No, I think you should avoid bringing the house down. Just be careful."

Toby slipped first the blade and then his fingers under the loose board and began to lift.

He heard Slater breathing heavily beside him. "You've got something, mate. That's definitely a hidey-hole."

"Probably for the family silver," Toby said. "Shine the light down there."

Slater shone the light down into a shallow cavity. "See anything shiny?" he asked.

"Nothing shiny, but I see something," Toby replied. He stretched his arm down into the hole and felt something solid beneath his fingers. He moved his head out of the way and studied the object in the beam of Slater's light.

"Well?"

"I think it's leather. It feels like a suitcase."

"You sure?" Slater asked, and Toby could hear suppressed excitement in his voice.

"I'll have to pull it out," Toby said. He lay flat on his stomach and extended both hands into the hole. The object was heavy. He pulled upward and heard an ominous groan from the surrounding floorboards.

The beam wavered in Slater's hand. "Careful."

"I'm being careful."

Toby pulled again and brought the box out of the hole. He set it on the floor and used his hands to wipe away the accumulated dust. It appeared to be a small leather suitcase.

"Do you want me to open it?" he asked.

"I want you to be very, very careful," Slater replied. "It could be booby-trapped."

"Why would someone booby-trap their suitcase?"

"Because that's not a suitcase," Slater said. "That's a radio, made in Deutschland."

A gust of wind blasted through the door opening, and the rafters shook. Thunder rolled in the distance.

"We can't open it here," Slater said. "Come on. Let's get out of here while we can."

Toby looked up and saw lightning crackling overhead. He was stumbling to his feet, clutching the suitcase, when the roof beam broke loose from the crane and crashed down into the house.

Detective Inspector Percy Slater

Instinct told Slater to protect his head, and instinct was stronger than memory. The muscles in his right shoulder twitched and trembled in their attempt to move the arm that no longer existed. Rubble crashed down around him. Something sharp struck him on the back of the head and drove him facedown into the ground. He turned his head sideways and saw Toby drop the suitcase.

"No!" The fall had not knocked all the air out of his lungs. He could still shout. "Hold on to that. Don't lose it."

Toby dithered, dancing from one foot to the other. Slater knew that the lawyer didn't have a policeman's instinct. He would put the suitcase down so that he could use both hands to pull Slater free of the rubble that was still showering down on him.

"Don't you dare lose that radio," Slater shouted. "Get it out of here."

"What about you?"

"I'll get myself—"

Something heavy landed on Slater's back, and this time, it knocked the wind out of him and robbed him of speech.

Toby's glasses and hair were white with dust, but he was still holding the suitcase.

Slater drew in a ragged breath. "Put the damned thing outside. We can't lose it."

Toby darted out of sight, and when he returned, he was empty-handed and he had wiped his glasses. Slater saw the fear and concern on his face. "How bad is it?"

Toby sounded thoughtful but unafraid. "I'm not sure. You have a good-sized pile of rubble on top of you. I'm not sure what will happen if I pull you out. I might bring the whole house down."

"Where's the radio?"

"Forget about the radio."

"Where is it?"

"Outside, well clear of the building."

"All right, then. Pull me clear if you can. Make it quick."

Slater extended his left arm and was suddenly reminded of the skeletal arm that had reached out from beneath the dresser just days before. Of course, the owner of that skeleton had a bullet in her head, and she had already been dead when the dresser had fallen on her. She would have known nothing. He, on the other hand, would feel every brick.

Toby was still standing and showing no signs of grabbing Slater's extended hand.

"Hurry up."

Toby shook his head. "Wait. I'm working this out. It's like a puzzle."

"We don't have time for a damned puzzle."

Toby bent down with his head tipped to one side so he could look Slater in the face. "I don't want to mention the obvious problem here, but I will. If you had two arms, I could pull you out, but you only have one, and—"

"I know that."

"And all I'll do is pull you sideways, which won't help at all. I have to move some of this stuff. Hold still and try not to move."

The wait seemed interminable, and while he waited, he thought of Dorothy. He had finally found someone who saw him as a whole man despite his disability, and now he would have to leave her. Well, at least she would have a police widow's pension, and that was better than nothing.

He could hear Toby muttering to himself. He closed his eyes and fought for patience. He knew from experience that Toby often acted without thinking, and not always with satisfactory results. On the other hand, when Toby did take time to think, the results were usually impressive. Slater would never say it aloud, but Toby was the smartest man he knew. He hoped that Toby would soon prove him right. He hoped that Dorothy would not be a widow.

Toby's voice came from nearby. "All right, are you ready?"

"What do you mean? How am I supposed to be ready? All I can do is lie here and hope you know what you're doing." Slater tried to make light of the moment. "I don't know what the world's coming to when I have to trust you."

Toby gave a bark of laughter, but his voice was shaky. "Here goes."

Slater felt some of the weight being lifted from his back. He tried to move, but Toby pressed down on his shoulder. "Not yet. Couple more to go."

Another weight lifted, and Slater was able to draw in a lungful of dusty air. He suppressed the urge to cough and managed to choke out an instruction. "If anything happens to me—"

"Nothing's going to happen to you."

"If it does," Slater gasped, "you have to get that radio into the right hands. Don't give it to anyone else, not even the chief constable. Get it up to—"

"Stop talking."

The weight was gone from his back. The air was filled with a rumbling, cracking sound, and Toby was dragging him upright.

Pain, scattered and unfocused, absorbed every ounce of his attention as Toby dragged on his left arm and supported him in a stumbling lurch out into the open air. Behind them the house gave up its long battle with the elements and caved in on itself.

Toby deposited Slater on his back among a patch of weeds and left him to the mercy of the rain. He could not say how long he had been lying there when Toby finally swam back into view, with his wet hair plastered down onto his head and his spectacles beaded with water.

"The radio's safe."

"Good."

"Can you move?"

Slater made small, experimental movements with his legs. "I can move. I don't think anything's broken."

"You're bleeding," Toby said. He wiped his spectacles with his handkerchief. "From what I can see, most of the blood is coming from a head wound, but you have a couple of gashes on your back, and one big one on your leg. You're going to need an ambulance."

"What? No. We can't call an ambulance. We can't say what we found."

Toby kneeled down next to him. "We don't have to say what we found," he replied. "I've put the … item … in my car, and now you have to let me call for help. I know that head wounds bleed a lot, but you're losing blood all over, and you're looking very pale. There's no way we can keep this quiet."

"What do you mean by a lot of blood?" Slater asked.

Toby turned his head away. "You're leaking like a sieve, mate. I'm going to get on the radio in your car and call an ambulance, and there's nothing you can do about it. So while we wait for the men in white coats, do you want to tell me what to do with the radio? I can keep it safe until you've been stitched up."

"No, you have to get it to the right people. My people."

"What's the hurry? It's been there for years, and even if a spy was operating out of the house, there's nothing for him to spy on now."

Slater's world was receding around the edges. He felt as though he had entered a tunnel. His voice had taken on an echo.

"Stop talking and listen. Go to my house, and ask Dorothy for the tea caddy."

His fuzzy vision showed him that Toby was shaking his head.

"I'm not delirious. Get the tea caddy. There's a phone number for Dorothy to call in case of an emergency. She put the paper in the tea caddy for safekeeping. Phone that number and ask for Daphne."

Toby was still shaking his head. "You're going to be all right."

Slater summoned the last of his energy. "Don't argue. Just do it."

The tunnel was closing in on him. "Tea caddy," he said weakly. "Daphne. Do it."

He heard Toby's reply from far, far away. "I'll do it."

Toby Whitby

The ambulance attendants went about their work in urgent and efficient silence. Toby saw the way that their attention flickered from the bleeding man to the crumbled remains of the house. They wanted to be out of the way before anything else happened, and so did Toby, but he couldn't leave until they had loaded Slater into the ambulance. He hovered anxiously as they lifted the stretcher into the back of their vehicle.

"Is he going to be all right?"

The answer was noncommittal. "He's still breathing. Where's there's life, there's hope. Stand out of the way, sir."

Toby stepped back and remained silent and watchful until the ambulance disappeared from sight with the sound of its alarm bell sending seagulls soaring from their rooftop perches. As the sound of one bell faded, another bell stirred the morning air. A police car was approaching.

Toby ran for the Morris. He did not have time to talk to the police. He had to reach Slater's house and find the phone number that Dorothy kept hidden. He looked at the fuel gauge on his dashboard. The needle hovered on empty. Slater lived on the other side of Brighton. Toby swore quietly, using some words he had not learned from his mother and father. He would have to stop at a petrol station. At least he no longer needed a ration book, but he still needed money. Did he have enough? He had given Carol the housekeeping money. What did he have left?

He pulled into the forecourt of the petrol station and reached for his wallet. Empty, as usual. He searched his pockets for change and came up with five half crowns, two sixpences, a threepenny bit, and a handful of pennies. He waited impatiently for an attendant to come out to pump the fuel. Eventually, a mechanic, gray haired and limping, appeared from the gloomy depths of the garage, pulled on a raincoat, looked up at the sky in disgust, and sauntered out to the pump.

Toby gave him the handful of change. "That much," he said.

The mechanic turned the money over in his greasy palm. "That'll get you three gallons," he said. He looked up at the rain, now descending in a steady stream. "They should leave well enough alone," he declared.

"Who?"

The mechanic set his face in a suspicious frown. "The government," he muttered.

"What about the government?"

The mechanic's face twisted. "Making it rain."

Toby couldn't help himself. He was in a hurry; he wanted the man to get on with filling the tank, but he couldn't just ignore the mechanic's claim. "The government is making it rain?" he queried.

"Seeding the clouds," the mechanic said. "They couldn't even allow us a spell of nice weather. They have to go and send the RAF up to seed the clouds. Playing God!"

He turned away and busied himself with the pump, and Toby sat looking out of the windshield at the curtain of rain. He thought of Slater's shadowy taskmasters, who trafficked in radios and cyanide pills, and concealed numbers in the bottom of tea caddies in case of an emergency. Supposedly, the task force had been created to prevent any interference with the coronation, but what else were they doing? He remembered the suspicion that twisted the mechanic's face. The silence of the war years had come to an end. People were free to talk and free of the enforced patriotism of war. The bombing was over, and now they licked their wounds and searched for someone to blame for the austerity of day-to-day life. Why not blame the government for all of it, even the weather?

The mechanic thumped the roof of the car. "You're good, mate."

Toby stuck his head out of the window. "Thanks."

He drove out of the forecourt and into a curtain of rain that threatened to defeat his windshield wipers. He navigated with only limited moments of visibility and kept a tight grip on the steering wheel as a gusty wind tugged at the car. If the RAF was causing the rain, they were certainly doing a good job.

Toby's route took him past the offices of Champion and Company. The windows were dark. Anthea had not yet arrived. She usually arrived on the first bus. He wondered what was delaying her.

He turned into the street where Slater shared a flat with his wife and his stepson, and saw that a taxi was waiting at the curb. Was Dorothy leaving? He parked behind the taxi and climbed out. The Slaters lived in the upstairs of the hastily divided house, with a front door that opened onto a staircase. The door stood open.

Toby climbed out and started toward the front gate.

"Hey, mate!"

He turned back and saw that the taxi driver was leaning out of his window, rain beating down on his head.

"Tell them to get a move on. The clock's ticking here."

"Who are you waiting for?"

"I don't know names. I picked up an old gentleman in Hove, very military type. He told me to come here and wait, and then we're to go to the hospital."

Toby looked at the open front door. An old military gentleman? That would have to be Colonel Trewin.

The taxi driver's voice followed him as he ran through the rain to the front door. "Tell him the meter's running."

Toby paused to wipe the mist from his spectacles before he bounded up the stairs. At the top of the stairs, he was met by Anthea Clark.

"Mr. Whitby, I am ashamed of you," she declared.

He stared at her. "Miss Clark, why are you here?"

"The colonel and I have a taxi, and we are taking Mrs. Slater to the hospital."

Toby thought of the tea caddy. He had to get to the kitchen and find the phone number for Slater's mysterious associate, but he couldn't just push past Anthea, who was formidable in her fury. "Is this about Slater's accident?"

"Accident?" Anthea queried. "I wouldn't call it an accident; I would call it reckless irresponsibility. You and Inspector Slater are married men. You have responsibilities. I didn't think you could be so thoughtless."

"Now wait a minute," Toby protested. "I didn't ask him to come with me."

"It doesn't matter who asked whom," Anthea sniffed. "The fact is you were both where you shouldn't be, and now Inspector Slater is—"

"Is what?" Toby asked, the tea caddy forgotten. "What? Is he—?"

"He's not dead, if that's what you're asking," Anthea hissed, "but no thanks to you."

"Now hold on," Toby protested. "I pulled him out of there."

"What were you doing there in the first place?" Anthea asked. "Who asked you to investigate? You should be looking for our client, not risking other people's lives in collapsing buildings."

"Steady on, old girl." Hugh Trewin advanced down the hall and laid a hand on Anthea's shoulder.

It occurred to Toby that the colonel had not shaved this morning and his shirt had lost some of its usual crispness. As for Anthea, she seemed to be missing a few of the hairpins that normally held her gray hair in place. It would seem that they had both dressed in a hurry. He discovered a rogue thought at the corner of his mind and dismissed it immediately. Ridiculous.

Hugh gave Anthea a warning glance. "We can't hold Mr. Whitby responsible for everything," he said firmly.

"No, you can't," Toby agreed. "So will you please stop nagging at me, Anthea, and tell me what the hospital says about Slater."

Anthea stiffened at the use of her first name and pursed her lips in an angry line. Hugh took command of the conversation. "They say it's too soon to tell."

Dorothy Slater, in a raincoat and headscarf, pushed past Hugh, her face pale and devoid of makeup.

She looked up at Toby. "Why do you do it?"

"I didn't—"

"Oh, don't give me that." Dorothy's London accent surfaced as her anger increased. "I knew he was up to something when he left before dawn this morning. You two had this planned, didn't you? I didn't know anything until Sergeant Pierce rang to say that they had Percy in the hospital. Well, I hope you're happy now he's going to lose his leg."

Hugh shook his head. "Now, now, Dorothy, don't jump to conclusions. They're doing the best they can. Maybe they'll be able to save it."

Tears streamed down Dorothy's face. "And what if they can't? How's he going to live with one arm and one leg? He'd sooner kill himself." She buried her head against Hugh's shoulder. He patted her back tentatively and shook his head. "It won't come to that, my dear."

"How will we manage?" Dorothy wailed. "And me with another one on the way."

"Another what?" Toby asked.

"What do you think?" Anthea snapped. "Another baby."

"She's having a baby?"

"Yes, she's having a baby."

"Does Slater know?"

Dorothy's voice was muffled by the sleeve of Hugh's raincoat. "I haven't told him."

"Well, then," said Toby, trying to sound reasonable, "if you haven't told him, you can't blame him for taking risks."

Hugh looked at him over the top of Dorothy's head. "Just be quiet, Whitby. You're making matters worse. We have a taxi waiting, and we're going to take Dorothy to the hospital. We're leaving now."

"Yes, of course." Toby stood back to let the trio pass him.

"We're leaving," Anthea repeated. "Why are you standing there?"

"Well, I ... uh ..."

"What?"

"I need the tea caddy."

"Are you mad?"

"No, I need it." Toby touched Dorothy's shoulder. "Look, I'm sorry about your husband, I really am, but something's come up. We found a radio."

Dorothy shook her head. "I don't care what you found."

Toby wasn't sure that he should be telling Dorothy anything, but he needed to say something to convince her. "It was a German radio, hidden under the floorboards. A German agent had been living in that house, probably spying on the shipping in the Channel. I think it was Buddy's father. Please, Dorothy, I need the tea caddy."

Hugh's eyes were bright with curiosity. "What's in the tea caddy?"

Dorothy sniffed and wiped her eyes. "He said I was only to call that number if he died, and he's not dead. Not yet."

Anthea pushed her way in front of Hugh and put an arm around Dorothy's shoulders. "Don't talk like that, dear. He's not going to die. Negative thoughts bring negative results. I don't agree with all this cloak-and-dagger nonsense, but if your tea caddy contains some kind of secret information, and if there is any connection to a German agent, I suppose you'd better tell Mr. Whitby where it is."

"It's just a phone—"

Anthea silenced Dorothy with the touch of a finger to her lips. "Don't say it, dear. Just tell Mr. Whitby where it is. We don't want to know why he needs it; none of us need to know that. Come along, let's go and see your husband. I'm sure it can't be as bad as you think."

Toby remembered the rubble that had rained down on Slater, the flow of blood from his head, and the gash on his leg that had left a trail of blood as the attendants had carried him to the ambulance. What if he lost that leg? Would that be more than he could bear?

"In the pantry," Dorothy said. "It's just an old tin, doesn't look like anything special. The paper is hidden at the bottom." She turned toward the stairs. "Why do you do it, Toby? Why can't you leave things alone? I feel sorry for your wife. If you carry on like this, she'll be the next one going to the hospital in a taxi, or maybe to the mortuary." She started down the stairs. "Lock the door behind you."

Toby wanted to call out to her and give her a message for Slater, but what could he say? Slater had struggled to accept the loss of his arm; he would never accept the loss of a leg.

Toby watched from the kitchen window as the taxi pulled away from the curb. The frying pan was on the stove, and three breakfast dishes were still on the table, one of them untouched. Dorothy had made breakfast for her son and sent him off to school and had waited for her husband. He put a hand on the teapot. Still warm. He looked at the loaf on the table. Home baked. His stomach growled. Would it be too awful if he …?

First the tea caddy.

He found the pantry, just a small cupboard with a very meager supply of foodstuffs: a few tin cans, a package of flour, a container of sugar, some baking dishes waiting for the day when food would be plentiful, and pies and cakes could return to the menu. A metal container sat on the top shelf. It was definitely prewar and bore the remnants of a colored label proclaiming it to be filled with Lyons Red Label tea. He reached up and took down the tin, opened the lid, and examined the tea inside. The earthy smell of the fresh leaves told him the container was in daily use. Dorothy said that the paper was at the bottom, beneath the tea. Without thinking, Toby upended the caddy and showered tea leaves onto the kitchen floor.

He stood still for a moment, looking at the mess he'd made of Dorothy's kitchen. He took a deep breath. He needed to pull himself together. He could not concern himself with Anthea's irritation, or Colonel Trewin's bluster, or even Dorothy's anger; he had a task to complete, and he needed to stop bumbling around like an idiot and get on with it.

He picked the slip of paper out from the mess on the floor and carried it over to the window so that he could read the number written in small, cramped writing.

Toby had expected that he would have to find a public phone box in order to make the phone call and was surprised to find that the Slaters had a shiny black telephone on a shelf in the corner of the kitchen. With phones in short supply, and the availability of phone lines in even shorter supply, the presence of the phone underscored Slater's importance as an agent, and the importance of the shadowy agency itself. Someone had pulled strings to get this phone installed.

Toby dialed O and gave the number to the operator. He waited, listening to the clicks and buzzes of innumerable connections until finally he heard a voice.

"Yes?"

Toby waited. He had expected more.

"Yes, what is it?" A woman's voice. She sounded old and tired.

"I need to speak to Daphne."

"How did you get this number?"

"From Percy Slater."

"I see. Is Mr. Slater dead?"

"No."

Toby waited, but the woman remained silent. Toby spoke into the silence. "Are you still there?"

A long pause, and then the woman spoke again. "If Mr. Slater is not dead, why are you phoning?"

"He's in the hospital."

"This number is for use in case of his death."

"Dammit," Toby said, surprised at his own vehemence. "Can't you just be glad he's not dead?"

"To whom am I speaking?"

"To someone who was with him when he very nearly died."

"But he is not dead?"

"No."

"I see. Well, that is all we need to—"

Toby grasped at the only straw available. "Arundel."

"I beg your pardon."

"Arundel. I know about Arundel and the Duke of Norfolk. Now, will you listen to me? My name is—"

"Don't tell me your name. Just tell me what you want."

"I have a radio."

"Many people have radios."

"Found in a hiding hole in a bombed house, and most probably of German manufacture."

"The war is over, sir."

"Not according to Slater. He wants you to have the radio."

"Hold, please."

Toby waited. Although he could not hear voices, he could sense that the line was not dead. After what seemed like hours, but was probably no more than a few minutes, the woman returned.

"Do you own a car?"

"What the hell does that have to do with anything?"

"Just answer the question."

"Yes, I have a car."

"I suggest that you take it to be repaired."

"There's nothing wrong with it."

The woman sighed. She sounded tired and impatient. "Nonetheless, you should take it to be repaired. What model is it?"

"It's a Morris Oxford."

"I see that you are calling from Mr. Slater's phone. You are in Brighton?"

"Yes, I am."

"You are fortunate. You will not have far to travel. Hold."

Before he could speak, the woman's voice was gone, replaced by an echoing silence occasionally punctuated by voices too distant for him to discern words. Eventually, the tired woman returned, sounding wearier than before. She spoke slowly, as though addressing an idiot.

"Listen carefully and do exactly what I say. Take your car to Tulich Tyres and Radiators, three fifty-nine Carew Road in Redhill."

Toby thought that the shock of finding the radio and having the house fall on Slater had affected his ability to function. He could not think of any good reason to take his car all the way to Redhill, and it did not need to be repaired. He felt dull and stupid as he asked the woman to repeat the address.

"Three fifty-nine Carew Road. It is just off the Brighton Road in Redhill. You should be there within the hour. Report to the service bay."

"Should I bring the—"

The woman's voice was an impatient snap. "Of course you should. Why else would you go there?"

The line went dead in his hands. Toby returned the receiver to its cradle. He stood for a moment in the middle of the kitchen, allowing the conversation to play out in his mind. If he was expected in Redhill, he should leave now, so why wasn't he moving? He eyed the fresh homemade loaf Dorothy had left on the table, and the crock of butter beside it. She had been making breakfast for Slater, a breakfast he would not come home to eat. Would he ever come home again?

He picked up the bread knife. He appreciated that Carol had given him two slices of dry toast, but here was fresh bread and golden creamery butter. He was about to do Slater's work, so why not eat Slater's breakfast? Perhaps a slice of bread and a cup of tea would settle his mind and banish the image of blood pumping from Slater's leg, and the memory of Dorothy's angry, accusatory face.

CHAPTER TWELVE

Toby drove through the rain. If the rain was the product of a cloud-seeding experiment, he would have to say that the experiment was a success; maybe too much of a success. He had been given an hour to drive the thirty miles from Brighton to Redhill. On a good day, that would be more than enough time, but not today. The wind rose to gale force and buffeted the Morris, causing it to skitter from side to side on the busy road, while the rain pooling on the surface sent it into bursts of hydroplaning. With every other vehicle on the road behaving in an equally irresponsible manner, Toby took two hours to reach the outskirts of Redhill. He spent another fifteen minutes peering through steamed spectacles for a sight of Tulich Tyres and Radiators.

At last he drove into the forecourt of a small and unprepossessing cement block building. The building seemed abandoned. If Tulich Tyres and Radiators did in fact sell tires and repair radiators, they were not doing so today. A solid metal door, protected by a suggestion of a porch roof, proclaimed itself as the entrance to the office. Toby, stiff from sitting hunched over the steering wheel, climbed out of the Morris and stretched his arms, careless of the rain pouring down on his head.

The office door opened, revealing a dimly lit interior and the silhouette of a woman. Her greeting wafted to him through the rain. "You're late. What took you so long?"

"The RAF," Toby replied.

The woman in the doorway took a step forward while remaining in the protection of the porch. She was tall and slim, wearing black pants and a cornflower-blue cardigan. Her dark hair swept across one eye, surely impeding her vision, and fell in a smooth curtain to her shoulders.

"I don't understand you." Her voice rang like pure crystal. It was a trained voice, with all hints of a regional accent ironed out by rigorous elocution.

Toby looked up at the sky, not caring about the rain that washed across his face. "Word is that the RAF is seeding the clouds," he said.

The woman in the doorway shook her head impatiently. "That is nothing to do with me. Bring the radio inside. Hurry up. We don't have all day."

Toby shrugged and leaned into the back of the Morris to pick up the leather case. He sloshed through a puddle to carry the radio into the shelter of the porch. The woman held the door open and ushered him inside, where the warm air immediately rendered his glasses opaque.

He paused to get his bearings, and the woman snatched at the case, trying to drag it from his hand.

As Toby tightened his grip, someone pushed past him. He turned his head and saw that a tall, broad-shouldered man had moved into position to bar the outer door.

"Arundel?" the woman said, still wrestling for control of the suitcase. "How do you know about Arundel?"

"I'll tell you what I know about Arundel if you tell me what this is all about."

"You are in no position to bargain," the woman hissed.

"And yet I'm bargaining. Why does Slater have your number hidden in the bottom of a tea caddy?"

"We are not responsible for Inspector Slater's choice of a hiding place."

Toby ignored the interruption. "Instructions to call only in the event of a death, or moldering radios found under floorboards." He took a calming breath. "Are you Daphne?"

"You may call me that."

"But is it your name?"

"It is the name by which you may address me. Now please, give me the radio before my colleague takes it from you."

"Not until you tell me your real name."

"Daphne. My name is Daphne. Now give me the radio."

The last shreds of steam evaporated from his spectacles, and he was able to take a good look at the woman who called herself Daphne. The cloud of dark hair and the convention-defying pants had brought him to the conclusion that Daphne was no older than he was, but now he saw that was not the case. The layer of makeup on her face could not disguise the lines around her mouth or the blurring of the sharp angles of her jawline, and the hair falling across one eye did not completely conceal a thin scar that ran the length of her cheek. He looked at the hand she had extended to receive the case and saw twisted fingers and missing fingernails, and shame sent a rush of blood to his face as he recognized her for what she was. She was a survivor. Whether she had been a spy dropped behind enemy lines or a victim of one of Hitler's concentration camps, this woman had suffered and was still suffering.

He dropped his gaze and handed over the suitcase. "I'm sorry."

"For what?" she snapped, and Toby knew that he should not put his feelings into words. She did not need to be reminded.

He changed the subject. "Is there any word on Slater? Is he going to be all right?"

"I am not able to give you that information."

"I was with him when it happened," Toby said. "I need to know."

Daphne looked at him from beneath her veil of hair. "Wait here. Don't leave."

Toby looked at the large man barring the door. "I don't think your friend will let me."

"Just wait," Daphne snapped, turning on her heel and leaving him alone with his guard. As she walked away, he thought he detected a limp, a favoring of her right leg. Gestapo?

As he waited in the corridor, he could hear voices from behind the closed doors. Phones rang, heels clicked on tiled floors, a typewriter's rhythmic clacking was interrupted by the ding of the bell at the end of a line and the racket of the carriage return. In all the busy noise, he heard nothing that sounded like the work of an auto mechanic, not so much as the humming of an engine.

At long last Daphne returned, minus the suitcase.

"Well?" Toby asked.

"You are Toby Whitby?"

"I am."

"A lawyer at Champion and Company of Brighton?"

"How do you know?"

"We began with the registration of your car, and the rest was easy. I understand that you are not only a personal friend of Percy Slater, but you have been able to assist him on several assignments."

"Yes, I—"

"However, this is not yet an official assignment, and Mr. Slater has not requested your assistance, although he seems to have told you more than was necessary about our work."

"It's hardly a secret that something big is happening at Arundel Castle," Toby said. He took a wild guess. "Everyone in the village knows you have extra police up there. Don't blame Slater for that."

"So why were you together?" Daphne asked.

"We just ... well ... we were just trying to find out ..." He took a deep breath. "Is he okay? Is Slater going to be okay?"

Daphne raised her one visible eyebrow. "A house fell on him, Mr. Whitby."

"I know that. I was there. Answer the damned question."

"He is undergoing surgery. The outcome is not clear." She shrugged. "Let us hope for the best. This unfortunate incident leaves us a man short. We need him."

Toby was stung by Daphne's cool assessment of Slater's situation. "You're not the only ones who need him. He has a family."

Daphne shrugged again. "That was unwise of him. The work he is doing is not compatible with family life." She raised an eyebrow, the only one he could see behind the curtain of hair. "Britain is not out of the woods yet, Mr. Whitby. In fact, the trees grow thicker every day. Do you have a family?"

"Yes, I do."

"Best not to be involved, then," Daphne said. She waved to the guard, and he moved away from the door, pushing past Toby and returning to the inner offices.

Daphne gestured to the door. "Time to leave, Mr. Whitby. I suggest that you forget everything Slater may have told you about Arundel. It's nothing to do with you."

Toby took a step forward. "No, no, wait. Whether you like it or not, I am involved. My client, a young boy from Canada, lived in the house where we found that suitcase. I'm trying to establish his identity and—"

An impatient smile curled the corners of Daphne's lips. "Yes, we heard from Slater about this case and about some jewelry he had retrieved. When it comes to the welfare of your client, I suggest that you allow me to talk to the boy briefly and—"

Toby shook his head. "He doesn't remember anything."

"There are ways of—"

Toby could hardly believe that Daphne would say such a thing. "No! Don't you dare."

An angry flush suffused her pale face and defeated her makeup. "What are you suggesting?"

"Methods of making people talk."

She took a step forward. She was almost Toby's height. She lifted her head, and they were eye to eye. He saw the milky surface of her right eye behind its veil of hair and felt a wave of shame. What was wrong with him? How could he be so unaware? She wasn't suggesting torture. She would never suggest torture. He had been thoughtless, maybe worse than thoughtless, and he deserved her cold stare.

He didn't give her an opportunity to speak. "I don't know where my client is."

"Mr. Slater said that he had run away, but surely he's been found by now."

"No, not so far as I know."

"I see."

Toby waited, letting Daphne absorb the information, and determined not to make any more foolish and hurtful comments.

"And you have no idea where he is?" she asked.

"No. I assume that the police have people out looking for him, but I've heard nothing."

Daphne gave a grunt that could have been amusement, or it could have been disapproval. "Of course you have heard nothing. I am sure that you have not informed anyone of your whereabouts, and even if you were foolish enough to tell someone where you were going, we would have denied all knowledge of you. You have been out of communication, Mr. Whitby, and you do not have the latest intelligence."

"Is that what you do here?" Toby asked. "Do you gather intelligence?"

Daphne shrugged. "That is one of our duties."

"And what does your intelligence tell you about that suitcase?"

He waited for Daphne to tell him that the suitcase was none of his business, but she stayed silent for a long, uncomfortable moment. She shook her head, and a sudden teasing smile lit her face. In that moment, he saw the girl that she had once been, before a terrible thing had been done to her. "Oh, Mr. Whitby," she said, "you surely don't expect me to answer that question."

Toby thought of his office at Champion and Company, the rain streaming down the windows and blocking the daylight. By now Mr. Champion would be coughing and wheezing behind his oversize desk and waiting for Toby to answer his question about Rhodesia.

He considered the fact that Anthea Clark was probably back from the hospital by now and waiting to sit in judgment on him for taking Percy Slater, a family man, on a fool's errand. He couldn't go back there. He couldn't face Roy and Evvie Stewart and tell them that their son had not been found. He had to do something.

He took Daphne's smile as a sign of encouragement.

"I could help you."

"We are a highly specialized unit."

"And you are one person short. I saw what happened to Slater. He won't be back on duty anytime soon, and I could take his place."

"You could take the place of a trained investigator?"

"Yes, I could, and …"

Daphne frowned. "You're very sure of yourself."

Toby shook his head. "Not really, but I'm very sure of my duty to my client."

"Your client is nothing to do with me."

"Of course he is. Buddy is the only one who can tell you who that radio belonged to. If Buddy could give you a name—"

"But you say that he doesn't remember."

"I think he wants to remember; that's not why he ran away. I think he overheard my conversation with Slater. He heard me saying that eight is the age of legal responsibility. We talked about whether he could be charged with murder."

"Surely that couldn't happen."

"Unfortunately, there is a visiting inspector from Yorkshire who wants us to press charges, and the chief constable may possibly agree with him."

"And that's why your client ran?"

"Yes, I think it is."

Anger flashed on Daphne's face. "This is an absurd waste of time. We need to know who was living in that house, and we have no time to waste. Just because the war is over doesn't mean that whoever it is has now settled down to a nice quiet, law-abiding life. Someone in that house was communicating with German forces, the same someone who was issued a cyanide capsule in case of capture. Whoever it is will be very unhappy with the outcome of the war. Perhaps he's been lying low for a while, but he will surface. Our intelligence tells us that the Soviets are making contact with former German spies. Britain is vulnerable, Mr. Whitby. We're still at war."

"Then let me help," Toby pleaded.

"Do you know where to look for your missing client?"

"If he was somewhere in the town, he'd have been found yesterday. I think he's run up onto the Downs."

Daphne nodded thoughtfully. "I'll need to look at an Ordnance Survey map. The Downs are riddled with footpaths. He'll probably follow a path without even realizing what he's doing."

"Are you going to let me come with you?"

"Do you really think we are so short-staffed that we need an amateur to help us?"

"I think some of your staff are at Arundel."

Daphne glared at him. "I told you to forget Arundel."

"But I can't forget, can I? So either you lock me up, or you let me help."

Daphne nodded. "Oh, very well. Let's get staretd. I am told that the rain won't last much longer."

"How do you know that? Is it really the RAF seeding the clouds?"

126

"I know nothing about the RAF, Mr. Whitby, so stop asking. Just take it from me that the rain will soon be over. The ground will be wet. I'll find you some boots."

Royal Sussex County Hospital, Brighton
Anthea Clark

Anthea heard the sound of high heels clicking along the marble corridor. She looked up to see the familiar figure of Carol, Toby Whitby's wife, coming toward her, dressed in an oversize raincoat that probably belonged to her husband. Carol's red curls brightened the gloomy waiting space and sent out a spray of droplets as she shook the rain from her hair. Apparently, Carol felt no need to wear a plastic rain hat to preserve her hairstyle. Anthea registered a new level of approval for Toby's wife, obviously a no-nonsense young woman who did not set her own appearance as a priority. Of course, when one was young, redheaded, and endowed with an hourglass figure that could not be disguised by an old raincoat, it was hard not to look lovely.

Anthea touched her own crown of gray hair and felt the prickle of misplaced hairpins. Hugh Trewin had patted her arm before stepping away with Dorothy Slater to find a doctor. The gesture had felt extraordinarily intimate and out of place. It would mean nothing to a casual onlooker, but if anyone knew … *Someone is sure to find out. He answered the phone when Dorothy called at my house this morning. What on earth must Dorothy be thinking?*

Anthea knew that now was not the time to worry about last night. She should concentrate on reassuring Toby's wife. Despite Carol's jaunty manner, she must be full of concern for Dorothy Slater. The two women were the same age, each with a child born in unfortunate circumstances, and each in a new marriage. Anthea thought that, given Toby's propensity for finding trouble, Carol must be putting herself into Dorothy Slater's shoes already.

Carol's face lit up in recognition, and a smile spread across her freckled face. "Oh, Miss Clark, I'm so glad I found you. I looked everywhere, and no one would tell me where he is."

"Inspector Slater is in an isolation room," Anthea said, "and I don't think the police want anyone to know he's here. Wouldn't want it to get in the papers."

"Mr. Champion himself phoned me and told me to come here. Do you have any idea what's going on?" Carol asked. "Is Toby here?"

Anthea tried not to purse her lips or to let sourness seep into her voice. "No, Mr. Whitby is not here. He's … well, he's …"

Carol's brown eyes widened in horror. "He's what?"

Anthea shook her head. "Oh, nothing's happened to him, so far as I am aware, but he was behaving very strangely. He came into Mrs. Slater's kitchen and demanded that she give him her tea caddy."

"What?"

"We were all anxious about Inspector Slater, and we had a taxi waiting, but all your husband wanted was to find the tea caddy."

Carol gave Anthea a wry smile and settled herself onto the bench beside her. "That's my Toby," she said. "He'll have a good reason for what he's doing."

"Well, I can't imagine what it is," Anthea sniffed.

Carol's voice was determinedly cheerful. "Neither can I, but I trust him."

"Of course."

"That's why I married him," Carol said. "He always has a good reason, but he can't always tell me what it is." She settled her purse on her lap. "Now, tell me about Percy. Is he going to be all right?"

"The inspector is badly injured," Anthea replied. "I'm afraid Mrs. Slater is very upset and only thinking of the worst possible outcome. If he loses his leg …"

"Do you think he will?"

"We don't know. Colonel Trewin and Mrs. Slater have gone in search of a doctor to answer their questions. This new National Health Service is all very well, but the doctors don't seem to feel any responsibility for keeping the family informed. It's not like the old days, when doctors were obliged to give service in return for payment."

"But at least it's free," Carol said.

"Sometimes you get what you pay for," Anthea muttered. She raised a hand to her lips. "Oh, I'm sorry. I should never have said that. I don't know what's the matter with me."

Carol patted her hand. "You're just worried, that's all."

Anthea looked away as she heard measured footfalls coming toward them. "That must be Hugh … the colonel."

The old soldier was alone, walking toward them with his head up. His military bearing gave no hint as to what he was feeling, but Anthea saw the flash of a smile beneath his bristling military mustache.

Carol bounced to her feet. "Well?"

Hugh inclined his head in a slight bow of greeting. "Mrs. Whitby, so good of you to come. I think that Dorothy will appreciate your company. I'm too much of an old stiff to keep her entertained."

"How is he?" Carol asked. "His leg? What about his leg?"

Hugh shrugged. "Time will tell. They didn't amputate, and that's always a good thing. Once the limb is off, well, there's nothing to be done, but while there's life, there's hope. He's still sleeping. When he wakes, we'll have to see if he can wiggle his toes, and if he can, well, all well and good. If he can't …"

"Don't talk like that," Carol said, shaking her head and making her curls bounce. "I can see why Dorothy needs someone different to keep her company. He'll be fine, and don't you dare say anything to the contrary. Point the way, and I'll go and sit with her. Is anyone here from the police?"

"A very interfering police officer from Yorkshire came by," Hugh said, "but he didn't stay. He says he's going to launch a manhunt for young Buddy, and he won't be distracted by anything, not even the almost death of a colleague."

"That man needs to mind his own business," Anthea declared. "This is all his fault. If Inspector Slater loses his leg—"

"He will not lose his leg," Carol declared. "Why don't you go back to the office, Miss Clark? I'm sure Mr. Champion needs you. I will stay with Dorothy."

Hugh waited until Carol had retreated along the corridor and out of sight before he spoke. "Well, Anthea, what are we going to do now?"

Anthea lowered her head, unable to meet his gaze. In the long years since she had learned to read, she had devoured hundreds of romance stories in women's magazines; she had watched any number of romantic movies and witnessed screen kisses rendered in sepia and in black and white, but nothing had prepared her for what came next. In fairy tales, the kiss was followed by marriage and a happy ever after, but here and now, in the sterile hospital corridor, with its odor of disinfectant and its harsh lights, she had no idea what would come next for her. Hugh had not said anything about marriage.

She needed time. She needed to return to familiar activities and forget for the moment the deeply unfamiliar, although not at all unpleasant, activities of the night before.

She rose and patted her hair, feeling the prickle of misplaced hairpins. "I shall go to the office," she declared. "Mrs. Whitby has reminded me of my duty."

Hugh frowned and took a step back. "Of course."

The Montard Estate, Brighton
Buddy

Buddy struggled to control his breathing and his rising panic. He looked down at Winnie's body lying amid the varied colors of her flower garden. The light was gone from her bright, inquisitive eyes, and she returned his gaze with a dull, meaningless stare. Without really thinking, he stooped down and straightened her dress and apron. She wouldn't want to be seen like this, with her bony knees on display.

He took a sudden step backward. He shouldn't have done that. HShe should have left her just as she was. Now the police would come, and they would see how her dress had been arranged, and they would know that someone had touched her; someone who had cared enough to make her decent.

A raindrop landed on the path beside him, then another. Thunder rumbled again. He hated the idea of Winnie lying on the path with rain pouring into her wide-open eyes. Should he close her eyes? He'd already rearranged her dress; would it matter if he also closed her eyes?

A sudden fierce wind gusted through the flower garden and sent a rainbow swirl of flower petals to blanket the body on the path. Buddy turned away, strangely comforted by the idea that the dead eyes would see nothing now except the soft colors of rain-drenched flowers.

He looked at the open door of the cottage. The oil lamp still flickered and beckoned him in out of the rain. He looked back at the path he had followed from the boathouse. Everything had changed. Winnie could tell him nothing now. Was that why she had been killed? Perhaps he should go back to his hiding place and wait for Leo to bring Mr. Whitby to him. Nobody would need to know that he had even tried to talk to Winnie. No one would know the connection. *Someone knows. Someone killed her.*

He took a deep breath and pushed down panic and despair. Winnie could tell him nothing, but he couldn't give up. He had planned to go to London, and now was not the time to abandon his plan. He could still go to see Mrs. Powley. He could still ask her what happened at the train station and why she had been willing to give him her son's name.

Money! He couldn't get to London without money. The oil lamp flickered, luring him into the cottage. Surely Winnie would have some money somewhere in the house. He wouldn't take much, just enough for the train fare.

The interior of the cottage was uncomfortably warm. The fire was alight in the big old Aga, and two trays of bread dough were arranged on the warming surface. Buddy shook away his regret that the bread had not yet been baked. He should not be thinking about food. He studied the small room, a cozy combination of kitchen, living room, and dining room, beneath ancient blackened beams.

Winnie's shopping bag stood on the table. He glanced out of the door, guilt already rising and threatening to paralyze him. Surely she wouldn't mind; not now. He found her coin purse, small, black, and heavy with coins. He tipped the coins onto the table and studied them. He knew enough to know that the big copper coins were pennies and would not be worth loading down his pocket. He studied the other coins and selected five half crowns, a handful of shillings, and a couple of sixpences. He had hoped for paper money, a ten-shilling note, or even a pound, but apparently,

Winnie didn't have that kind of money. Guilt stabbed at him again. Winnie wasn't a wealthy woman, and he was taking the last of her money. He heard Ma's voice, no longer soft, but very determined. *Needs must when the devil drives. Just get on with it, son, and get out of there before someone else finds her and calls the police.*

He found an ancient army-issue raincoat on a peg by the front door. Ma's voice chimed in again. *You can't go out like that. Wash your face and comb your hair.*

No bathroom here, Ma.

Wash yourself in the kitchen sink. Get a move on.

He splashed water on his face. Perhaps Winnie had a comb, but he wasn't willing to go upstairs to her bedroom. He had stolen her money, but he would not invade her privacy.

The raincoat had been made for a big man; perhaps it had belonged to Mr. Widdicome. He dropped the stolen coins into the deep pockets, turned up the collar, and stepped out into the rain.

CHAPTER THIRTEEN

Toby Whitby

Toby brought the Morris to a halt. Beside him Daphne unfolded a section of the Ordnance Survey map and held it close to her good eye. Toby wiped his glasses on his handkerchief and then used the handkerchief to wipe the mist that had collected on the inside of the windshield. St. Godric Street, with its demolition equipment, was behind them. They had followed a wide road past St. Swithin Primary School and a general store whose lights bravely pierced the damp fog, and eventually turned onto St. Athanasius Close. Here the road came to an end, leaving nothing ahead but the rain-soaked emptiness of the South Downs.

Toby interrupted Daphne's study of the map. "We should walk from here."

"Perhaps."

"If he didn't go into the town, this is the way he would go."

"I know."

"So why are waiting? Let's get on with it. The rain has more or less stopped."

Daphne refolded the map with a defiant flourish. "I agree that he probably came this way. The map shows a public footpath leading across the hillside over there and following the boundary of Montard Hall. If he followed this path for any length of time, he wouldn't still be here, he would be somewhere on the Montard estate."

Toby's heart sank. He had no way of knowing if Cameron had already found Buddy, but it was beginning to sound very likely. If the boy had followed the path onto someone's private property, he would have been seen. If he was trespassing, the police would have been called, and if Buddy had been arrested, Slater would be no help; not now. The case would be passed up the chain of command and to a prosecutor, who would bring charges.

He readjusted his spectacles. "We should find a phone box. I'll call the office and see if he's been picked up."

Daphne looked at him from beneath her veil of black hair and sniffed disapprovingly. "Really, Mr. Whitby? Would you really give up so easily?"

"I'm not giving up, but I don't see any point in following the path from here. If this is the closest we can come to the footpath, and if the path leads to someone's house—"

"The path leads to Montard Hall, a massive Tudor pile surrounded by acres of parkland, a lake, a managed forest, and any number of outbuildings, plus a boathouse and a folly. If he followed the footpath, he wouldn't even be seen by anyone at the house. We can drive along one of the farm lanes and pick up the footpath closer to the house."

Toby gave his companion a curious glance. "You could tell all of that from looking at the map?"

Daphne smiled. "I can. The Ordnance Survey map marks every outbuilding, every gate, and every legal footpath."

"It doesn't tell you that the house is Tudor."

"No," Daphne agreed. "That is something I know from personal experience. I was at school with Daisy Montard. I used to visit the estate long, long ago. My parents were in the Foreign Office, and I was, of course, abandoned at a boarding school."

"Abandoned?" Toby asked.

Daphne shrugged her shoulders. "One felt abandoned," she said in a small voice. "One felt alone." She recaptured her smile. "Daisy Montard was my best chum, and I always spent my long hols at Montard Hall. Did I mention that they also have a tennis court and a walled maze?"

"No, you didn't."

"It doesn't matter. I expect the place has changed."

"You haven't been there recently?"

"No."

"Not to see your friend Daisy?"

"No," Daphne snapped, "I have not."

Toby turned the key in the ignition, and the motor coughed into life and took up an uneven rhythm. He suspected that the Morris did not like rain any more than he did.

Daphne raised her voice to be heard above the unhappy engine. "The point is that I know the property, and I can show you how to approach the footpath, and we can trace it backward. I should have realized it before we even left the office. There was no need to come all the way out here."

She spoke as though Toby was at fault for not knowing of Daphne's prewar friendship with the wealthy inhabitants of Montard Hall.

"However," Daphne said, "I think it was good to see the neighborhood where our young friend lived and the place where you found the radio." She reached out to smear mist from the side window, and the hillside came into view. "The German agent on St. Godric Street, whoever he was, wouldn't have to go far to get a signal. He'd have great reception up here on the Downs, and no one to see him." She nodded. "It all makes sense."

"It doesn't explain why Buddy was sent to Canada or why he can't remember his own name, or why there was a dead woman in the house."

"No," Daphne agreed. "To understand that, we have to find the boy, so we had better get a move on. Your engine doesn't sound healthy; are you sure we'll get there?"

"Are you sure you should look a gift horse in the mouth?" Toby snapped. "If I hadn't offered to drive, you'd still be sitting in your office in Redhill, waiting for a car and a driver."

Daphne smiled, and her smile went a long way to soothe Toby's irritation. She nodded. "Touché, Mr. Whitby."

Toby turned to ask Daphne for a route to follow, but before he could speak, the engine of the Morris gave a despairing cough and died.

He cranked the starter motor and listened to its pointless whining. Nothing. No spark. No anticipatory cough from the engine.

He adjusted the choke and tried again. The Morris wreathed itself in petrol fumes and remained stubbornly uncooperative.

"You've flooded the carburetor," Daphne said.

"I know that," Toby snapped. He opened his door and stepped outside. The rain had reduced to a fine drizzle, and the ground was slick with mud beneath his only good pair of shoes. Polishing would be required before he entered Mr. Champion's office. The thought of Mr. Champion led him to thoughts of his unannounced and unsanctioned absence from the office, and following that train of thought brought him to the memory of Percy Slater being loaded into an ambulance.

He shook his head, made his way around to the front of the car, and felt for the latch to open the bonnet. Daphne called out to him from the passenger window. "That won't do any good. All you'll do is get the distributor cap wet, and anyway, your battery's flat."

"No, it isn't," Toby argued.

Daphne's head disappeared into the car, and after a moment, he heard a reluctant whine from the starter motor; a whine that stopped almost before it started. He flushed in angry embarrassment. She shouldn't have done that. He felt a surge of anger, and he dredged up a resentment he must have been nursing unawares for months. He realized the feeling had started with his initial encounter with aristocracy in the person of Sylvia, Countess of Southwold. Standing in the rain beside the dead car, he now widened his annoyance with Lady Sylvia to also include Daphne, who spoke of herself in the third person. He added in Daphne's chum Daisy, who spent her "hols" frolicking on the tennis court and running around in the maze. To make matters worse, Daphne had added to her sins by thoughtlessly and arrogantly running down the car battery. So now they were stuck.

Daphne reached into the back seat and brought out two pairs of wellington boots and two raincoats.

"We'll have to walk," she said. "I assume you're fit enough."

"Of course I'm fit," Toby barked. "I'm not the one who ..." He silenced himself. He couldn't say what he had been about to say. *You're the one with the limp and the blind eye and the broken fingers. You've been tortured. I haven't. All I have to show for the war is a bit of shrapnel in my leg. I'm fine. I can walk for miles.*

Shame drove out his resentment. He had no idea what Daphne had suffered, but apparently, she had not given up. She had made a place for herself in the shadowy world of counterespionage, and fate had decreed that he would be here at this moment to assist her. Unreasonable shame lived with him every day. He had not done his "bit." He had not put on the uniform and crossed over into Europe. He knew he would spend the rest of his life proving to himself that he had courage to equal that of people like Daphne with her ruined body, or Percy Slater with just one arm, or even Randall Powley with his bitter memories of Dunkirk.

He took off his shoes and put on the sturdy wellington boots. His socks were thin, and Carol had not yet darned the holes in the heels. He suspected that he would have blisters before the end of the day. He shrugged into the raincoat, government issue, dark green, and rubberized. If the sun came out, he would be baking. *Stop complaining.*

Daphne handed him a canvas messenger bag. "You can carry this."

"What is it?"

"A radio. We should get a good signal from the top of the hill. I'll let my people know what's happening, and they'll let me know if Buddy's been found."

Toby slung the satchel across his chest. "Lead the way."

They climbed a stile set in a barbed wire fence and set off uphill. They walked in silence, and Daphne kept up a fast pace. Toby was fighting for breath by the time they reached the hilltop and could look down on the town streets and suburbs spread far below them. The sea was no more than a smudge where the gray of the waves met the gray of the clouds.

Daphne stopped at a circle of rocks and held out her hand for the radio. "I should get a signal from here."

She sat on a smooth rock and opened the satchel. Toby examined his surroundings. The rocks had not been cut or shaped, but they had obviously been placed. In one area, they were black with soot. Someone had camped here.

He looked at Daphne. The radio was perched on a rock, and she had extended the antenna. Her fingers seemed to flicker as she worked the Morse key. Her shoulders were hunched, and he saw that her head moved constantly, sweeping the horizon. For what? Enemy agents? Planes? Troops? This was probably the first time in her tortured existence that she had been able to send and receive signals without expecting the imminent arrival of the Gestapo.

The radio chattered into life, sending a stuttering response to Daphne's questions. She listened, nodded, and immediately folded the antenna and began to pack the radio into the satchel.

"Well?" Toby asked.

"We have a problem."

"Have they found him?"

She shook her head. "No, not yet, but we have another murder, a woman named Winnie Widdicome, found dead outside her cottage on the Montard estate. I'm afraid your boy is a prime suspect. There's a full police search of the whole area, so we'd better get a move on if we want to find him before they do."

Buddy

The wind died down. A watery sun broke through the clouds, and Buddy began to regret taking the raincoat. He crossed a stile. The existence of a stile meant that he was still on the well-traveled footpath. He was not sure how he knew that fact, but he did know it, and that was all that mattered. Apparently, his eight-year-old self had known many things about living among these grassy hills and sheltered valleys, and those memories had not been forbidden; they just hadn't mattered until today. Now that he needed the knowledge, it was there for the taking.

The footpath skirted a field of wheat and led down into a village of thatched cottages huddled together at a crossroads. The lights were on at the village store, and the proprietor was standing outside beneath a striped canopy, arranging a display of vegetables. Buddy hesitated. His plan to talk to Edward Powley's mother relied on taking a train to London. He had the money for the train ticket, but no idea where he would find a station. Train stations were not something to be casually stumbled upon. A station was not going to magically appear out among the sheep on the Downs, and he did not have all day to wander in search of one. Winnie's body had probably been found by now, and the police would believe the worst.

Ma and Pa would be frantic with worry, but he couldn't stop to think about that now. He crossed the street and approached the storekeeper. The man looked up.

Buddy ironed every possible trace of Canadian from his voice, replacing it with a weak imitation of Leo Montard's aristocratic voice. "Good morning, sir. Excuse me for asking, but can you point me to the nearest railway station?"

The storekeeper gave him a quizzical and slightly amused glance. Perhaps he had overdone the accent. Well, too late now. He had asked the question.

"Railway station?" the man repeated.

"Yes, please."

The man scratched his head. "Well, it's here, isn't it?"

"Is it?"

"Of course it is." The storekeeper raised his hand and pointed to a post with four arrow-shaped white signs pointing in different directions: Brighton, Devil's Dyke, footpath, station.

Buddy felt a flush of embarrassment rising in his cheeks. He should have read the sign for himself, but it was too late now. Now he had made himself conspicuous by asking a stupid question in a ridiculous accent. Well, he'd done it now. Ma was there again with one of her sayings. *Might as well be hanged for a sheep as a lamb; you've already talked to him, so buy yourself something to eat. No good trying to do anything on an empty stomach.*

The storekeeper was still looking at him. "Do you want to buy something?"

"Oh, yes ... um ... an apple."

"Is that all? Healthy young lad like you needs more than an apple."

Buddy considered his collection of stolen coins. Best not spend too much. "No, just an apple."

He followed the storekeeper into the cramped interior of the store, selected an apple from a basket by the door, and paid with a shilling piece. He was rewarded with two brass threepenny pieces and two massive copper pennies as change. He turned to leave the store. The proprietor stopped him with a question. "You taking the train to Brighton?"

The response was out of his mouth before he could stop himself. "No. I'm going to London."

"Better hurry, then. She'll be here in a few minutes. Not the express, mind you, that don't stop here, but the slow train stops."

Buddy bit into the apple and mumbled his reply as he left the store. "Thank you."

He took his direction from the signpost and hurried uphill along the deserted street, with the oversize raincoat flapping around his ankles. Was it just his imagination, or could he hear the rattle of a train in the distance? He turned to look back, searching anxiously for puffs of steam from beyond the rise in the ground. As he looked down on the village, he could see the side wall of the village store. He saw a name in bright new paint: "Hunter's Village Shop and Post Office; Greg Hunter – Proprietor." Below the new name, he could make out the shadow of an old name, faded by time, no longer relevant: "Powley and Sons, Greengrocers."

His feet turned in the direction of the village street as he made the connection. Perhaps the answer to his question was not in London; perhaps it was here, at the store that had once been owned by someone named Powley; someone who had sons.

He still couldn't see the whole picture, but one part was certainly becoming clearer. Edward Powley was not some random child Buddy's mother had found among the children waiting to go to Canada. The Powley family, father and son, had a presence here, among the hills and valleys that Buddy found so hauntingly familiar.

Buddy turned indecisively. He was sure that Mrs. Powley in London knew something, but maybe he wouldn't have to go so far. He could go back to the store and talk to the proprietor. Were there other people named Powley still living in the village? Did the storekeeper know anything about a boy being sent to Canada? Did he remember a kid named Henry?

He turned again as his ears picked up the rattle of a train. This time, it was not his imagination; the train was definitely coming through the valley, belching steam as it approached. He hesitated. He could hear Ma in his mind. *Get on with it, Buddy. Stop shilly-shallying about.* Perhaps the man in the store knew something about the Powleys, but perhaps he didn't. On the other hand, Buddy was more and more certain that the expression on Mrs. Powley's face had been fear and not surprise. She was afraid of Buddy. Why? Well, the man in the store couldn't answer that question. That was something that only Mrs. Powley could answer.

Buddy turned toward the station. The train gave a great sigh and sent up a cloud of steam with a chaser of coal smoke. The brakes squealed. With his mind made up, Buddy picked up the hem of his stolen raincoat and ran onto the platform as the train chugged to a halt.

Toby Whitby

"No!" Toby knew he was shouting, but he could not stop himself. It was enough that Buddy had been accused of one murder, but now another and much more recent death was being laid at his feet.

"He's not a killer," Toby protested. "Just because someone on the Montard estate has been killed, it doesn't mean Buddy did it. What reason would he have for killing someone? This is Cameron's fault. He has some kind of vendetta against Buddy."

"Cameron?" Daphne asked. "Who is Cameron?"

"A visiting police officer from Yorkshire. He says he's here to help out with the Arundel business."

"Arundel?"

Toby felt his patience slipping. "Yes, Arundel. The Coronation Commission meeting. I know all about it, and so do you."

"Who told you about it?"

"It's not exactly a secret," Toby replied. "The whole neighborhood is crawling with police."

"So where does this Cameron come into it?" Daphne asked.

"Detective Inspector Cameron had time on his hands, waiting to take up his duties at Arundel, so he presented himself at Brighton to see if he could help, and ran right into the Edward Powley case. He's been showing an interest ever since."

Daphne frowned as she packed away the radio. "Did anyone check his credentials?"

"I assume so. The chief constable made no objection, and even Slater said that there wasn't much we could do about him. Of course, we thought he'd be on his way as soon as he was needed at Arundel. Now I'm not so sure. Brighton is short-staffed, and Cameron is very keen to be helpful. Maybe he's hoping for a transfer."

Daphne buckled the satchel and handed it to Toby. "I suggest we get started."

Toby remained in place. "Look, even if Cameron is working with the approval of the chief constable, you can stop him, can't you?"

"I don't know. I will have to find out what he really wants, but I don't have time right now. We need to move."

"Well," Toby said, "can't you just order Cameron to leave this to you? You outrank him, don't you?"

Daphne shook her head. "We do not always like to draw attention to ourselves. I would need to discuss this with Slater. It's his assignment."

"What about Slater?" Toby asked. "When you talked on the radio, did you ask anyone about him? Is he going to be all right?"

"I'm sorry, I don't know. I didn't think to ask."

Toby bit down on his annoyance. "Did you ask for another vehicle?"

Daphne shook her head again. "No point. It will be quicker just to walk. I know the way."

As Toby lifted the satchel onto his shoulder, he looked around at the circle of stones. "Any idea what this is? It's not natural."

Daphne pursed her lips. "I imagine it's the place where Buddy's father came to send signals to German agents. It's a good location and a good strong signal."

"What about before the war? This isn't a wartime installation."

Daphne shrugged. "Could be tramps. We had a lot of tramps up here during the Depression, and Gypsies, of course." Her voice took on a tinge of bitterness. "The Gypsies came every year, and ..." She shook her head. "What does it matter? We have to go."

Toby followed her as she set off along the white chalk footpath. After a few moments, Toby tried to resume their conversation about Cameron, but Daphne cut him off with a shake of her head. "Later."

The path followed a fold in the hills, dipping down into a protected valley. Daphne barely broke stride as a small posse of animals broke cover from a patch of gorse and scuttled across the path. It took Toby a moment to realize that the skinny white creatures were just sheep, raggedly sheared and apparently still upset about the indignity of losing their wool. They lowered their heads and blew down their noses at him.

Daphne halted and looked back at him. "They're all ewes. They won't hurt you."

"I know that," Toby replied. "I'm wondering why they've been shorn so late in the season."

Daphne stopped abruptly and stared at the sheep. Toby could not read the expression on her face. "He didn't do a very good job," she said at last.

Toby studied the sheep, arranged behind them in a sullen, angry group. It was obvious that their wool had been removed in uneven clumps, leaving behind patches of gray.

"You know the shepherd?" Toby asked.

Daphne nodded. "Yes, I know him."

"We should ask him if he knows anything," Toby suggested. "This is the most obvious way for Buddy to come. Perhaps he saw him. What's the shepherd's name?"

"Leo."

"Well, let's go find Leo."

"You won't find him. He won't talk to you."

Daphne swiped a hand across her face. Was she crying?

Toby took a step forward. "Daphne?"

She sighed. "He won't see us. He won't see anyone. It's no good trying."

"Why?"

She shook her head and turned back to the path. "For some people, the war will never be over," she said softly. "Some people will never have a second chance."

The footpath brought them to a spillway where water flowed over a low dam and into a shallow stream. Toby assumed that this was the dam that had created the ornamental lake of Montard Hall, where Daphne and Daisy and their chums had frolicked in the long-ago summertime.

Toby's thoughts of Daphne's privileged vacations were interrupted by the frenzied barking of a dog and the sound of raised voices coming from the path ahead. Daphne held up a hand for silence. Toby shrugged. The dog was making enough noise to drown any sound that he and Daphne could make.

They found the dog almost immediately. She was a black-and-white border collie, barking and leaping frantically in an attempt to free herself from the rope that attached her to a small oak sapling.

The arguing men were just a short way ahead, hidden by a sharp turn in the path.

"Let my dog go, damn you."

"Don't worry about your dog, sir. She'll be taken care of."

Toby recognized the second voice. Cameron.

The first voice spoke again. "She's a working dog. You can't tie her up. For God's sake, man, let her go before she chokes herself."

"All in good time. Just come along quietly, and don't give me any more trouble."

Daphne's voice was soft in his ear. "See if you can untie that dog before she chokes herself. What kind of fool ties up a working dog?"

"I know exactly what kind," Toby replied. "That's Inspector Cameron. I'd know his voice anywhere. I have to——"

"No, you don't."

Toby grunted in frustration as Daphne held on to his arm and pulled him backward. "See if you can untie the dog," she whispered.

"I'm not wasting time on that," Toby hissed. "I'm going over there and——"

"No, you're not. Not until I have instructions. I want to know more about Cameron. Just untie the dog, and she'll go straight to Leo. That will be enough of a diversion, and I can——"

"Is that Leo up ahead? Is that the man you were talking about?"

"Yes, he's the man that fool of a policeman is trying to arrest. He's Leonard Montard, who used to be the viscount."

"And he's not now?"

"No."

"Why?"

"You will see for yourself soon enough. Just get on with it while I get the radio out and try to get some instructions. Try to keep them busy until I get back."

Toby watched as Daphne walked across the ankle-deep stream and began to climb toward the top of the dam. When she was hidden from sight, he approached the dog. She greeted him with a frustrated whine and wriggled in anticipation as he struggled to untie the rope around her neck.

Leonard Montard's voice was choked with anxiety "Hey. What's happened to my dog? Why is she whining? She's going to choke herself. Let me go."

Toby was holding the wriggling dog under one arm when the sound of a scuffle broke out close by. The rope collar was finally loose, and the dog bounded from his arms just as a tall man stepped out onto the path. The man and dog collided in a joyful reunion.

Toby rose from his knees. So this was one of the Montards, one of the chums of Daphne's golden youth.

"What are you doing with my dog?"

The words of explanation died in Toby's throat. She should have warned him. She should have said something.

Daphne

Daphne set the radio on a tree stump. Aligning the antenna, finding the frequency, even the need to hide her position and scan the woods for enemies brought a flurry of remembrance. She decided to plug in the microphone. Morse code was all very well, but she had too many questions. She would have to risk voice communication.

Her heart pounded with a sudden onrush of cold fear as the radio emitted a burst of static. She reminded herself that she was safe. No one was listening. She was back at Montard Hall, where she had once been happy. The war was over and she had survived.

The sound of men arguing drifted to her through the trees. Toby Whitby, calm and measured, the police inspector, rough and demanding, and Leo, angry and frustrated. She wanted to go to him, but what would Leo do if she revealed herself now? Would he refuse to see her? Was he still blaming himself?

She slipped on the headphones, adjusted the frequency, and sent out her call sign, just as she had been trained.

September 1943
RAF Tempsford, England

The officer's mess of No. 138 Squadron was little more than a few chairs and tables set in a curtained corner of a Nissen hut. Daphne took a deep breath, parted the curtains, and stepped inside. She wanted to meet the man who would fly her over to France. She was afraid, of course, but she was trained and ready, and now she was impatient.

As she held the curtain aside and looked at the two men leaning against the makeshift bar, she realized that she was not only impatient, she was also bored. She needed something to take her mind off what lay ahead, and a handsome RAF pilot could be just what she needed. The art of seduction had been part of her training, and putting her training into practice would help to pass the short time until the full moon and her flight to France.

The two pilots were equally attractive, and thank goodness, neither one of them had grown an absurd RAF handlebar mustache. She could not imagine fighting her way through so much undergrowth for the sake of a kiss, but these two men were clean-shaven. She considered testing her skills on the shorter of the two men. He was broad shouldered, with curling chestnut hair and a broad grin. She thought he would be fun. The other man was tall, slim, and blond, and his expression was far too serious. No, not just serious, shocked!

His name came to her in a choked gasp. "Leo!"

Leo Montard had kissed her on her seventeenth birthday. A peck on the cheek, a wink, and an admiring glance that had led to a warning from Daisy: "Don't let my brother break your heart. He's sowing his wild oats all over the south of England, everything from a duchess to a Gypsy, and he'll ruin your reputation."

But Daphne, perched on the edge of adulthood, could not stop thinking about Leo and replaying his admiring glance. She had wasted the golden days of that summer keeping close to the house and hoping that Leo would notice her again; that she would be the one to tame him. She wanted to be the girl beside him in his open-top MG, with her hair blowing in the wind, smiling, laughing, kissing. She knew what those girls were giving him, and she trembled in anticipation.

And then came the day that he saw her watching as he saddled his mare.

"Hello, Daphne."

She could feel the heat rising in her cheeks. "Hello, Leo."

He laid a hand on her shoulder, and she trembled. He shook his head and gave her a sad smile that would haunt her for many years. "Don't waste your time on me, Daphne. I'm not worth it."

"Don't say that. I ... I ..."

He laid a finger on her lips. "Shh. Don't say it. You're not safe with me."

"I don't want to be safe."

He shook his head again. "I won't do it, Daphne. You have a reputation to maintain, and one day you'll marry some thoroughly decent chap and forget all about me."

"I won't."

He swung himself up into the saddle and looked down on her. "The girls I go with know how to play the game, but you don't, and I won't teach you. For your own sake, leave me alone."

That had been her last summer at Montard Hall. The next summer, she went to finishing school in Switzerland, and then on to study French at the Sorbonne. For years she had searched the scandal sheets, devouring news of Leo. He had not changed his ways. He blazed his way through debutante society, with occasional diversions into the lower classes: chorus girls, actresses, exotic dancers. Despite the best efforts of his own father and several other outraged fathers, he did not marry.

Now the world had changed. Leo was here, and he was to be her pilot. He took a step toward her. "Daphne, I didn't know you ..."

She put a finger to her lips. "It's a secret."

The other pilot broke the silence. "Well, it seems you two know each other already."

Leo nodded. Daphne said nothing.

She watched as the other man set his glass down on the counter. She waited until the curtains closed behind him, and then she stepped into Leo's arms.

August 1952
The Montard Estate, Brighton

The radio stuttered into life. Daphne dragged her thoughts back to the present and made her report.

While she waited for a response, she heard the sound of a vehicle coming down into the valley. Her heart leaped.

Why are you afraid?

Germans.

There are no Germans in these woods.

The old injuries to her fingers sent her a sudden stab of pain to remind her to loosen her grip on the microphone. She saw the face of the Gestapo officer who had done this to her. It had not been Leo's fault. She had known the risks. If only he would stop blaming himself, then perhaps they could talk.

She peered through the trees and saw a black police car nosing its way along the path. Cameron had called for reinforcements. She should go down now and put a stop to this before he could take Leo away.

The radio came to life again.

Even with the headphones, even with the voice of command in her ears, she could still hear car doors slamming, raised voices, and the dog barking again. Time was running out. She should go down now. Leo needed her.

Toby Whitby

Toby focused his attention on the burned man's eyes and tried not to look at the strangely oversize pink nose, the web of scars across his cheek, and the cruelly distorted mouth.

The police car had delivered two uniformed constables, who now waited uncertainly for instructions from Cameron.

"Get him into the car," Cameron commanded for the second time.

The constables still hesitated. After a quick glance at the suspect, they had both averted their eyes. Now they shuffled their feet and stared down at their muddy boots.

One of them ventured a question. "What about the dog, Inspector?"

"I don't give a damn about the dog. Secure the prisoner."

Toby had hoped to see Daphne coming across the stream and waving a warrant card that would put an end to the situation, but so far she had not arrived.

"Mr. Montard," Toby said.

The pale eyes turned toward him.

"Do you need a solicitor?"

Cameron's voice was scornful. "You stay out of this, Whitby, before I arrest you as well."

"On what charge?"

"Interfering with a police action."

"I am asking your prisoner if he needs a solicitor. He has a legal right to a solicitor." Toby tried to meet Leo's pale gaze. "I can help you. Let me help you."

Leo's eyes were focused on something beyond Toby's shoulder. Toby turned and caught a glimpse of Daphne watching from the opposite bank of the stream.

"No, no." Leo's voice was a pained whisper as he lowered his head and turned abruptly away. "Don't let her come."

Cameron sniffed suspiciously. "What are you talking about?"

Leo looked down at the ground. "It's nothing."

Toby glanced back across the stream. Daphne was now nowhere in sight, and her absence somehow imbued him with confidence. She had been trained to work undercover in occupied France, and he had a strong feeling that she was about to put that training to good use. Her interaction with Toby had been cold and impatient, but he had heard real pain in her voice when she'd spoken of Leo Montard, and he had seen her wipe away a rebellious tear.

He caught a hint of movement in a bramble thicket beside the stream and felt reassured. Daphne was still nearby. Leo had a guardian angel.

He turned back to the prisoner. He could not know what Daphne planned to do, but he knew what he needed to do. Leo Montard needed legal representation, but he could not represent a man who didn't want to be represented.

Leo was still facing away from the stream and the place where Daphne had made her brief appearance, and he did not turn when Toby spoke to him.

"Mr. Montard, will you allow Champion and Company to represent you?"

Without turning, Leo nodded his head. "Yes, very well. Get me out on bail if you can, and tell ... tell her ... I'm sorry to ... to ..." His voice faded.

Cameron broke the silence. "Tell who?"

Leo turned back, the rain-washed light catching the full horror of his face. He looked across the stream. "I thought I saw ..."

"I'm alone," Toby said. "I came alone."

Cameron's voice was brusque and impatient. "All right, Whitby, you got what you wanted. We won't lose track of this client the way you lost track of the last one." He beckoned the two constables forward. "What are you waiting for? Get him in the car."

The dog lunged as the two constables took hold of Leo's arms, and the rope slipped through Toby's hands. Leo took a step backward as the dog hurled herself at his knees. He broke free of his captors, and his hands reached down and caught the rope. He looked up at Toby.

"Take her to my brother," he said. "He'll keep her until I come back; if I come back."

Toby attempted to reassure the prisoner. "You'll be back. You've done nothing. We'll have you out in no time."

He met Leo's steady gaze and saw him raise the remnants of his eyebrows and stretch his damaged lips into an expression that could have been a smile. "Nan follows me everywhere," he said, "and I don't want that. I don't want her to follow where I'm going."

"Get that damned dog under control," Cameron snarled, "before I have her taken away and shot."

Toby took the rope from Leo's hands, noting the way the burned fingers were fused together. Nan strained against the leash as Leo shook off the constables' attempt to hold his arms and walked alone to the black Wolseley police car.

He waited while the car labored through a five-point turn, and all the while, his eyes scoured the woods, looking for a sign of Daphne. The police car slithered perilously on the path and finally gained traction. Perhaps Daphne would do nothing. She was not the sentimental type, and perhaps Leo Montard meant nothing to her. He gripped Nan's rope and set off toward the main house to inform the Viscount that his brother was under arrest.

September 1943
The Skies above France
Daphne

They flew low across the moonlit mountains and dark valleys of enemy territory. She had flown before, of course. Her training had been as thorough as time allowed and had included low-level flights across the darkened English countryside, but this was not England; this was occupied France. The people below them were prisoners of the Germans. They were not locked into their homes and villages, but they were still prisoners in a landscape alive with German troops.

Despite the drone of the Lysander's engines, and the acid fear in the pit of her stomach, she had managed to sleep for an hour. Perhaps she had been lulled by the knowledge that Leo was flying the plane. They had maintained radio silence, but just knowing that he was there in front of her, glimpsing the outline of his head and shoulders in the splash of moonlight, had been enough to calm her fears. Leo would not allow anything to happen to her, not while he was in control.

Of course, he would not be in control for very much longer. She shook her head to clear away the last remnants of sleep and looked out through the domed window. The mountains were behind them, and they were flying low to the ground across a patchwork of fields interspersed with occasional ribbons of road and dark clusters of buildings.

She felt the pull of gravity as the Lysander banked into a steep turn and dropped abruptly. This was it. In a few short minutes, they would be on the ground. She would pull back the hatch, scramble down the ladder, and become just another Frenchwoman, as docile as a lamb in the face of the German occupation.

The plane dropped again and made another turn. She saw lights marking a runway among the lavender fields. The lights flared, the Lysander dropped abruptly, her stomach heaved, and then they were on the ground, and someone was thumping on the hatch above her head. She opened the hatch and smelled the lavender. She fought down her panic. Be quick. You only have a few seconds to get out of the plane. He has to leave. You will not see him again until this is over.

She dragged at her suitcase, heavy with the weight of the radio, and thrust it out of the hatch.

What if they were not French Resistance outside? What if the people who had been sent to meet her had been captured and replaced with Germans? What if it was Germans who had lit the flares and brought the Lysander into a trap?

Leo opened the cockpit. His head was shrouded in a flying helmet, but he had pushed back his goggles. His eyes were on her. His body leaned toward her. She knew what he wanted. She wanted the same thing. She wanted one more kiss, one more moment to stand with his arms around her, one more assurance that at the end of the war, they would …

August 1952
The Montard Estate, Brighton

Daphne crouched among the bushes and waited for the sound of an approaching police car. She had seen Leo taken into the back seat and seen the police driver make his laborious turn and set off down the steep path. The main road was just a short distance ahead. If she did not stop the car here, she would not have another opportunity.

Her orders were to find the boy, not to attempt to rescue Leo Montard. Leo was not important to anyone except her, but what did that matter? She knew what she owed him. If she had not been so sure that she could outsmart the Germans, if she had not been confident that she could pass as a Frenchwoman, if she had not thrown herself into his arms, he would not be here now, hiding from the world. It was her fault that he had renounced his title. It was her fault that he would never again find peace and acceptance. The past was the past, and she could do nothing about that now, but she could disobey orders, and she could do this. She heard the thrum of the Wolseley's engine struggling along the muddy path. She smiled. She still had a few tricks up her sleeve.

CHAPTER FOURTEEN

Brighton, Sussex

Anthea Clark

Anthea arrived at the office just in time to find Mr. Champion making his own tea.

"Oh, I am so sorry. I should have been here."

She looked into the teapot and saw a few tea leaves floating on the surface of the water. Perhaps she should add another spoonful. Would Mr. Champion be offended?

Her employer joined her in looking at the weak tea. He gave a papery little laugh. "That doesn't look right. I should have waited for you, but I didn't know how long you would be. How is Slater?"

"Too soon to know," Anthea replied. "He was quite a long time in the operating theater. His wife is very worried, but Mr. Whitby's wife is with her now."

She took the tea caddy from the shelf and stood for a moment, remembering Toby's insistence that he should be given Dorothy Slater's tea caddy. She wished she knew what was going on. She should have insisted that he tell her so that she could pass the information to Mr. Champion. Of course, she had been quite distracted at the time. She felt a flush rising in her cheeks at the memory of what had distracted her. Her hand flew to her hair, and she patted at the stray hairs and loose hairpins. She really should go home and get dressed properly.

"Miss Clark. Miss Clark."

She flushed again, realizing that she had been standing with the tea caddy open, struck like a statue; like a pillar of salt; like Lot's wife. Oh dear, now was not the time to be thinking of the Bible.

She shook the caddy. "I'll add another spoonful," she said. "I'm sorry I wasn't here."

Mr. Champion waved away her apology. "I'm sure you were needed," he said. "Do you know where Whitby is?"

She shook her head and felt a stray lock of hair fall across her forehead. "He wasn't at the hospital," she said. "I don't know where he went. I thought he would be here."

Mr. Champion frowned. "So did I. He's gone off somewhere, Miss Clark, and I don't like it. He is so very reckless, and I'm afraid that something will happen to him. We've already had to pull him out of the sea, and out of an airplane, I can't help wondering what he'll do next. I'm not sure he's suited to legal work. You're the one who suggested we employ him."

Anthea spooned the tea into the teapot. "When I met him during the war, he struck me as a very bright young man," she said. "I'm sure he will have an explanation."

Mr. Champion stroked his chin. "I've been thinking of retiring and handing over the reins. I talked to him about it last night."

Last night! Anthea hastened to set the lid on the teapot. She would not think about last night.

"Hello! Anthea! Are you in here?"

As if in answer to her stray guilty thought, Hugh Trewin appeared at the door of the little kitchen nook. His smile was somewhat tentative. She wondered if he was feeling as uncomfortable as she was. *No, he's a man. It means nothing to him.*

"You have two people in your outer office," Hugh said.

Mr. Champion straightened his cravat. "Clients?"

Hugh shook his head. "No, I doubt it, but they do have information that will benefit one of your clients." He gave Anthea a conspiratorial smile, which she tried to ignore. "It's Elspeth, the young lady we went to London to see, and she's brought a young man with her."

Mr. Champion refastened the buttons on his old-fashioned morning coat and nodded to Hugh. "Well, Colonel, let us go and talk to her. Miss Clark, will you please bring tea."

"No!" The words were out of Anthea's mouth before she could stop herself. "No, I won't bring tea. I am the person who found Elspeth Aleshire. I am the one who went to London to interview her, and I want to know why she's here. I won't be relegated to tea girl."

Hugh patted her arm. "Well done, old girl."

Mr. Champion was momentarily rigid with shock. He looked from Anthea to Hugh to the teapot and back again. He pursed his lips, and his gray eyebrows shot up to meet his neatly combed hair. "I see."

He turned and walked out of the kitchen. Anthea dithered, moving from one foot to another.

Mr. Champion returned. "Miss Clark, we are waiting for you."

"The tea?"

"We don't need tea; we need the benefit of your wisdom. Come along."

Anthea was relieved to see that Elspeth Aleshire had covered her legs. She wore a stylish yellow cotton frock to set off her suntan, and she had a small yellow bow in her dark hair. It would seem that she had gone to some lengths to make the most of her appearance. Perhaps, Anthea thought, that was because the young man who accompanied her was very handsome with his broad, freckled face, cropped brown hair, and a grin that lost its confidence as he surveyed Mr. Champion.

Mr. Champion ushered the guests into this office. After a moment's hesitation, Hugh left and returned with additional chairs. They were all seated, all waiting for whatever Elspeth had come to tell them, when it occurred to Anthea that she should have brought her notebook. It would not, she told herself, be a diminishment of her status if she took notes. Someone would have to take notes, so why not her? She was the only one who could write shorthand, and shorthand would surely be needed.

She hurried out of the room and returned with a stenographer's notepad and a pen. She made a notation of the date and created her own Pitman's outline for the names of the visitors. Elspeth and ...? She looked at the young man questioningly.

"Sidney," he said. "I'm Sidney Rutherford. I was on the boat with Elspeth and ... him. We called him Eddie because that's what it said on his label, but he kept telling us his name was not Eddie."

Sidney's accent betrayed an upbringing somewhere north of the Thames. "We weren't very nice to him," Sidney admitted. He looked down at the floor. "He was an easy target, and we needed something to take our minds off ... well, you know ... the U-boats, the bombers, leaving home."

August 1940
North Atlantic
Sidney Rutherford

Sidney waited impatiently in the doorway of the cabin. "Come on, Pete. Stop messing with that. The sun's out, and we can go up on deck."

Peter Martin turned his acne-pocked face toward Sidney. "Hang on a tick; I'm going to look in his suitcase. There's something going on with that kid, and I want to know what it is."

Sidney stepped back into the cabin and closed the door behind him. "You don't really think he's a spy, do you?"

Peter undid the clasps on the suitcase and lifted the lid. "He talks in his sleep, and it ain't English."

Sidney shrugged. "I don't think it's German. I mean, he doesn't say 'Sieg Heil' or anything like that."

"There's more to German than saying 'Sieg Heil' and 'Jawohl, mein Führer,'" Peter declared. He pulled a piece of paper from his pocket. "I've been writing down what he says."

"Everything?"

"No, not everything, just what he says in his sleep, or as much as I can remember of it. Sometimes he says the same words over and over, so I keep a pencil under my pillow, and I write it down."

"You're weird," Sidney declared.

"I'm not the weird one," Peter replied. "He's the weird one. I don't think he even knows his own name, which means that he's using someone else's name."

Sidney looked down at the meager contents of the suitcase. He picked up a shirt and examined the label sewn inside. "Edward Powley," he said.

Peter pawed through the remaining clothing, examining the labels. "They all say Edward Powley, so why doesn't he want to be called Edward, or Eddie, or Teddy or anything that has something to do with his name? I'm telling you, Sid, he's a spy."

"So who is he spying on?" Sidney asked. "We're just a bunch of kids being sent to Canada. We don't know anything."

Peter tapped his nose. "That's what you think. Perhaps one of us is the son or daughter of a really important person, maybe even a royal. We haven't seen the girls, not since we came on board. Suppose one of them is a princess."

"You mean like Princess Elizabeth or Princess Margaret?"

Peter nodded. "Exactly. Maybe they're sneaking the princesses across the Atlantic. Maybe the rest of us are just decoys to hide the fact that the royals are running away."

Sidney sat down on his bunk. "Would they do that?"

"They would if they think we're going to lose."

"Are we going to lose?"

Peter shrugged. "My dad says that things don't look good."

"So does mine," Sidney agreed. "That's why they're sending me to my mum's brother in Winnipeg. My mum says that Hitler wouldn't want to invade Winnipeg, so I'll be safe there. Where are you going?"

"Got an aunt in Calgary," Peter said.

Sidney gestured to the suitcase. "Where is he going?"

Peter rummaged through the clothing and produced a large brown envelope. He lifted the flap and pulled out a sheaf of papers. "He's going to someone called Malcolm Powley in Vancouver." He riffled through the papers. "Letter of introduction, gives his name as Edward Powley, some photographs of his family, medical certificate, list of vaccinations."

Sidney held out his hand and took the papers. He studied the photographs. "These are weird."

Peter shrugged. "That's 'cause he's weird."

"No, not just that." Sidney held up a picture. "I mean, look at these people. Do they look English to you?"

Peter pounced on the photos. "See, I told you. He's not English."

"But they don't look German," Sidney argued. "I mean, they look sort of foreign."

"Germans are foreign."

"Not that kind of foreign," Sidney said. "Germans are all blond and blue-eyed, aren't they? These people are all kind of dark."

"Spanish," Peter declared.

Sidney continued to look at the pictures, seeing two elderly people, a man and a woman, with dark, beady eyes, standing in a field with a horse grazing in the background. Another picture was a younger man and woman standing in front of a painted background. The man was round faced, with a receding hairline. The woman was thin and straight faced, with a feathered hat perched on her dark hair.

He heard the double click of Peter closing the locks on the suitcase.

"Wait a minute. We should put these back. He'll need them when we land."

Peter tapped his nose again. "And what if he doesn't have them?"

"No one will know what to do with him."

"Exactly. They won't know what to do, so they'll start asking questions. And that means he won't go where he's supposed to go, and he won't be able to spy. They'll probably give him the third degree, and he'll fess up, and the whole plot will come out."

Peter flung his arm around Sidney's shoulders. "We'll be heroes. We'll be the lads who saved the princesses."

Sidney was momentarily overwhelmed by the idea that the two young princesses might be on the ship with them, might even now be up on the deck, taking in the sunshine. Peter had the right idea. The authorities might not listen to the theories of a couple of thirteen-year-old boys, but if the kid had no papers, they'd have to start asking questions.

"We should throw the papers overboard," Peter suggested. "Just chuck them in the ocean."

Sidney shook his head. "That would be destroying the evidence. We should keep them as proof. I'll put them in my suitcase, and if anything happens, you know, if we hear about the princesses being kidnapped or anything, we'll have the proof."

Peter slapped him on the back. "Good idea. Put them in your case, and put my notes in the case, and then we'll go up on deck and look at the girls."

August 1952
Brighton, Sussex
Anthea Clark

Sidney reached into the inner pocket of his jacket and pulled out a brown envelope.

"I kept them."

Anthea's mind was racing to put all the pieces into place. Evvie Stewart had said that Buddy had no papers, and that was why he had been left behind in Toronto to be given to the first family who offered to take him.

She held out her hand, and Sidney gave her the envelope. His broad, honest face was flushed.

"It was all stupid," he said. "We went up on deck and looked at the girls, and none of them looked like the little princesses."

Anthea smiled with the confidence of her own memories of London. "The little princesses remained in the palace," she said. "I know that for a fact."

She had almost forgotten about Hugh, but now he looked at her with interest. "You know that for a fact?"

"I had a position in the palace during the war," she said. "I saw the girls quite often."

Sidney was still speaking. "When we went up on deck, I saw Elspeth and I ... uh ... sort of ... forgot about the spying and everything, especially when she said she was going to Winnipeg just like I was."

It was Elspeth's turn to blush. "We lost track of each other before we got to Winnipeg," she said, "but he wrote to me in London after the war. It took a while for the letter to find me. When you and the colonel came to see me, I wanted to tell Sid what you had told me. I thought he'd be interested, but I didn't think that he would really know anything." She smiled at Sidney. "Turns out that he knows a lot."

Anthea pulled the pictures from the envelope and stared at the black-and-white images. She knew why Sidney and his bunkmate had called the people foreign: dark hair, dark eyes, and the woman with her hair loose, the horse grazing in the background, and not a building in sight. Who were they?

Her thoughts were interrupted by the urgent clangor of the telephone in the outer office. She rose automatically. She had asserted her right to be in Mr. Champion's office and to hear what Elspeth had to say for herself, but she was still the secretary; she was still the person who answered the phone.

Mr. Champion leaned back in his chair and steepled his fingers. "I sincerely hope that's Mr. Whitby," he said dryly. "I can't imagine what's keeping him."

Anthea lifted the receiver and heard Toby Whitby's familiar voice. "Mr. Whitby, where are you? Mr. Champion is asking for you, and—"

"Not now, Anthea. Don't talk; just listen. I'm up at Montard Hall with the Viscount, and my car is ..."

Toby's voice trailed away, and Anthea hissed at him in irritation. "What about your car?"

Toby was speaking again but not to her. His voice echoed as though he was standing in a large room. "That was a gunshot, wasn't it?"

Another voice, presumably the Viscount's, answered Toby's question. "Yes, I would say so. Wonder what's going on."

"There it is again," Toby said. "Someone's shooting. I don't suppose it's poachers, not at this time of day."

"Well, let's go and find out what's going on," the Viscount suggested. "We'll take the Land Rover. Are you finished on the phone?"

"Almost finished," Toby said. His voice was in her ear again. "Can you get someone to fix my car?"

"But where is—?"

"Thanks, Miss Clark. You're an absolute brick. I'll explain everything later."

And just like that, he was gone.

The Montard Estate, Brighton
Toby Whitby

Lord Victor Montard was a tall, handsome man with a mop of blond hair and an air of easygoing privilege. He was, Toby thought, the man that Leo should have been. He remembered Leo's ruined face, his mouth that could not smile, and the patches of yellow hair on his scalp. Only the eyes were the same, blue and honest. The Viscount's eyes had flashed with anger as Toby told him of his brother's arrest.

Victor was already dressed for the outdoors, in a green Barbour anorak and wellington boots, and now, with the sound of gunfire still reverberating, he whistled for his dogs and strode out of the door.

Toby and the two springer spaniels followed him across the stable yard and into a dark green Land Rover, where the dogs scrambled into the back seat, leaving room for Toby in the front.

"If they have done anything to my brother ..." Victor muttered.

Toby could not find words to reassure him. Inspector Cameron's behavior had been erratic and spiteful from the moment he had presented himself at Brighton Police Station. Toby suspected that Cameron's cases in North Yorkshire were not nearly as exciting as the case he had stumbled upon in Brighton. If he'd been sent down to help with security at Arundel, why wasn't he at Arundel now? Why was he still interfering in the Powley case? Toby could only assume that Cameron was trying to make a favorable impression on the chief constable, hoping for a promotion and a permanent transfer to Brighton.

Slater had not said when the Arundel meeting was to occur, but Toby hoped it would be very soon and that Cameron would start fulfilling his original assignment.

Toby looked at Victor's hands gripping the steering wheel impatiently. With the Viscount crashing through the gears and the dogs panting eagerly down his neck, he had trouble marshaling his thoughts, but he thought he should try to phone the office as soon as possible. Thinking back on his brief exchange with Anthea Clark, he realized that he had not told her where to find the car, or what he was doing, or what had happened to Leo. Come to think of it, he had not even told her that Leo existed, and of course, he'd said nothing about Daphne.

A silent alarm sounded at the back of his mind. Did Daphne have a weapon? Was she the one doing the shooting? He wouldn't put it past her. He wouldn't put anything past her.

Victor ground the gears impatiently as he turned the Land Rover onto the narrow path that led downhill to the base of the dam.

"I thought the police car would come up past the house while I was walking up the road," Toby said. "I expected Cameron to pass me before I reached you."

Victor shook his head. "He didn't need to. There's a shortcut that will take them to the main road. It's steep and rocky, but I expect they're giving it a try. I can do it in the Land Rover, but I'm not sure about a police car. With any luck, they'll be stuck down there, and we'll get to them before they reach the main road."

"Then what?" Toby asked.

Victor jerked his head toward the back seat. "I have my gun. I'm prepared to use it. My brother is my responsibility, and I'll take care of him."

The Land Rover careered over a rock and knocked Toby's breath out of his lungs before he could reply. All he could do was cling to the door handle and try to remain in an upright position as Victor flung the Land Rover around a sharp corner and onto a precipitous rocky path.

"Do you really think they went down here?" Toby asked.

"I think they tried," Victor said grimly.

Toby tightened his grip on the door handle and raised his voice to get the Viscount's attention. "You need to slow down."

"We'll be fine," Victor responded. "Land Rover's made for this."

Toby reached out and gripped Victor's arm. "No, we won't be fine. Someone's shooting and we'll be next."

Victor jammed on the brakes, and Toby barely avoided slamming his face into the dashboard. With the Land Rover at a standstill, Victor turned off the engine, and the world was suddenly silent, apart from the heavy breathing of the spaniels.

Victor turned in his seat. "Sorry, old chap. I'm acting the fool and I should know better. It's just that Leo ... well ... you know ... I worry about him, and the thought of them taking him somewhere public. He's not up to it. He's just not up to it. You saw him. You know."

Toby nodded. "Yes, I know. It was a shock. I can't say that it wasn't. Daphne didn't tell me. She hinted but she didn't really say."

"Daphne?"

"Yes. She was the one who brought me here. She's an old friend of your family, apparently."

"Daphne Raleigh?"

"I don't know if that's her last name, or if it's even a real name. It was all very hush-hush."

"But she's here somewhere?" Victor asked.

"Yes. She has a radio. She was reporting to someone."

"Who?"

"I don't know."

Victor turned away and stared ahead through the windshield. "Did Leo see her?"

"No, I don't think so."

"What about the arresting officer? Did you say his name was Cameron?"

"He was too busy arresting your brother to see anything else."

"The man's a fool," Victor muttered. He turned to look at Toby. The anguished expression was still on his face, but he seemed calmer, less frantic. "Leo will be released, won't he? I mean, there's no evidence."

"None that I know of," Toby agreed. "I offered your brother my legal services, and he accepted. I'll do my best to get him released without charge, and Cameron will be gone soon. He's only temporary."

Victor nodded. His breathing had stilled and his expression was thoughtful. "I suppose Leo would be all right for a while, so long as he doesn't have to appear in court. He would hate that."

"I'll do my best," Toby said. He thought of the gunshots that had reverberated through the morning air. He wondered if Leo was still in police custody or if he and Daphne were even now escaping across the Downs.

The dogs in the back seat whined impatiently. Toby assumed that they were conditioned to the sight of Victor's rifle, and now they were impatient for Victor to shoot something for them to retrieve.

Voices drifted toward them, and the dogs began to bark. Victor silenced them with a sharp command.

The voices came closer. Two men arguing.

"Up this way. This'll take us up to the big house. We can call from there."

"We should go down to the road. We can stop a car. We're in uniform."

"Leave that to the inspector. He's gone down there."

Victor climbed out of the Land Rover, and the dogs scrambled out behind him. Toby heard the click of Victor releasing the safety on the rifle and made his own hurried exit.

He clutched at the back of Victor's Barbour jacket. "It's okay. It's the police. Something's happened to the car. They probably have Leo with them. I'll take care of this."

Victor's shoulders relaxed, but he kept the rifle at the ready as two uniformed policemen came into sight on the rocky path. Toby immediately recognized them as the constables who had been with Cameron when he had made his arrest. They were a mismatched pair, one young and gangling, with legs that were too long for his uniform pants, and one with a middle-aged face and a uniform jacket that strained at its buttons. Although they bore no resemblance to each other, their faces reflected the same expression of shock and bewilderment.

Victor straddled the path, rifle at the ready. "Where's my brother?"

Toby pushed past him and faced the two constables. "Viscount Pulborough wants to know what you're doing on his land and what you have done with your prisoner," he said.

The gangling youth, PC 24, according to his badge, looked at Toby suspiciously. "You was with him," he said. "You said you was his lawyer."

"I am," Toby agreed. "Now tell me where he is."

"Damned if I know," said the fat one, whose badge identified him as PC 17. "Did you have something to do with this?"

"This what?" Toby asked.

PC 24's voice was an indignant squeak. "She shot at us."

Victor maintained his position on the path, with his rifle still at the ready. "Who shot at you?"

"Don't know," PC 24 declared. "She came out of nowhere. Shot out our tires and shot up the radio."

"She?" Victor asked. "You're saying a woman shot at you?" He turned his head slightly to look at Toby.

Toby nodded, all of his suspicions confirmed. Daphne's satchel had contained more than just a radio.

"What did she look like?" Victor asked.

PC 24 shook his head. "Dunno."

PC 17 grunted his disapproval of his companion. "PC Wainwright's just a baby," he declared. "Ain't never been shot at. He wasn't in the war, but I was, and I don't fall apart when some woman comes out of the woods with a pistol. I kept my eyes open."

"And what did you see?" Toby asked.

The older man pursed his lips. "Not sure I should tell you. This is police business, and you might be involved. Maybe I should bring you in. Maybe I should bring both of you in."

"I'd like to see you try," Victor hissed.

Toby nodded his agreement. "I don't think you should be making any more arrests. The last one didn't go well for you, did it?"

PC 17 bristled. "Are you threatening me?"

"No," Toby said. "I am just asking you what happened to my client. It seems that he's no longer in custody."

"No longer in custody?" the young constable said. "No, he ain't. He's gone off with that woman, and good luck to him. I thought she was going to kill us all."

PC 17 shook his head. "She wasn't shooting at you, son. If you'd kept your eyes open, you'd have seen for yourself. She was after the inspector."

"Is he shot?" Toby asked, somewhat ashamed of his fervent hope that Cameron was indeed injured.

"Don't think so," PC 17 replied. "He was up and running, last we saw of him."

"Running?" Toby asked. "Running where?"

PC 17 squared his shoulders and made an attempt to take charge of the situation. "I believe that Inspector Cameron has gone down to the main road to requisition a vehicle and call for assistance. The woman shot out our tires to make us stop, and then she leaned in and shot up the radio. After that she pulled our prisoner out of the car and fled the scene. It will all be in my report."

Victor lowered the rifle. "So you are saying that Inspector Cameron has abandoned you and gone down to the main road, and that my brother is somewhere in the woods with the woman who shot at you?"

"I am. As soon as I get to a phone, I am going to call it in, and we'll get ourselves a search party. She won't go far."

Victor laughed and shook his head. "They'll be long gone before you can find them. What are you going to do? Do you plan to search the whole of the South Downs?"

"But she has a gun," PC 24 complained. "She can't be running around with a gun."

"I wouldn't be so sure of that," Toby said. "I think that she may be one of the few people allowed to carry a gun."

"But she shot at a police officer."

Toby smiled. "That's what you say, but you admit that your eyes were closed."

"Vernon had his eyes open," the youth declared, nodding his head at his companion. "He saw what happened. He knows. We'll phone it in, and we'll have a search party out here in no time."

Toby fought against his momentary joy at the idea of Cameron running for his life while his prisoner escaped, and remembered instead that a brutal murder had been committed. If Leo was not the murderer, then the killer was still on the loose. He wanted to ask, but he could not remember the victim's name. It was a woman, but …

Victor supplied the name in a sharp question. "What about Mrs. Widdicome?"

PC 17 stumbled at the question. "Mrs. Who?"

"The victim. The woman who was killed. The murder you are supposed to be investigating."

PC 17 puffed out his chest. "That's all under control," he declared. "Inspector Cameron says it was a murder committed by another one of Mr. Whitby's clients, a boy from Canada."

"And yet you arrested Leo Montard," Toby said. "Why did you do that?"

"Inspector's orders. We just follow orders."

"That's what happened in Germany," Victor muttered, "and we all know what that led to."

PC 17 shook his head. "I ain't arguing with you. I'm going to requisition the use of your phone and report in for my orders."

"Of course you are," Victor agreed. He tossed the rifle into the back of the Land Rover and whistled for the dogs, who had lost interest in the lack of a victim to retrieve and were snuffling around in the bushes.

"Get in," Victor said, holding the door open. The dogs rushed to obey. Toby hesitated. "Get in," Victor repeated. "Our friends in blue will have to walk. I won't prevent them using the phone, but I won't give them a ride up the hill. I'm giving Daphne as much time as I can. Get in, Whitby, or I'll leave you behind."

January 1944
Bellerive, Provence, France
Daphne Raleigh

Frost lay heavily on the bushes and sparkled in the moonlight. The lavender perfume of a hundred summers rose up around Daphne as she walked toward the landing strip. She realized that she would miss the scent that had permeated her time in Bellerive. She would never again wash with lavender soap or fold sprigs of lavender into fresh laundry without thinking of her time with Henri and Marcel.

She turned to her companions, walking in single file behind her.

"I am sorry. Je suis désolée.*"*

Marcel shook his head. "You are not safe here. Ça va mieux.*"*

Henri raised a finger to his lips. "Tais toi."

Daphne forced herself to be silent. She had said all that needed to be said, and all that was left to do was to listen for the approach of the Lysander that would carry her away from here. The last communication from London had been brief and to the point. One of her fellow agents had been taken, and given the Gestapo's methods, it would not be long before Daphne's cell would be revealed. She must leave France and return to England with her cover intact.

Her handler had even taken the time to add a personal message. Her heart had leaped as she had decoded it. The pilot will be familiar to you. *Leo? Was Leo coming to get her? The thought of seeing him softened the sorrow of leaving, but not the guilt. She would soon be safely across the Channel, but Marcel and Henri and dozens of other Resistance fighters would be on the run. The word was out; the Gestapo was closing in.*

They reached the grassy landing strip, and Marcel ran ahead to place the lanterns. He would not light them until the plane was almost overhead, but he would be ready.

Marcel had children. What would happen to them when their father was taken? No, don't say when. Say if. There is still time.

Daphne ran along the edge of the field and caught up with Marcel as he was setting out the last of the lamps.

"Vas t'en. Vite."

He shook his head, but she would not leave him. "You go, Marcel. I will do this." She pointed to herself. "Moi. Depeche toi."

"No." Marcel rarely revealed his knowledge of English. From the day she had arrived in Bellerive, Daphne had spoken only French. Now Marcel took her by the shoulders, stared into her face and spoke in English. "We will do our work until the end. You must leave before anyone realizes that you are not a Frenchwoman, but we must stay. We will not be treated as you will be treated, so you go and let us do what we have to do."

He jerked the lantern from her hand and set it on the ground. "You will leave. We will stay. Vive la France.*"*

And so they waited, with the moonlight beaming down on the dormant fields and the scent of lavender filling the cold night air. They listened for the sound of Leo's plane and heard nothing but the rustling of field mice and the calling of night birds. They waited until a pink dawn replaced the moonlight, and still the plane did not come.

Marcel and Henri retrieved the lamps. Henri set a hand on her shoulder. He did not need to speak; she knew that she only had one hope now. She must hope that the Gestapo would not realize who she was. She must not break. Whatever they did to her, she must not scream out in English. She must be a Frenchwoman. She must know nothing; just an innocent caught up by mistake.

She looked up at the arc of cold blue sky, searching one last time for the sight of a plane. She listened for the distant thrumming of an engine. Yes, there it was; not a plane but a German staff car, and behind it, a canvased truck to take the prisoners.

August 1952
The Montard Estate, Brighton

Nine years had passed since she had seen him. They had both suffered, and they had both changed, and yet Leo recognized her as soon as she pulled him out of the wrecked police car. Their eyes met as she clasped his hand, and for one brief, joyful moment, nothing else mattered. She ignored the burned flesh, the terrible nose, and the twisted mouth. The spark of recognition in his eyes was enough for that moment. Words would come later, but for now it was enough that he knew who she was, and knew that she had come for him.

She was tempted to shoot the grubby little police inspector, but some level of her training still remained. Shooting him would bring on a massive manhunt. Whatever the circumstances, and however unreasonable Leo's arrest had been, nothing would be solved by killing a police officer. Maybe she should have wounded him, just to slow him down, but she knew that she couldn't trust herself. If she shot, she would shoot to kill, so best not to be tempted.

She dragged Leo for some distance uphill until they reached the concealment of a thicket of brambles and spindly alders. She pulled Leo down beside her and parted the leaves. When she had shot out the tires, the big police car had rolled onto its side and jammed itself onto a rock. The two uniformed constables were already on their feet and trying to extricate the inspector, who was turning the air around the car blue with his use of unofficial language.

Daphne looked at Leo lying on his belly beside her. "I shot out their radio. He won't be calling anyone for a long time. We'll have time to get away."

He was staring at her, and she was suddenly aware that he did not know the extent of her injuries. They were nothing compared to his scars, but this was the first time he had seen her damaged face. He reached up with a scarred hand and pushed back her hair. He touched the scar on her cheek, and his finger flickered lightly just above her blind eye.

"I didn't come," he said.

"You couldn't. I understand."

He rolled away from her, hiding his face and revealing the patchy hair on the back of his head. Remembering how his hair had been, thick and yellow, her heart ached for him.

"Leo, please, it's all right. Look at me."

He spoke without turning to her. "You don't have to pretend. I know what I look like, but I didn't know that you …"

"I'm at peace with what happened to me," she said. As soon as the words were out of her mouth, she knew how ridiculous they were, how trite, how meaningless. She could hide her scars under a veil of hair. She could put on dark glasses or a shady hat, but Leo had no place to hide.

She parted the grass again and looked down at the police car. The inspector was standing in the road and taking stock of the situation.

She kept her voice to a low, urgent whisper. She would find words later for all the things she wanted to say, but for now she could only give instruction. "Leo, we have to move. We can't let him find us."

"You go. He doesn't know who you are."

"I'm not leaving you here. I am not going to allow him to take you. Get on your feet, Leo, and we'll make a run for it before he gets his wits back."

"Run where?"

"I know a place. It's quite a hike, but it will be worth it. Do you trust me?"

He turned to face her for a brief moment. "What's in the bag?"

"A gun and a radio."

He laughed softly. "Daphne Raleigh, secret agent."

CHAPTER FIFTEEN

Toby Whitby

The Viscount released the disappointed dogs and ushered Toby into a whitewashed room at the end of the stable block. With ledgers piled on the desk, and a bulging filing cabinet set against the wall, Toby assumed that this was the estate office and this was where he would find a telephone.

When he saw the dusty black instrument squatting on the desk, he found that he was uncertain how to proceed. Should he call Miss Clark and tell her where he was and where to find his car? Should he call the hospital and see if Slater had come around from his anesthetic? He was well aware how very much he needed Slater's advice. Should he try to recall the number he had dialed to contact Daphne? Should Daphne's superiors, whoever they were, be told that their agent was out in the woods, shooting at the police? Should he call Mr. and Mrs. Stewart and see if they had heard from Buddy? The number of questions competing for answers held him in momentary suspension. There was the phone, but where should he begin?

Victor pulled open a drawer in the filing cabinet and produced a bottle of whiskey and two glasses. "I don't like gunfire," he said. "Takes me back to places I don't want to go. I'm sure you feel the same way, old chap." He rubbed his hands together. "So, we'll have a quick snifter, just to settle the nerves, and then you can tell me what this is all about."

Toby accepted the glass and waited while the Viscount poured a generous measure of whiskey. Victor swallowed his drink in one long gulp, and Toby followed suit, delighting in the heady feeling as the liquor made its way into his stomach and the fumes made their way into his brain. He resisted the urge to ask for a refill. He shuffled his thoughts and attempted to present them to Victor in some sort of logical order.

He began at the beginning, with a boy from Canada whose name was not Edward Powley.

"We still don't know his real name," Toby said, "but he comes from the Brighton area. He lived in a house on St. Godric Street, and according to Daphne, who is now running around the woods shooting up police cars, the boy's father was a German spy."

Victor held up a hand to silence him. "The war's over; nothing left for a German to spy on."

"Not according to Daphne," Toby replied.

Victor frowned. "Daphne was always very excitable."

He poured himself another drink and raised an inquiring eyebrow at Toby. Toby shook his head. He was still shuffling information and realizing that Buddy's simple question—*Who am I?*—had opened a Pandora's box of questions, and Toby could not see how he would ever be able to close the lid. Where was Buddy? Who had killed Winnie Widdicome? Who had killed the woman in St. Godric Street? Was that woman Buddy's mother? Who had taken Buddy to the train? Why was Cameron so set on arresting everyone involved in the investigation? What did Cameron expect to learn from Leo?

"We have not even passed the first hurdle," Toby complained. "We've established the boy is not Edward Powley, and that is the only thing we know for a fact. Mrs. Elizabeth Powley is supposedly his mother, but Mrs. Powley denies all knowledge of him and says that she changed her mind and never sent her son to Canada."

"And you believe her?" Victor asked.

"Buddy's foster parents believed her," Toby said. "I've never met her myself."

"Maybe you should."

Toby stared into the Viscount's challenging blue eyes with sudden alarm. "You're right. I just took Roy Stewart's word for it that Mrs. Powley denied all knowledge of the boy. But why would she—?"

Victor interrupted abruptly. "Powley? Powley? It's not a common name, and it's too much of a coincidence."

"What is?"

"You say that the boy knows that he lived somewhere around here?"

"On St. Godric Street in Brighton."

Victor nodded. "That's not far. It's within walking distance for a sturdy young boy."

"Is it?"

"Footpaths," Victor explained. "Long way by road but not so far as the crow flies."

"So you know the name Powley?" Toby asked.

Victor took a measured sip of his whiskey. "Before the war, we had a handful of shops in the village, now we have only one. What is now the post office and village shop used to be Powley's greengrocer's. I remember them being there when I was a kid. You're looking for a young man who says his name is not Edward Powley, but if he comes from around here, the name Powley is not just a coincidence."

"Greengrocers?" Toby said thoughtfully. "I didn't see Mrs. Powley, but I saw Randall Powley, her ex-husband. He's growing watercress in Surrey, and who sells watercress?"

Victor raised his glass in a salute. "Greengrocers."

Toby had a sudden memory of his mother working patiently to unpick a ball of yarn that had been tangled by the cat. He remembered her triumph when she finally found a thread; a place to begin. He had that same feeling now. The first thread was in his hand. *Gently. Don't pull too hard, or it turns into a knot. Patience.*

Patience? No, Toby was not willing to be patient, not when Buddy was still on the loose, Winnie Widdicome was dead, an unknown woman was lying in the mortuary, and Slater's life hung in the balance.

"Is there someone in the village who …?"

The Viscount grinned. "Every village has a gossip hiding behind a lace curtain and watching. We have Mrs. Stackpole. I'll drive you to her house."

The bright flower garden surrounding Muriel Stackpole's brick bungalow failed to hide the raw ugliness of the house itself.

"She came into some money when her husband sold the shop," Victor said as he parked the Land Rover beside the front gate, "and she built this monstrosity. Her husband's gone now and she's on her own. When she's not in the garden, she's upstairs, looking out of the attic window."

Toby climbed out of the passenger seat and surveyed Mrs. Stackpole's garden, bright with roses and hollyhocks and blooms he could not recognize. He wished Carol could see this garden. She was longing for a house of her own with a patch of lawn and maybe a swing or a Wendy house for Anita, not that she would find anything like that in Africa. The thought of his wife brought a renewed feeling of guilt. He really should tell someone where he was and what he was doing.

He looked up and saw a lace curtain blowing and billowing in the morning air, but no sign of the gossipy Mrs. Stackpole.

Victor came up beside him. "She knows we're here. Give her a minute to get down the stairs. No need to knock."

As if on cue, the front door opened to reveal a tall, sturdy woman in a flowered dress and a clean white apron. Her iron-gray hair was bundled up in a hairnet. She bobbed a curtsy. "Your Lordship."

"Mrs. Stackpole."

"I wasn't expecting you."

Toby thought he heard a note of rebuke in her voice.

Victor nodded agreeably. "I am so sorry to disturb you."

Mrs. Stackpole wiped her obviously clean hands on her obviously clean apron, as if to give the impression that the Viscount had disturbed her while she was about some very important household task.

"This is my friend Toby Whitby," Victor continued. "He's a solicitor."

Mrs. Stackpole lifted her head like a spaniel scenting a rabbit, and her eyes glinted. "A solicitor," she repeated.

Toby handed her his business card, and she studied it with delight. He thought he could see the woman's mind at work. A solicitor meant legal trouble for someone. A divorce? A legacy? Jail?

"We've come to ask for your help," Victor said.

Mrs. Stackpole nodded, her eyes still on the business card. "Of course, Your Lordship. If there's anything I can do …"

"Mr. Whitby needs some information," Victor said, "and I understand that you have an excellent memory, Mrs. Stackpole, and you like to keep an eye on what's happening in the village."

Mrs. Stackpole squared her shoulders indignantly. "Are you suggesting that I'm nosy," she asked. "That's not true, Your Lordship. I have enough to do with my own business, without minding other people's business."

"Just information about people who used to live here," Victor said soothingly. "So many people have left, but you're still here, and we're hoping you will remember."

Mrs. Stackpole sniffed. "Remember what?"

"The Powley family," Toby said, cutting short the slow dance between Mrs. Stackpole and the Viscount.

"Powley," Mrs. Stackpole repeated. "Oh yes, I remember them. They're gone now, although I saw a boy this morning …"

"A boy?" Toby repeated.

"Not so much a boy," Mrs. Stackpole amended. "A young man really, and he reminded me of …"

She fell silent.

"Of what?" Toby barked. "What did he remind you of?"

"Well …"

Toby turned to Victor with an imploring look. Was this going to take all day?

"We shouldn't talk out here, where everyone can hear us," Victor said. "Why don't we go inside, Mrs. Stackpole, and you can tell us all about the Powleys?"

Toby tried to pour all of his frustration into a long sigh. If Mrs. Stackpole had seen Buddy, he needed to know when and where and ...

Victor laid a hand on Toby's shoulder. "Mrs. Stackpole will make us a nice cup of tea, and we'll hear all about it."

July 1932
Muriel Stackpole

Muriel hesitated outside Powley's greengrocer's store, taking in the heady scent of the fresh fruit and vegetables displayed in boxes beneath the awning. She'd done her best to grow a few vegetables in the patch of dirt behind the Stackpole Hardware Store, but the hard ground had yielded nothing but weeds. What the ground needed was some good manure. The milkman's horse dropped the occasional contribution as it passed through the village, and Muriel was always ready to dash out with a bucket, but the contribution of just one horse was nowhere near enough. Unfortunately, horses were rare these days, with delivery vans taking their place.

She wished that Jethro would stir himself to give her a hand, but he rarely came out from the seclusion of the stockroom, leaving her to sell the occasional hammer or garden fork or handful of penny nails.

Jethro wasn't an invalid; he had the energy to walk down to the pub every night and spend the day's takings on drinking. It was fourteen years since he came back from France, but he wasn't the same man she had married. Perhaps if they'd had children ... No hope of that now. Those days were behind them. Maybe it was for the best with the country in the grip of the Depression and unemployed men lingering on every street corner.

She glanced wistfully at the display of strawberries, longing for the taste of summer sweetness, but who could afford strawberries these days? She found her hand making an involuntary movement, stretching out ... just one. She jerked back. No, she would not be reduced to stealing. Tomorrow she would follow the bridle path up onto the Downs, where wild strawberries were free for the picking; if the Gypsies had left any for anyone else. They were like a plague of locusts, she thought, picking the wild berries, filling the air with the smoke of their fires, and setting their horses to graze the summer grasses. Well, they'd move on soon enough; they always did.

She looked in at the store door and noticed Randall Powley leaning on the counter and watching the two girls his father had taken on as store assistants. Jethro, in one of his rare moments of good humor, had told her that old Mr. Powley was not even paying the girls. Room and board and no questions asked as to where they came from. It seemed that they'd come to Winnie Widdicome's door, begging for food, and she was the one who'd brought them into the village and asked if anyone had work for them.

"Jim Powley knows a good thing when he sees it," Jethro had said. "He got himself two good-looking girls, and all he has to do is let them sleep in the back of the shop."

Muriel, with a clear view from the window of the hardware store, had seen for herself that Jim Powley had made a wise decision. Curiosity about the girls had led to an immediate increase in Powley's revenue, with men and women alike stopping in to buy a couple of tomatoes or a head of lettuce, and to take a look at the girls.

Muriel hovered in front of the strawberries, breathing in the scent and planning her trip up to the wild strawberry patch. One of the girls, the one who was not engaged in flirting with Randall Powley, leaned forward and looked at her with dark, suspicious eyes, as if she expected that Muriel was about to steal the fruit.

Muriel took a step back and saw the expression on the girl's face turn from interest to alarm, and in that moment, she was aware of the rumbling of an engine behind her. She staggered and tripped, colliding with the boxes of vegetables and landing amid an avalanche of carrots, potatoes, and soft fruits.

Someone's hands were on her. She lifted her head and tried to stand, but a firm hand kept her on the ground, and a girl's voice, cheerful and unsympathetic, assured her that she was all right. "Nothing broken."

The hand tugged at her skirt, and Muriel tried to slap it away. The girl spoke again, just a whisper in her ear. "Just pulling your skirt down. Don't want everyone looking at your unmentionables."

Muriel sat up abruptly. Her head was swimming, and she felt a sharp pain in her left arm. One of the girls from the greengrocer's store was kneeling beside her, and vegetables were scattered all around.

A stocky, blond-haired man loomed above her with his arms folded across his chest and a scowl on his face. She knew who he was. He had come to her door last week, trying to sell life insurance; two shillings a week. She didn't know his name, but she recognized the car that was now stalled in the middle of the road. Jethro had been envious of that motor: "He sells insurance door-to-door, so how does he afford a Hillman?"

"I'm not paying for these vegetables," the insurance salesman said. "Fool woman stepped right out in front of my motor. She's lucky she's not dead. Make her pay for the damage."

The store girl put an arm around Muriel's shoulders. "I'll pick them up," she said. "No need for anyone to pay. No harm done. Just a few squashed strawberries, and not as good as wild ones."

How did she know? *Muriel wondered.* How did she know I was thinking of wild strawberries?

The girl rose in a graceful movement that somehow caused her hips to sway and her skirt to ripple with the movement. The blond man's anger seemed to evaporate as he turned to watch the girl gathering the vegetables from the pavement. Muriel nursed her bruised elbow and realized that the salesman had forgotten all about her as he watched the dip and sway of the store girl's hips.

Randall Powley abruptly blocked her view as he leaned over her. "You all right, Mrs. Stackpole? Want me to help you up?"

Muriel extended her right hand, and Randall pulled her to her feet. "I'm sorry about your vegetables," *she said.*

Randall shook his head. "Don't worry about it." *He looked at her thoughtfully.* "I know times are hard everywhere, and if you need a few squashed vegetables—"

"We're fine," *Muriel snapped.* "We don't need anything."

Randall grinned. "If you're fine, you're the only people who are." *He leaned toward her and spoke softly.* "We're not even paying these two girls, but I expect you know that already."

"The whole village knows it," *Muriel replied.* "Where did Winnie Widdicome find them?"

Randall shook his head. "They found her; that's what I hear." *He nodded toward the girl who had come to Muriel's rescue.* "That one's Nina."

The insurance salesman was now helping the girl to gather some straying King Edwards that had rolled into the gutter. She held out her skirt, and her admirer dropped the potatoes in one by one with occasional misses as his glance strayed from the skirt to Nina's legs.

"And the other one?"

"Elizabeth."

Muriel assessed the value of the information. So now she knew the girls' names, but anyone could discover their names. It wasn't enough. She needed more.

"Where have they come from?"

Randall shrugged. "I didn't ask."

Muriel raised her eyebrows. Men! A woman would have asked. A woman would have asked a great many questions.

"They have a kind of West Country accent," *Randall volunteered.* "That's all I can tell you. I think they're sisters, although they haven't said."

Muriel heard a horn blaring on the street behind her and turned to see a green Southdown bus whose path was blocked by the insurance salesman's Hillman. The salesman looked up from his potato gathering and made an impatient gesture. The bus driver returned the gesture and blared the horn again.

The salesman dropped the last of the potatoes into Nina's skirt. He moved toward his car, and Nina said something to him. Her hand rested on his arm, and they spoke in urgent whispers. The bus driver sounded his horn, and the salesman finally climbed into his vehicle and accelerated away in a cloud of exhaust fumes. Nina turned away and emptied her harvest of potatoes into a cardboard box beneath the awning. When they had all been returned, she straightened her skirt, flicking away dirt and smoothing it across her stomach.

Muriel took note of the gesture. It was something she had done in years gone by; the hand that caressed the belly, feeling for that first slight rounding, that first proof that this time there would be a baby.

August 1952
Toby Whitby

Toby resisted a sudden urge to kiss Mrs. Stackpole. He was quite certain that a kiss would be unwelcome and could possibly result in physical consequences. Mrs. Stackpole was a big woman with broad shoulders beneath her flowered dress, and she did not have a face that encouraged kissing.

Well, he couldn't kiss her, but he could take her hand and thank her. She looked at him suspiciously as he lifted her hand from her lap.

"What's all this about?"

"You, my dear Mrs. Stackpole, have given me the first piece of good news in days. I finally have a name for my client's mother. Her name is Nina. I don't suppose you know the name of the insurance salesman, do you?"

She released her hand from Toby's grip and chewed her lip thoughtfully. "Jack," she said at last. "Jack Farren."

"Jack Farren," Toby repeated. "So Buddy's real name is Farren."

"Who is Buddy?" Mrs. Stackpole asked disapprovingly. "It sounds like a dog's name."

"Yes, it does," Toby agreed, "but thanks to you, we'll soon have a real name for the poor boy."

"What poor boy?"

"The son of the girl in the greengrocer's and the insurance salesman."

Muriel cocked her head to one side and gave Toby a look of feminine contempt. "I don't understand what this is all about, but I am quite sure that Nina's baby was nothing to do with Jack Farren. She was already pregnant when she met him." She hesitated thoughtfully. "Of course, she may not have told him that. Many a baby has come a few weeks early, if you know what I mean, and men don't always understand these things."

"So who was the father?" Toby asked.

Muriel smiled triumphantly. "I'm right. I knew I was, not that I've ever said anything to anyone. I would never gossip—"

"Of course not," Toby agreed, trying to keep the impatience from his voice.

"I saw that boy this morning, running to catch the train, and I thought for a moment that I saw something in his face, something wild."

"Wild?" Toby repeated.

"Gypsy!" said Muriel.

Toby clamped his mouth shut. This conversational detour was going somewhere important, and he had to let Muriel Stackpole set the pace.

"We haven't seen Gypsies up here in years," she said, "not since before the war, but I saw that boy today, and I saw his wild face, and I thought there's a Gypsy if ever I saw one. He came out of the village shop, where the greengrocer used to be, and he ran up the road to the station. He's not as dark as some, but Gypsy was still my first thought, and then I thought about that girl Nina. He looks like her, you know. He's nothing like Jack Farren, of course, because he's not Farren's son, but he looks like his mother, and that's when I knew I was right. I've always thought Nina and Elizabeth were Gypsies, but I've never said anything. Don't like to make waves, you know, and most people don't want Gypsies around, so I kept it to myself. But when I saw that boy and his Gypsy eyes, I knew it. He's got his mother's Gypsy blood."

"And what about his father?" Victor asked.

Muriel shook her head. "I don't know. I'll have to think about that. I have a suspicion, but I won't say it yet, not in front of you, Your Lordship."

Toby waited, but Muriel apparently meant what she said. She was not going to voice her suspicions ... not yet. Nonetheless, he felt he had enough to go on for the time being. He nodded to Victor, who rose from his seat and offered Muriel a gracious smile.

"Thank you, Mrs. Stackpole. We are most grateful for your honesty and your interest in local events."

Nicely put, Victor. What a tactful way to thank her for being the village gossip. Every village has to have one.

Outside the cottage, and beyond the range of Muriel's sharp ears and eyes, Victor raised a querying eyebrow.

"Where to now?"

"Are you offering to drive?" Toby asked.

"I don't see why not. Where are we going?"

"Surrey. I have to see a man who lied through his teeth about knowing Buddy's mother."

"Who would that be?"

"That would be Randall Powley, the greengrocer's son, who told me he has no connections in Brighton and his wife has no relatives."

He looked beyond the Land Rover to a red telephone box set at the edge of the village green. "I should call my office." He thought for a moment about calling the number from the tea caddy. Surely Daphne's shadowy superiors would want to know what she was up to. She had destroyed a police car and interfered in a murder inquiry by making away with a prisoner. Was that something they should know about? On the other hand, she still had the radio, and she wasn't the kind to welcome assistance, however well-meant.

Daphne, he decided, could take care of herself.

Daphne Raleigh

Leo stopped on the wooded path and held out his hand. "Let me carry the radio."

Daphne shook her head. "I'm fine."

"No, you're not. You're limping."

"So what? I've been limping since February 1944. I'm used to it."

Leo forgot to hide his face as he moved toward her. At the last moment, common sense overcame his instinct to take her in his arms. He stepped back and lowered his head. "How bad was it?"

Daphne's shoulders slumped. "It was bad. I thought I could lie my way through it. I went to the Sorbonne; my French was perfect. Apparently, it was too perfect. I didn't have the right accent for that part of France, and I couldn't come up with a reasonable explanation for what I was doing in Bellerive."

She swept her hair back from her blind eye. "It's hard to think when ..."

"Did they do that to your eye?"

She gave a bitter little laugh. "No, the Germans didn't do this. They did a lot of other things, but I have the RAF to thank for this. I was one of the prisoners in Amiens when Operation Jericho came to bust us out. The Gestapo had drained me of everything I could give, and I was a day away from execution when the RAF sent in a couple of dozen bombers for a last-minute attempt to stop the executions. There were a hundred of us due to die the next day."

She shook her head, and the dark hair fell back into place, shielding her blind eye. She gave him a rueful smile. "I suppose it was the best the RAF could do, but it wasn't much. I took a splinter in the eye, which was mild considering what happened to some of the others. The bombers broke down the walls and killed guards and prisoners alike. It was left to us to escape on our own. Not many of us made it. It wasn't really much of a plan."

"I'm sorry."

"If you apologize again, I am going to submit you to some of the painful tricks I learned in spy school," Daphne promised. "I'm not blaming you, so stop blaming yourself. You were coming for me and you were shot down. It's not your fault, Leo. When I look at you now, I can see that you got the worst of the deal. You're not a pretty sight."

Leo turned his head away. "I know."

Daphne circled around in front of him. "I've been trying to see you ever since you came out of the hospital. Why can't you understand that you lost your face, not your soul? I was in love with you, not your face. Look at me, Leo. Why won't you look at me?"

Leo hung his head. Since his discharge from the burn ward, very few people had managed to look him in the eye without revulsion. The kid Buddy had been unusual, somehow steeling himself not to look away. Victor had done his best, but Victor's children never visited. Winnie had been kind. *She was paid to be kind, and now she's dead.* Now Daphne was doing her best not to be shocked, but how could she pretend that nothing had changed? She said he had not lost his soul, but it wasn't true. Perhaps his soul was in there somewhere, still cowering in horror at what had been done to his face, but it wasn't the same soul. He was not the man who had planned to make Daphne Raleigh his bride.

He shook his head. What was the point of talking about all the time that had been wasted? He remembered Daphne's seventeenth birthday. He had kissed her on the cheek and seen her blushing confusion. He could have sweet-talked her into his bed that summer, but he had resisted the temptation; there were other, less complicated girls to be had. Now he could not even remember their names: a couple of debutantes, a secretary from Brighton, a barmaid, a Gypsy girl. They had fallen willingly into his arms and helped him to forget Daphne's blushing innocence.

He was no longer that shameless youth, and he was no longer the bold pilot who had flown Daphne into enemy territory. He was not the same, and neither was she. He glanced up at her, seeing her confidence as she stood before him with the satchel on her shoulder and a pistol in her hand. She belonged to the shadowy world of espionage, and he belonged ... nowhere.

He waved his hand and dismissed the past. "You don't have to stay here with me. I imagine a lot of people will be looking for you. You made quite an impression."

She grinned. "I enjoyed it. What's the point of training, if you can't use what you've learned?"

"What will you do now?"

"I plan to take you to a safe place, and then I'll get on with what I came to do. I'm looking for a missing kid. He's the only one who can tell me the name of the agent, or at least give me a description."

"He doesn't remember," Leo said.

Daphne drew in a sharp breath. "You've seen him?"

"Yesterday," Leo confirmed. "He helped me shear the sheep."

"Why didn't you tell me?"

"I didn't know you were looking for him."

Daphne nodded. "Well, now you do know. So where is he?"

"I took him to the boathouse last night and left him to sleep there. He's a good kid, but he's in deep trouble. I was going to contact his lawyer this morning and see what could be done, but by strange coincidence, the lawyer found me."

He looked at Daphne. "That wasn't a coincidence, was it? The lawyer was with you. Is he—?"

"No, he's not. He's not an agent; he's just a lawyer, and I have no idea where he is now, but maybe I can find out." She set the satchel on a rock and pulled out the radio. "If he has any sense, he will have called the number again and—"

"What number?"

Daphne shook her head. "You don't need to know. First let me get you to a safe place."

"A safe place?" he queried. "You want to put me away, like an imbecile or a doddering old man?"

"No! It's just that ..."

"It's just that I'm no use to anyone." His eyes were wide and angry in his ruined face. "You don't need to take me anywhere, Daphne. I'll find my own safe place. I don't need you to lead me by the hand."

"Leo—"

"No, you carry on with your spying for Britain, and I'll take myself out of your way. Forget about me, Daphne; everyone else already has."

She tried to stammer out a protest, but he held up a finger to silence her. He stood with his head cocked to one side, listening. From somewhere far away, a bell began to chime. He nodded his head and strode away in the direction of the sound.

She should run to him, put her arms around him, and apologize. She should say that the scars didn't matter, but that would be a lie. They mattered; not just the scars on Leo's face and hands, but also her scars, the ones she hid behind a veil of hair.

She had to let him go. She still had a mission to accomplish on behalf of the nation. If she walked away from her mission now, the scars they had both endured would be in vain. Britain was still in danger, not of war but of anarchy, and she was hunting an agent of chaos; that was her priority. When it was all over, when the new queen was on the throne, and the Communist menace was beaten back behind their Iron Curtain, then she would have time to think of Leo, but not now.

CHAPTER SIXTEEN

London, England

Buddy

Buddy was hungry, thirsty, and frustrated by the time he arrived in south London and began his search for Mrs. Powley, the woman who had sworn she did not know him. The train ride to London had seemed interminable. The train stopped at every little village as it crawled through the leafy countryside. It halted even more frequently as it approached London and the countryside gave way to landscaped backyards and eventually to rows of industrial buildings. Here the city crowded in along the railway line, with the sky only occasionally visible where a building had been blown to rubble and stood forlornly awaiting demolition.

When the train disgorged him at Victoria station, he left the borrowed raincoat on the seat. If the man in the village post office, the man who had told him to take the train, were to give a description of him, he would start with that raincoat, and now Buddy was no longer wearing it.

Walking out of the station in his stained and rumpled clothing, but without the telltale coat, Buddy felt as though no one in the world would be able to identify him. Eventually, of course, someone would think of his connection to Mrs. Powley's house in Tooting, but not yet. First they would search the Downs and maybe question Leo, but he was certain that Leo wouldn't tell them anything. Of course, if they went into the village and spoke to the man in the shop … He felt a moment of added anxiety. The man in the store would tell them that a strange boy had come in and asked about the London train. Eventually, someone would trace him to London.

But not yet. Not until he'd spoken to the woman who held the key to his past. She'd said she didn't recognize him. She'd said she knew nothing about him, but he'd seen the flicker of alarm in her eyes. She was the key, and he was going to find her.

The address was emblazoned on his memory. Mrs. Elizabeth Powley, 42 Cadogan Street, Tooting, SW17. How many times had he seen Ma write that address on an airmail envelope with her lips pursed in annoyance? *"Why doesn't she ever answer? Has she forgotten that she has a son? She doesn't deserve him."*

Inquiries outside the train station, making certain to remove every trace of a Canadian accent as he asked, brought him the information that he should catch the number 44 bus to Tooting Broadway. The red double-decker delivered him to a street crowded with market stalls, where women with shopping bags queued for groceries.

He was surprised to see that the sun was low in the sky and casting long shadows. He glanced at the clock that hung crookedly in a wrought iron frame above the marketplace. Its cracked face and bent hands told him that the time was six o'clock. He thought back on the long day that had started with a rifle shot to jerk him into wakefulness, followed by a dead body to send him running. He decided that the clock was telling him the truth. The day was almost over.

He made his way along the crowded street, pushing past women with ration books and worried faces, waiting their turn at the market stalls.

"Hey, *chavo!*"

The voice brought him to an abrupt halt with the word reverberating in his ears. *Chavo!* The word bathed his spirit and filled him with sudden confidence. He was a child again, and someone spoke the word in love.

A woman's voice, cracked with age, whispered in his ear, and her hair tickled his nose as she leaned over him. "Ah, chavo, such a handsome boy."

He looked around. The voice he heard now had belonged to a man. Perhaps the word had not been intended for him; perhaps someone else was being addressed as *chavo*. It made no difference. He still had to know who had spoken. Where did this word come from?

He glanced along the market stalls. The women, concentrating on retaining their place in line, ignored him, but one stall drew his attention. This trader was not selling vegetables or dented canned goods that had "fallen off the back of a lorry." This stall was bright with beads, mirrors, and colorful scarves, and it drew him like a beacon. A dark-haired man with a red scarf at his throat stood beside his glimmering wares, with his eyes fixed on a small boy who was scampering through the crowd. A hand-painted sign nailed to the stall identified the owner of the stall as Bruno Blackmore, licensed trader.

The child, with his eyes fixed on some unknown objective, barreled into Buddy's legs and sent him staggering.

"Sorry, mister."

Buddy nodded. "It's all right. Nothing broken."

The man, presumably Bruno Blackmore himself, stepped forward and grasped the boy's collar. "Say sorry to the man."

"I did."

Bruno's voice had a hint of an exotic accent hidden beneath the cockney vowels. "Say it again. We don't want no trouble."

"It's all right," Buddy repeated. He studied Bruno, seeing now that the man was older than he'd first appeared. His deeply wrinkled face belied the black of his hair. He was slightly built, but his rolled sleeves revealed corded muscles, and his eyes flashed enmity.

"You called him *chavo*," Buddy said. "Why?"

Bruno cocked his head to one side. His tone was aggressive. "Why not?"

"What does it mean?"

As Buddy advanced on him, Blackmore took a step back, and suddenly and inexplicably drew a knife.

Buddy held up a hand in what he hoped was a peaceful gesture. "No, please, I don't want any trouble. I just want to know about the word. You called him *chavo*."

Blackmore scowled. "What of it? Who are you to tell me I can't speak my own language? Is that what it's come to now? Hitler didn't do it, so now you're doing it?"

"I don't know what you're talking about."

Bruno scowled. "We won't let it happen; not again. We'll fight back."

Buddy's attention was so focused on the knife in Bruno's hand that it took him a moment to notice that a much younger woman had emerged from behind the scarves that draped the stall.

She laid her hand on Bruno's arm. "It's all right, Dad. I'm sure he doesn't mean any harm. He's just curious."

"About what?" Bruno asked. "He has no business being curious. You tell him, Cherry. You tell him to be on his way."

Buddy looked helplessly at the woman. "I asked him what *chavo* meant, and he pulled a knife on me."

Cherry smiled. "It's a Roma word. It means 'boy.'"

"Roma?" Buddy queried.

"Romany. It's what we call ourselves. You call us Gypsies, but we call ourselves Roma."

Buddy was momentarily speechless. Gypsies! He thought of the stone circle high up on the Downs, the scorch marks from a fire … the horses …

The caravans stood in a circle high up on the crest of the Downs. His grandfather's black-and-white horse was cropping peacefully alongside the horses that would be sold at the next fair. His grandmother sat knitting on the steps of the caravan, with the bright blue wool moving smoothly between her fingers, and the sleeve of a sweater slowly taking shape. He couldn't stay long. Momma said that Purodad and Puridaia were a great secret, and he must never let anyone know that he knew where they were. His father would not understand. His father must never know that he visited his grandparents.

"What are you doing here?" Cherry asked. "You sound American."

"Canadian," Buddy said. "I'm from Canada."

"And why are you so interested in us?"

Buddy scratched his head. "I knew someone who called me *chavo*. I think she was my grandmother."

Bruno surveyed Buddy suspiciously, his eyes lingering on Buddy's face. "Could be," he said eventually. "Could be he's a mongrel pup with a *gorja* father or mother. Half Roma, like that other boy, not that his mother will ever admit it."

Buddy was instantly alert. "What other boy?"

"Eric, no, Edward," Cherry said. "Edward Powley."

"Is his mother Elizabeth Powley?"

Bruno Blackmore spat contemptuously. "That's her. She married a *gorja* and gave birth to a pale boy who doesn't even know what he is."

Buddy thought of the woman who had answered the door at 42 Cadogan Street. Her hair had been bundled under a hairnet, but it was dark, just like Cherry and her father. Her unfriendly eyes were equally dark. He tried to imagine what she would look like with earrings and bracelets and with her hair loose like Cherry's and like …

His mother's hair had been long and dark. He remembered the way she would sit on the edge of his bed and brush and brush until every strand was smooth and glossy. Then, one day, the long hair was gone, cut short and hidden under a scarf, and she no longer sat on his bed with her hairbrush.

"I think you're right," Buddy said. "I think my mother was one of you."

"What's her name?" Bruno asked.

Buddy shrugged. "I don't know. I don't remember."

Bruno scowled at him. "Is she another Roma who won't admit what she is?" he asked.

"I don't know." Buddy was suddenly angry with Bruno and his implied contempt. "She's dead. Someone shot her. Do you understand? She's dead and I can't ask her. I can't ask anyone."

He fought to keep his anger alive. Anger was better than fear, better than sorrow. "I don't even know my own name, so how can I know her name?"

"You don't know your own name?" Cherry queried. "How can that be?"

"Someone told me to forget," Buddy said. He looked at Cherry, remembering something he had heard about Gypsies. "Did you do that? Was it one of you? Was it some kind of Gypsy magic?" He glared at Cherry and her father. "It didn't work. You gave me another boy's name, but I knew it wasn't mine. I knew I had another name. I want to know who I am. Just tell me."

Cherry laid a gentle hand on his arm. "I'm sorry, *chavo*."

Chavo! That word again. His knees were suddenly weak. The exhaustion of the long day, which had begun with a murder and ended in a sudden understanding of who he was, overcame him.

"I have to sit down."

"Come."

Cherry led him behind the wall of scarves and mirrors, and guided him into a canvas deckchair.

"I don't know who you are," she said softly, "and my family does not practice that kind of enchantment, but I know of other families who do. It's possible that you were made to forget, but even so, the forgetting doesn't last forever. With the right triggers, the memory will return. Don't fight against it."

"I'm afraid of what I'll remember," Buddy confessed. "My mother sent me to Canada for a reason. She gave me Edward Powley's name. Why would she do that?"

Cherry frowned. "Edward Powley? You were given the name of that pale boy?"

"His name, his suitcase, his place on the boat. I was given everything."

"But you're here now," Cherry said. "You're not in Canada, so why don't you just ask Mrs. Powley?"

"I did," Buddy replied. "We went to her house and asked her. She said she didn't know who I was, but she knows something. I could tell from the way she looked at me that she knows something."

Cherry pulled a boldly painted wooden stool from beneath the stall and sat down beside him. She took his hand. "Do you have a silver coin?"

"I have a sixpence. I'm not sure it's real silver."

"It contains some silver," Cherry said. "It may work." She held out her hand. "I have some powers of divining. We can try. Cross my palm with silver."

Before Buddy could reach into his pocket, Bruno appeared from around the side of the stall. "The pale boy is here," he declared. "Very frightened." He looked at Buddy. "You want to talk to him?"

Buddy was on his feet with all thoughts of magic banished from his mind and replaced by everyday common sense. "Yes, I want to talk to him. Where is he?"

"I'll bring him."

Edward Powley appeared to be the same age as Buddy, but there the resemblance ended. Edward was stocky and broad shouldered, with overlong brown hair that fell forward across a wide forehead. With his light eyes and lightly freckled skin, Buddy understood why Cherry and her father referred to him as "the pale boy."

If he takes after his father, Buddy thought, *who do I take after?* He grabbed at a memory. Cherry had been right; his memories had become easier to find. *What if I remember killing my mother? I didn't. I know I didn't.* Buddy pushed his fears aside and dragged out a memory of a forbidden face. He saw a round, florid face flushed with anger, a bulbous nose, and light eyes beneath thick sandy eyebrows. He thought of his own face, the one he had studied in the mirror for years, looking for the first stirrings of a beard and mustache. The man he remembered had not contributed anything to that face. That man, the angry, red-faced man, could not be his father.

"Who is he?" Edward Powley's voice interrupted his thoughts.

Buddy stared at the newcomer. So this was the boy who should have been sent to Canada and safety. Someone had given Buddy this boy's name, and this boy's clothes, and sent him to Canada instead. Why?

"Don't worry about him," Bruno snapped. "Tell me what you want."

"The police are at our house."

Bruno shrugged. "What do you want me to do about it?"

"My mother said that I should come to you. She said I could trust you. I don't know why."

Buddy stayed silent, listening to Edward's voice. He lacked the London accent of the women in the market, and it had no resemblance to the intangible accent of Bruno and his daughter. He sounded a little like Leo. Buddy thought longingly of the shepherd in his hidden retreat. If he could only have stayed there.

"So your mother has never told you what you are?" Bruno asked.

"No. I don't know what you mean."

"I mean that blood is thicker than water. You're one of us, boy, and be glad you are, because we look after our own. So, what's got you so upset?"

"I was in my bedroom, and I heard someone at the front door. My mum looked out the window. She said there was a police car outside and what had I done? I told her I hadn't done anything. Then she looked again, and she said, 'That's not a policeman.' I didn't know what she meant. I mean, if it's a police car, why isn't it a policeman? Anyway, she told me to go out the back and run here and not to let anyone see me."

"And what did your mother do?" Bruno asked.

"She said she'd find me here, but she's not here."

Bruno shook his head. "No, she's not here."

Edward looked at Buddy again. "Who are you?"

Buddy took a deep breath. "Until a few days ago," he said, "I thought I was you. I thought I was Edward Powley."

Edward stared at him. "You're that boy, aren't you? The one at the station?"

July 1940
Euston Station, London
Edward Powley

Eddie Powley clutched his mother's hand as they stood in the queue. He was a big boy for his age, almost nine years old, but he saw that boys from his school who were even bigger were clutching at parental hands. Most of the girls were crying. The pandemonium of voices joined the background sound of clanking rails and hissing locomotives.

"Do I have to go, Mum?"

"Your father wants you to be safe."

Eddie sensed a chink in his mother's armor. "Do you want me to go, Mum?"

"No, of course not, but London isn't safe. If Hitler comes, God only knows what will happen to us, and if Hitler finds out that ..." His mother slapped a hand across her mouth as if to stifle her own speech.

"If Hitler finds out what?" Eddie whined. "What is Hitler going to find out?"

His mother shook her head. "He won't. I've never told anyone. He won't find out."

"So I don't have to go?"

"I didn't say that. Your father wants you to be safe." She pursed her lips. "Of course, crossing the Atlantic is ... well ... I suppose I shouldn't worry. You'll have an escort, or so they say, and they'll go fast. You'll be in Canada in no time at all."

"I don't want to go to Canada."

His mother's arms tightened around him. "I don't want you to go, but we'll have to do what your father wants. It won't be for long. This war is going to be won or lost in a very short time."

"What happens if we lose?"

"We all learn to speak German."

Eddie looked up at his mother's face. "Will I come back from Canada if we lose?"

He saw the flash of worry on her face as her mouth fell open in surprise. "I don't know. I didn't think. They may not let you come back. If Hitler's here in England, the Canadians might keep you."

Eddie's whine rose to a crescendo. "I don't want to stay in Canada. I don't want to stay forever. Why can't I stay here?"

A woman in the queue turned an angry face toward his mother. "Can't you stop him whining?" she asked. "He'll set all the other children off. Our Frankie doesn't want to go either, but we've made all the arrangements, and he's taking it like a man."

Eddie studied Frankie, a spindly boy with a blotchy face, wearing an unfamiliar school uniform. Not all the children in the queue were from Eddie's school. In fact, most of them were strangers.

"What will happen to them if Hitler wins?" Eddie's mother asked. "Has anyone told you."

Frankie's mother turned away. "He won't win," she said over her shoulder, "and I'll thank you not to talk like that." She put her hands over her son's ears. "Little jugs have big handles," she hissed.

The line shuffled forward. Eddie's mother hesitated, allowing the gap between her and the other mother to become wider. "I don't know," she muttered. "I just don't know."

Eddie shuffled his feet and kicked at his suitcase. Waiting was the worst part. If he really had to go to Canada, he wanted to go now, and if he didn't have to go, he wanted to go home. Standing here in the late-summer heat with the station's massive glass dome trapping the sulfurous smoke was becoming unbearable.

"Mrs. Powley."

Eddie looked up and saw a small woman in a blue cotton frock. Her hair was tied in a headscarf, and she carried a large straw handbag. He had never seen her before, but the boy she was dragging behind her looked vaguely familiar.

"Elizabeth, it is you, isn't it?" the small woman asked.

Eddie's mother released his hand as she took a step toward the other woman. "Stay there, Eddie. Don't lose your place in line."

"But, Mum ..."

"Stay there." Her voice was harsh and impatient. "Stay there and don't you dare move."

The small woman seemed to dance with impatience. "You remember me, don't you? Winnie Widdicome."

Eddie's mother looked over her shoulder at him and then turned back. "Yes, I remember. Is that ...?"

"Yes. That's Henry."

"Why is he here?"

"He has to go to Canada."

Eddie saw his mother's shoulders stiffening. "How do you know about Canada?"

"Nina told me. She was wishing that she could go."

Eddie heard the chill in his mother's voice. "She's free to make her own arrangements. It's up to her and her husband."

"It's too late for that. Nina ..."

Eddie shuffled sideways. He had an aunt Nina and a cousin Henry he had met only once. The boy, small and dark haired, was probably Henry. He wondered why they had come. Were they here to say goodbye?

He took another sideways step and heard a scrap of whispered conversation.

"Shot ..."

"Did he see?"

"I don't know."

His mother turned suddenly and saw that he was listening to the conversation. She gestured impatiently for him to leave and get back into line. Although he returned to take his place among the children, the stranger's words were still in his mind. "You have to let him go to Canada." He felt a flame of hope. Perhaps he wouldn't have to go to Canada. Perhaps Henry would be sent in his place.

He watched his mother from the corner of his eye. She was arguing now, her face both angry and fearful; her attention fully focused on the white haired woman. He edged closer.

The words he overheard made no sense but his mother seemed to understand. . "Did she use the candle and the glass?" she asked.

"I don't know. I didn't watch. All I know is that she took him inside her caravan, and they were in there a long time, and now he doesn't remember who he is or what happened."

Eddie heard a man's voice behind him. "You boy, are you supposed to be looking after this suitcase."

Eddie turned to see a man kicking at this suitcase. The man's angry complaint about disobedient boys drowned out the rest of his mother's whispered conversation. He knew nothing more until his mother stood beside him holding Henry's hand.

"Take off your blazer Eddie and give it to your cousin. He's going to Canada."

August 1952
Buddy

Cherry parted the scarves and looked out at the market. "People are closing down for the night. If she's coming, she'd better hurry up. We can't stay here all night. It's not allowed."

Buddy was still sitting in the deckchair with Edward's words whirling around in his head.

Edward stared at him.

"So you're my cousin," Buddy said.

Edward shrugged. "I suppose so. It was years ago, but I remember the whole thing. We went to the station, and I was so sure that I was going to Canada, and then suddenly I wasn't. My mother said to keep quiet and never tell anyone what had happened. When my dad came home, there was a hell of a row. My mum showed him the bag of jewelry, but it didn't help. He took it, and I don't know what he did with it. A couple of days later, he was gone. He shipped out with his regiment. He didn't come home again. Mum tells people he's dead, but he's not. I see him sometimes, but I don't tell Mum about it."

Buddy sat back in the deckchair and stared up at Edward. "The woman who brought me to the station said that someone had been shot," he confirmed.

"I always supposed that it was your mother who'd been shot," Edward said. "Was it?"

Buddy nodded. "I think it so."

"Who shot her?"

Buddy was silent, seized by sudden doubt. He thought of what Edward had overheard. Winnie Widdicome had said that Buddy's mother had been shot; she had not said who had done the shooting.

"Did he see?"

"I don't know."

Cherry leaned toward him and softly interrupted his thoughts. "It sounds as though your grandmother used the old candle flame magic; these days they call it hypnosis. The memory is in there. It will come back."

"Couldn't you ask the woman who brought you to the station?" Edward said. "She said her name was Winnie Widdicome. That's the kind of name you don't forget."

Buddy shook his head. "I can't ask her. She died this morning. Someone murdered her."

Cherry parted the scarves again.

"There's a man looking behind all the stalls."

"Policeman?" Bruno asked.

"I don't know." She stepped back and motioned for Edward to take a look. "Well?"

"Yes, that's him. I think he's still looking for my mother. I don't know where she's gone."

Buddy rose from the deck chair on shaky legs. He felt exhausted physically and emotionally. He knew more than he had known in the morning, but he still didn't know everything, and he still didn't know why his mother had died or who had killed her.

He elbowed Edward aside. "Let me see."

"He's just coming out from behind the fish stall," Edward said.

Buddy focused on the squat figure of a man emerging alongside the nearly empty stall; short and balding, with small eyes buried in a puffy face, a mouth that turned downward, and thick sandy eyebrows set in a frown.

"Close the door. Stay in your room."

Screams. Terrible screams.

A crack that echoed through the house.

Silence.

CHAPTER SEVENTEEN

Brighton, Sussex
Anthea Clark

Elspeth and Sidney had departed long ago, leaving the brown envelope behind on Anthea's desk and walking hand in hand toward the promenade and the delights of the pier.

Anthea remained at the window, watching the sun sinking toward the horizon and painting a golden path across the waves. She wondered how to make a graceful exit. Hugh was still in the office. He should leave. He should go home, to his own home and not to hers. Another night was rapidly approaching, and what would he expect?

She wished she hadn't ... No, that wasn't true. She had wondered, and now she had no need to wonder. After a lifetime of reading romances, now she had practical experience. She wished she knew what she was supposed to do next.

Hugh came to stand beside her, and she took an instinctive step sideways. He was too close for comfort.

"Look at this," Hugh said. He pulled a paper from the envelope and held it out to her. "I've been studying the words that Sidney's bunkmate wrote down, the ones that Buddy spoke in his sleep."

Anthea lifted the glasses that she kept on a chain around her neck and examined the paper. She shook her head. "I don't recognize them. It's not German, or French, not even Spanish. I don't know what it is."

"But I do," Hugh said. "I've had some experience with these words."

"Really?" Anthea asked. "I know you were in Flanders in the Great War. Is this Flemish?

Hugh turned his gaze back to the window, focusing his eyes somewhere beyond the horizon. "No, not Flemish." He spoke softly. "When my son was lost on Bodmin Moor …"

Anthea touched his arm. "You don't have to talk about it. I already know of your loss."

He grasped the hand that she had laid on his arm. "I'm at peace with it, Anthea. I know what happened to him. I never saw him again, but I know he survived, and I have seen his children. I can talk about it."

Anthea remained silent, enjoying the warmth of his grasp.

"When Jacob was taken, I went to the Gypsies. I have never forgotten that day."

"Of course not. You told me that the old Gypsy woman gave you hope."

Hugh continued to stare out of the window, not looking at her but tightening his grasp on her hand. "She spoke to me in English, but all around me, the Gypsies were speaking their own language."

"Gypsy language?"

"Romany. They call it Romany. The words on that paper are Romany."

"Are you sure?"

"Yes, I'm quite sure. I don't know what they mean, but the boy who wrote them spelled them phonetically. If I speak them aloud, I recognize the sound."

Anthea looked down at the paper and began to read aloud. "*Chavo, puridaia, groi, tikni* …" She shook her head as she scanned the scrawled list of words. "What do the words mean?"

"I don't know," Hugh admitted, "but they sound familiar. I remember every detail of that day: the old woman who insisted that I cross her palm with silver, the daughters who glared at me like they wanted to kill me, the children playing in the dirt, and the people talking, calling to each other, calling to the children. I remember it all, and those words belong in that memory."

"So you're saying that our client Buddy is a Gypsy."

"Yes, that's what I think. I think that at least one of his parents was a Gypsy. It explains everything."

Anthea looked at Hugh's excited face and was momentarily distracted by his broad grin beneath his military mustache. She had kissed that mouth, and the mustache had tickled. She had … *No, no, stop thinking about that. Concentrate. Ask a sensible question.*

Before she could recover her equilibrium, she heard Mr. Champion's wheezing voice. "What does it explain, Colonel?"

Mr. Champion had emerged from his office and was looking at Hugh with a puzzled expression. How long had he been there? Had he seen Hugh clasping her fingers? Did he suspect …?

Hugh straightened his shoulders and turned away from the window. "I think that Buddy was sent away, not just to save him from the bombing but to save him from the invasion. No one wants to talk about it now, but in 1940 our chances did not look good. Defeat was a possibility. People talked of surrender. Even the Duke of Windsor—"

Mr. Champion interrupted abruptly. "The man's a traitor, and we're not done with him yet."

Hugh nodded. "I quite agree, Edwin, and maybe that still has some bearing on the situation. Hitler despised the Gypsies just as much as he despised the Jews, and he treated them the same way: labor camps, slavery, and ultimately the gas chamber. He intended to wipe them from the face of Europe. He would have done the same thing here. So if Buddy's mother was a Gypsy …"

"But Toby found a radio hidden at Buddy's house," Anthea protested, "and he said that Buddy's father was a German agent. He would never have married a Gypsy."

"Perhaps he didn't know she was a Gypsy," Hugh suggested. "Gypsy life is hard for girls. They're made to marry at a very young age, and they don't choose their own husbands. Some of them run away and try to find work and don't tell anyone where they come from. They could pass as a shop assistant or a secretary—"

Anthea bristled with resentment. Secretary indeed! "It's not so easy to be a secretary," she protested.

Hugh did not pause to register her protest. "If Buddy's mother was working in town, his father wouldn't have known what she was, but maybe he found out later, and she sent Buddy away to save him."

"From his own father?" Anthea asked. "Surely not."

Mr. Champion coughed and raised a finger. "Although the law does not recognize the possibility, not every man is the father of his wife's child."

Anthea's heart was pounding, and her mind was racing with endless possibilities. She saw the excitement in Hugh's eyes, and she recognized that Mr. Champion was in imminent danger of passing out. She made an unceremonious grab for her employer's arm and guided him to a chair, where he collapsed in a fit of coughing.

"Shall I get you some water, Mr. Champion?"

"No, don't waste your time. Do you know where Whitby is?"

"No, I don't."

Mr. Champion's mumbled complaints were interrupted by the jangling of the phone on Anthea's desk.

Anthea took a deep breath to calm herself and lifted the receiver. "Champion and Company, Solicitors."

A woman's voice. "My name is Muriel Stackpole, Mrs. Muriel Stackpole, and I'd like to speak to Mr. Whitby."

Speak of the devil. "Mr. Whitby is not here. May I take a message?"

Muriel Stackpole's voice was an ingratiating whine. "But he does work there, doesn't he? He is a real solicitor?"

"Of course he is."

"Well, you can never be too careful. He came to see me——"

"When?"

"This morning. He said he was working on a case. I'm sure you understand …" The whine increased in intensity. "I'm sure you realize that it is very worrying to have a solicitor come to your house and say he is working on a case and then not give you any details. Perhaps you could tell me why he would come and bother me. I'm very worried."

No, Anthea thought, *you're not worried; you're just very curious.* She wanted to slam down the receiver and return to the problem of finding Toby. *No! Wait! Get this woman on your side. She knows something.*

"Well, Mrs. Stackpole …"

"Yes?"

"We're a little worried about Mr. Whitby ourselves."

"Worried?" Mrs. Stackpole's curiosity seemed to radiate through the telephone wires. "Why are you worried?"

Anthea could see Hugh looking at her with raised eyebrows. She ignored him and returned to Mrs. Stackpole. "Mr. Whitby hasn't returned to the office. Did he happen to tell you where he was going next?"

"Well, he didn't exactly tell me, but …"

"Yes?"

"I did happen to overhear him talking to His Lordship."

Lordship? What lordship? Anthea did not dare to interrupt with a question.

"And," Mrs. Stackpole whined, "I heard them say something about going to Surrey to see Randall Powley. He's the greengrocer's son. I remember him, of course. Would you like me to——?"

"No, thank you. There's no need. Thank you for calling."

Anthea replaced the receiver and instinctively looked up at Hugh, her partner in crime. "I know where he is. Should we go?"

Hugh shook his head. "We have to talk to Slater."

"I don't see why."

"Chain of command, old girl. Chain of command."

Anthea's frustration surfaced with an angry snap. "Don't call me old girl."

Hugh took a step back. "I'm sorry."

"And so you should be," Anthea hissed. She turned away, wondering at her own words. Why should he be sorry? Why should she be sorry? This was all foolishness. What should it matter that Hugh had spent the night? She should not let that fact distract her.

She turned back to Hugh. He was right, of course. The soldier in him had cut through sentiment.

"We'll go to the hospital," Hugh said. "I'm sure Mr. Whitby can manage without us."

Mr. Champion's voice was a weak groan. "He always does."

Royal Sussex County Hospital, Brighton
Detective Inspector Percy Slater

Slater decided that it was almost time to open his eyes. He had put it off for too long, hiding behind closed eyelids while people around him talked in whispers. Dorothy was here. He recognized her London accent. His wife had made an effort to change her speech and make it more suited to the wife of an inspector in a very special branch of the Metropolitan Police. When all was going well in her life, she was usually able to iron out the cockney vowels and remember to pronounce her *h*'s, but when she was under stress, she was every inch a Londoner. Listening to the whispered conversations around his bed, he had to assume that Dorothy was highly stressed.

With his eyes still closed, he wiggled the toes of his left leg. He was not reassured even when he felt them move. Eight years before, he had come around from surgery in a field hospital in Normandy. On that occasion, he had been certain he could feel pain in his right arm and cramping in his fingers. He had been wrong. His right arm existed only in his muscle memory. His brain had taken years to forget the missing limb and cease attempting to move it.

No, he was not comforted by thinking his toes were moving. He would have to open his eyes and look. Would he see the sheet draped over a cage that protected the stump of his limb, or would he see the mound under the bedclothes that showed he still had two legs? He took a deep breath. He had never been a coward, and he would not be one now. He would look.

His eyelids fluttered. He heard Dorothy's voice. "He's coming round. Percy, Percy, we're here."

He couldn't look at her. Not yet. First the leg. He forced his eyes open and strained to lift his head from the pillow, and there it was: not the cage but just a sheet draped over his legs. Two legs. For a horrible moment, he thought he was going to cry. He blinked, swallowed hard, and reached out for Dorothy's hand.

At first her smile was all he could see, but after a moment of grinning like an idiot, he looked past her and saw that the room was crowded.

"What's all this, then?" he asked. His throat was sore and his voice was raspy. He remembered the shower of brick dust that had engulfed him when the roof had fallen. His lungs were probably full of cement and heaven only knew what else. He would be coughing for weeks.

"What's all this?" he repeated. "Is this a deathwatch?"

Dorothy squeezed his hand. "No, you big silly. You were never going to die."

"I'm not so sure about that," Slater said, "but I'll take your word for it. So who are all these people?"

He struggled to sit upright and take a better look at the shadowy figures on the edge of his vision.

Dorothy slid a pillow behind his back as he edged himself upright. He exchanged a glance with her. "Is my leg really okay? I'm not dreaming, am I?"

"You lost a lot of blood, and you'll need to convalesce before you go back to work, but your leg is going to be fine. The surgeon's coming to talk to you in a minute. In the meantime, here's Mr. Champion and Miss Clark, and Grandpa Hugh."

Grandpa Hugh! Dorothy had finally settled on a title for the old colonel who was grandfather to her son. Well, it was better than calling him Colonel Trewin, and the old man was sure to like it.

"Why are they here?" Slater asked. "Where's Whitby?"

Miss Clark stepped forward, an angular figure in a tweed skirt and a dun-colored cardigan. He thought that her hair looked unusually untidy, and her face was flushed. "We don't want to worry you."

"You're already worrying me," Slater snapped. "Has something happened to Toby?"

"Not yet."

"Not yet," Slater repeated. "What does that mean?"

"He came to the flat to get the number from the tea caddy," Dorothy said, "and no one's seen him since, and that was hours ago. You've been unconscious for a very long time. How do you feel?"

"Like a house fell on me," Slater replied.

"You're going to be all right," Dorothy whispered. "Give it time."

"Don't worry about me. Just tell me what you know about Whitby." He looked up at the small window set high in the wall. "What the hell time is it? It's almost dark."

Dorothy made a disapproving face. She didn't like to hear him swear, but he was past caring. Now that he was fully awake, he was aware of the pain in his leg and a throbbing headache. As he struggled to remain sitting, another wave of pain attacked his chest. Cracked ribs, he knew the symptoms.

"Dorothy didn't want us to worry you," Hugh said, "but this won't keep any longer. We think we have a photograph of Buddy's father."

Buddy? Yes, the missing boy. *So they haven't found him yet, and it's growing dark again.*

He tried to ignore his headache and concentrate. *First things first.* "Did Toby make the phone call? Did he report what we found?"

Anthea shook her head. "You mean the radio?"

"Yes, I mean the radio, although he wasn't supposed to tell anyone what we found."

"I made him tell me," Dorothy confessed. "I was trying to protect you. I know I'm not supposed to ring that number unless ..."

Slater turned his mind from his own pain long enough to comfort her. "It's all right, love. You did the right thing. So did he report it?"

"I don't know. I left and came here, and I've been here ever since. Carol Whitby was here with me for a while, but she's gone home to take care of Anita and our Eric. Toby was still at our house when I left, but that was this morning, and no one's heard from him since."

"Well," Anthea amended, "we did have a phone call from him, but it made no sense, something about losing his car."

Hugh Trewin loomed behind Anthea and rested his hand on her shoulder. "There's something else," he said. "If the village gossip is to be believed, and village gossips are generally correct, we know that Whitby's on his way to Surrey to talk to Mrs. Powley's husband."

Slater fought against his brain's sluggishness. "Randall Powley," he muttered. "Hackbridge. Why is he going there?"

His question was met with silence. He tried another. "What about Cameron?"

Hugh shook his head. "Haven't seen him. Haven't heard from him. But we do have something. We have a photo of Buddy's parents. Take a look."

Slater freed his hand from Dorothy's grasp and held it out to the colonel. "Where did you get it?"

Dorothy leaned in close, speaking in a whisper. "Miss Clark and Grandpa Hugh went to London and met someone who was on the boat with Buddy, and then that person came to Mr. Champion's office and brought some papers."

"I don't care about papers. Show me the photograph."

Dorothy scowled at him. "Percy, darling, don't get excited. Let me explain."

"All right, explain, but do it fast."

"Some boys on the boat stole Buddy's paperwork. That's why he arrived in Canada without the name of his host family. No one knew where he was supposed to go, and so the Stewarts took him in."

Hugh Trewin placed an impatient hand on Dorothy's shoulder. "Let me explain, dear. Some of the boys on the boat thought he was a spy."

"Spy?" Percy repeated.

Hugh nodded knowingly. "Boys will be boys. They heard him talking in his sleep and decided he was talking German. He wasn't, of course. He was speaking Romany."

Slater groaned as a wave of pain made its way down his leg. "Just get on with it."

Hugh handed him the picture. "We think that these are Buddy's parents on their wedding day. Take a look."

Slater squinted at the faded black-and-white photo. The woman was young and pretty, far younger than the man, and the way she held her small bouquet of flowers in front of her made him think she was concealing a problem. *Getting married in the nick of time.* He could see something of Buddy's features in her tentative smile. As for the man, round face, receding hairline, bushy sandy eyebrows; no smile and no hint of Buddy in his features.

And something else. What? He wished he could think clearly. It was the damned anesthetic making him stupid. He grasped the corner of the picture so tightly that it trembled in his grip. *Think. Think.* And there it was. He knew that unhappy face.

He flung off the bedclothes and swung his legs out of the bed. "I have to get to a phone. I have to take care of this."

His head started to spin. Dorothy's face swam in and out of focus. Her hands pressed him back against the pillows. He fought against her and against his own weakness.

"I have to take care of this."

Dorothy nodded reluctantly. "I know. We'll bring the phone to you. And there's a woman to see you. She says her name is Daphne."

CHAPTER EIGHTEEN

Tooting, London
Buddy

Voices reached him from a distant, faraway place. A hand on his arm guided his stumbling feet.

"Get him in the van."

Another voice. "We should wait for my mother."

"Your mother knows where to find us, Eddie."

The hand that guided Buddy gave him a rough slap on the side of the head, or maybe it was another hand. It didn't matter. The slap did the trick, and Buddy was himself again, memories banished to the back of his mind, and the current danger clear and crisp in his mind.

Bruno was beside him, his hand raised for another slap.

"It's all right," Buddy said. "I'm okay now. It's just that ..."

Cherry was beside him, holding the hand of a small boy. "Your memory's coming back, but we can't talk, not now. That man is telling people that he's Inspector Cameron of the Brighton Police, and he's here to take you in for murder. You need to get into my father's van, and we'll take you away from here."

"No," Buddy gasped. "It's not true."

She ignored his interruption. "We can't hide you here. Get in the van and come to the camp. You'll be safe there."

Edward tugged on Cherry's shawl. "What about me?"

"You can come too."

Buddy hung back. "Where's your camp?"

"On Tooting Common. It's the only place we're allowed to stay."

196

Buddy shook his head. "Then it's the first place he'll look." He turned to Edward. "He knows what we are. He knows the Gypsies will try to hide us."

"But we're not—"

"Yes, we are," Buddy insisted, "and he'll come looking for us at the camp. We have to go somewhere else."

Bruno turned away and pointed at a decrepit old Bedford van idling nearby. "I'm packing everything up now. Get in if you're coming, because we're leaving."

Edward took a step forward, and Buddy pulled him back. He pushed the whispering memory voices to the back of his mind and concentrated on the plain common sense he'd learned from Ma and Pa. "We can't go with them. The camp is the first place he'll look. Is there anywhere else we can go?"

Edward hesitated.

Bruno reached up and began to remove the screen of scarves, pulling them down and stuffing them into a box. "I'm shutting up shop and we're leaving. Come now if you're coming."

"We can't go with you," Buddy insisted. "He'll be sure to look there."

"We could go to my father," Edward said. "My mother tells people that he's dead, but he's not. I don't know why she says he is. Anyway, I know where he lives."

"Is it far?" Buddy asked. "How do we get there?"

Bruno flicked down the last of the scarves, and Edward dropped to his knees behind the market stall. "I have a motorcycle. It's in the shed behind the house."

Bruno folded the canvas deckchair. "Make up your mind."

Buddy joined Edward as he crouched behind the stall. He moved on his hands and knees to peer around the corner of the cart. The man he had once thought of as his father was engaged in heated conversation with the fishmonger, who was shaking his head vigorously.

Buddy crawled back and nudged Edward. "Let's go. He's still talking."

Bruno stood with the folded deckchair in one hand and a box of scarves in the other. "You go, *chavo*. I'll keep him occupied if he comes this way. Go on, get going."

Edward nodded. "Follow me."

Buddy followed Edward in a low crouch as they left the shelter of the market stall and ducked behind the low brick wall that surrounded the market square. Still crouching, they ran the length of an alley and finally halted in a patch of gathering darkness behind the public conveniences.

Buddy drew in a ragged breath and immediately regretted it as the stench of drains and urine overwhelmed him.

He punched Edward's arm. "Why are we stopping?"

"I was just looking," Edward replied.

"For what?"

"For my mother."

"Oh, sorry."

"It's all right. I'm sure she's somewhere safe. I mean, the policeman didn't find her, and—"

Buddy spoke with sudden confidence. "He's not a policeman."

"That's what she said," Edward agreed, "but how did you know?"

Buddy gripped the other boy's arm. "Because I know who he is, and I know what he did. I can't talk about it now. How far is your house?"

"It's just round the corner. I keep the motorcycle in the shed. It's a Bantam. It's not very fast with two people, but it'll get us there."

"All right," Buddy said encouragingly. "Just take a deep breath, and …" He remembered where they were. "No, don't take a deep breath. Just get us out of here."

They ran, scampering along back alleys and dodging between parked cars, until they reached the house that Buddy remembered: 42 Cadogan Street. Was it really just a couple of days since he'd stood outside this house, dreading the moment that would bring him face-to-face with the mother who had abandoned him? Things looked very different now that he knew he was not, and never had been, Edward Powley and Elizabeth Powley was not his mother.

He wanted to feel something for the mother he was now discovering, the one who had been a Gypsy, but someone had robbed him of that memory. Instead, he found himself thinking of Winnie Widdicome. He knew now that she was the person who had taken him to the station and put him on a boat to Canada.

She had kept her secret all these years while the body of a murdered woman lay undiscovered in a ruined house. Now Winnie had been murdered. Who would be next?

Edward sprinted down a narrow footpath beside the house and finally came to a halt in front of a dilapidated wooden shed. The padlock on the door gleamed brightly in the last rays of sunlight.

Edward looked nervously over his shoulder. "Keep an eye out, Henry."

"I'm called Buddy."

Edward shrugged. "Yeah, okay. Keep an eye out, Buddy." He fumbled in his pocket for a key, and within moments, he had the door open and was wheeling out a small green motorcycle.

He patted the bike with pride of ownership. "Army surplus. Great little bike. I got pulled over by the police yesterday because the rear light's not working. I'm not supposed to drive it until I've had it fixed, so let's hope we don't get caught."

For a moment, Buddy wanted to respond that he'd like to get caught, by a genuine policeman but not by a homicidal maniac masquerading as a policeman. On the other hand, if the police caught him, there would still be the matter of the murder charge against his eight-year-old self.

Edward buckled on a white crash helmet and shrugged as he looked at Buddy. "I don't have one for you."

"I don't care. Let's just go."

With nothing but fear to motivate him, Buddy climbed onto the pillion of the Bantam and wrapped his arms around his cousin's waist. Much as he wanted to roar off at top speed and put distance between himself and the fake policeman, the Bantam was not capable of roaring off. With Edward leaning low over the handlebars, and Buddy silently urging the little motorcycle onward, they puttered away into the night.

Before long the crowded streets gave way to a wider highway, a broad, straight road where the Bantam picked up a little speed, and Buddy stopped looking over his shoulder. The last of the daylight gave way to darkness punctuated by streetlights. Eventually, Edward brought the Bantam to a halt in the forecourt of a train station, where a light glowed in the windows of the ticket office. Buddy climbed off the pillion and stretched his legs. Edward still sat astride the bike, holding up his hands and uncramping his fingers.

"Are we there?" Buddy asked.

"This is Hackbridge station. We're almost there. I've never driven this in the dark. I might need to ask for directions."

"No!"

Edward glowered at him from beneath the brim of his crash helmet. "What do you want me to do? You want me just to drive up and down until I find it? It's a little place, out of the way, stuck in the weeds. I can't find it just like that in the dark."

"But if you ask," Buddy said, "then you'll leave a trail, and the police will—"

A voice came from behind him. "The police will what?"

Buddy turned to find a uniformed police constable approaching him across the forecourt. "The police will what?" he repeated.

Once again Buddy was tempted. This was a policeman, a genuine constable, in his uniform, with the force of the law behind him. He could provide protection, or of course, he could throw both of them into jail.

The policeman drew closer. "I saw you drive up. Your rear light's not working, laddie."

"I'll get it fixed," Edward promised.

The constable's tone was officious. "You'll get off and walk."

Edward's voice was a low hiss as he locked eyes with Buddy. "Get on. Quick!"

Edward's hands were already on the handlebars, his right hand twisting the throttle and the engine working itself up to a high-intensity whine. Buddy leaped on and flung his arms around Edward's waist. They left the constable behind in a spray of dust and gravel.

As they hurtled onto the road and around a sharp bend, they came close to a collision with a Land Rover. Edward swerved and lost control. The little motorcycle jumped a ditch and buried itself in a hedge, pinning Edward underneath.

Buddy rolled onto his side and staggered to his feet. He looked back down the road and saw the red brake lights of the Land Rover. They were stopping, and they were coming back to investigate. In the distance, he heard a police whistle; the constable at the station, rising to the occasion.

He leaned down and grabbed the handlebars of the motorcycle. Panic lent strength to his lift, and Edward wriggled out, apparently uninjured.

Darkness beckoned to them from the other side of the hedge.

Buddy had no time to ask questions. Edward was on his feet; he didn't seem to be injured. They had to move.

Buddy tapped Edward's head. "Take off your helmet."

"Why?"

"It's white. It's easy to spot."

Edward fumbled with the strap and flung the helmet aside. They dived together through the hole they had made in the hedge and emerged into an open space.

"Now what?" Edward asked.

Buddy pointed to a deeper darkness beyond the wide expanse. "Looks like trees over there. We'll make a run for it. Go!"

As they ran, Buddy observed that despite his shorter legs, Edward was quite a runner, or maybe it was the sound of the police whistle and the raised voices that lent him speed.

They were soon on a paved path that ran through a stand of trees, and beyond the path, he saw the gleam of a river. The sound of the police whistle died away. Apparently, the constable had failed to gather reinforcements. Of course, the motorcycle was still in the ditch, and eventually, Edward's ownership of the little Bantam would be revealed, but not yet. As for the Land Rover, presumably, the irate driver had moved on. No harm had been done, and surely he had somewhere else to be.

Buddy came to an abrupt halt, bending over to catch his breath. Edward leaned against a tree, and his words were punctuated by long, gasping breaths.

"I think they've gone ... My mother will ... I wish I knew where she was."

"I wish I knew where we were," Buddy responded. "What is this place?"

"It's a park," Edward gasped.

"So where's your father's house?"

Edward pushed himself away from the tree and pointed toward the river. "My father grows watercress along the Wandle."

"Huh?" Edward's statement made no sense to Buddy's exhausted mind. He grasped at the only word he understood. "Watercress?"

"He sells it to hotels, you know, for sandwiches."

Sandwiches? "But where," Buddy said between gritted teeth, "does he live?"

"Somewhere along there," Edward repeated, pointing at the river again. "That's the River Wandle, and that's where he grows the watercress."

"All right, so you know where we are?"

"Not exactly," Edward admitted. "I usually come along the road, not through the park, in the dark. But if we follow the river, we'll come to his house."

An expanse of open ground lay between the stand of trees and the river. Buddy looked back the way they had come and saw no signs of life. He reasoned that the police constable had no reason to continue the chase. He had no idea that Buddy had been accused of a long-ago murder. The only thing he'd seen was a passenger without a crash helmet.

They reached the river, a small, shallow stream. For Buddy, accustomed to the roaring river of his Canadian home, the River Wandle was not worthy of its title. They followed the gurgling water upstream along the manicured banks of the parkland until the landscaping ended abruptly in a tangle of bushes.

"Are we going the right way?" Buddy asked.

"This is it," Edward replied, pushing through the brambles. "I can see his house."

Buddy followed behind with thorns snatching at his clothes. Adrenaline was giving way to exhaustion as he saw a light up ahead and made out the shape of a house that seemed balanced on the water's edge.

Edward, who was just ahead of him, stopped abruptly. "Why are they here?"

Buddy took an exhausted step forward. "Who?"

"Them," Edward said softly. "The people in the Land Rover."

Royal Sussex County Hospital, Brighton
Detective Inspector Percy Slater

As Daphne Raleigh slipped into the room, Slater acknowledged her presence with a nod of his head, but he was not in a mood to interrupt his phone conversation with the chief constable. Giving vent to his anger had blown away the last vestiges of anesthesia, and he was finally able to think. He would speak to Daphne in a minute, but meantime, he had Reginald Peacock, the chief constable, to deal with.

Peacock's voice was thick with outrage. "You may not address me this way, Slater. I'm the chief constable, and don't you forget it."

Slater gripped the photograph as he spat out his reply. "You're not my chief constable, *sir*. I don't answer to you, or anyone else under your command. What the hell were you all thinking to let someone just walk in and tell you he was Inspector Cameron of the North Riding of Yorkshire Constabulary? And you let him take over your most sensitive case."

"We're short of people," Peacock said accusingly, "since you went off to do whatever it is you're doing. He showed me his paperwork. He came here to—"

"To help with the meeting at Arundel. Yes, I know. Nothing in his paperwork says he's to take over cases in Brighton, and did you even look closely at his assignment papers?"

"Well, I, uh ..."

"Obviously, they're forgeries," Slater raged. "Not only did you accept an imposter, you let him work on a murder case in which he is quite possibly the guilty party."

"I don't know about that."

"I do," Slater replied. "I have here a photograph of that Canadian boy's parents, a wedding picture of a Gypsy woman and a man who is, without a doubt, the man who is now calling himself Robert Cameron; the man you accepted into your station without even a question. It's no wonder he was so keen to hunt down that boy. He knew the kid would recognize him and ..."

Slater sighed and stopped speaking. What was the point of shutting the stable door after the horse had bolted? It was done now. Buddy had run to London, and Whitby was giving chase. There was precious little that he could do from this hospital bed.

"Slater, are you still there?"

He turned his attention back to the chief constable. "I'm here."

"What you're saying ignores one primary problem. You think that Cameron, or whoever he is, came to Brighton to insert himself into the Stewart case, but that's not possible. He was already in Brighton before Whitby turned up with his client. He already had the papers, forged or not, assigning him to work security at Arundel Castle. Arundel is why he's here.

202

The missing boy is just a bonus. We have to concern ourselves with Arundel. We have to know what Cameron was planning to do at Arundel."

Slater felt a shiver run down his spine as his fury dissipated. Peacock was not wrong. The meeting at Arundel should be his focus, not the problem of one nameless evacuee.

He replaced the phone receiver and turned to look at Daphne. She had arrived in a flurry of authority and cleared the room. She had been the only witness to his phone call with the chief constable; the only witness to his revelation that Detective Inspector Cameron was an imposter.

"Do you feel better now?" Daphne asked acerbically.

"Not yet," Slater replied. "Where have you been? Why are you here? Why aren't you with Whitby?"

Daphne hesitated. "I had … things … to do."

"Things?"

Daphne straightened her shoulders. "May I remind you that I am not under your command and I don't appreciate being questioned?"

"And I don't appreciate being left here with no information."

"You were unconscious."

"Well, I'm not unconscious now, so tell me what you know."

"There's been another murder. A woman on the Montard estate by the name of Winnie Widdicome."

"Is it connected?"

"Undoubtedly. She saw the boy yesterday in the company of a shepherd."

"A shepherd? Who is he? Can we bring him in?"

Slater saw a flush of something like guilt on Daphne's face. "No, we can't, and don't ask me any questions about him, because I won't answer them. They're not relevant to this case."

Slater looked at the set of Daphne's lips and knew that he would get no answers. He changed the subject.

"What do you know about Toby Whitby? According to my informants, he's on his way to London, possibly in the company of a member of the aristocracy."

Daphne nodded. "Yes, he's with Lord Victor Montard, although I can't imagine why Victor has involved himself in this case, apart from idle curiosity."

"So you know this man?" Slater asked. "You know the Viscount?"

"I do." Daphne looked at him speculatively. "I could go and look for them."

"Go where?"

"London."

"London," Slater snorted, "is a big place."

Slater thought he saw sympathy in Daphne's face. So she thought he was still groggy from anesthesia, or maybe from the bump on his head. He marshaled his thoughts. "He's either gone to see Elizabeth Powley, the woman who claims that the boy is not her son, or he's gone back to see Randall Powley."

"So what do you suggest?" Daphne asked.

"Pick one, and let's get Peacock on the phone again. You'll need transport, and we'll need to get all of this out of the way before the meeting at Arundel Castle."

He looked at Daphne, noting for the first time that she was wearing wellington boots and her clothes were spattered with mud. "Where have you been?"

He watched her face crumple as if she was attempting to hold back tears. "Daphne?"

"A war wound," she said. "I was taking care of an old war wound."

Hackbridge, Surrey
Toby Whitby

Toby recognized the forecourt of Hackbridge station, with its light providing a welcoming beacon in the gathering dusk. This was where he had come to meet Percy Slater. Was that only yesterday? So much had happened in such a short time since the first time he had driven up here from Brighton.

He looked across at Victor Montard, who was driving the Land Rover with speed and confidence. "We're nearly there," he said.

Victor nodded and took his eyes off the road. "I know my way around this part of the world. I used to—"

Whatever it was he used to do remained unspoken as a motorcycle hurtled out of the station forecourt with a uniformed police officer running behind. Victor swerved but not before the motorcyclist had lost control and driven his motorcycle into a ditch at the side of the road.

Victor satisfied himself with a glance in the rearview mirror and did not even apply his brakes.

"Hold on a minute," Toby protested. "They could be injured."

Victor Montard shook his head. "We didn't even hit them. They had a soft landing on the side of the road. They'll be right as rain. You saw that policeman running along behind them. They're fine; just a couple of boys out on a lark. Don't worry about them."

Victor bumped the Land Rover along a rutted lane with bushes closing in and scraping on each side. Toby's Morris had fitted easily between the obstructions, but the Land Rover was wider.

"This seems to be the right way," Toby offered. He remembered driving up and down country lanes with Slater in search of Randall Powley's cottage. He was surprised that the Viscount had found the path so easily.

Before the surprise had time to take hold, Victor waved his hand expansively. "I know this part of the country fairly well. That's Beddington Park. I played cricket there in the good old days, before everything went up the spout. There's a river that runs through the park and comes out along here. I'm just guessing where it goes, but I seem to be on track. It's like you said: watercress requires running water, and we're following the running water."

The lane took a slight turn, and Toby glimpsed the shape of Powley's cottage, with a light in an upstairs window and the gleam of water beyond. As they turned through the gap in the hedge, the upstairs light was suddenly extinguished.

When the headlight beams lit up the lawn surrounding the cottage, something moved across Toby's line of vision; two dark human shapes darted behind the outbuildings. He remembered the motorcycle in the ditch and the two riders who had crashed through the hedge in panic. They'd had no cause to run. There had been no collision, no damage, no one injured. Why were they fleeing?

Time was running out. He made an intuitive leap. "Buddy and Edward Powley!"

Victor brought the Land Rover to a halt with his headlight still trained on the front of Powley's cottage. "What did you say?"

"The two people on the motorcycle. That was Buddy and his cousin. That's why they ran. Didn't want the police to stop them and turn them in."

"But why come here?"

"Buddy's running from Cameron and his absurd murder charge. Maybe they think Randall can keep them safe. Maybe they think he knows something about what happened."

"What would he know?" Victor asked.

"He knows the name of Buddy's father, his supposed father, and he may not realize what danger that puts him in. If he knows the name of Buddy's father, he knows the name of the German agent, because the man was obviously a German agent."

"But the war's over," Victor said mildly.

"If the agent was an enemy of Britain in the war," Toby said, "he's still an enemy of Britain now, and he's still active. Think about it: someone killed poor Mrs. Widdicome just this morning. That's not old news; that's not like the body in the house on St. Godric Street. This is something that's still going on. Slater knew it and so does Daphne. I'm betting she'll turn up here sometime soon but not in time to save Powley. We'll have to do that ourselves."

Victor turned off the Land Rover's engine and extinguished the headlights, leaving Toby momentarily blind.

"So someone needs to let Powley know we're here," Victor said, "and someone else needs to get hold of those two boys."

Toby looked at the darkened cottage. "Powley knows we're here. You shone your lights in his windows. We could probably just knock on his front door. He has no reason to be suspicious."

Victor nodded. "You're right. Good thinking, old chap. Of course he knows. On the other hand, those two boys are obviously in a complete panic, and they're not going to let me near them. Fortunately, the Canadian boy knows you. Why don't you go after them, and I'll go knock on Powley's door and see if I can get him to listen to me?" He gave a slight laugh. "It's a handy thing to be a viscount. The title still makes people sit up and take notice."

Toby felt Victor's hand giving him a slight push in the direction of the outbuildings. His eyes had grown accustomed to the darkness, and he could make out a paved path across the lawn.

He took out his handkerchief and polished his glasses. From the corner of his eye, he saw Victor reaching into the interior of the Land Rover. "Going to comb my hair," Victor said. "Want to make a good impression."

Well, combing his hair would have been very low on Toby's list of priorities, but he left the Viscount to his primping and strode across the lawn to the deeper darkness of the outbuildings. As he walked, he called softly.

"Buddy. Buddy, it's Toby Whitby. It's all right. You can come out. Everything's under control."

A rustling sound reached him from somewhere behind the shed. Voices whispered.

"It's all right. It's my lawyer."

"The one who set the police on you?"

"He's okay. We can trust him."

Toby picked up on his cue. "You can trust me, Edward."

Someone behind the hedge hissed in alarm. "He knows my name."

"Yes," Toby said. "I know your name. You're Edward Powley. Are you all right? Does your mother know you're here?"

"My mother?"

A groan, a rustle in the undergrowth, and the shape of a boy revealed itself. "What do you know about my mother? Is she all right?"

Toby felt a sinking in the pit of his stomach. Why were Edward and Buddy here at Randall's cottage, and why were they worried about

Edward's mother? With no love lost between Randall and Elizabeth, and Elizabeth even saying that Randall was dead, why had Edward left her and come here?

"Has something happened to your mother?" Toby asked.

"I don't know."

Edward was visible now, a stocky boy with wide shoulders, and behind him the taller, thinner shape of Buddy.

"His mother didn't come," Buddy stammered. "She told us to ... She said we should ..."

"We didn't go with the Gypsies," Edward said, his voice rising to a nervous squeak. "We didn't go, because ..."

Buddy interrupted in an exhausted voice. "Because that's the first place he would look. We didn't think he'd look here. He doesn't know about Edward's father, does he?"

"My mother tells everyone he's dead," Edward said, "but the police would know he's not, but he's not a real policeman. That's what Buddy says, and we didn't know what to do."

They were both out in the open now. Although there was not enough light to study their faces, Toby could read fear, confusion, and exhaustion in their voices.

He chose a tone of authority. Edward and Buddy were obviously on the edge of panic, but they were young men, not children. Ten years ago, boys their age were being turned into soldiers and sent to fight.

"Calm down, both of you. Buddy, I know you were a Boy Scout; you know better than to panic. So slow down and speak clearly."

"You accused me of murder," Buddy said truculently. "I heard you."

"And so you ran away?"

"Yes."

"And terrified your poor foster mother."

"Is she all right?"

"She'll be better when I tell her that I found you."

"But you can't turn me in. He'll say I'm a murderer."

Toby saw Edward tugging on Buddy's arm. "No, he won't. Not now we know who he is."

Toby reached out a long arm. The boys ducked, but Edward was slower than Buddy, and Toby grabbed him by the back of his shirt. He spoke through gritted teeth. "Tell me."

"The policeman," Edward said, "is not a policeman. Leastways, he might be a policeman, but that's not important, because he's really Buddy's father."

"What policeman?" Toby queried, but before the boy could reply, he already knew that there could only be one answer. "Cameron? Are you saying that Cameron is Buddy's father?"

Buddy kept a safe distance as he spoke. "He came to the market outside Edward's house, and he was looking for us, and I saw him, and I recognized him. I remember that face from when I was little. He told the Gypsies that he was Inspector Cameron. I don't care what he says, or even if he is a policeman. I know who he is; he's my father, and he killed Mrs. Widdicome. She was just a nice old lady, but he killed her. I found her, outside her cottage. I wanted to close her eyes, but ..." He sniffed quietly. "I should have closed her eyes."

Gears shifted in Toby's mind, and he felt the beginning of understanding. "You're sure about all of this?" he asked.

Buddy nodded his head vigorously. "My memory is clearing. I'm remembering a lot of things, and I remember everything about that man; even his voice."

Toby recalled that he was still holding Edward's collar, and released him abruptly, leaving him to collapse in a heap on the ground.

"I know for certain," Buddy repeated.

Toby nodded. "I believe you. It's starting to make sense, but you're wrong about the man you remember being your father. Maybe you were told he was your father, but he isn't."

Buddy gasped. "He's not?"

"No."

Toby could not begin to imagine how Buddy was feeling as once again his understanding of who he was slipped away to be replaced by uncertainty.

"If he's not my father, who is?" Buddy asked.

"I don't know, but we'll find out between us."

"I didn't shoot my mother," Buddy said. "I know I didn't."

"Even if you did," Toby replied, "no one can prove it, and—"

Buddy's reply was an angry hiss. "Don't say that. I didn't. I know I didn't. Edward knows what happened. He was at the station and he heard."

Edward scrambled to his feet. "It was Mrs. Widdicome," he said.

"Mrs. Widdicome shot Buddy's mother?" Toby asked incredulously.

"No, of course not," Buddy replied, his voice filled with youthful scorn at Toby's slow wits. "Mrs. Widdicome took me to the station when the children were being sent to Canada, and she told Edward's mother what had happened."

"I heard her," Edward said. "I didn't really know what they were talking about, but I understand now. Buddy's father shot his mother and ran off."

"Mr. Whitby said that man isn't my father," Buddy corrected.

"No, he's not," Toby confirmed, and took a moment to wonder if anyone would ever know the name of Buddy's true father.

"Anyway," Buddy continued breathlessly, "it seems that Mrs. Widdicome found my mother dead, shot by that man, and took me out of the house, and we went to London and traded places with Edward, and that's how I got to Canada."

"And that's why my mother wouldn't even tell my dad, even though they argued and he left home," Edward said. "She didn't want anyone to know where Buddy was."

Toby nodded. "That makes sense, and it explains a lot. We've talked long enough out here, and we should go into the house now and talk to Edward's father. Perhaps he can fill in some of the gaps."

Buddy shrank back slightly. "What if Cameron has followed us? I'd rather stay out here."

"We'll be safe," Toby assured him. "I have a good man with me. Viscount Pulborough was a soldier in the war, very brave. I think he won himself some medals. We'll leave here as soon as we've collected Edward's father, and we'll take you all to a safe place."

"What about Edward's mother?"

Toby wished he could find a reassuring answer, but nothing came immediately to mind, and he settled for chivvying the boys toward the front door.

"Can I get my Bantam out of the ditch?" Edward asked.

"Later," Toby said. "The Viscount has a Land Rover with plenty of room for all of us, so we'll worry about your bike tomorrow. Tonight I just want to get you all to a safe place."

They rounded the corner to the front of the house. Toby was surprised to see that no lights were shining at the windows. Maybe Victor was just being cautious. The front door stood open; obviously, Victor was inside.

As he crossed the threshold, his foot encountered an obstacle.

Victor's voice came to him from the darkened interior of the house. "Careful, Whitby."

Toby's heart sank as he explored the obstruction with the toe of his shoe and realized that it was the shape and consistency of a human body.

Victor's voice was closer now. "Best to leave the lights off, old chap, and get the boys out of here."

"Is it …?"

"I think so, although, of course, I've never met him."

A hand tugged at Toby's sleeve, and Edward tried to push past him. "What's he talking about? What is it?"

Toby held him back. "There's something here. I'm afraid it's another body. The Viscount will take care of it. No need for you to come any closer. We'll go back to the Land Rover."

Edward's voice quivered slightly. "Is it my father?"

"I don't know. It's too dark to tell. Come away now. No need for you to look."

A strong hand pulled Toby backward, and Toby was surprised at the sound of Buddy hissing indignantly in his ear. "We're not children, Mr. Whitby. I've already seen one dead body today."

"You told us not to panic," Edward added, his voice firmer now, "and I'm not panicking. I want to see."

Toby looked toward the interior of the cottage. "Victor?"

"I'm here."

"Can you find the light switch?"

"Righty-ho!"

The Viscount's cheerful acquiescence seemed out of place in the presence of the dead body just inside the doorway. Toby had only a passing acquaintance with the aristocracy, but he suspected that Victor was hiding his emotions behind a veil of upper-class sangfroid. And there was his battle experience to be taken into account. Viscount Pulborough was familiar with violent death. Toby tried to suppress his old sense of shame. He had not risked his life in battle. He had not led men and seen them die. He had no business judging a man who had been awarded medals for valor.

Before he could sink into the vortex of his own insecurities, light flooded the scene, and he saw the body. Randall Powley lay facedown in a pool of blood that had collected beneath his head. His bald scalp gleamed in the bright light of the living-room lamps. Victor stepped over the body and extended his arms to block the doorway.

Toby felt the weight of the two boys pressing against him. "I don't think you should—"

Edward pushed hard and broke through. "I'm not a kid. I want to see." Toby stepped back, and Edward took a hesitant step forward. Victor stopped him with a barked command. "Don't touch him. It's a crime scene. We have to leave it alone."

"He's not an *it*," Edward protested. "He's my father."

Toby caught Edward's arm. "The Viscount's right. We can't disturb the scene."

"He's my father," Edward repeated in a choked voice.

Toby's instinctive attempt to comfort the boy was preempted by Buddy, who put an arm around his cousin's shoulder and led him away, murmuring the words of comfort that Toby should have been able to muster up if his mind had not been so busy with questions.

"Victor."

The Viscount lowered his arms. "Yes?"

"When we pulled in here, I saw a light in the window upstairs, and then it went out. If Powley was already dead, why was the light on and then off?"

Victor shook his head. "I didn't see anything."

"I thought you did."

"No, it was all dark."

"But we agreed he was home, because we saw the light."

Victor shook his head again. "We agreed that if he was at home, he would know we were here, because we shone our headlights into the front windows. I didn't see a light upstairs. Are you suggesting that whoever did this is still here?"

"He could be."

"I've had a good look around," Victor said, "and I haven't run into anyone." He looked down at the body on the floor. "This could have been done a couple of days ago for all we know. Best to wait for the medical examiner. He'll be able to give us a time of death."

Toby nodded. "We'll need to phone the police."

"I doubt Randall has a phone," Victor said. "I haven't seen one. Still, we know where to find a policeman. I'll go back to the train station and stir up that whistling constable; he'll be glad of some real excitement instead of chasing boys on motorcycles."

"What shall we do with the boys?" Toby asked.

"I'll take them with me," Victor offered. He held up a hand to halt Toby's expected protest. "I won't give them away either for putting their motorcycle in a ditch or for being somehow or other wanted murderers."

"They're not—"

"That's not quite true, is it? Our young friend from Canada is wanted on a murder charge."

"No," Toby protested. "Look, I've been thinking about that and him saying that Cameron is the father he remembers."

"Do you believe him?"

"It's a possibility. From the first time I met him, I didn't like Cameron's behavior or the way he went after Buddy or the way he went after your brother."

"No," Victor agreed, "I didn't like that either."

"So," Toby continued, "if you call the police, you have to make sure it's not Cameron who turns up here. I just don't trust him, and you have to keep the boys out of sight."

"Righty-ho. I'll take the boys with me, but I won't tell anyone I have them. I'll get onto the local constabulary and report the body, and you wait here."

Toby reached into his pocket for a business card and a pen. He set the card down on the wide stone windowsill beside the front door, where a light shone out from the living-room window. "I'll give you a number to call to say that Buddy is all right. His foster mother must be beside herself."

He hesitated with the pen poised above the paper. Who should be told? He thought of Percy Slater and the mysterious tea caddy number. No, not that one; Victor could not be told about that number. Anthea? Yes, Anthea was reliable, and Hugh Trewin would also ... Why was he assuming that Hugh would be at Anthea's house? Even in the stress of the moment and the presence of so many questions with so few answers, he took a moment to grin. Would Hugh be at Anthea's house *again*?

He handed the card to Victor and herded the boys into the waiting vehicle. The Land Rover bounced away, leaving Toby alone with nothing but the gurgling of the river for music, and the dead body of Randall Powley for company. He turned off the living-room lights and settled down to wait. He wondered who would come first: the local constable with his whistle, or the German agent with the Luger.

CHAPTER NINETEEN

Tooting, London
Daphne Raleigh

Daphne wrestled with the controls of the adapted police car. Slater had told her that the car was, in his words, "a bugger," and she couldn't disagree. In fact, she had a few French words to add to the description.

She winced as she crashed her way through a gear change. She had always dismissed the idea of a car with an automatic transmission as lazy American nonsense and "not real driving," but grinding through the gears on her way to Tooting had given her a reason to change her mind.

The street market adjacent to Tooting High Street stood forlorn and empty in the dim light of the streetlamps. The market stalls were shuttered, and nothing moved except scrap paper dancing in the light breeze and a rat that scuttled across her path as she climbed out of the car.

There had been rats at Amiens, brown and thin, as sickly as the prisoners in the medieval cells.

Amiens was where she had abandoned hope. Her torturers had extracted what they could, but not enough to be useful. What did they expect from her? She had only a handful of names to give, and the owners of those names were here already. Marcel, Henri, Adélie, Simone had all been taken. Maybe they were already dead. Tomorrow she would join them. The firing squad would be a blessed relief. Just a few hours to wait, and it would all be over. And then, as she sought to remember comforting words from the *Book of Common Prayer*, the drone of engines, the falling bombs, the walls collapsing, and the terrible pain in her right eye.

Daphne pulled the *London A-Z Street Atlas* from her pocket and folded it open at the page showing Cadogan Street. She had come as far as she intended to come in the noisy, conspicuous Wolseley. From here she would go on foot. Her path to Elizabeth Powley's house would take her past the public conveniences, still open and glowing with a faint light, although the market was closed. Somewhere along the way from the rat-infested prison at Amiens, to the months of hiding in Resistance safe houses, to the final, stormy Channel crossing, she had acquired a persistent urinary tract infection, mild but incurable. She was no longer Daphne the secret agent, the combat-ready spear tip of the Resistance. She was a one-eyed woman with a weak bladder who now had to waste valuable time visiting the dubious comfort of London County Council's public conveniences.

She opened the heavy outer door and found herself in an odiferous tiled interior illuminated by a single flyspecked bulb. Three closed stalls faced her, two of which had a mechanism requiring a penny piece to open them, and one of which was the legally required "free" compartment. She groped in her pocket for a penny, and finding nothing, rattled the door of the free compartment. She was surprised by a faint sound from within, as though someone had taken a sudden, terrified breath.

She rattled again. "Come on out. I need to get in there."

A woman's voice reached her through the stout door. "Is anyone out there? Is there a man?"

"No, just me. Come out. I don't have a penny, and I need to use the ... you know."

"Did you see a man in the market?"

"No, there's no one in the market. Everything's locked up. Will you please come out?"

"No."

Daphne's anger had been simmering all day, from the moment Toby Whitby's car had faltered in the rain, to the first sight of Leo, to his angry departure when all she wanted to do was help him. That anger now came to a boiling point, and she aimed a frustrated kick at the door of the stall.

The woman inside gave a scream of fear. Daphne did not care. This woman was coming out, and she was going in, and that was all there was to it. "If you don't come out now, I am going to hurt you."

"Why?"

"Never mind why. Just come out."

The door rattled open, and Daphne came face-to-face with a stocky, dark-haired woman in a wraparound apron. She didn't pause to ask what the woman was doing and simply dashed inside to take care of her needs.

When she reemerged, the woman was still there. Her features were not easy to read in the dim light, but Daphne knew fear when she saw it, and this woman was fearful; terrified in fact. Daphne pushed the woman aside, heedless of her obvious terror, and attempted to wash her hands in the rust-stained sink.

"It won't work," the woman said. "We've told the council, but they don't care. All those public health signs telling us not to spread germs, and still they …" She shook her head, impatient with herself. "What does it matter? He didn't get my Eddie. I saw him go, and that man didn't get him; that's all I care."

Daphne was about to dismiss the woman and "her Eddie" when the words suddenly took root in her mind. "Eddie?" she asked. "Edward?"

"Yes."

"You're Edward Powley's mother? You're Elizabeth Powley?"

Suspicion warred with fear on Elizabeth's face. "So what if I am? He's done nothing. And that man is not a policeman."

Daphne abandoned her attempt to get water from the corroded tap. She had suffered through far worse things than failure to wash her hands. She took a stab in the dark, realizing that the darkness was no longer complete. The fog of incomprehension was lifting rapidly on many levels.

"Are you talking about Inspector Cameron?"

"Don't know what he calls himself," Elizabeth said. "He's been telling people in the market that he's a policeman, but he's not, and his name isn't Cameron. He's a few years older and has a lot less hair, although he never did have much to begin with, and his name is Jack Farren."

Daphne paused for a short, triumphant breath as she caught hold of the information she had spent all day chasing. The enemy agent who had lived in the house on St. Godric Street, the man whose impersonation of a detective inspector had driven Percy Slater into a paroxysm of rage, was named Jack Farren.

"What do you know about him?" she asked.

Elizabeth scowled. "Nasty piece of work. He murdered my sister."

"And you're sure that the man who came here calling himself a policeman is the same man?"

Elizabeth gave Daphne a shrewd glance. "Yes, I'm quite sure, but I'm not saying another word until you tell me who you are."

"It doesn't matter who I am. I want to know—"

"I don't care what you want to know. Why should I tell you anything?" Elizabeth pulled her lips into a thin, straight line and stared at Daphne with hard dark eyes. "You come in here, kicking down doors and making threats …"

"I needed to use the—"

Elizabeth waved Daphne into silence. "I tell you someone murdered my sister," she continued, "and all you say is 'Are you sure it was him?' Most people would say they're sorry; they'd ask how it happened; they'd ask how long ago; but you didn't, did you?"

"No, I didn't."

"So, who are you?"

"I'm an agent of the government."

"Police? You're police. That's why you knew about Jack pretending to be a policeman."

Daphne wished that this conversation could be held somewhere other than the smelly confines of London County Council's public conveniences, but she didn't dare take Elizabeth outside. Cameron, or Farren, to give him his true name, could still be out there somewhere. Of course, if he was who she thought he was, he would not be deterred by the fact that this was the ladies' side of the toilet block. Elizabeth was nursing a false sense of security if she thought she could hide from the likes of Jack Farren by locking herself in the loo.

"I'm not police," Daphne said. "I'm someone the police go to when they have a case that involves national security, and what happened to your sister, and what's happening now, involves national security."

"Why?"

"Because Jack Farren was a German agent."

Elizabeth's mouth fell open in surprise, and she uttered a long-drawn-out "Ohhhh!"

Daphne waited for the next, inevitable remark.

Elizabeth recovered from her surprise. "But the war's over."

Daphne shook her head. "No, it isn't. No one's dropping bombs on us, but we're still at war. We still have enemies, and if Jack Farren was our enemy when we were fighting Hitler, he's still our enemy now; he just has new masters."

"But why is he skulking around here looking for me?"

"He's looking for your sister's son, the one you sent to Canada. He knows that Buddy can identify him."

"Buddy? You mean Henry?"

"His Canadian parents call him Buddy."

Elizabeth's eyes softened. "They looked like nice people. I felt bad telling them that I didn't know anything about poor Henry."

"Why didn't you tell them?"

Elizabeth leaned her ample backside against the sink. "Winnie brought him to me at Euston station ..."

July 1940
Euston Station, London
Elizabeth Powley

The air trapped under the dome of Euston station was hot and sulfurous. Poor Eddie was perspiring in his school blazer, but wearing the uniform had been part of the instructions: "Bring your child to Euston station at 10 a.m. sharp with suitcase packed and label attached. Maintain a cheerful air at all times. We do not want the children upset. Say goodbye firmly but cheerfully."

Elizabeth had been prepared to be firm and cheerful, but now she was embarrassed. It seemed that all the other children were taking the situation in their stride, but Eddie was dragging on her hand and whining. It occurred to her that maybe the other neatly dressed boys and girls, each with a suitcase packed and a label tied around their neck, had not been told where they were going. Perhaps they thought they were being sent to a safe place in the English countryside and they'd be home in a couple of days. They didn't know, because their parents hadn't told them, that they were being put on a ship and sent across the Atlantic to live with strangers in Canada. Well, she'd been honest. She'd told Eddie where he was going, and this was the result.

"Mrs. Powley."

Elizabeth turned away from her grizzling son and studied the birdlike woman who was advancing on her, dragging a small, dark-haired boy. The woman was dressed in a blue cotton frock, and her wispy gray hair peeked out from a scarf knotted loosely under her chin. The boy was empty-handed; obviously, he was not boarding the train to Liverpool to catch the boat to Canada.

"Elizabeth, it is you, isn't it?"

The small woman dragged the boy forward, and Elizabeth stiffened in recognition. Henry. What was he doing here?

Eddie tugged at her hand but she shook it free "Stay there, Eddie. Don't lose your place in line."

"But, Mum …"

"Stay there." She knew her voice was harsh and impatient and not the way a mother should speak to her child when he was about to leave her for a long, long time, but she couldn't help herself. This woman and her forlorn charge had to be dealt with. She bent down and looked Eddie in the eye. "Stay there and don't you dare move."

She looked up and saw that the small woman was dancing with impatience. "You remember me, don't you? Winnie Widdicome."

Elizabeth glanced back at Eddie. He was stiff with resentment, but he was maintaining his place in line. She knew Winnie, of course. She was a cook at Montard Hall, but she hadn't seen her, not in years. Winnie was part of her former life, when

Elizabeth and Nina had been working in the greengrocer's that belonged to Randall's family, and pretending they were not what they actually were. That was where Nina had met Jack Farren, and this dazed-looking boy was Nina's son.

"This is Henry," Winnie said. "

Elizabeth looked back at the line of children. Eddie was holding his place. She grasped Winnie's arm and drew her aside. "Why is he here?"

"He has to go to Canada."

"How do you know about Canada?"

"Nina told me. She was wishing that she could go."

Elizabeth forced herself to be calm. Something was very wrong, but she didn't want to hear it. She just wanted to get Eddie on the boat and then go home and have a good cry.

She spread her hands in a helpless gesture. "She's free to make her own arrangements. It's up to her and her husband."

"It's too late for that, Nina is…" Winnie lowered her voice to a whisper glancing sideways at Eddie. Her next words were little more than a breath in Elizabeth's ear. "Your sister's dead."

Elizabeth's felt the cracking of her heart in the sudden realization of loss, and then a swoop of hope. Nina was gone. Now no one knew their secret. Words came haltingly. "What? How?

"Shot …"

Elizabeth's next question remained unasked.in her sudden awareness of her sister's boy. She looked down at Henry. "Did he see?"

"I don't know. Elizabeth, you have to let him go to Canada. He'll be safe there."

Elizabeth looked back at Eddie who had edged toward her. How much had he heard? She gestured for him to re-join the line of children.

She turned back to Winnie. "Safe from what?"

Safe from his father."

So you think it was Jack. You think Jack shot…"

Winnie clawed at her arm impatiently. "Of course I do. This is no time to argue Elizabeth. Young Henry knows what happened, and now we have to keep him safe. Jack will come for him; you know he will, and what with him not really being Henry's father—"

"Jack doesn't know that."

"He's starting to suspect. Look at the poor little mite. He looks nothing like Jack."

"But …"

Winnie tightened her grip on Elizabeth's arm. "Listen to me. I've come with instructions from your people."

"I don't understand. What people?"

Now Winnie slapped at her impatiently. "Your people. The Gypsies up on the Downs."

"I'm not one of them."

"Of course you are. I've always known it. Your mother sent me to you because she couldn't come herself. Gypsies would stand out like a sore thumb in this crowd, and she doesn't want young Henry to even know what he is."

"How did you know I was—?"

Winnie slapped her again. "It's as plain as the nose on your face. Nina and me were friends. That's why I went. I was taking her a few strawberries from the garden; she always liked strawberries. It was early in the morning, and the front door was open, so I went in, calling out the way you do, so I wouldn't surprise her, but she didn't answer, and then I saw her, on the floor. I didn't have to look too close to see what had happened. Shot in the head. There was nothing I could do. Shot in the head is shot in the head. Nothing anyone can do. I was going to leave, but I heard someone crying, and I knew what it was. It was poor little Henry, hiding under his bed. He said his parents had been fighting and his mother had told him that he should never come out of his bedroom if he heard his father shouting, and so he stayed there, and he heard a bang. And he still didn't move, bless him. He waited for his mother to come, but of course, she didn't."

Elizabeth's hand moved involuntarily to stroke Henry's head as he looked up at her with wide, blank eyes. "How long has he been like this? Is he in shock? We should give him something, tea, or brandy; I don't know."

Winnie shook her head. "It's not shock, not now. It's something else, something your people did to him."

"You took him to my people?"

"Of course I did. What else was I going to do with him? I took him up to the camp, and I talked to your mother. She told me what to do. She said I was to bring him to you and to tell you, not to ask you, but to tell you, that it was your duty to put young Henry on the boat to Canada."

Elizabeth's heart sank. She wanted to refuse. She was beyond the reach of her parents and their mysteriously compelling ways. She lived in Tooting and pretended she was like everyone else, but here was the boy with his blank face, providing evidence that Gypsy magic still worked.

"Did my mother do this to him?" Elizabeth asked. "Did she use the candle and the glass?"

"I don't know. I didn't watch. All I know is that she took him inside her caravan, and they were in there a long time, and now he doesn't remember who he is or what happened."

Winnie reached into her capacious handbag. "Before I left your sister's house, I went into the bedroom and collected Nina's jewels from the dressing table. I thought they might be important to you, something to remember her by."

Elizabeth took the knotted handkerchief and stuffed it into her pocket. Later ... she would look at them later, but jewels or no jewels, she was not giving up Eddie's chance of safety.

Winnie reached into her bag again and produced an envelope. "Your father sent you a note."

Elizabeth took the note and looked at the writing scrawled in a foreign alphabet. She saw the words of the promise and the words of the curse. She breathed deeply and reached for Henry's hand. "Come with me. We need to change your clothes."

Winnie stopped her again. "I took a couple of photographs from the dresser. One day, the boy will want to know about his grandparents and his mother." She sniffed disapprovingly. "Maybe he'll even ask about this father." She pressed an envelope into Elizabeth's hand. "You should put these in the suitcase he's taking with him. I expect his memory will come back one day, won't it? It's not permanent, is it?"

Elizabeth shook her head. "I don't know. Might be best if he never remembers." Henry's hand trembled slightly as she caught hold of it. Fear? Shock? It didn't matter. It was all over now. She turned back to Winnie one last time. "Where is my sister's body? Did my people come for her?"

Winnie shook her head. "They were going to, but the Germans came first. The houses on St. Godric Street were bombed two nights ago. There's nothing left for them to bury."

August 1952
Tooting, London
Daphne Raleigh

Daphne wished that Toby was still with her. Here was the explanation he had been seeking. If Elizabeth Powley would testify to what she had been told, the charge of murder would no longer hang over Buddy's head. Jack Farren had shot his wife, and Nina's Gypsy family had wiped away Buddy's memory of the event. Probably hypnosis, she thought, and now that Buddy was here, where it had all happened, his memory would soon return.

She looked at Elizabeth leaning gloomily against the sink. Winnie Widdicome knew what had happened; Winnie would have known that the man who called himself Robert Cameron was in fact Jack Farren, a murderer and a German agent. Now Winnie was dead, and Farren was already here in Tooting, looking for anyone who could identify him, and that included Elizabeth Powley. She sighed. Roy and Evvie Stewart's simple desire to adopt their British foster child had already resulted in one death, and it would result in many more if Jack Farren had his way.

The Gypsies had moved on from their encampment on the South Downs and wouldn't be Farren's first priority. He was focusing on the easy targets: Elizabeth Powley and her son, and Buddy, whose memory was returning; who would soon remember the face of his childhood tormenter.

"Well?" Elizabeth asked. "Now I've told you what's what, are you going to do something about it?"

"Of course I am. Jack Farren is still a danger to Britain, and I intend to bring him in, with your help."

Elizabeth shuffled her feet. "I can't help you."

"If you don't help me, I'll leave you here for Jack Farren to find when he's good and ready. Tell me where your son went."

"I don't know."

"Think. Where would he go to feel safe?"

Elizabeth's habitual scowl gave way to an expression of something like regret. "He'll go to his father. I told him Randall was dead, but he knows that's not true."

"Why did you tell him that?"

"Randall was angry with me. I wouldn't tell him why I didn't send Eddie to Canada. He found Nina's jewelry, and he thought I'd sold Eddie's safety for a handful of gemstones. When he stormed out of the house and said he'd never come back, I took him at his word. I told people he was dead; I even told Eddie he was dead. It was the best way to keep my secret. Henry was safe in Canada, with no idea of his real name, and if I kept quiet, no one would ever find out. So I kept quiet and let Eddie believe his father was dead. It didn't last. Eddie knows his father's alive, and he knows where he lives. That's where they've gone."

"Right!" Daphne grabbed Elizabeth's arm. "Take your apron off. We're going for a ride."

Hackbridge, Surrey
Toby Whitby

Toby turned on all the lights. He told himself that he wanted to be certain that the police could find the place, but he secretly acknowledged that the presence of Randall Powley's dead body was the real reason why he didn't want to sit in the dark.

The body was still where he had found it, facedown on the rug just inside the front door. He imagined that Randall had opened the door to someone and only had time to take a quick step backward before the fatal attack.

Although he had not actually moved the body, he had made a close examination, lifting the head and finding that rigor mortis had not yet set in, meaning that Randall had died within the last couple of hours; and not from a gunshot wound. The dark slash across his throat and the pool of blood beneath his head told their own story. A sharp knife, expertly used.

He left the body to its lone vigil behind the front door and sat down in the easy chair beside the kitchen stove. He tried to think logically. Farren had a gun. He'd used it to kill Winnie Widdicome, so why had he come here with a knife? Randall Powley was a strong, healthy man, and Farren, in his disguise as Inspector Cameron, had seemed pudgy and out of shape, not really capable of wrestling a man to the ground and cutting his throat.

He shook his head. Nothing made sense. Perhaps he was just too tired to think logically. He had started his day before dawn with a house falling in on him. He'd spent hours wandering the Downs in the company of a belligerent secret agent, followed by a visit with the village gossip and a mad dash up the London Road. And now he was playing babysitter to a dead body. No wonder he was tired. He leaned back and closed his eyes.

He awoke with a start, not knowing for a moment where he was. He sat up and straightened his glasses. Yes, now he knew. He was in Randall Powley's kitchen. He stumbled to his feet and looked out into the hallway. No, it had not been a dream; Randall Powley was indeed dead. But where were the police? Surely they should be here by now. He glanced at his watch. That couldn't be right. If Victor had gone straight to the train station, the young constable on duty should have been here hours ago, blowing his whistle and threatening to arrest everyone in sight.

Toby stared down at the body. His mind, no longer completely befuddled by his exhausting day, offered him a thoroughly unsettling thought. If Farren had been in Tooting, looking for Buddy, he could not also be here, murdering Randall Powley, which meant that either he had an accomplice or Randall had more than one enemy. And where was that enemy now?

He resisted the sudden urge to turn off the lights and hide. Too late! Anyone watching the house would know Toby had been there for hours, not keeping watch but snoring away in an armchair.

He drew in a sharp breath as he heard a car approaching, gears crashing as it navigated the narrow lanes. If he didn't know better, he would say it was Slater driving his abominable adapted police Wolseley, but Slater was still in hospital. So if it wasn't Slater, who was it?

He sidestepped the body and looked out of the living-room window in time to see Daphne emerging from the driver's seat, followed by the squat shape of a woman in an apron.

He hurried to step outside the front door and closed the door behind him so that the newcomers would not immediately see the dead body just inside the doorway.

Daphne shaded her eyes. "Is that you, Whitby?"

"It is."

The woman in the apron ran toward him. "Where's my boy? Where's Eddie?"

Toby held up a hand to stop her. "Are you Mrs. Powley?"

"Yes, of course I am. Where's my boy?"

"He's all right, Mrs. Powley. He's safe but he's not here." Even as he spoke, Toby wondered whether or not he was telling the truth.

Daphne was almost at the door now, and the light streaming from the living-room windows illuminated her puzzled face.

"We assumed the boys came here."

"They did. They came here, but they're gone now. Don't worry, they're in safe hands. Why have you come? Where are the police?"

Daphne shook her head. "Why did you call the police?"

"Well, you know, because … Not me, actually, Victor … I don't understand … Slater's car."

The impatient expression on Daphne's face reflected the fact that Toby was burbling, unable to complete a sentence. Perhaps it was the relief that he was no longer alone with Randall Powley's body. Perhaps it was the guilt of knowing that he had slept for several hours instead of watching the minutes and hours tick by and wondering what had happened to Victor and the boys. The police should have been here long ago. The young constable should be blowing his whistle and taking charge. Victor Montard should have returned with a Land Rover full of reinforcements, but Daphne was here instead, driving Slater's car and dragging Elizabeth Powley along with her.

"What's going on?" Daphne asked.

She made an attempt to push him aside, but he held his ground. "Not now, not with Mrs. Powley listening."

"What are you talking about?"

"There's a …"

"A what?"

Toby grabbed Daphne's arm and ducked before she could aim a reflexive blow at him. "Listen to me," he hissed between gritted teeth. "Just stand still and listen to me. There's a … there's someone … inside. Keep Mrs. Powley away."

"Keep me away from what?" Elizabeth asked, grabbing at Daphne's coat and attempting to drag her away. "What don't you want me to see? Is it my Eddie? Is it?" Her voice rose to a hysterical scream. "Is it my Eddie?"

"No, Mrs. Powley, your son is fine. I'm afraid it's your husband."

"Randall? What's happened to him? Where is he?"

"He's just inside the door," Toby said, still standing in the doorway. "There's been an accident."

Daphne pushed past him and opened the door, revealing Randall Powley's obviously lifeless body.

While Elizabeth filled the night air with startled screams, Daphne knelt beside the corpse. She looked up at Toby. "That's no accident. Did you—?"

"No, of course not. That's how we found him. Someone got here ahead of us."

Daphne ignored the screeching of the bereaved woman. "Farren?" she asked.

"No, there wasn't time."

"Then who?"

"I don't know."

Elizabeth's screams died away as suddenly as they had started, and now she was running down the lane.

"What on earth?" Toby muttered as he set off after her, easily overtaking her short, frantic steps with his long-legged stride.

"It's him," she shouted. "I can hear him."

"Hear what?"

Elizabeth held up a finger to silence Toby and cocked her head to one side. "That's my Eddie's motorbike," she said. "I'd know that sound anywhere."

Toby listened to the rapidly approaching whine of a two-stroke engine. "It's my Eddie's Bantam," Elizabeth confirmed. "He's here. He's safe."

Toby kept his doubts to himself. He was not at all sure that Eddie was safe or that it was Eddie approaching on the motorcycle. Eddie had left with Victor, so why was he back here now, and where had he been?

The beam of a headlight flickered among the trees as the motorcycle rounded the turn.

"Eddie," Elizabeth screamed. "Eddie, don't go in there."

She turned to Toby. "You can't let him see."

"He's already seen," Toby replied, "before you got here."

The motorcycle wobbled to a halt, and Eddie let it drop to the ground as his mother hurled herself at him. He was riding without a helmet, and his face was pale and drawn.

"It's all right, Mum. I'm all right. Not hurt."

"Your dad ..."

"I know. That's why I came back, but I didn't think you'd be here."

Toby interrupted the reunion and the garbled explanations flying back and forth between mother and son. "Eddie, where are the police? Why aren't they here?"

Eddie turned a startled face toward him. "I don't know."

"You were going to get the police," Toby reminded him. "What happened?"

Eddie shrugged. "I didn't go with them. That man—he's a viscount, you know—suggested I should get my bike out of the ditch. He said I shouldn't leave it there all night, in case someone stole it. He helped me get it started. He said I should go home." Eddie took a deep breath. "I ... well ... I ..."

Toby waited quietly for Eddie to speak.

"I went back to Tooting, but I couldn't find my mother, so I started just driving round in circles, trying to get up my courage to come back here, even if it meant facing the police. He's my dad; I couldn't just leave him." He turned to his mother. "Mum, something's happened to Dad."

"I know. I'm sorry."

Eddie pushed his mother away with an abrupt gesture. "Why would you be sorry? Why would you even care? You told everyone he was dead."

Elizabeth shook her head. "I had my reasons," she said softly. "I had to keep away from him."

"Why?"

"Because of Henry."

"Henry?"

"Yes, your cousin Henry. The boy from Canada."

"I know who he is. I came here with him."

Elizabeth swiped a hand across her eyes. "I had to keep him safe. I couldn't let anyone know where he'd gone, not even your father, so I made your father leave."

"But you said he was dead."

"But you found him anyway," Elizabeth reasoned. "You didn't believe me."

Toby heard Daphne's cool voice in his ear. "He's dead now."

He turned toward her. "Don't say it like that."

She shrugged. "This is all very touching, but it doesn't solve anything. Why aren't the police here? Who went to fetch them?"

"Victor Montard. He drove me here, and when we found the body, I stayed here to make sure no one touched anything, and he went with the two boys to fetch the police. He was only going as far as Hackbridge station. I don't understand."

"So Eddie got out to rescue his motorcycle, and Victor and Buddy went on toward the train station?"

"Yes."

"And never arrived there."

"That seems to be the case."

Daphne sighed. "This isn't going to be easy," she said, "and if we don't want to be tied up here for the rest of the night, I'm going to need to pull a few strings." She squared her shoulders. "Let's begin by calling the police ourselves. I've no intention of leaving Eddie and his mother alone. I'll use the radio in Slater's car."

"And then?" Toby asked.

"Then we find out how a Land Rover containing a member of the aristocracy and a resourceful young fugitive has managed to disappear somewhere between here and Hackbridge station."

CHAPTER TWENTY

Royal Sussex County Hospital, Brighton
Detective Inspector Percy Slater

The Scottish staff nurse bustled into Slater's room, with her starched apron crackling in outrage. The dull glow of the night-light revealed a mouth set in a grim line.

"You have a visitor," she declared, in a tone that suggested that the having of a visitor was akin to the stealing of the Stone of Scone.

Slater's mind pounded with questions. Good news or bad news? Daphne Raleigh to tell him the agent had been captured, or someone to tell him that Daphne was dead and the agent was in the wind? He pushed himself upright and gave a one-word response. "Good."

The nurse shook her head, her white cap bobbing. "We do not encourage visitors in the middle of the night."

Such a long night, he thought, and still not over. "What time is it?"

"It's past midnight, and you should be asleep."

"I was asleep until you came to tell me I had a visitor," Slater lied. Despite the drugs that served to put a distance between his brain and the pain in his injured leg, he had not been asleep.

The nurse sniffed and tugged fiercely at the blue counterpane until it lay across his bandaged leg without a wrinkle. "You must be very special," she said sourly, "to be allowed visitors this time of night."

A hand appeared from the darkness and rested on the nurse's shoulder, and a woman spoke. "Yes, he's very special. National security. You can leave us now. Close the door behind you."

Daphne waited until the door had clicked shut before she spoke again. "Your man Whitby is pretty damned good," she said.

"I told you."

Daphne perched on the edge of the bed. "I thought he was a bit of a prat at first."

"Most people do," Slater agreed, "but then they realize their mistake. Have you found what we're looking for?"

"No, not yet. It's a bit of a bollocks-up right now, and ..."

Her voice trailed away, and her hand plucked nervously at the bedclothes above his injured leg.

Slater resisted the urge to reach out and slap her hand away. "Daphne."

"What?"

"What's happened?"

She shook her head until her dark hair fell across her blind eye. "Sorry. I'm tired. It's been a long day."

Slater thought back on his day, which had started with a house falling on him and was finishing now with Daphne telling him that despite her admiration for Toby Whitby, the mission had fallen apart.

Daphne sighed. "Sorry, Slater. I should have asked you ... How are you feeling?"

"I'll live. So, tell me ..."

"Whitby found the boy, well, two boys, the Canadian and his cousin Eddie Powley."

"Cousin?"

"Oh, yes, I have a lot to tell you."

"Never mind that. Where are they now?"

"I know where Eddie is, and his mother, and unfortunately his father."

"What about his father?"

"Someone slit his throat and left him on his own doorstep ..."

Percy spared a thought for Randall Powley, the watercress farmer. He'd made it home from Dunkirk and survived the war, but not the peace. "What about the other boy, Whitby's client?"

"Disappeared."

"Again?"

"Yes, again, and he's not alone."

"Tell me."

"He left Randall Powley's house in the company of Victor Montard."

"Don't know him."

"I do. He's Viscount Pulborough has a big house on the South Downs; old family friend. I went to boarding school with his sister."

Slater couldn't keep the sarcasm out of his voice. "Of course you did."

"Hey," Daphne snapped. "I can't help the fact that my parents sent me to a fancy school. Do you want to know the rest of the story, or do you just want to sulk because you didn't go to boarding school?"

"Sorry. Tell me the rest."

"Buddy and Victor left in Victor's Land Rover. They were supposed to fetch the police. They never returned."

Slater shifted uneasily in his bed. "That's it? That's all you know?"

"Yes, that's all I know. Edward Powley said that they dropped him off to retrieve his motorcycle, and they were continuing on to Hackbridge station. The police say that they never arrived at the station, and they never alerted the police. I had to do that myself. We've searched the road between Powley's cottage and the railway station, but no sign of them. We've even had the dogs out. Nothing. It's too dark now. We'll start again in the morning."

Slater considered for a moment. "Tomorrow's Friday, isn't it?"

Daphne's shoulders slumped as she looked at her watch. "No. It's tomorrow already. Today is Friday. Leave it to me. We'll widen the search as soon as its daylight."

"You can't be involved," Slater said. "If it's Friday already, you're due at Arundel. Much as I'd like to find Whitby's client and your friend the Viscount, Arundel is more important. You'll have to let the locals deal with the missing viscount."

Daphne rubbed a weary hand across her eyes. "Arundel," she said. "How did I manage to forget about that?"

"Because you've allowed yourself to become personally involved," Slater said. "Obviously, you and the Viscount are friends, and—"

Daphne straightened her shoulders. "Leave it alone, Slater. My personal life is nothing to do with you. I'll be at Arundel in the morning. Will you?"

Slater glared at her. It was late; she was tired, but really ... "No, I won't come," he snapped. "I won't be going anywhere. I damned near lost my leg, and I need a couple of days off, if it's all right with you."

Daphne said nothing. She was just a dim shape at the end of his bed. He wondered if she'd fallen asleep. He tugged at the blanket and saw her lift her head.

"You could take Whitby," he suggested.

Brighton, Sussex
Toby Whitby

The Land Rover skewed sideways, sending up a cloud of red dust and hurling Toby against the door. The African driver hunched over the steering wheel, not daring to look behind. Toby looked. The bull elephant was closing the gap. He didn't know elephants could run so fast, and as for the noise … He thought that elephants trumpeted, but this one seemed to be knocking.

"Toby!"

Carol's voice banished the elephant and brought the glad awareness that he was not being chased by a bull elephant. He was, in fact, in his own bed with his wife beside him. He turned on his side and inched closer to her warm body.

"Toby, someone's at the door."

"What on earth?"

She was right, of course; someone was knocking. The last shreds of dream vanished. High noon on the sunbaked African plain was replaced with the tentative sunlight of an English morning.

Carol poked his arm. "Door," she said sleepily.

Toby blinked at the alarm clock on the bedside table. He had found one whose numbers could be read even without his glasses.

He sat up. "It's six o'clock," he complained. "Who on earth is it at this hour of the morning?"

He slid out of bed and reached for his glasses.

Carol pulled the eiderdown up around her shoulders. "You should answer the door before he wakes Anita."

"I'm going. I'm going."

He shrugged into his dressing gown and stumbled down the stairs toward the front door. Memory returned in an angry flood as he shuffled along the hall. He remembered the police arriving at Randall Powley's cottage, the questions, the protestations of innocence, and eventually Daphne flourishing her warrant card and silencing all complaints. Eddie and his mother had waited at the cottage, where Randall's body was now draped in a sheet, but Daphne and Toby had taken to the road in search of Victor Montard's Land Rover or any sign of Victor and Buddy.

That's why I was dreaming about a Land Rover, Toby thought as he set about releasing the chain and unlocking the dead bolt. He hesitated for a moment with his hand on the doorknob. What was wrong with him? He should ask who was knocking. He shouldn't just open the door to anyone. He had a wife and daughter to protect. He blamed his carelessness on lack of sleep. It had been way past midnight when Daphne had dropped him off at his front door, having failed to find any trace of the Land Rover.

Of course, if he shouted through the door, he would probably wake Anita, and if he didn't, maybe he would be admitting a murderer. He weighed the two probabilities and opened the door.

Colonel Hugh Trewin stood on the doorstep with his mustache bristling energetically and a navy-blue blazer held up for Toby to inspect.

"Morning, young Whitby."

"Good morning … uh … what … why?"

Hugh thrust the blazer forward. "Try it on. I think it will do the trick. He didn't think you would have one."

"One what?"

"A blazer with a regimental badge. You can't go in a lawyer's suit. That would be sure to attract attention. Tweeds would be acceptable, but you're not a tweedy kind of person, are you? So Slater thought this would do nicely. Mind if I come in? Can't stand here on the doorstep all day."

Toby stepped back and allowed Hugh into the hallway. Carol's voice floated down the stairs.

"Grandpa Hugh, what a surprise."

Toby shook his head. Colonel Trewin was grandpa to Slater's stepson, Eric. He was not Anita's grandpa. No one ever spoke of Anita's parentage and the fact that her father had been a German prisoner of war. Toby's mind was wandering. He brought it back under control. If Carol wanted to address the colonel as Grandpa Hugh, that was not a matter to discuss now, and it surely had nothing to do with the fact that Hugh was holding up a regimental blazer as if measuring Toby for size.

Carol drifted down the stairs with her red hair picking up the early morning sunlight streaming in from the landing windows.

"Cup of tea?" she asked casually, as if this early morning visit was nothing unusual.

Toby did not have her patience. "What do you want?" he demanded as he followed Hugh and Carol into the kitchen. "Do you know what time it is?"

"Yes, I know. We'll have to get a move on if we're to have you ready in time. Do you have a good pair of gray flannels?"

Carol bustled over to the sink and began to fill the kettle. Toby faced the colonel. "What's this all about?"

"Well," said Hugh, "I'm sure it's on a need-to-know basis, and I obviously don't need to know. I'm just following orders."

"Whose orders?"

"Inspector Slater. I've been staying with Dorothy and Eric, trying to keep their spirits up. So, Slater rang me this morning and told me to get over here with my regimental blazer and tie, and get you kitted out for the morning meeting at Arundel Castle."

Arundel Castle! Slater had told him about Arundel. The Duke of Norfolk, Earl Marshal of England, was heading the committee to plan the coronation. The planning committee was meeting at the Duke's castle in Arundel. The Duke of Edinburgh would be in attendance, not to mention any number of other aristocratic notables. Was today the day?

"Slater said to tell you that he couldn't be there, but he trusted you to take his place, and you'd have another of his people with you; someone called Daphne. He didn't give me a last name."

"I know who she is."

Behind him, Carol turned off the water and placed the kettle on the stove. Toby licked his dry lips. Perhaps a cup of tea would help him bring the morning into focus.

"Why do I have to wear your blazer?"

"Ah." The colonel nodded knowingly. "A regimental blazer will see you through all kinds of difficulties with no questions asked."

"But I'm not in your regiment. I don't even know—"

"Duke of Cornwall's Light Infantry," Trewin said. "Distinguished ourselves on the Western Front."

"I can't ..."

"No, of course not. No one would take you for a veteran of the First World War," Hugh agreed. "We showed up again for the second, Egypt mainly. No need to say anything. Just wear the blazer and keep quiet. Slip your arms in, and let me see if it fits."

Toby reluctantly removed his dressing gown. He emphatically did not want to wear Hugh's blazer. As he slid his arms into the sleeves, he was suffused with angry embarrassment. He had no right to wear the insignia of this regiment, or of any other regiment. He had not served.

Carol was suddenly beside him with her hand on his arm. "It's all right, love. I know how you feel, but if Percy wants you to do this, he has a good reason. He trusts you, Toby. He can't go himself, so he's sending the very best person he can think of, and that's you. So just put the blazer on. It's all in a good cause."

Toby managed a reluctant laugh. "I'm not doing a Cornish accent."

Hugh waved a dismissive hand. "If you're mixing with the hoi polloi, they wouldn't know a Cornishman from a Scouser."

He smoothed the blazer over Toby's shoulders. "Fits a treat." He took a step back and nodded approvingly. He reached out and touched the gold-encrusted badge. "That badge would stop a bullet."

"I hope it won't have to," Toby admitted.

The kettle shrieked a warning, and Carol poured hot water into the teapot. "Drink that, love, while I go upstairs and iron your shirt. I've made you a sandwich."

In a morning of surprises, Daphne provided yet another surprise by arriving outside Toby's house in his Morris Oxford.

He stood on his front doorstep, arrayed in Hugh's regimental blazer and tie and his own gray flannel pants, and stared at his car. The paintwork shone in the sunlight; the chrome gleamed; and the engine ticked over with the precision of a metronome.

"How did you do that?" Toby asked, remembering how he had left the Morris, mud caked and completely dead at the edge of the Downs.

"A clean car draws less attention than a dirty one," Daphne replied, "and no one should be asked to drive that dratted Wolseley, so this is what we're using."

Toby stared at her. "When did you have time to do this? Didn't you sleep?"

She curled her lip. "I didn't do it myself. We have people to do this sort of thing. And no, I didn't sleep. I have trained myself to do without."

Toby considered his own attire, gleaming shoes, pressed flannels, a white shirt that Carol had starched until it crackled. Daphne wore uncompromising black, a loose black shirt, black pants, serviceable shoes. "Are you going in like that?"

"I'm not going in. You are. I can be recognized, but no one knows you. You're a minor flunky in the Duke of Edinburgh's entourage. Don't speak to the Duke. He doesn't know you and doesn't know why you're there, but you will have an appropriate pass."

"What about you?"

"I will be ... around."

"What am I looking for?"

"I'm not sure. The people outside can take care of anyone lurking in the bushes or crawling through the long grass. You are looking for someone who doesn't fit in."

"I don't fit in," Toby protested.

Daphne surveyed him. "You fit in surprisingly well. I'm willing to believe that you're holding a position at Buckingham Palace, equerry, private secretary, something like that." She smiled. "You'll do very well, but what's in the parcel?"

Toby felt a flush of embarrassment. "It's a sandwich for my lunch. My wife is trying to fatten me up."

They walked to the car. Daphne reached into the back seat and emerged with a small canvas bag. "Take your jacket off."

"I just put it on."

"Well, you can just take it off again. This is a small two-way radio. It's called a walkie-talkie."

"I know what it's called," Toby replied.

"But you don't know how it works. I mean, you were never in uniform so ..."

Toby felt the familiar sting, a mixture of shame and resentment. "I know how it works," he insisted. "I was on fire watch in London." He knew that he was raising his voice in pointless anger, but he could not stop himself. "In London," he repeated, "on a rooftop in Whitehall, every night while the city burned around us. Yes, we had radios, and yes, I know how this bloody thing works."

Daphne's injured fingers pressed buttons and turned dials. The radio squawked. She nodded. "All right, we're set up. Take your jacket off, and for goodness' sake, get rid of that sandwich."

No, Toby thought, *not while Carol's watching*. She makes me sandwiches because she cares. He was smiling as he reached into the car and put the wrapped sandwich into the glove compartment.

With the sandwich safely stowed away, he shed the blazer and stood patiently as Daphne buckled him into a harness that had probably been designed to conceal a handgun. It worked surprisingly well to conceal the radio and allowed his borrowed blazer to hang smoothly with no unsightly bulges.

Daphne stood back and admired her handiwork. "Looks good. Now get into the passenger seat. I'm driving."

Toby resisted the urge to argue over trivialities and allowed Daphne to have her small victory. He settled into the passenger seat; the first time he had been a passenger in his own car. He waited until Daphne was behind the steering wheel before he spoke.

"I don't mind doing this, but …"

"But what?"

"This won't get us any closer to finding Buddy and Victor. I'm concerned that something really bad has happened to them."

Daphne put the Morris in gear and drove smoothly away from the curb. "I agree, it probably has, but for today at least, you'll have to leave it to the local police to find them."

"Local police? You mean the Surrey police?"

"Yes. They're searching the woods around Powley's cottage and the road between the place where Eddie retrieved his motorbike and Hackbridge station, which is where Victor failed to appear."

"It was a massive great Land Rover," Toby complained. "How hard is it to find something like that? If we couldn't find it last night, what makes them think they can find it this morning? Meantime, I don't know what to tell Buddy's foster parents. They must be beside themselves with worry."

"I'm sure they are, but they're not your concern."

"They're my clients."

"They're not your priority this morning. We're after bigger game. There's a reason why Jack Farren was calling himself Robert Cameron and had papers assigning him to duty at Arundel, and it was not because he was looking for Buddy. There is no doubt that Farren's an agent of a foreign government. Discovering that Buddy is here was a bonus, but it's not his main purpose."

Toby could not imagine why it had taken him so long to see the whole picture. "You're expecting him to turn up at Arundel?"

Daphne nodded. "Jack Farren may have been planning on using his Inspector Cameron disguise to get in, but he won't be doing that now. He knows we're onto that game, but he's not going to give up. He'll be there, and he's already killed three people."

"Three?"

"Buddy's mother, Winnie Widdicome, and Randall Powley."

Toby frowned. "I'm not so sure about Powley. I don't see how Farren had time to get from Tooting to Hackbridge. You said Mrs. Powley was hiding in the ladies' loo because Farren was outside, looking for her."

Daphne kept her concentration on the road ahead. "Mrs. Powley was scared to death, and I have no idea how long she'd been hiding. Farren was probably long gone, but she just didn't know it."

"But why kill Powley?"

"Because Powley would recognize him." Daphne turned her head briefly to look at him. "You need to concentrate on what we're doing here and stop trying to make a mountain out of a molehill. Farren killed all three people. Problem solved. Concentrate on the task ahead."

Toby reluctantly set aside the problem of Randall Powley's murder. Perhaps Daphne was correct. No doubt Farren had been long gone when Daphne arrived to rescue Mrs. Powley. Of course, there was the question of rigor mortis. Powley's body was limp. Rigor had not set in.

"What's your rank?"

Toby's brain snapped to attention. Now was not the time to wonder about Powley.

"Well?"

Toby touched the badge on Hugh's blazer. "Lieutenant?"

"No, you're too old to be a lieutenant. You're a captain. Now stop daydreaming, and put the rest of your story together, just in case."

Toby fought down his rising panic. Having never even met the Queen's husband, he was to pass himself off as a member of the Duke's staff. Worse than that, he was to pretend to be a Cornishman who had served as a captain with the Duke of Cornwall's Light Infantry in Egypt. Egypt? Pyramids, sphinx, the Suez Canal. Cornwall? Tin mines, moors, and King Arthur. He knew nothing in any detail about any of those things.

They left the outskirts of Brighton on a road that climbed upward and skirted the edge of the South Downs. Arundel's Norman Keep was the first part of the castle to come into view. It sat on a high bluff protecting the River Arun and the valley below. As they drew closer, he saw the castle in all its glory of high stone walls, gothic ramparts, and the stunning Victorian addition, where the Duke had his residence. It was a castle out of every child's fairy tale. Toby wished that Anita could see it. Well, maybe one day, but definitely not today; not when the approach road was alive with limousines and police cars.

Daphne slowed for a checkpoint. A constable inspected her warrant card. Instead of waving her forward, he indicated a parking place at the side of the road.

"Now what?" Toby asked.

"I don't know," Daphne replied. "I'll give them five minutes, and then …"

What she would do next remained a mystery. They had waited no more than thirty seconds before Reginald Peacock, the chief constable, came into view, dressed in full uniform, with medal ribbons and a military air he had never displayed in his office.

He looked in at the window and gestured to Toby. "Out!"

Toby hesitated.

"Get out," Peacock insisted. "I want to look at you."

Daphne shrugged. "You'd better do it."

"I thought you weren't under police command."

"I'm not," Daphne replied, "but Peacock's the one who is going to get you into the castle, so you'd better get out."

Toby climbed out and stood at the side of the road. The chief constable circled him disapprovingly. "Stand up straight. No one's going to believe you're on the Duke's staff if you stand like that. They're all ex-military. Shoulders back. Chin up."

He circled again and tugged at the set of the blazer across Toby's shoulders. "All right. You'll do, but for goodness' sake, stand up straight, and don't speak unless you're spoken to." He stepped back. "You can't arrive in that car. We don't have a spare Bentley, so I'll ride up with you in a police vehicle. Say goodbye to Miss Raleigh. You're on your own now."

A broad road wound its way through landscaped grounds, revealing sunlit vistas across the river valley. The massive stone walls of the Norman Keep towered above them at first and then gave way to the gothic arches and mullioned windows of later additions. The car continued to climb until it passed beneath a stone arch and came to a halt in a stone quadrangle, a Victorian fantasy of delicate stonework, fountains, and flower beds. The beauty of this interior garden was somewhat masked by the presence of a dozen vehicles, ranging from Bentleys to delivery vans.

Toby stepped out of the police car. Peacock accompanied him to the open front door and returned the salute of the police constable on duty. "Duke of Edinburgh's staff," he said. "Missed his train. Duke's probably looking for him."

"Should I escort him to the Duke, sir?"

Peacock shook his head. "Good heavens, no. You can't leave your post for the sake of one of the Duke's minor flunkies. He can find his own way."

Toby tugged at his blazer, worried that the bulge of the radio might put the constable in mind of the bulge of a weapon. He nodded curtly to Peacock and strolled in through the front door, attempting to look both casual and military at the same time.

The entryway buzzed with activity, men in tweeds, blazers, and military uniforms all moving slowly in one direction. He followed and soon found himself in a long gallery lined with portraits of the Duke's ancestors. Every painted face seemed to wear a look of suspicious disapproval.

The long gallery brought him to a cavernous reception room with arched windows, oriental rugs, and a scattering of red velvet chairs and brocade sofas. Perhaps the Duke of Norfolk himself, the Earl Marshal of England, was in this room, but he was most definitely not the center of attention. That honor belonged to the Queen's husband. Toby had seen pictures of the Prince, but he was unprepared for the impact of the man himself. Philip carried himself like a Greek god. Tall and bronzed, with his blond hair catching the sunlight, he dominated the room with his physical presence and impatient gestures.

Toby made his way to a shadowy corner, where a massive Chinese vase cast a deep shadow. He stepped into the shade, watching and listening.

At Philip's urging, a group of men broke free of their various conversations and followed a servant in formal morning dress toward a gilded door flanked by a pair of marble statues. The Prince raised his voice to call to a middle-aged man in a tweed suit who was still engaged in conversation.

"If His Grace, the Duke of Norfolk, would care to join us, we can begin our meeting," Philip said. His tone, his accent, everything about him spoke of barely concealed contempt.

The Duke of Norfolk turned a sour expression on the young prince, but he abandoned his conversation and joined the waiting group.

The servant opened the gilded door for the committee members. Toby caught a glimpse of another room, lit by floor-to-ceiling windows and dominated by a long table. The men, led by Philip, filed in through the door, with the host hurrying to catch up with them. The door closed. Toby assumed that the committee was now in session.

"Do you see what I mean?" a voice asked in rising anger. Toby shrank back. The speaker was very close to him and still complaining. "Did you hear the way that upstart talked to the Earl Marshal, ordering him about in his own home? Philip might be the Queen's husband, but that's all he is; he's a nobody."

"Careful, old chap," another voice soothed. "Come over here. We don't want any of Edinburgh's people hearing us."

Toby took another step backward until he was crammed against the wall. A group of men formed a knot in the shade of the Ming vase. If they looked behind the vase, they would see him, but they were not looking. They stood in a huddle, speaking softly. Their complaining voices flowed back and forth.

"He's made himself chairman of the Coronation Committee."

"Disgraceful. The Duke is the Earl Marshal. He planned the last coronation. He doesn't need that upstart foreigner to tell him how to do it."

"I heard that Philip is pushing to have the whole thing televised."

"Oh, really. Whatever will he think of next?"

"He'll have himself crowned king if we're not careful."

"Oh, I don't think so, old man. Prince consort maybe, but not king."

"Not yet, but one day. He'll bide his time and be the power behind the throne for a while, and when it's obvious Elizabeth isn't up to the job, he'll step in."

A hissing command cut through the whispered complaints. "Stop talking. You never know who may be listening. It's all under control. We have our man in place, and I suggest we move out of here before something nasty happens."

Toby drew in a silent breath. Casual complaining conversation had suddenly become a conspiracy.

The owner of the commanding voice was no longer speaking softly. His voice was loud and hearty, and he seemed to be moving into the center of the room.

Toby took a tentative step forward and peered around the vase. A squat, gray-haired man in an abominable tweed suit was forcing his way through the waiting knot of secretaries, equerries, and supporters.

"Drinks in the Long Gallery," Tweed Suit announced. "Don't be shy. Come along. No point in waiting around here. Someone will fetch us if we're needed. Meantime, I could use a snifter."

The announcement was greeted with a murmur of voices that eventually crystalized into a general agreement that the meeting would last for a while and drinks would be a really good idea. Toby watched from the shadows, trying to pick out the conspirators. He knew he could give a good description of the man in the tweed suit: sixtyish, red-faced, and a bulbous nose; almost a caricature of an English squire. As for the others, he could say nothing. They had already merged into the crowd that moved purposefully toward the Long Gallery. They were all men, not a woman among them. Although they were obliged to put a woman on the throne, apparently, they felt that no women should be involved in planning the event.

Toby reached under his jacket to retrieve the radio. The threat had been clear and simple and not open to misinterpretation: *We have our man in place, and I suggest we move out of here before something nasty happens.* Toby analyzed the conspirator's words. Tweed Suit only wanted to move as far as the Long Gallery. Obviously, he was expecting the nasty event to be something small and contained, not a major explosion that would kill Tweed Suit and the rest of his conspirators but something that would remove any possibility of the Duke of Edinburgh becoming king. An assassination?

As the last of the drinkers made their way out of the room, a servant appeared, swimming against the tide and holding a tray of glasses. Toby sank back into the shadows and watched the man's progress through the empty room. In stark comparison to the tweed-suited and blazered gentry who had been occupying the room, the servant was formally dressed in a starched white shirt and a black cutaway coat with brass buttons. He was an unusual-looking man with a round, perfectly bald head. The lack of hair extended to his eyebrows but not to a thin dark pencil mustache.

Toby froze in place as the man passed by with the glasses clinking and covering the sound of Toby's sudden intake of breath. He noted little nicks and drops of blood on the bald head. This man was not naturally bald; he had shaved his head. He had no hair and no eyebrows, but if this man had eyebrows, they would surely be thick and sandy, and if he had hair, it would only be a small amount. Dress this man in a raincoat, and he would be Inspector Robert Cameron; remove the raincoat, and he would be Jack Farren, German agent. He had rid himself of his most prominent features and squeezed into a servant's uniform, and now he was walking through Arundel Castle as if he owned the place.

With one eye on Farren's rapidly retreating back, Toby pressed the talk button. He grimaced at the radio's sudden squawk. Farren walked past the door of the committee room and continued on along the carpeted hallway.

CHAPTER TWENTY ONE

Daphne Raleigh

Daphne watched from the deep shadows of a clump of willows. She felt nothing but disdain for the security arrangements that had resulted in the Coronation Committee meeting not only in a first-floor room but in a room where ornamental shrubs, ideal for concealment, grazed the windowsills, and trees crowded in against the walls.

The committee room was part of the updated Victorian addition to the castle. No doubt it had adequate lighting and electricity and good acoustics that would allow every quarrelsome member of the committee to be heard. It did not, however, have the security of the massive stone walls and high-set windows of the original castle.

Well, no one had consulted Daphne about the choice of room, or anything else. In fact, very few people knew that she was here today, representing a branch of the government that had not yet been given a name. She was not MI5 or MI6, and no longer even MI19, the shadowy group that had engineered her final escape from France.

She flexed her right leg, feeling the familiar scratch of pain in her ankle. The pain and the limp served to remind her of the months she had been sheltered in Perpignan, waiting for her ankle to heal; waiting to be led like a child along the escape route to Spain.

She parted the concealing leaves and looked out at the landscape. Oh, how she had longed to be back here, away from the dust and heat of that attic apartment in occupied France. If she could no longer serve the Resistance, then she wanted to be home again. She needed to see Leo and to know why he had not come for her. Was he even alive? No one in the shadowy underworld of the Resistance could take the time to find out what had happened to him. It was enough that they risked their lives day after day to shelter downed airmen, escaped prisoners, and betrayed Resistance workers, and guide them into Spain. She could not ask them to find out what had happened to the man who was supposed to fly her out.

It was not until she was home that she discovered the truth.

June 1944
Sussex

She could hear her father rattling the lawnmower back and forth across the remaining patch of lawn. Most of the garden had been given over to vegetables and to the chicken coop, where a hen was clucking loudly to announce the advent of an egg. Daphne's mother would no doubt present the egg scrambled or poached as a supplement to build up her daughter's health.

Daphne was a stranger in this house, where her parents had come to live in exile from their diplomatic post. Ambassadors were not needed now that the whole world was at war. Her parents lived in Sussex now, in unaccustomed poverty, while Adelaide Raleigh nursed the daughter who had never been more than an occasional visitor in her mother's far-flung life.

A knock at the bedroom door, and Adelaide entered with a teacup. Her hand was trembling, and the tea slopped onto the saucer, wasting both the milk and the tea itself. Daphne leaned forward to take the cup, but her mother resisted and set it down on the bedside table.

Daphne retrieved the cup and took a sip of tea. "I'm going to get up," she announced.

"The doctor—"

"Please, Mother, don't worry about the doctor. I feel fine, and the doctor should not waste any more time with me. Whatever is going to heal has healed, and the rest of it is something I just have to live with."

Sympathy radiated from Adelaide's eyes. "There's nothing to be done about your eye," she said, "but the scar on your face, well, we could maybe find a good surgeon, and—"

"It is what it is," Daphne declared.

"Perhaps you could grow your hair."

Daphne tugged at her tangled hair. "It's already grown. I just have to get it styled."

Her mother opened her mouth to make another suggestion, but Daphne forestalled her. "I'm going to Montard Hall. I want to find out about Leo. I know he's

241

not dead, but he doesn't answer my letters, and no one will tell me anything, so I'm going in person. Someone there will tell me."

"Oh, Daphne." Adelaide's hand, yellowed by years in the tropics, stroked ineffectually at the bedclothes. "Don't go there. It won't do any good."

Daphne swung her legs out of the bed. "I'm going. If Daddy doesn't have enough petrol to drive me, I'll take a train, or a bus or whatever is available."

She felt an unwelcome prickling in her eyes, astonished that even the damaged eye still retained its ability to shed tears. "I'm not angry with Leo," she insisted. "I know now that he was shot down over the Channel. None of my injuries are his fault. I just want to see him."

Her mother's voice was suddenly firm and insistent. "No, you don't. You don't want to see him, and he doesn't want to see you."

"Of course he does."

"No, Daphne, he doesn't. Your father has tried to see him, and Leo has made it clear that he doesn't want visitors."

"But if I go to Montard Hall—"

"He's not there. He's at the Queen Victoria Hospital in East Grinstead."

"So I'll go to East Grinstead."

"It's a hospital for burn patients."

Daphne reached for her slippers. "I'm going."

"It's a hospital for men who are badly burned; very badly burned."

Daphne hesitated. "How badly?"

"They're doing their best. They have all kinds of new treatments."

"How badly?"

"He won't see you."

"How badly?"

"He has no face."

August 1952
Arundel Castle, Sussex

The radio clipped to her belt emitted an urgent squawk. Toby's voice, distorted by the radio, was surprisingly calm, and his radio protocol was faultless, but what he said made no sense.

"Jack Farren is here. He's going to assassinate someone, over."

Toby Whitby

"Say again, over." Daphne's voice was sharp and urgent.

"Jack Farren is here. I'm going after him, over."

"Farren? Say again. Farren? Over."

Daphne's voice was too loud. What would happen if Farren heard her and turned to look? Toby groped for the volume control. Yes, he had told Daphne that he had used a walkie-talkie in the war, but that was ten years ago, and this radio was nothing like the one he had carried on the roof of the Ministry of Defence. He looked up and caught a glimpse of Farren disappearing through a doorway.

He keyed the microphone. "I'm going after him, over and out."

"No."

Her voice died abruptly as Toby depressed the off button and stuffed the radio back into its harness. He kept his eyes focused on the place where Farren had disappeared. The corridor was lined with closed doors, and he could not afford to go through the wrong doorway.

He found the door that Farren had used. It was an inconspicuous baize service door that opened smoothly at his touch and gave him a view of a long corridor with a tiled floor, dim electric lights, and dingy plaster walls. Here was the place where the grandeur of the castle ended abruptly and upstairs met downstairs. This was where servants would bustle about with their coal scuttles and brooms and trays of refreshments. From these corridors, they would appear when needed and vanish when not needed.

Toby had only very limited experience with castles, mansions, and manors, but he knew enough to guess that the Victorian reception rooms at Arundel would have inconspicuous doors set into the paneling or concealed behind columns; doors that would allow a servant to glide in and out without disturbing the guests.

Toby came close to stumbling over the tray that Farren had abandoned on the floor. The walls here were smooth, uninterrupted by doorways, and leading away into darkness. Toby paused automatically and polished his glasses. He was replacing them when a light flared at the end of the corridor, revealing a passage turning to the left.

Toby approached cautiously, sidling along the wall in the hope that Farren would not be tempted to look behind him. His groping fingers found the light switch Farren had used to light up the corridor ahead. He considered turning off the light and plunging Farren into darkness. He peered around the corner. Too late. Farren was nowhere in sight. Baize doors were lined up on either side of the empty corridor. Farren could have gone through any of these doors and could be anywhere in the labyrinth of service tunnels. Turning off the light would accomplish nothing.

He leaned against the wall and forced himself to think. Why was Farren here? Why had he gone along this corridor? The tweed-suited conspirator had promised that something nasty was about to happen; something that would solve the problem of the Duke of Edinburgh. The conspirators were not planning to blow themselves up, so whatever was about to happen would be confined to damaging the Queen's husband, or at least confined to the committee room, and that probably meant a well-placed bullet or two.

Toby drew a map in his mind and mentally retraced his footsteps. He had entered through the baize door, followed a long corridor, and turned left. If his calculations were correct, none of these doors would open into the committee room. He would need to make another left turn. Of course, any of these doors could be concealing another corridor that would lead to yet another and eventually to the committee room. He shook his head. That kind of thinking would only serve to paralyze him. He had to go with his first thought. Follow this corridor until it turned to the left, and be quick about it. He'd spent too much time thinking.

Throwing caution to the wind, he ran the length of the corridor until he came to a junction with another dimly lit passageway. He paused, peered around the corner, and was rewarded by the sight of Farren just ahead, standing outside another baize door.

He hesitated. Farren had not yet seen him. He did not know he was being followed. If he turned now, Toby would be a sitting duck, but if Toby stayed silent, nothing would prevent Farren from entering the committee room, and even if he called out and challenged Farren, it would make no difference. Farren could kill Toby and still kill the Duke. On the other hand, Farren couldn't kill Toby if he couldn't see him.

Toby removed his glasses and tucked them into his pocket. He would not need glasses for what he was about to do. He ran his hands along the wall, trusting that he would find a light switch at the junction of the passageway. Aristocrats were notably miserly with their money when it came to servants. They would not permit lights to blaze night and day along empty corridors, and so there would be a switch. He breathed a sigh of relief as his fingers found the metal plate. He squinted to bring Farren into fuzzy focus. Farren's hand was now on the door.

Toby flicked the switch and plunged the corridor into darkness. Without waiting for his eyes to adjust, he hurled himself forward with his head and shoulders down. For a moment, he was a schoolboy again, deep into a rugby grudge match and proud to play in the first fifteen for his school. Farren grunted as Toby barreled into him at waist level. Struggling to stay upright, Toby caromed off Farren and fell through the door into the committee room. Angry voices assaulted his ears; feet shuffled; chairs scraped against the floor; and light flooded the corridor as Toby wedged his body into the doorway. Flat on his back, panting for breath, Toby waited for the inevitable gunshot, but nothing came, only hands reaching for him.

He scrambled away, ignoring the voices behind him, and flung himself back into the corridor. In the light that spilled from the committee room, he caught an unfocused glimpse of Farren running. The door closed again, and darkness descended for a brief moment. He heard raised voices behind him, and the door opened again; light returned. The voices behind him increased their volume, and the door closed again. Toby could only imagine the chaos of the committee room, filled with opinionated aristocrats opening and closing the door, and all trying to work out what had just happened. Was this a disturbance among the servants or a threat to their own lives? Should they open the door, or should they keep it closed?

Toby took advantage of the chaos and sprinted through the dark in the direction he had last seen Farren running. Ahead of him another door opened, adding bright light to the corridor; brighter than the electric lights, brighter than the committee room. Had Farren chanced upon a door to the outside? No, not chanced; there was no element of luck involved. Of course Farren had an escape route planned. He had not intended to be a martyr.

If Farren had planned a way to leave the castle, he probably had someone waiting for him. Toby increased his pace. Farren had gained a head start while Toby was wedged in the doorway of the committee room, and Farren had the advantage of knowing where he was going. The corridor was suddenly dark again. The door to the outside had closed. Toby could hear voices behind him. The committee members were taking action, and the chase was on, not for Farren but for Toby. No one had seen Farren, but they had all seen Toby in his borrowed regimental blazer. The lights in the corridor flicked on. Someone had found the light switch.

Toby saw the fuzzy outline of a door ahead. This must be the door to the outside; Farren's escape route.

He groped for the door handle, hoping that Farren had panicked and failed to lock the door behind him. He flung the door open and squinted in the bright sunlight. He blinked and tried to bring the world into focus. He seemed to be in a cobbled courtyard. He could discern Farren as a running figure. He fumbled for his glasses, but before he could find them, Farren dropped out of sight.

Toby ran forward and suddenly found the ground falling away beneath him. He stumbled and fell onto his hands and knees. He lifted his head. He could still see Farren flailing his arms as he raced down a steep grassy slope.

Toby scrambled to his feet. Farren was a dark shape in a world of misty green and blue, but a flash of white shirt told Toby that Farren had turned to face him. Toby waited for the impact of a bullet. Surely Farren had a weapon. How else had he intended to carry out an assassination of the Duke of Edinburgh? Farren turned away again. *He must have dropped the gun. He's not going to shoot me.*

Confident now that he was not going to be taken out by a bullet, Toby leaped down the slope and hurled himself at Farren, bringing them both crashing to the ground.

They rolled downhill together, Farren cursing and shouting, and Toby hanging on to Farren's coat with fierce concentration. Their tumble brought them to the edge of the road, both gasping for breath. Farren surged to his feet and aimed a kick at Toby's head. Toby rolled, and Farren's kick caught him on the side of his head, and for a moment, the world faded.

Farren's voice reached him through the ringing in his ears. "I'm taking my boy."

Toby rolled over onto his hands and knees, and struggled to bring Farren's fleeing figure into focus. A vehicle, no more than a dark, blurry shape screeched to a halt beside them. Farren climbed in, and the vehicle accelerated away.

As the sound of the engine faded, it was replaced by a babble of excited voices. Toby reached into his pocket for his glasses.

"He has a gun."

Toby abandoned his attempt to retrieve his glasses and raised his hands high in the air as the angry faces came into view.

He kept his hands in the air as rough hands explored his blazer and his pockets. One of the voices spoke above the general babble. "Duke of Cornwall's Light Infantry? I don't think so. The blighter's not from my regiment."

A rough hand ripped the walkie-talkie from its pouch with a shout of triumph.

Toby said nothing. He decided to let Daphne deal with them.

Detective Inspector Percy Slater

"You didn't have to come. We have everything under control."

Slater wheeled himself forward and looked up at the chief constable's face. "You have nothing under control."

"The Prince is safe."

Slater spun the wheelchair in a circle, taking in the view from the terrace. The grounds of Arundel Castle swarmed with blue-coated officers and green-coated soldiers.

"If my man Whitby hadn't intervened, the Prince would be dead."

"Your man?" Peacock expostulated. "He's not one of your men. He's a lawyer, that's all. Just a lawyer."

Slater smiled inwardly. Too many people had made the mistake of thinking that Toby Whitby was just a lawyer. At that moment, seeing Toby conversing with Prince Philip, Slater was inordinately proud of his friend. He was equally proud of himself for suggesting that Daphne Raleigh should take Toby on as her partner.

He watched as Toby shook hands with the Duke of Edinburgh. The men were the same height and the same build, tall and rangy. The Prince had the burnished good looks of a man who had been born into privilege and married into unimaginable wealth by winning the heart of the Queen of England. Toby, on the other hand, was sporting a cauliflower ear, and his glasses sat awkwardly on his swollen nose. He had abandoned Colonel Trewin's regimental blazer, and his white shirt was ornamented with grass stains. His brown hair was desperately in need of a barber.

Toby approached with a grin on his face. "How's the leg?"

Slater returned the grin. "How's the hero?"

Toby shook his head. "I'm no hero. I let him get away, and your friend Daphne is hopping mad with me."

"Because the Prince wants to give you a medal? Daphne has her own fair share of medals."

Toby shook his head. "The Prince didn't say anything about a medal. He was more interested in inviting me to join in one of his drinking parties. I told him I was married, and he laughed and said so was he, and so what? I'm not sure I like him."

"So you won't be going drinking with him?"

"No, I won't. I've had enough of the aristocracy, thank you very much."

Slater heard Daphne before he saw her. "Do we have to report Mr. Whitby's anti-royalist tendencies? Perhaps he's a communist."

Slater swiveled in his chair, and his frustration gave way to a grin. Daphne had a limp and a blind eye; Toby could not see without his glasses; and Slater was temporarily in a wheelchair and permanently without one of his arms. They were not exactly the three musketeers, but somehow they had managed to foil an assassination attempt.

Daphne rested her hand on the back of the wheelchair. "That wonderful old colonel and his girlfriend are here to see you," she said.

"Colonel Trewin?" Slater asked.

Toby grinned from ear to ear. "His girlfriend?"

"She works in your office."

"Girlfriend?" Toby repeated. "I thought so."

Slater met Toby's eyes. "Miss Clark?"

Toby raised his eyebrows. "Yes, indeed. Miss Clark." He looked at Daphne. "Why are they here?"

"They came to get me," Slater said. "I am required to take sick leave. Dorothy, Eric, and I are going to Hugh Trewin's house in Cornwall so I can convalesce. I was not aware that Miss Clark was coming with us.

Toby continued to grin and shook his head. "I can't wait to tell Carol."

Daphne's smile faded as she looked at Toby. "You need to learn radio protocol," she said.

Slater looked up at her, sensing the change in mood. "What's going on?"

Toby shrugged. "I failed at being a secret agent. I panicked. I dialed Daphne up on the radio, squawked into the microphone, and then just let her drop. She had no idea what was going on until all hell broke loose. She's right; I messed up. If I'd told her what I'd seen, she could have alerted the security forces, and whoever drove Farren away would not have had such an easy time of it."

"And who was that?" Slater asked. "Who drove him away? Who is his accomplice?"

Toby's eyes were thoughtful behind the thick lenses. "I don't think it's an accomplice. I think it's the other way around. This has something to do with Farren's son. I didn't hear much after he kicked me in the ear, but I did hear him say that he was taking his son."

Slater took a deep breath as the pieces of the puzzle began to fall into place. "He wants to take Buddy?"

Toby nodded. "I think that once Farren discovered that his son had come back from Canada, he decided to kill two birds with one stone. He was here to worm his way into the Arundel meeting, but while he was waiting, he turned up at Brighton Police Station with his forged papers and took over the search for Buddy. He knows we're onto him now that he's blown his assassination attempt, but I don't think he'll leave without his son."

"Of course he will," Daphne said. "He doesn't want him. He murdered the boy's mother, and Buddy had to be spirited away to Canada to keep him safe. Why would Farren want him now?"

Slater thought back on the many abusive men he'd encountered in his career. "Just because he liked to beat up his wife, doesn't mean he'd hurt his son. The two things are separate in his mind. Buddy never said anything about his father harming him, did he?"

"He was afraid of him," Toby replied.

"Of course he was afraid. He saw what was happening to his mother, but I don't think Farren ever laid a hand on the boy himself. I've seen it before. He's not going to harm his own son."

"Until he discovers that Buddy isn't his son," Toby said.

Slater felt his carefully constructed jigsaw puzzle begin to fall apart again. "What do you mean?"

Toby shrugged. "According to Muriel, the village gossip, Jack Farren wasn't Buddy's father. Nina was already pregnant when she met

Jack, but she didn't tell him. He may not have suspected anything when Buddy was a little boy, but he will now. Don't forget, Farren hasn't seen him yet. He's been looking for him, but he hasn't seen him, but when he does, he'll know."

"So who is his real father?" Slater asked.

Toby looked at him thoughtfully. "I don't think it matters."

"Of course it does."

Toby shook his head. "No, it doesn't. His real father is the man who raised him, and that is Roy Stewart. We need to find Buddy, return him to the Stewarts, and get him on the next boat back to Canada."

Slater opened his mouth to disagree, but Toby silenced him with an angry hand gesture.

"Nothing good has happened to Buddy since he arrived here, and I have a duty to my clients. His foster parents haven't seen him in four days. It's no good me telling them that I saw him yesterday and lost him again as soon as I found him. And by the way, we seem to have lost a viscount. Is anyone looking for him? Do you think there might be some significance in him going missing?"

"Perhaps Farren's done something to him."

Toby shook his head. "No, I don't think so. I think it's the other way around."

Slater longed to leap out of the wheelchair and release his frustration by grasping Toby's throat. He made do by curling his hand into a fist and looking meaningfully at Toby's nose. "If you've got something to say, just say it. I can't do anything from this wheelchair, so it's all up to you. If you've got a theory, just spit it out. Farren's already committed three murders, and—"

"No," Toby argued. "Not three."

Daphne moved in beside Toby and looked at him curiously. "Nina Farren, Winnie Widdicome, and Randall Powley."

Toby shook his head again. "Two. He didn't murder Randall Powley."

Slater held his breath. Now was not the time to interrupt.

Toby repositioned his spectacles before he spoke. "There was no way that Farren could have come from Tooting to Hackbridge in time to kill Powley. I've known it all along; I just haven't stopped to see what it means. It's perfectly obvious, isn't it?"

"Not to me," Slater said, "but I wasn't there."

Toby's eyes were bright with excitement. "We saw a light upstairs when we drove up to the house, and then the light went out. That means Powley was alive, and he turned out the light so he could hide from us. Victor Montard sent me to find Buddy and Eddie, and he went into the house. When I arrived on the doorstep with the boys, Victor told me that

Powley was dead. Of course, I assumed Farren killed him. Farren's a killer, so why not think he killed Powley? And then Victor drove away with Buddy and Eddie to get the police, or so he said, and yet he stopped to let Eddie out and even helped him to start his motorcycle, even though he was supposed to be in a hurry.

"It all adds up when you stop to think. Farren didn't kill Powley; Victor Montard did."

CHAPTER TWENTY TWO

Montard Hall, Brighton
Lord Leonard Montard

Leo surveyed the stable yard at Montard Hall. He was hot and thirsty from his walk across the Downs in the afternoon sun. He was looking forward to dunking his head in cold water from the tap in the yard. The skin grafts on his face and scalp had no ability to sweat, and he felt as though his head was on fire. *No, not on fire. I know what a real fire feels like, and this is not it.*

Seeing that the stable yard was empty and there was no one to gasp at his disfigurement or shy away as he approached, he walked in through the arched gateway. He was greeted immediately by an anxious whine from one of the stalls. He had already guessed that he would find Nan locked up here. This was where his family always kept stray dogs or dogs that tended to roam. He felt a pang of guilt. He should have come for her last night.

As Nan's whining turned into impatient barking, he forgot about dunking his head and followed the sound into the stable. The air in the old stone building was heavy with the scent of hay and manure. He passed a row of empty stalls. The Montard estate no longer kept carriage horses or hunters. A duet of whinnies revealed the presence of the pair of ponies Victor kept for his children, and he paused to pat two inquisitive noses.

Nan was dancing with impatience by the time he reached the stall where she was confined. When he opened the door, she hurled herself at him, her whole body wriggling with delight. When she was finally calm, he led her from the stable and out into the bright, clean air.

He squatted beside her and stroked her head. "Well, old girl," he said, "we have a new home."

She cocked her head to one side. He pretended to himself that she could understand him, pretended that she might even be concerned. He continued to stroke her head. "I told them you were part of the deal," he said. "You and the sheep. I wasn't going to come without them. They said we're all welcome."

He leaned back on his haunches. "It was the bells," he said. "I heard the bells. I don't know why I didn't think of it before. The Benedictines, Nan. We're going into the monastery, and we're not coming out. It's the best thing for us." He ruffled the hair on her neck. "They don't mind you being female, but there'll be no women."

Nan's tail thumped on the cement floor. Leo shrugged. She didn't understand a word, but he had to tell her. He had to say it aloud so he could believe it himself. At long last he had found his hiding place. He wondered what Nan would make of her new home. She was accustomed to the isolation of his cottage and the rhythm of his days, with only an occasional visit from Winnie Widdicome.

Leo shook his head in puzzlement as he thought of Winnie and of Inspector Cameron's accusations. He had seen no one on his walk from the monastery to Montard Hall. Cameron had accused him of murdering Winnie, and Daphne had more or less blown up a police car, but today there was not a policeman in sight, and he could think of only one explanation.

He patted Nan's head. "I think Daphne's saved our bacon," he said. "Somehow or other she's called off the chase."

He stood up and looked down at Nan's inquiring eyes. He smiled as best he could, feeling the skin tightening around his lips. "Sorry, old girl. If I'm not talking about sheep, you have no idea what I'm saying. I'm just telling you that our girl Daphne must be some kind of superspy." He patted Nan's head again. "I think we're safe."

Safe? Daphne had offered to take him to a safe place, and he'd responded by angrily refusing her help. Now, after a long night of reflection in the monastery chapel, he had managed to come to terms with his feelings for Daphne. He knew that he could never give her what she wanted. She was still in love with him. She still thought they could have the life they'd dreamed of in the brief interlude before she had gone to France, but he knew the reality of his dreadful disfigurement. Perhaps he could have a few more surgeries, but what difference would that make? He would always have the face of a monster. Did Daphne really think they could marry and live a normal life? Did she imagine that they would have children? What child would want a monster for a father?

The sound of a vehicle interrupted his thoughts. He caught hold of Nan's collar and drew back into the shadows. The vehicle drew closer. Leo recognized the rackety sound of his brother's Land Rover. He waited to see if Victor was alone. He would see his brother one last time, but not the children. He didn't want the children to see him; not ever again.

He caught a glimpse of the Land Rover as it passed the entrance to the stable yard and continued down the road. He stepped out of the shadows and looked out through the gate to follow the vehicle's progress. He saw the Land Rover turn onto the graveled track that skirted the lake and come to a halt next to the boathouse. The driver's door opened, and Victor stepped out. Leo waited and hoped that Victor was alone. The passenger door opened. Leo felt a pang of disappointment. He really had wanted to say goodbye but not if …

Cameron? Why was the police inspector climbing out of Victor's Land Rover, and why was he dressed in a black tailcoat with brass buttons, making him look like a footman from a grand house? He watched as Victor and Cameron entered the boathouse. He looked from the boathouse to the Downs, where his sheep were waiting for him. With Nan to help him, he and his flock would reach the monastery before dark, and there he would stay. Why should he care what Cameron was wearing? Whatever Cameron and Victor were doing in the boathouse was none of his business.

He passed through the gate with Nan at his heels and turned onto the narrow chalk track that would lead him past his cottage and into a new life. The track meandered uphill and threaded its way through a grove of oak trees. Leo's curiosity got the better of him, and he paused in the shade to look back at the lake and the boathouse.

Victor's Land Rover was still parked in the center of the track. As he watched, Victor and Cameron emerged from the boathouse, both shouting and gesticulating. Although Leo could not make out the words, it was obvious that the two men were engaged in a furious argument. The confrontation soon turned to blows. Leo watched in amazement as his brother attacked Cameron.

Although it was probably not a good idea to assault a police officer, Leo thought back to the indignity of his own arrest and silently rooted for his brother. He was certain that Victor would stop short of actually killing Cameron, and so he enjoyed the sight of the Viscount using all the skills they had both learned at school, dancing lightly and aiming lightning blows at the older man.

He grinned as Victor landed a blow that sent Cameron into a stumbling fall onto a pile of broken and abandoned equipment. Victor stood upright, rubbing his bruised knuckles and looking down at the defeated police inspector. Leo's mind had already turned to wondering what Victor would say when he was brought up on charges when Cameron suddenly surged to his feet. Victor took a step backward as Cameron swung a canoe paddle at Victor's head. Victor tried to duck the blow, but Cameron came at him furiously, smashing the paddle into his head, not once but twice. Victor fell backward, and Cameron landed another blow as Victor dropped to the ground.

Leo did not even realize that he was shouting as he charged out of the thicket, but Cameron heard him and looked up.

Leo's words were a jumble of threats and a promise of what he was about to do to the police officer. Cameron stood for a moment, obviously assessing the distance that Leo would have to travel to reach him. Leo could not see the expression on his face, but he could see the inspector's right hand stretch out stiffly in a Nazi salute before Cameron disappeared back inside the boathouse.

What the hell? Leo started to run, with Nan leading the way in a streak of black-and-white fur. The path folded itself into a dip in the hill, and Leo lost sight of the boathouse. He ran in a way he had not run in since before the war, pounding into the valley and up the other side, trying to drag in oxygen through his reconstructed mouth and his useless nose.

He paused to gasp for air as he crested the next rise. He was closer now, but to reach the boathouse, he would have to run around the perimeter of the lake. He could see Victor on the ground. He was not moving.

Cameron emerged from the boathouse, dragging a struggling figure. Leo could only watch, knowing that he would not be able to prevent whatever was going to happen next. He could see Cameron clearly now, but Cameron was fully occupied in dragging the struggling figure into the Land Rover and did not look up at him or repeat the Nazi salute. Cameron's prisoner had his hands bound behind his back, and his head was concealed beneath a burlap hood, but Leo recognized the clothing. Buddy!

As Cameron manhandled his prisoner into the back of the Land Rover, Leo saw his brother begin to move. He crawled toward Cameron with his hand outstretched. Cameron turned and stomped on the hand. Victor's agonized cry blended with the sound of the Land Rover's engine as Cameron roared away.

Toby Whitby

He did not know the Morris was capable of such speed. Whoever cleaned the paintwork and polished the chrome had also tuned up the motor, and the car attacked the short distance between Arundel Castle and Montard Hall with a greedy roar.

Daphne gestured impatiently from the passenger seat. "Turn here. It's a shortcut."

Toby swung the Morris around a sharp bend and onto a narrow country road with hedges on either side. A tractor chugged toward them, and Toby saw the driver's look of increasing alarm as Daphne urged him forward.

"Don't stop. He'll get out of your way."

The tractor veered to the right, tipping precariously as the driver struggled for control. Toby glanced in his rearview mirror as they passed, and saw the tractor lurch onto its side and come to rest in the roadside ditch.

Daphne showed no interest in the welfare of the driver. "Keep going. He'll be fine. He's not our concern."

Toby shook his head to clear away stray thoughts. Yes, the tractor driver would be fine, but what about Buddy? What had Victor Montard done with Buddy?

Daphne's instruction broke through his thoughts. "Turn right. Now!"

He spun the wheel and broke free of the concealing hedges onto a paved road that ran across the crest of the Downs. "This will bring us around the back way into Montard Hall," Daphne said, "and with any luck, Victor won't see us coming."

"If he's there," Toby cautioned.

Daphne ignored Toby's doubts. "He'll be there."

Toby's thoughts were on Buddy. Victor had driven away with the two boys. He'd stopped to let Edward retrieve his motorcycle, and he'd driven off into the night with Buddy still in the Land Rover. He wondered how long it had taken for Buddy to become suspicious. They were supposed to stop at the train station and report to the police constable there. Failing that, they would go to a phone box and call the police. How long had it been before Buddy realized that none of those things were happening, and what had he done about it? Why hadn't Victor thrown Buddy out of the Land Rover? In fact, why hadn't he killed Buddy? He had already killed Randall Powley, so what was to stop him from killing Buddy?

Toby clung to the thought that Victor had let Edward go free, even helped him start his motorcycle. So he wasn't a man who killed for no reason at all. On the other hand, why hadn't he simply released Buddy when he released Edward?

The answer had come from Farren himself: *I'm taking my boy.* So long as Farren still thought that Buddy was his son, Victor would have a hold over him. Buddy was, once again, the key to everything.

Daphne grabbed Toby's arm, bringing an end to his speculation. "Stop. Wait. What's going on down there?"

Toby brought the Morris to a halt and followed Daphne's pointing finger. He noticed that her hand trembled slightly. "That's Leo's dog. That's Nan." She did not even attempt to hide her anxiety. "What's she doing?"

Toby looked down into the valley. He saw the lake spread out below them, and the unmistakable shape of the sheepdog racing in circles, although he could see no sign of sheep. He wound down his window, and the dog's agitated bark reached him clearly above the background hum of insects and the distant calling of seagulls.

Daphne opened her door and stepped out.

"Hey, come back," Toby protested. "We don't have any time to waste. We may already be too late."

"Something's happening down there," Daphne said. She took several steps forward and lifted her hand to shade her eyes. Toby shook his head and climbed out of the car, uncertain how much Daphne could see with her one eye. She turned to him. "Turn off the engine. I can't hear."

He reached back and turned off the ignition. The dog was still barking, but now he could hear voices drifting up to them from the lakeside.

"Two men," Daphne said. "Down there in the grass, and one of them is Leo."

"Are you sure?"

"That's his dog," Daphne replied, "and there's nothing wrong with my good eye." She shrugged. "Leo's easy to recognize."

Toby polished his glasses and followed her gaze. He could make out two men fighting at the edge of the road that circled the lake. *No*, he thought, *they're not fighting*. Even from this distance, he could make out Leo's features, or more accurately, his lack of features: the painfully pink nose, the scarred blurring of his face, and the burned scalp with its patches of blond hair. The other figure had collapsed to the ground, and Leo was struggling to lift him.

Toby pulled Daphne backward. "It's Victor," he whispered. "Don't let him see you."

"Too late," Daphne replied. "Leo's already looking at us, and Nan is headed this way."

Nan arrived in a flurry of fur and looked at them entreatingly. Toby caught Nan's collar while Daphne raised her hand to signal to Leo. Victor lifted his head for a moment and then let it fall back.

Daphne slapped Toby's arm impatiently. "Come on. I'll drive. I know the way."

Toby took another moment to see if he could make sense of the scene below. Leo was lifting Victor now and draping his brother's arm around his neck.

Daphne honked the horn impatiently. Leo looked up and then returned to his task of trying to get his brother to stand on his own two feet. With the Morris already in motion, Toby ran to catch up and flung himself into the passenger seat. With her knuckles white on the steering wheel, Daphne floored the accelerator.

The Morris skidded and bounced down the paved road and onto the gravel path around the lake, spewing stones and clumps of grass from beneath its wheels. Daphne screeched to a halt beside Leo at the same moment that Leo gave up trying to get his brother to walk and let him drop to the ground.

In the sudden silence after Daphne killed the ignition, Toby heard Leo's pleading voice. "Come on, old man, you have to try. We need to get you to a hospital. What on earth's going on? That was Cameron, wasn't it?"

"Name's not Cameron," Victor muttered. With agonizing slowness, he curled himself into a fetal position. "I've made a complete hash of everything. Just leave me here."

Nan nosed at Victor's face, and he pushed her away, covering his face with his hands.

Leo knelt beside his brother and gently parted his hands. "What is it, old man?"

Daphne dropped to her knees beside Leo, and there was nothing gentle in her voice or her actions. "Where have they gone? Where is Farren taking him?"

"Farren?" Leo queried. "Who is Farren?"

"Cameron is Farren."

Leo shook his head. "I don't understand, but it doesn't matter. We have to get Victor back to the house. He needs a doctor."

Daphne's voice was a malevolent hiss. "He needs a hangman."

Leo rounded on her. "What the hell are you talking about?"

Daphne sprang to her feet and looked down at Victor. She moved her right leg. For a moment, Toby thought she was going to kick the Viscount, but she restrained herself and settled for resting her hand on Leo's shoulder in a suddenly solicitous gesture. "Your brother has just attempted to assassinate Prince Philip, the Duke of Edinburgh."

"The what?"

"The Queen's husband. Your brother has attempted to assassinate the Queen's husband."

"No."

Victor's hands were still covering his face, and his voice was muffled. "No, not me. It was Farren."

"Farren's a pawn," Daphne said. "A low-level nothing, but you're the brains, aren't you?"

Leo sat back on his haunches. His stiff, scarred face was barely able to register emotion, but Toby could see horror in his eyes and hear a grudging belief in his voice.

"Victor, what did you do?"

"We talked about it," Victor muttered. "You know we talked about. The country's going to hell in a handcart, and we'll never recover with that stupid chit of a girl on the throne and her Nazi husband pulling the strings."

Leo shook his head. "He's not a Nazi, and he's not going to be king."

"Power behind the throne," Victor said. "You'll see. Once he's gone, she won't know what to do. She can't manage without him. The good English gentry will never bend the knee to her." He extended an arm toward his brother. "Once we were great. Think of it, Leo. Agincourt, Crécy, Poitiers. We won and we were great. But what have we won this time? What's happening to us? We need a man on the throne, and with her gone, we'll have one."

Daphne leaned forward. "Philip is alive and well, and you'll hang for what you tried to do."

Leo stumbled to his feet. "I don't believe this. Are you telling me that my brother—?"

"I'm telling you that Toby Whitby saved the day," Daphne said. "Without him, we would be looking at a state funeral and not a coronation."

Victor uncurled himself and sat up. The expression on his face was a cross between abject fear and a kind of sullen pride. "It had to be done," he said, "but I didn't do it."

"But you killed Randall Powley, didn't you?" Toby said. "Did that have anything to do with your grand plan?"

Victor ignored the question. His attention was only on his brother as he pleaded with Leo for understanding and approval.

Toby tuned out Victor's voice and set his mind to work on what he knew and what he didn't know. He knew that Inspector Cameron was actually Jack Farren, who had been a German agent during the war and was now most likely an agent of the Soviets. He knew that Victor was not interested in the Soviets. The Viscount had his mind set on restoring England to the kind of glory that had once been the heritage of the Montard family and the other great aristocratic families. So who had been the puppet master? Had Jack Farren played Victor Montard, or was it the other way around? Well, one thing was certain: Victor Montard had been left to face the music, and if he stalled much longer, Farren would get clean away and would take Buddy with him.

Toby pushed Leo aside and squatted down next to Victor. "Was Buddy the bait?" he asked.

Victor curled his lip. "Is that his real name? Sounds like a dog's name. That boy is too trusting. It took him a good half hour to realize I wasn't about to send the police up to Randall Powley's place, and by then we were well clear of Hackbridge. He's a tough kid. I had quite a struggle to subdue him."

"You could have put him out of the car when you put Eddie out," Toby said.

"Why would I do that," Victor asked, "when I could use him as bait to get Farren under control? No need for both of us to go blundering around Arundel. All I had to do was promise Farren that I'd turn over his son once the deed was done.

"Of course," he added, "I didn't expect Farren to take one look at Buddy and realize that the boy is not his son. I knew he had a cuckoo in his nest, because old Mrs. Stackpole told us, but Farren didn't know, so I thought I could get away with it. No such luck. He took the sack off the boy's head, and all hell broke loose. I thought he was going to kill me. He's gone to great lengths to get his hands on Buddy, and now he's found him, he doesn't want him. He was going to take him to Moscow, you know, so they could help the Soviets take over the world. That's not going to happen now that he knows Buddy isn't his son. I don't know what he'll do with the boy. I imagine he'll use him as a hostage, and then he'll dispose of him."

Daphne leaned down to speak to Victor. "Do you know how they were going to leave the country?"

"Farren has paperwork for himself. He can get on any ferry out of Dover. He obviously has connections with forgers, and I'm sure he has a believable passport."

Toby thought of the documents that Farren had shown Chief Constable Peacock to establish himself as Robert Cameron from North Yorkshire, sent south to help with security at the Arundel meeting. Yes, Farren knew a good forger, and maybe he had intended to get a passport for Buddy and take him to Moscow, but he wouldn't do that now that he knew Buddy wasn't his son."

Victor offered his brother a mocking half smile. "Don't scowl like that, old man. It can't be good for your skin grafts."

"To hell with my skin grafts," Leo hissed. "Do you realize what you've done?"

Victor spread his hands, wincing as he opened the damaged fingers of this right hand. "I've done nothing. The Duke is still walking around unscathed. I didn't even go into the castle. You've got nothing on me for that. Besides, I'm Viscount Pulborough and I have friends in high places. Nothing will happen to me."

Toby thought of the man in the tweed suit who had ushered his followers away from the committee room. *Drinks in the Long Gallery. Don't be shy. Come along. No point in waiting around here.* Who was he? How much power did he wield?

"I'll give evidence against you," Leo threatened.

Victor shook his head. "I don't think so, brother dear. You're not really going to take that face into a courtroom and present evidence, are you? Why don't you go back to your hiding place and let me get on with running the estate? As for Daphne, well, she's not going to show herself either, not now that she's a secret agent and her identity can't be revealed."

What about me? Toby thought. *I may not be an aristocrat, but I'll tell the world what I know.*

Victor's glance slid past Toby as he raised his right hand and looked up into the sky as if to invoke some heavenly power. "I solemnly swear not to involve myself in any more plots to keep that wretched girl off the throne. She can have her moment in Westminster Abbey, and then we'll see what happens next. Now leave me alone."

He turned his head away from Leo and finally acknowledged Toby. "Are you going to give me a ride up to the house in your car? I'm afraid our phony police inspector gave me a very real beating. Walking is somewhat of a problem."

Toby stared at Victor's extended hand. Did he really think he was going to get away with this? Apart from everything else, there was the murder of Randall Powley to consider, and the abduction of Buddy. Toby was suddenly impatient with the whole situation, with the blaming and explaining and the fact that they were all standing at the side of the road, doing nothing, while Farren was making his escape with Buddy in the Land Rover.

"No," Toby said with a burst of fierce anger, "I'm not taking you anywhere. I'm going to get my client back. You three can debate all you like about the rights and wrongs of monarchy, or whatever it is that's disturbing your aristocratic heads, but I'm not going to stand here and listen to you. Farren killed Buddy's mother, and now that he knows that Buddy isn't his son, he won't hesitate to kill Buddy as well, so I'm going to find him before that happens."

He strode rapidly to the Morris. The keys were still in the ignition. He turned to look back at Daphne and the Montard brothers. "Is anyone coming with me? Is there anyone who cares what happens to that poor kid?"

Victor and Leo lifted their heads in unison, and for a moment, Toby did not see Leo's scarred face and patchy hair; he saw only the true twin resemblance in the way they angled their heads to look at him with wide blue eyes. Despite Leo's terrible disfigurement, nothing could hide their similarities.

Understanding came in a flash. He drew in a sharp breath as another piece of the puzzle slid smoothly into place, and he recognized that Buddy's features were mirrored in the lift of Victor's chin, the line of his nose, the shape of his eyes, and the hair that flopped across his eyebrows. The resemblance was suddenly so obvious that Toby could not imagine why he had not seen it before, when he had first met Victor.

Daphne left Victor at the side of the road and approached Toby with a grim expression on her face. "Can you believe it?" she asked. "He thinks he'll get away with it. He really thinks we won't try him for what he's done." She shook her head. "I can't go with you. I hope you find the boy, and I wish I could help, but I have to take care of this business."

She turned away, and Toby called her back impatiently. "You don't see it, do you?"

"See what?"

"The resemblance."

"I don't know what you're talking about."

Toby glanced back at Leo and Victor. "Were you staying with the Montards in the summer of 1932?"

Daphne nodded, and a pained expression crossed her face. "I was. It was the summer of my seventeenth birthday."

"And were the Gypsies camped on the Downs?"

"They came every summer."

"And my client Buddy, whose real name is Henry Farren, was conceived in the summer of 1932."

"I don't see what that has to do with ..." Daphne's voice died away, and she turned to follow Toby's gaze as he gestured at the two brothers. "What are you suggesting?"

"I'm suggesting that there is resemblance between Victor Montard and young Henry Farren. I know that Jack is not Buddy's father. Mrs. Stackpole made that quite clear. Nina was already pregnant when she met Jack Farren. So I have to ask myself if it is possible that Buddy is Victor's son."

Daphne shook her head. "No, not Victor. Victor wasn't at home that summer. He was in America. Leo was home."

Toby remained silent, allowing Daphne's words to take hold. Of course, Victor and Leo were twins, but their resemblance had ended the day that Leo was shot down.

Daphne's eyes were brimming with tears, but her voice was steady. "I'll tell him."

CHAPTER TWENTY THREE

Toby Whitby

Victor lay in a huddled heap, emitting an occasional groan and ignored by everyone. Toby's eyes were fixed on Daphne as she took Leo aside and told him what she suspected, that the boy from Canada was his son. For a long moment, Leo said nothing. Toby tried to read the expression on his face, but the scars hid all but the strongest emotions.

"You know I'm right," Daphne said. "I know you went to the Gypsy camp." She ducked her head and spoke without looking at him. "That was the summer that I followed you everywhere. You didn't see me, but I was always watching, even when you went to the Gypsies."

"Nina," Leo said. "Her name was Nina." His mouth twisted as he spoke. "I abandoned the boy. I told him to sleep in the boathouse and left him to his own devices. I should have seen it in his face."

"You couldn't have known," Daphne said.

"You knew," Leo snapped.

"I saw *your* face, not his mother's face," Daphne replied.

Leo extended a scarred hand and let it rest against Daphne's cheek. "I'm sorry for what I did to you."

Toby sensed that they were caught up in an emotion that had nothing to do with Buddy's plight, but this was not the time or the place to say whatever it was they needed to say to each other.

He stepped up to Leo and looked him in the face. "There's still time. Come on. If you can fly a Spitfire, you can certainly drive my old Morris fast enough to catch up with Farren. Let's go. Leave the explanations for another day."

Leo nodded. "You're right. Come on. Chocks away."

As Leo sprinted to Toby's car, Toby thought of Leo's other life, the life when he had been a Battle of Britain pilot, racing from the hangar to his Spitfire to take to the skies against the Luftwaffe.

Leo flung himself into the driver's seat and had the engine running by the time Toby had scrambled into the passenger seat. Leo's scarred hand rested impatiently on the gear lever as he revved the engine. He turned to Toby. "Whatever happens, don't tell him I'm his father."

Toby opened his mouth to protest, but Leo cut him off. "Let him go back to Canada. Don't tell him."

Toby's chance to object was cut off by the protesting whine of the Morris engine as Leo floored the accelerator. The Morris leaped forward, and Toby turned his attention to trying to remain upright.

Leo drove with the same skill that he had brought to piloting his Spitfire, and Toby hoped that the car engine would not explode under the strain of his demands. Unable to cope with the speed and fury of Leo's driving, Toby's mind escaped into thoughts of how he would tell Carol that the car was gone; always assuming he was alive to tell her anything.

Leo took one hand off the wheel and tapped the dashboard. "Fuel?" he barked. "How much? Is this accurate?"

Toby thought back on the last time he had put petrol in the tank: in the rain with the attendant who blamed the RAF. No, that was yesterday. The long days were beginning to run together in his mind. He forced himself to think as Leo flung the car around another bend in the road.

"How much?" Leo barked again.

Toby remembered the knocking at the front door and Daphne waiting for him in the Morris. The mechanics who had cleaned the car and tuned the motor would surely have filled the tank.

"Well?"

"Full tank this morning," Toby replied.

Leo nodded. "All right. Good enough. If he's heading for Dover, he'll be on the A27, past Eastbourne. I'm going to take the back road and cut off some corners. Just hang on tight. We should catch up with him somewhere around Beachy Head."

Toby looked at Leo in admiration. The pilot had set aside his guilt and brought all of his skill to bear on hurling the Morris at top speed along winding country lanes, never slowing, never hesitating, and somehow knowing at what time and at what point he would reach the main road.

Toby's stomach lurched, and he was glad he had not eaten the sandwich Carol had made for him. He closed his eyes and gave himself up to the task of staying in his seat and trying not to retch.

After what seemed to be an interminable time, Toby felt the car slowing. He opened his eyes.

Leo looked at him from the corner of his eye. "We're joining the A27 now. Sorry about the rough ride."

"I'm fine," Toby lied.

Leo nodded. "I've calculated the Land Rover's speed. It's a slow vehicle, and your little car is quite nippy. We should be seeing him up ahead any moment. We should catch up with him well before Eastbourne. I'm going to cut him off before he gets into heavy traffic, where we can lose sight of him. I need you to keep a look out for him."

Leo slid the car smoothly from the narrow country lane onto a wide highway and passed a heavily loaded lorry with only inches to spare. Toby squinted at the highway ahead and made out the unmistakable shape of a Land Rover in the distance.

"That's him," Toby said.

Leo nodded, and Toby wondered why Leo had even asked him to keep a lookout. Leo had spent the war years searching the skies for enemy planes; he didn't need Toby to tell him about a vehicle that was no more than a half mile ahead and now plainly visible in the bright afternoon sun.

Leo shifted his hands on the steering wheel and leaned forward. "All right," he said, "I'm going to force him off the road." He glanced sideways at Toby. "Things might get a bit hairy."

Toby nodded. "Do what you have to do."

The engine whined, and the car shook as Leo floored the accelerator and slowly closed the gap between the Morris and Land Rover. Toby imagined Farren looking into his rearview mirror and seeing another vehicle eating up the road behind him. He wouldn't know, of course, that this was Toby's car or that Leo was bearing down upon him with the cool, calculating skill of a fighter pilot and the hot fury of a father.

The Land Rover was slowing now, getting out of the way of the Morris with its reckless driver.

A small white signpost indicated a narrow road ahead on the right. "This is it," Leo said. "Hold on."

He came abreast of the Land Rover and spun the wheel. Toby spared a thought for his newly restored paintwork, but that thought lingered for no more than a moment as the two vehicles collided. He caught a glimpse of Farren's shocked expression. What had shocked him most? Had it been the crashing of the cars, or had it been the horror of Leo's scarred face? With the shock came recognition. Toby saw the light dawn on Farren's face as he locked eyes with him. He knew Toby; he knew what Toby wanted, but he could not know what Leo wanted, or the depth of Leo's anger.

Toby looked past Farren to see if Buddy was in the passenger seat, but the seat was empty. Either he had ditched Buddy, or Buddy was in the back seat. Toby strained to see what was in the back, but Farren didn't give him time. He made a hard turn away from the Morris and onto the narrow side road. Leo followed. Toby caught a glimpse of the black writing on the white signpost. Beachy Head, just as Leo had predicted.

Farren sped along the narrow road with Leo in pursuit. The hedges gave way to a chalk road across a broad swathe of jewel-green grass leading inevitably to the sudden expanse of wide blue sky, where seagulls dipped and wheeled. Toby caught hold of Leo's arm. Leo had said that things would be "a bit hairy," he had not said that he was willing to hurl the Morris over the highest headland on the south coast.

"Stop," Toby gasped, grabbing Leo's arm. "Don't chase him. He'll go over the edge."

Leo kept his eyes on the road and shook his arm free. "No, he won't. It takes guts to kill yourself. I don't have the guts, and neither does he."

The Land Rover stayed ahead of them, and despite Leo's prediction, Farren showed no sign of stopping.

Toby was shouting now. "Don't push him. He has a hostage. He'll negotiate."

Leo slowed the car a fraction and looked at Toby. "All right. What do you want me to do?"

"I want you to stop," Toby gasped. "Let's talk to him. We'll see what he offers."

Leo stamped on the brakes, and the engine of the Morris gave a despairing cough and stalled. Leo turned his face toward Toby. The fire in his eyes still smoldered, but his voice was calm. "If I get near him, I'll kill him with my bare hands. You'd better do the talking."

Toby saw the Land Rover swerve abruptly away from the edge of the cliff. It halted perilously close to the place where the cliff top met the sky. Farren left the motor running, the rattle of its engine blending with the sound of waves crashing against the shingle beach far below, and the wild calling of seagulls gathering hopefully above them. Toby shuddered, remembering the way the seagulls had attacked in a blur of wings as he had tried to rescue Anita. There would be no picnic food for them today. As the memory of that afternoon threatened to overwhelm him, an idea forced its way through, and he knew what he had to do.

He opened the car door and climbed out. He stood for a moment, feeling the security of the ground beneath his feet and wondering what it would feel like to lose that security and step off the cliff. Would there be time to think? Would there be a moment of elation?

"What now?" Leo asked.

"Look in the glove compartment. You'll find a sandwich."

"For heaven's sake," Leo exploded. "I'm not hungry."

"But the seagulls are," Toby said. "They're always hungry. They'll come at the first sign of food."

Leo looked at him thoughtfully and then leaned forward and unlatched the glove compartment. He set the sandwich on the seat and unwrapped the paper.

"This isn't going to be easy," Toby admitted, "and it may not even work, but I'm going to distract him while you toss crumbs into the air. He won't be looking at you, because ..." He paused, ashamed of what he had been about to say. *He won't look at you, because no one can bear to look at you.*

Leo nodded his understanding, and words were unnecessary. "Leave it to me. You talk, and I'll do what I can, but whatever happens, grab the boy. I'll go over the cliff if I have to, but don't let anything happen to him." He looked down at the sandwich, two thick slices of bread. "This should be enough," he muttered. He looked up at Toby. "Don't tell the boy who I am."

"I won't."

Toby raised his hands in the air and walked toward the Land Rover. His stomach churned as he realized how close Farren had come to the edge of the cliff. The Land Rover had slewed sideways, with the passenger side just a few feet from the precipice. If a passenger stepped out that side, he would ...

Toby shuddered and refused to finish the thought. *Just keep Farren distracted. Leo's a fighter pilot. Nerves of steel. He can do it.*

Farren leaned out of the open window and watched Toby's approach. *Look at me; don't look at the man with no face.*

Farren spoke first. "Give me your car keys."

"Why would I do that?"

"Because if you don't, I send this vehicle over the edge. The engine's running; I just have to nudge the gear lever. I'll get out, but the boy's in the back. He can't get out. Now give me your keys."

"What are you going to do with them?"

"I'm going to throw them off the cliff, and then I'm going to drive away."

"And what about Buddy?"

"Buddy! That's not the name I gave him."

"No," Toby said. "He didn't want the name you gave him."

"Give me the keys."

Toby slipped his hand into his pant pocket. No keys. Of course not. Leo had been driving. The keys were still in the ignition. *Keep him talking.*

"You think he's Victor Montard's son, don't you?"

"She was a slut. He could be anyone's."

"But you think it was Victor."

Toby moved slowly, edging sideways so that Farren's attention was drawn away from whatever Leo was doing. Toby did not dare to look, but he was keenly aware that the sounds of the seagulls had become louder and more urgent.

"Where are you going?" Toby asked. "They won't want you in Moscow. You failed in your mission. You won't get a second chance now that you've blown your cover."

"I don't need Moscow," Farren said. "Germany will rise again."

"We beat you once," Toby boasted. "We can beat you again."

He could feel the beating of the seagulls' wings. They were close overhead. He could not look up. He could not let Farren look up. Not yet.

Toby glimpsed movement from the corner of his eye. Leo was approaching the back of the Land Rover. *Keep his attention. Don't let him look.*

"You're wrong about him not being your son," Toby said. "Mrs. Stackpole told me."

Farren was angry now, and his eyes were still focused on Toby. "Who the hell is Mrs. Stackpole?"

"Village gossip. The woman you ran into the day you met your wife."

Farren leaned out of the window. "How does she know?"

"She knows all about it."

Farren shook his head. "Stop playing games. Give me the keys, or the boy goes over."

Toby felt the battering of seagull wings in the air around him. Their raucous complaining left no room for speech. Farren, finally aware that something was happening, looked up at the menacing cloud of birds.

"What the hell?" His eyes were on Toby as though somehow he knew that Toby had brought this cloud of wings down upon him. Toby shook his head. Farren was still looking at him, and he did not see Leo moving carefully in the small space between the passenger side of the Land Rover and the edge of the cliff.

Leo's voice rose above the cacophony of bird calls. "Now!"

Now what? Was there a plan?

Leo, with the birds circling within inches of his face, hurled a handful of sandwich bread into the Land Rover, where it hit Farren squarely on the back of the neck. The birds followed.

Toby didn't give himself time to think of Leo's danger, poised at the edge of the cliff while Farren flailed at the birds. At any moment, his wild movements could nudge the engine into gear, and the Land Rover would plunge forward with nowhere to go except straight down into the ocean below.

Toby had a promise to keep: not to save Leo but to save his son. He raced forward and pulled at the rear door. It began to swing open as the

Land Rover moved. For a brief moment, it ran parallel to the cliff edge. Toby reached inside, and his hands closed over rough fabric. He pulled, and the heavy bundle tumbled onto the grass. The Land Rover gained momentum. Toby closed his arms around the bundle and rolled away as the Land Rover veered toward the edge. Farren's screams were drowned out by the triumphant cries of the seagulls. They did not care that their lunch was going over the edge of the cliff. They could fly; they would come to no harm, but Farren was headed for a five-hundred-foot fall.

Would he have time for regrets before he crashed into the rocks? Would he know who had done this?

Toby dragged the wriggling bundle away from the edge, and when he looked up, there was nothing between him and the edge of the cliff. The Land Rover was gone, and so was Leo. Had Farren helped Leo to do what he really wanted to do, to end his life?

A voice drifted up to him from somewhere beyond the edge of the cliff. The tall grass that stood in a fringe to mark the joining of earth and sky started to sway. A hand appeared, scarred but strong, and then another.

"Is he all right? Tell me he's all right."

Toby looked at the bundle he had dragged from the Land Rover, man shaped, wriggling, and emitting loud complaints in a Canadian voice.

"He's all right."

EPILOGUE

Brighton, Sussex
Toby Whitby
The ancient stones of the Benedictine monastery glowed in the autumn sunlight as Toby parked the Morris and ran around to open the door for Carol. She was, as she herself said, "barely pregnant," but he could not help fussing over her.

"You'd better get used to this," she said. "Seven more months is a long time, and I refuse to be treated like an invalid." Nonetheless, she smiled as he helped her out of the car, and smiled again as he took her hand on the walk from the car park to the monastery entrance.

The gates that separated the monks from the world were old and formidable, but today they stood open for the small party of visitors.

Slater was here, walking with a cane but nonetheless walking. Daphne, elegant in a tweed skirt and pearls, had accompanied him.

A lay brother, distinguished by his gray robe, ushered them to a walled herb garden where wooden benches surrounded a carved statue of St. Benedict.

The lay brother was a middle-aged man with soft brown eyes and an expression not so much of happiness but of contentment. His hands, as he gestured for them to sit, revealed fingernails caked with dirt. He spoke with difficulty. Toby searched his face for signs of injury and detected a long scar running from his right ear to his jaw

"My garden," he said. "I work here. You sit. You wait."

Toby ushered Carol to a seat. She gave him an impatient glance. "Don't treat me like an invalid."

"If you sit, Slater will sit," Toby said softly. "And he needs to sit down before he falls down."

Carol smiled and seated herself on a bench. She patted the seat beside her invitingly, and Toby was relieved to see Slater sit down next to her. He wondered, not for the first time, how long it would be before Slater could be back in action or whether his future would be limited to patrolling a desk.

"Does … uh … Brother Leo know we're here?" Carol asked.

The lay brother's hands disappeared beneath the full sleeves of his robe as he clasped them together. He inclined his head toward Carol and smiled. Obviously, he had not heard the question. Toby thought with momentary longing of the peace that the brother enjoyed, tending his garden and living where his deafness would never put him at a disadvantage. It occurred to him that the brother may not have always been deaf. Was he another wounded warrior looking, like Leo, for a place where he could be at peace?

A bout of eager barking heralded the arrival of Leo's dog, Nan. She trotted into the herb garden and paused to take in the presence of four new faces and then rushed out again. She returned almost immediately with Leo walking beside her, wrapped in a long brown robe and with his face shrouded in a hood.

Toby heard Daphne catching her breath. She had been standing, but now she dropped down onto a bench as though she did not trust her legs to hold her.

Leo had noticed her sudden movement. *Of course he did*, Toby thought. *Leo notices everything; that's what made him a good pilot. He notices, but does he understand?*

Carol made a slight sound, and Toby looked across at her. She met his gaze and raised her eyebrows. They communicated in the unspoken language of husband and wife. She had already told him that Daphne did not believe that Leo would follow through with this, but now he was here, robed in brown, his feet in sandals and a wooden cross around his neck.

As if to drive home the point, Leo pulled back his hood. The monastery barber had done the best he could to tame Leo's patchy hair into a tonsure. The effect was far from perfect, but the message was clear. Here was a monk, a man who had turned his back on the world.

Daphne's voice was small and choked. "You didn't have to …"

Leo dropped to one knee beside her and lifted her hand, with its crooked fingers, to his lips. "I'm sorry," he whispered. "Some things take more courage than I possess." He kissed her hand again. "Be happy, dear girl."

He stood in an easy, athletic movement and turned to Slater. "What's happened to my brother?"

Percy's laugh was a derisive bark. "Oh, he's giving us all a run for our money. He wants to be tried by a jury of his peers and refuses to believe that we no longer allow aristocrats to be tried by the House of Lords. He'll fight us every inch of the way, but in the end, he'll come to trial."

"And then what?" Leo asked.

"I'm not sure. He didn't actually enter Arundel Castle, and the man who did went over the cliff at Beachy Head. Your brother will be found guilty of something eventually, of course. We're gathering evidence in the murder of Randall Powley and meantime, we're keeping him locked away. Your sister-in-law has sold the family silver and the paintings, and taken her children to America."

Leo turned away, shoulders hunched. "So the old place is empty," he said. "Nothing but memories of days gone by."

"I'm afraid so," Slater said.

Leo straightened his shoulders and turned to Toby. "Where is my ... where is Buddy?"

"Back in Canada," Toby said. "Inspector Slater pulled a great many strings to get him another passport. He's adopted now. His name is Stewart."

"Buddy Stewart?"

"No. I think he'll always be Buddy to his friends, but his legal name is Leo. Leo Roy Stewart. Named for both of his fathers."

Leo stared. "You told him?"

"No. He knows you as the man who saved his life, that's all. But he's proud to have your name."

Leo pulled up his hood, hiding the expression on his face, but not before Toby saw him twist his lips into a smile.

The chime of the chapel bell broke the silence that had descended on the walled garden, and Leo turned his head toward the gate.

"I have to go."

Toby nodded. "Of course."

"We don't normally allow visitors," Leo said, "but if you occasionally bring word of my ... of Leo Stewart, you will be welcomed."

"Of course," Toby repeated.

"Just the big events," Leo said. "A marriage, a birth, news that I am a grandfather."

"I will."

The bell chimed again. Leo bowed and called to Nan. "Time for prayers, old girl, and then we're off to round up the sheep."

He turned back to look at Daphne. "Forgive me if you can."

Toby watched him leave, and when he was gone from sight, Daphne rose shakily to her feet and held out her hand to Slater. "Come along, Inspector. We have work to do."

THE END

If you would like to know more about Toby's war years, you can receive a free copy of **Alibi** an introductory novella set during the early years of World War Two.
 To receive your free e-book novella visit www.eileenenwrighthodgetts.com and sign up for Eileen's newsletter.

We hope you enjoyed **Nameless.** This is the third novel in the Toby Whitby Mystery series. **Air Raid and Imposter** the first and second stories in the series are available in e-book format, paperback, and audio. Details are available at www.eileenenwrighthodgetts.com or purchase through your on-line book retailer.

Also available from the same author.

Excalibur Rising a four book edge-of-your-seat fantasy-suspense series laced with wit and history. If you like unusual characters, dramatic plot twists, and the myth of King Arthur, then you'll love *Excalibur Rising.*

You may also enjoy
Whirlpool – suspense and romance at the brink of Niagara Falls
The Serbian Solution – A whirlwind chase across England and Wales and out into the Atlantic in search of a man who may be king.
Afric When flooding traps two American women in an African village, they find themselves at the mercy of a war lord and in the center of the CIA's war on terror.

Made in the USA
Las Vegas, NV
24 November 2020